THE HORUS HERESY

Graham McNeill

FULGRIM

Visions of Treachery

For my friends, who kept me sane through the long, dark watches of writing the madness.

A BLACK LIBRARY PUBLICATION

First published in Great Britain in 2007 by
BL Publishing,
Games Workshop Ltd.,
Willow Road, Nottingham, NG7 2WS, UK.

10 9 8 7 6 5 4 3 2 1

Cover illustration by Neil Roberts.
First page illustration by Neil Roberts.

A CIP record for this book is available from the British Library.

ISBN 13: 978-1-84416-476-9
ISBN 10: 1-84416-476-4

Distributed in the US by Simon & Schuster
1230 Avenue of the Americas, New York, NY 10020, US.

See the Black Library on the Internet at
www.blacklibrary.com

Find out more about Games Workshop
and the world of Warhammer 40,000 at
www.games-workshop.com

THE HORUS HERESY

It is a time of legend.

Mighty heroes battle for the right to rule the galaxy.
The vast armies of the Emperor of Earth have conquered
the galaxy in a Great Crusade – the myriad alien races have
been smashed by the Emperor's elite warriors and wiped
from the face of history.

The dawn of a new age of supremacy for humanity
beckons.

Gleaming citadels of marble and gold celebrate the many
victories of the Emperor. Triumphs are raised on a million
worlds to record the epic deeds of his most powerful and
deadly warriors.

First and foremost amongst these are the primarchs,
superheroic beings who have led the Emperor's armies of
Space Marines in victory after victory. They are unstoppable
and magnificent, the pinnacle of the Emperor's genetic
experimentation. The Space Marines are the mightiest
human warriors the galaxy has ever known, each capable of
besting a hundred normal men or more in combat.

Organised into vast armies of tens of thousands called
Legions, the Space Marines and their primarch leaders
conquer the galaxy in the name of the Emperor.

Chief amongst the primarchs is Horus, called the Glorious, the Brightest Star, favourite of the Emperor, and like a
son unto him. He is the Warmaster, the commander-in-
chief of the Emperor's military might, subjugator of a
thousand thousand worlds and conqueror of the galaxy. He
is a warrior without peer, a diplomat supreme.

As the flames of war spread through the Imperium,
mankind's champions will all be put to the ultimate test.

~ DRAMATIS PERSONAE ~

The Emperor's Children

FULGRIM	Primarch
EIDOLON	Lord Commander
VESPASIAN	Lord Commander
JULIUS KAESORON	Captain, 1st Company
SOLOMON DEMETER	Captain, 2nd Company
MARIUS VAIROSEAN	Captain, 3rd Company
SAUL TARVITZ	Captain, 10th Company
LUCIUS	Captain, 13th Company
CHARMOSIAN	Chaplain, 18th Company
GAIUS CAPHEN	Second in command to Solomon Demeter
LYCAON	Equerry to Julius Kaesoron
FABIUS	Apothecary

The Iron Hands

FERRUS MANUS	Primarch
GABRIEL SANTOR	Captain, First Company
CAPTAI BALHAAN	Captain of the *Ferrum*

The Primarchs

HORUS	Primarch of the Sons of Horus, the Warmaster
VULKAN	Primarch of the Salamanders
CORAX	Primarch of the Raven Guard
ANGRON	Primarch of the World Eaters
MORTARION	Primarch of the Death Guard

Other Space Marines

EREBUS   First Chaplain of the Word
                            Bearers

Imperial Army

LORD COMMANDER THADDEUS FAYLE

Non-Astartes

SERENA D'ANGELUS   Artist and imagist

BEQUA KYNSKA   Composer and harmonist

OSTIAN DELAFOUR   Sculptor

CORALINE ASENECA   Theatrical performer

LEOPOLD CADMUS   Poet

ORMOND BRAXTON   Emissary of the
                           Administration of Terra

EVANDER TOBIAS   Archivist of *The Pride of the
                           Emperor*

Xenos

ELDRAD ULTHRAN   Farseer of Ulthwé

KHIRAEN GOLDHELM   Wraithlord of Ulthwé

PART ONE

THE PERFECT WARRIOR

'That which causes us trials shall yield us triumph, and that which makes our hearts ache shall fill us with gladness. For the only true happiness is to learn, to advance and to improve. None of this could happen without rejecting error, ignorance and imperfection. We must pass out of the darkness to reach the light.'

– The Primarch Fulgrim, *Attainment of Perfection*

'Perfection is achieved, not when there is nothing more to add, but when there is nothing left to take away.'

– Ostian Delafour, *Man of Stone*

'The only true paradises are those that are lost to us…'

– Pandorus Zheng, Philosopher Designate to the Autarch of the 9th Yndonesic Bloc

ONE

Recital/See it Through/Laeran

'THE DANGER FOR MOST of us,' Ostian Delafour would say on those rare occasions when he was coaxed to speak of his gift, 'is not that our aim is too high and we miss it, but that it is too low and we hit it.' He would then smile modestly and attempt to recede into the background of whatever conversation was underway, feeling exposed under the spotlight of adulation, and uncomfortable with the attention.

Only here in his chaotic studio, surrounded by scattered piles of chisels, hammers and rasps, chipping away at the marble with deft strokes to create wonders, did he feel comfortable. He stepped away from the block of stone that stood in the centre of his studio and ran a hand across his high forehead and through his short, tightly curled, black hair as he took in the measure of this latest session.

The marble column was a gleaming white rectangle, some four metres tall, its surfaces as yet unblemished by chisel or rasp. Ostian circled the marble, running his silver hands across its smooth surface, feeling the structure within and picturing where he would make the first cut into the stone. Servitors had brought the block up from the *Pride of the Emperor's* loading bays a week ago, but he had yet to complete his visualisation of how he would bring forth his masterpiece from the block.

The marble had come to the Emperor's Children's flagship from the quarries at Proconnesus on the Anatolian peninsula, where much of the stonework that comprised the Emperor's palace had been sourced. The block had been hand quarried from Mount Ararat, a rugged and inaccessible peak, but one known to contain rich deposits of pure white marble. Its value was incalculable and only the influence of the Primarch of the Emperor's Children had secured its shipping out to the 28th Expedition.

He knew others called him a genius, but Ostian knew that his hands were but the means of freeing what already lived within the marble. His skill (modesty forbade him from calling his talent genius) lay in seeing what the finished product would be before he laid so much as the first subbia upon the stone. The marble not yet carved could hold the form of every thought the artist could conceive.

Ostian Delafour was a slight man with a thin, earnest face and narrow, long fingered hands sheathed in silver metal that gleamed like mercury and which constantly fidgeted with whatever came to hand, as though the digits had a life beyond that dictated to them by their master. He wore a long white smock over a finely cut suit of black silk and cream shirt, the formal nature of his clothes at odds with the untidy workshop in which he spent most of his time.

'Now I'm ready,' he whispered.

'I should hope so,' said a woman's voice behind him. 'Bequa will have a conniption if we're late for her recital, you know how she gets.'

Ostian smiled and said, 'No, Serena, I meant I'm ready to begin sculpting.'

He turned and undid the ties holding his smock, lifting it over his head as Serena d'Angelus swept into his studio like one of the terrible matriarchs played so well by Coraline Aseneca. She tutted in distaste at the scattered tools, ladders and scaffolds. Ostian knew that her own studio was as neat and immaculate as his was disordered; the paints stacked neatly by colour and tone to one side, and her brushes and palette knives, as spotless and sharp as the day she had first acquired them, on the other.

Short and with the kind of attractiveness that completely eluded her as to why men found her desirable, Serena d'Angelus was perhaps the greatest painter of the Remembrancer order. Others favoured the landscapes of Kelan Roget, who travelled with the 12th Expedition of Roboute Guilliman, but Ostian felt that Serena's skill was the greater.

Even if she doesn't think so, he thought, stealing a glance at the long sleeves of her dress.

For Bequa Kynska's recital, Serena had chosen a long, formal gown of cerulean silk with an unfeasibly tight gold basque that accentuated the swell of her breasts. As always, she wore her hair unbound, the long, raven-dark tresses reaching to her waist and framing her long, oval face and dark almond-shaped eyes perfectly.

'You look beautiful, Serena,' he said.

'Thank you, Ostian,' said Serena, standing before him and fussing with his collar. 'You, however, look as though you've just woken up in that suit.'

'It's fine,' protested Ostian as she undid his necktie and painstakingly retied it.

'Fine, darling, is not good enough,' said Serena, 'as well you know. Bequa will want to preen once this damn recital is over and I won't have her saying we *artists* embarrassed her by looking shabby and bohemian.'

Ostian grinned. 'Yes, she does have rather a dim view of the practical arts.'

'It comes of a pampered upbringing in the hives of Europa,' said Serena. 'And did I hear you say that you were ready to begin sculpting?'

'Yes,' nodded Ostian, 'I am. I can see what's inside now. I only have to set it free.'

'Well I'm sure Lord Fulgrim will be glad to hear that,' said Serena. 'I hear he had to ask the Emperor personally to have that stone shipped all the way from Terra.'

'Oh, well no pressure then...' said Ostian as Serena turned away from him, satisfied that he was as presentable as he was going to get.

'You'll be fine, darling. You and your hands will soon have that marble singing.'

'And your work?' asked Ostian. 'How are you getting on with the portrait?'

Serena sighed. 'It's getting there, but with the pace Lord Fulgrim is setting for the fighting, it's a rare day I get him to sit for me.'

Ostian watched as Serena unconsciously scratched at her arms as she continued, 'Every day it sits unfinished I see more and more I hate about it. I think I may start again.'

'No,' said Ostian, prising her hands away from her arms. 'You're exaggerating. It's fine, and once the Laer are defeated, I'm sure Lord Fulgrim will sit for you as much as you need him to.'

She smiled, but Ostian could see the lie behind it. He wished he knew how to lift her from the melancholy that weighed upon her soul, and undo the harm she was doing to herself.

Instead, he said, 'Come on. We shouldn't keep Bequa waiting.'

OSTIAN HAD TO admit that Bequa Kynska, former child prodigy of the Europa hives was now a beautiful woman. Her wild blue hair was the colour of the sky on a clear day, and her features were sculpted by good breeding and discreet surgery, though she wore an overabundance of facial cosmetics that, to Ostian's mind, only detracted from her natural beauty. Just beneath her hair, he could make out aural enhancers and a number of fine wires trailing from her scalp.

Bequa had been educated at the finest academies of Terra and trained at the newly established Conservatoire de Musique – though, in truth, the time she had spent at the latter institution had largely been wasted, as there had been little the tutors there could teach her that she did not already know. People the length and breadth of the galaxy listened to her operas and harmonious ensembles, and her skill in creating music that could lift the soul and raise the rafters with its energy was second to none.

Ostian had met Bequa twice before aboard the *Pride of the Emperor*, and each time had been repulsed by her monstrous ego and intolerably high opinion of herself. But, for some unknown reason, Bequa Kynska seemed to adore him.

Dressed in a layered gown the colour of her hair, Bequa sat alone on a raised stage at the far end of the recital hall, head down and perched before a

multi-symphonic harpsichord linked to a number
of sonic projectors spaced at regular intervals
around the hall.

The recital hall itself was a wide chamber of dark
wood panelling and porphyry columns illuminated
by subdued lumen globes bobbing on floating
gravitic generators. Stained glass windows
depicting purple-armoured Astartes of the
Emperor's Children ran the length of one wall and
a row of marble busts said to have been carved by
the primarch himself lined the other.

Ostian made a mental note to examine them
later.

Perhaps a thousand people filled the hall, some
clad in the beige robes of remembrancers, others in
the sober black robes of Terran adepts. Others still
wore classically fashioned brocaded jackets, striped
trousers and high, black boots that marked them as
Imperial nobility, many of whom had joined the
28th Expedition specifically to hear Bequa play.

Amongst the crowd were soldiers of the Imperial
Army: senior officers bearing feathered helmets,
cavalry lancers in golden breastplates, and discipline masters in red greatcoats. A profusion of
different coloured uniforms circulated through the
recital hall, the click of sabres and spurs loud on
the polished wooden floor.

Surprised at the sheer number of uniforms he
saw, Ostian said, 'How can all these army officers
afford the time to attend events like this? Aren't we
at war with an alien species?'

'There's *always* time for art, my dear Ostian,' said
Serena, procuring two crystal flutes of sparkling
wine from one of the liveried pages that passed
quietly to and fro among the crowd. 'War may be a

harsh mistress, but she's got nothing on Bequa Kynska.'

'I don't see why I have to be here,' said Ostian, sipping the wine and enjoying the refreshing crispness of the beverage.

'Because she has invited you, and one does not refuse such an invite.'

'But I don't even like her,' protested Ostian. 'Why would she bother to invite *me*?'

'Because she likes you, you silly goose,' said Serena, nudging him playfully in the ribs with her elbow, 'if you know what I mean.'

Ostian sighed. 'I can't imagine why, I've barely spoken to the woman. Not that she let me get a word in edgeways anyway.'

'Trust me,' said Serena, placing a delicate hand on his arm, 'you want to be here.'

'Really? Enlighten me as to why.'

'You haven't heard Bequa play have you?' asked Serena with a smile.

'I've heard her phonocasts.'

'My boy,' said Serena, theatrically pretending to swoon, 'if one has not heard Bequa Kynska with one's own ears, *one has heard nothing!* You will need lots of handkerchiefs, for you will cry a great deal! Or failing that, take a sedative because you will be exalted to the point of delirium!'

'Fine,' said Ostian, already wishing he was back in his studio with the marble, 'I'll stay.'

'Trust me,' chuckled Serena, 'it will be worth your while.'

Eventually the hubbub of conversation in the hall began to subside. Serena took hold of his arm and placed a finger to her lips. He looked for the source of the gathering silence then saw that a vast figure in white robes with long flowing blond hair had entered the recital hall.

'Astartes…' breathed Ostian. 'I had no idea they were so huge.'

'That is First Captain Julius Kaesoron,' said Serena, and Ostian caught the smug tone to her voice.

'You know him?'

'He has asked me to create a likeness of him, yes,' beamed Serena. 'It transpires that he's quite the patron of the arts. Pleasant fellow and he has promised to keep me informed of opportunities that might arise.'

'Opportunities?' asked Ostian. 'What kind of opportunities?'

Serena did not reply and an expectant hush fell upon the privileged assembly as the lumen globes dimmed yet further. Ostian looked towards the stage as Bequa moved her hands across the keyboard of the harpsichord. A sudden, energetic and romantic feeling overcame him as the sonic projectors precisely magnified the intensity of her overture.

Then the performance began, and Ostian found his dislike of Bequa swept away as he heard the sound of a storm take shape in the music. At first he heard raindrops, then the symphonic wind picked up and suddenly there was a downpour. He heard torrents of rain, lashing wind and the throb of thunder. He looked up, half expecting to see dark clouds.

Trombones, a shrill piccolo and thundering timpani swelled and danced in the air as the music grew bolder, transforming into a passionate symphony that told its epic story in the tones and moods created, though Ostian would later remember nothing of its substance.

Vocal soloists combined with an orchestra, though he could see no trace of either, the soaring music yearning for peace, joy, and the brotherhood of Man.

Ostian felt tears pouring down his face as his soul was given flight, then plunged into despair, before rising towards a majestic, exultant climax by the power of the music.

He looked over at Serena, and seeing that she was similarly moved, wanted to pull her close and share in the joyous expression of his feeling. Ostian looked back to the stage where Bequa swayed like a madwoman, her sapphire blue hair whipping around her face as she played, her hands moving like dervishes across the keyboard.

Movement drew Ostian's eyes to the front of the enraptured audience, where he saw a nobleman in a silver breastplate and high collared jacket of navy blue lean over to his consort and whisper something in her ear.

Instantly, the music ceased and Ostian cried out as the beautiful concerto came to a crashing halt. Its absence left an aching emptiness in his heart and he felt an unreasoning hatred towards this boorish noble who had caused its premature end.

Bequa stood from her instrument, her chest heaving with exertion and an expression of fury plastered across her face.

She stared thunderously at the nobleman and said, 'I do not play for such pigs!'

The man stood angrily from his seat, his features flushed. 'You insult me, woman. I am Paljor Dorji, sixth Marquis of the Terawatt Clan and a patrician of Terra. You will show me some damned respect!'

Bequa spat on the wooden floor and said, 'You are what you are by an accident of birth. What I am, I created myself. There are thousands of nobles of Terra, but there is only one Bequa Kynska.'

'I demand you play on, woman!' shouted Paljor Dorji. 'Do you have any idea how many strings I had to pull to have myself assigned to this expedition in order to hear you play?'

'I neither know nor care,' snapped Bequa. 'Genius such as mine is worth any price. Double it, triple it, you have not even begun to place a value on what you have heard tonight. But it is irrelevant, for I shall play no more this day.'

A chorus of denials filled the air as the audience begged for her to resume playing. Ostian found his voice joined with that of the audience. It appeared, however, that Bequa Kynska was not to be swayed until a powerful voice at the door to the recital chamber cut through the clamour and said, 'Mistress Kynska.'

All heads turned at the commanding sound of the voice and Ostian felt his pulse quicken as he saw who had stilled the crowd: Fulgrim, the Phoenician.

The Primarch of the Emperor's Children was the most magnificent being Ostian Delafour had ever laid eyes upon. His amethyst-coloured armour shone as though fresh from the armourer's hand, its golden trims gleaming like the sun, and exquisite carvings twisted in spiral patterns on every plate of his armour. A long, scaled cloak of emerald green hung from his shoulders, a high collar of purple and the great eagle's wing sweeping over his left shoulder perfectly framing his pale features.

Ostian longed to render Fulgrim's face in marble, knowing that the coolness of the stone was perfect for capturing the luminosity of the primarch's skin, the wide, friendly eyes, the hint of a smile playing

around his lips and the shimmering white of his
shoulder length hair.

Ostian and the remainder of the audience
dropped to their knees in awe of Fulgrim's majesty,
humbled by perfection they would never come close
to achieving.

'If you will not play for the marquis, would you
consent to do so for me?' asked Fulgrim.

Bequa Kynska nodded and the music began anew.

THE BATTLE ON Atoll 19 would later be described as
a minor, opening skirmish in the Cleansing of
Laeran; a footnote to the fighting that was yet to
come, but to the warriors in the speartip of
Solomon Demeter's Second Company of Emperor's
Children, it felt considerably more intense than a
skirmish.

Shrieking bolts of hot, green energy flashed down
the curving thoroughfare, melting portions of the
angled walls and dissolving Astartes battle plate
whenever they struck one of the advancing Space
Marines. The hungry crackle of fires and the whoosh
of missiles mingled with the hard bangs of bolter
fire and the shrieking horns from the coral towers as
Solomon's Astartes fought their way up the serpentine street to link with Marius Vairosean's squads.

Coiled towers of glittering crystal coral reared
above him like the gnarled conch shells of some
great sea creature, with smooth rimmed burrow
holes piercing the spires like the touch holes of a
musical instrument. The entire atoll was formed
from the same lightweight, but incredibly tough
material, though how these structures floated above
the vast oceans was a mystery the Mechanicum
adepts were eager to solve.

Screeching cries echoed from the disturbingly alien architecture, as though the spires themselves were screaming, and the damnable metallic slither of the aliens' movement seemed to come from all around them.

He ducked back behind a sinuous column of pink veined coral and slammed another magazine into his customised bolter, its every surface and internal working hand-finished by his own artifice. Its rate of fire was only marginally faster than a regular issue bolter, but it had never once jammed, and Solomon Demeter wasn't the kind of man to trust his life to anything he hadn't worked towards perfection.

'Gaius!' he shouted to his second in command, Gaius Caphen, 'Where in the name of the Phoenician is Tantearon squadron?'

His lieutenant shook his head, and Solomon cursed, knowing that the Laer had probably intercepted the Land Speeder squadron en route to them. Damn, these aliens were clever, he thought, remembering the grievous loss of Captain Aeson's flanking force, which had revealed that the Laer had somehow managed to compromise their vox-net. The idea of a xenos species with the ability to wreak such a violation on a Legion of the Astartes was unthinkable, and had only spurred Fulgrim's warriors to greater heights of wrath in their extermination.

Solomon Demeter was the very image of an Astartes, his short dark hair kept shaved close to his scalp, his skin tanned from the light of a score of suns, and his animated features rounded and wide spread on thick cheekbones. He disdained the wearing of a helmet to prevent the Laer from deciphering his orders over the vox-network, and because he

knew that if he were hit in the head by one of the
Laer weapons, he was as good as dead, helmet or not.

Knowing he could not expect any immediate help
from the aerial units, he knew they were going to have
to do this the hard way. Though it railed against his
sense of order and perfection to undertake this assault
without the proper support in place, he couldn't deny
that there was something exhilarating about making
things up as he went along. Some commanders said
that it was an inevitable fact that they would often
fight without the forces they wanted, but such a belief
was anathema to most of the Emperor's Children.

'Gaius, we're going to have to do this ourselves!' he
shouted. 'Make sure we've plenty of fire keeping those
xenos heads down!'

Caphen nodded and began issuing curt, concise
orders, with sharp chops of his hand, to the squads
spread through the rubble of what could laughingly
be called their landing zone.

Behind them, the wrecked Stormbird still burned
from where the alien missile had blown off its wing,
and Solomon knew that it was a miracle the pilot had
managed to coax the stricken aircraft to stay in the air
long enough to reach the floating atoll. He shuddered
to imagine their fate had they plunged to the vast
planetary ocean below, lost forever amid the sunken
ruins of the Laer's ancient civilisation.

The Laer had been waiting for them, and now at
least seven warriors were down and would never fight
again. Solomon had no idea how the other assault
units had fared, but couldn't imagine they had suffered any less. He risked a glance around the column,
its height oddly distorted by the eye-watering curves
and subtly wrong dimensions. Everything on this atoll
jarred upon his sensibilities, a riotous excess of colour,

form and noise that offended the senses with their sheer frenzy.

He could see a wide plaza ahead, in which a flaring plume of searing energy was enclosed by a ring of bright coral that shone with a dazzling light. Dozens of such strange plumes were spread throughout the atolls, and the Mechanicum adepts believed that it was these peculiar devices that prevented the atolls from falling from the sky.

With no major landmasses on Laeran, capturing the atolls intact was deemed integral to the success of the coming campaign. The atolls would serve as bridgeheads and staging areas for all further assaults, and Fulgrim himself had declared that the energy plumes keeping the atolls in the air were to be captured at any cost.

Solomon caught glimpses of Laer warriors slithering around the base of the energy plume, their movements sinuous and inhumanly quick. First Captain Kaesoron had personally tasked the Second with securing the plaza, and Solomon had sworn an oath in the fire that he would not fail.

'Gaius, take your men right and work your way through cover towards the plaza. Keep your head down. They're sure to have warriors positioned to stop you. Send Thelonius on the left.'

'What about you?' Caphen shouted back over the din of gunfire, 'Where are you going?'

Solomon smiled. 'Where else but the centre? I'm going to take Charosian's lot, but make sure Goldoara are in position before I move. I don't want anyone moving before we've set down a weight of fire so heavy I could walk on it.'

'Sir,' said Caphen, 'without wishing to appear impertinent, are you sure that's the right choice?'

Solomon racked the slide on his bolter and said, 'You fuss too much over making the "right" choice, Gaius. All we need do is make a good choice, see it through and accept the consequences.'

'If you say so, sir,' said Caphen.

'I do!' shouted Solomon. 'We may not be able to do it by the book this time, but by Chemos, we'll do it well! Now pass the word.'

Solomon waited as his orders were issued to the warriors under his command, and felt the familiar thrill of excitement as he prepared to take the fight to the enemy once more. He knew that Caphen disapproved of his cavalier attitude, but Solomon firmly believed that only through such testing circumstances could warriors better themselves and so more closely approach the perfection embodied by their primarch.

Sergeant Charosian edged up behind him, his veteran warriors gathered around him in the shadow of a Laer burrow complex.

'Ready, sergeant?' asked Solomon.

'Indeed, sir,' replied Charosian.

'Then let's go!' shouted Solomon as he heard Goldoara squad open up with their support weapons. The bark and thump of heavy calibre shells thundering up the road was the sound he'd been waiting for, and he slid from the cover of the pillar and charged up the centre of the street towards the crackling energy tower.

Bolts of deadly green energy flashed past him, but he could tell they were not aimed, the weight of suppressing fire keeping the aliens from showing themselves. He heard gunfire from either side of him and knew that Caphen and Thelonius were having to fight their way towards the tower. The veteran Space Marines of Charosian followed him, firing from the

hip and adding to the weight of fire provided by
Goldoara.

Just as he thought they might reach the spire unmolested, the Laer attacked.

GATHERED TOGETHER IN a single system, the Laer had
been one of the first species encountered by the
Emperor's Children after taking their leave from the
Luna Wolves and the great triumph on Ullanor. The
cheers of that momentous day still rang in their ears,
and the sight of so many primarchs gathered together
remained a vivid, joyous memory in the minds of the
Emperor's Children.

As Horus had said when he and Fulgrim had shared
a heartfelt farewell, it was an end of things and a
beginning of things, for Horus was now the
Emperor's Regent, Warmaster of all the Imperium's
armies. Now that the Emperor had returned to Terra,
entire fleets, billions of warriors and the power to
destroy worlds were his to command.

Warmaster…

The title was a new one, created for Horus, and its
unveiling had yet to find its fit in the minds of the primarchs, who found themselves subject to the
command of one who had, until then, been their
equal.

The Emperor's Children had welcomed the
appointment, for they counted the warriors of the
Luna Wolves as their closest brothers. A terrible accident at the inception of the Emperor's Children had
almost destroyed them, but Fulgrim and his Legion
had risen, phoenix-like, from the disaster with greater
resolve and strength. In the process Fulgrim had
earned the affectionate sobriquet of 'the Phoenician'.
During this time, while Fulgrim rebuilt his shattered

Legion, he and his few warriors had fought alongside the Luna Wolves for almost a century.

With a stream of fresh recruits drawn from Terra and Fulgrim's home of Chemos, the Legion had grown rapidly and, under the aegis of the Warmaster, become one of the deadliest fighting forces in the galaxy.

Horus himself had praised Fulgrim's Legion as one of the best he had fought alongside.

Now, with decades of war behind them, the Emperor's Children had the numbers to embark on crusades of their own, to make their own way in the galaxy, battling alone for the first time in over a century.

The Legion was hungry to prove itself, and Fulgrim had thrown his all into making up for the time lost while he had rebuilt his Legion, seeking to push the boundaries of the Imperium yet further and prove the courage and worth of his Legion.

First contact with the Laer had come about when one of the 28th Expedition's forward scout ships had discovered evidence of civilisation in a nearby binary cluster and determined that it was a culture of some sophistication. Though initially not hostile to the Imperial forces, this alien race had reacted violently when one of the 28th Expedition's scout forces had been sent towards their home world. A small, but powerful alien war fleet had attacked the Imperial vessels as they approached the system's core world, destroying every one of them without the loss of a single vessel.

From what little information had been gathered before the scout force's destruction, the Mechanicum adepts had discovered that the aliens called themselves the Laer and that their technology was capable of matching and, in many cases, exceeding that of the Imperium.

The bulk of Laer society appeared to exist on numerous, city-sized atolls of floating coral that plied the skies of Laeran, an oceanic planet that bore all the hallmarks of a world submerged by the melting of its ice caps. Only the peaks of what had once been its tallest mountains and structures protruded from the mighty seas that covered its entire surface.

Administrators from the Council of Terra had postulated that perhaps the Laer could be made a protectorate of the Imperium, since conquering such an advanced race could prove a long and costly endeavour.

Fulgrim had rejected such a notion out of hand, famously saying, 'Only humanity is perfect and for an alien race to hold its own ideals and technology as comparable to ours is profane. No, the Laer deserve only extinction.'

And so the Cleansing of Laeran was begun.

TWO

The Phoenix Gate/The Eagle will Rule/In the Fire

OF ALL THE ships in the 28th Expedition, the *Pride of the Emperor* was the most magnificent, its armoured length inlaid with gold and armoured plates the colour of rich wine. It orbited the sapphire blue world of Laeran like the regal flagship of some ancient king, surrounded by an entourage of escorts, battleships, transports, supply vessels and army mass conveyers.

The shipwrights of Jupiter had laid its keel a hundred and sixty years ago, the design and creation overseen by the Fabricator General of Mars himself, and its every component crafted by hand to unimaginably exacting specifications. The construction process had taken twice as long as any other vessel of comparable displacement, but such was only to be expected for the flagship of the Primarch of the III Legion, the Emperor's Children.

The formation of 28th Expedition was a thing of martial beauty, perfectly anchored above Laeran in a textbook pattern of patrol and compliance that ensured nothing hostile could reach or leave the planet without being intercepted by the *Raptores* of the Imperial fleet. The vessels of the Laer that had proven so deadly to the expedition's scout fleet were now wreckage, drifting around the rings of the system's sixth planet, destroyed by the precise use of overwhelming force and Fulgrim's mastery of naval warfare.

Though the world below was known as Laeran, its official designation was Twenty-Eight Three, being the third world the 28th Expedition had brought to compliance. Though such an appellation was somewhat premature, given the ferocity of the opening battle attesting to its non-compliance, its usage was considered appropriate since compliance was deemed a certainty.

The *Andronius* and *Fulgrim's Virtue*, liveried in the purple and gold of the Emperor's Children, stood sentinel over the primarch's flagship, each with an exemplary legacy of victory behind them. Flocks of *Raptores* darted back and forth as they escorted the great and the good of the 28th Expedition to the *Pride of the Emperor*, for with the Laer fleet eliminated, the primarch was to unveil his plans to prosecute the war.

FIRST CAPTAIN JULIUS Kaesoron was a man not used to conflicting emotions, which made his current situation deeply uncomfortable. Dressed in the triumphal purple of his *toga picta* and the martial red of his *lacerna* cloak, he cut an imposing figure as he marched swiftly to the Heliopolis, followed by his equerry, Lycaon, and a retinue of bearers who carried his helmet, sword and trailing cloak.

A pendant of fiery amber hung around his neck and nestled between the carved pectorals of his golden breastplate. Nothing of his discomfort showed on his patrician features, for to display such emotion would suggest that he doubted the course his primarch had set, and that was unthinkable.

They marched along a wide processional way with pale walls of cool marble and towering onyx columns, their surfaces inlaid with gold lettering that spoke of battles won and glories gained during the Great Crusade. The *Pride of the Emperor* was to be Fulgrim's legacy to the future, and its walls bore the history of the Imperium carved into its very bones.

Statues of the Legion's heroes lined the processional way and gilt framed artworks commissioned from the expedition's remembrancers brought some much needed colour to the cold space.

'Are we in a hurry?' asked Lycaon, his armour shining and polished, though much less ostentatious than that of the first captain. 'I thought the Lord Fulgrim said he would await your arrival before presenting his course to the expedition.'

'He did,' snapped Julius, though he quickened his pace, much to the consternation of his bearers, 'but if we are to do what he demands, then the sooner I am down on Twenty-Eight Three the better. A month, Lycaon! He wants Laeran compliant in a month!'

'The men are ready,' promised Lycaon. 'We can do it!'

'I don't doubt we can do it, Lycaon, but the butcher's bill will be high, perhaps too high.'

'The Stormbirds are prepped on their launch rails and we await only your word to unleash them on the Laer.'

'I know,' nodded Julius, 'but we must await the primarch's order to launch.'

'Even though Captain Demeter's speartip has already launched?' asked Lycaon as they passed Emperor's Children armed with golden *pilum* spears at regular intervals along the triumphal way. Though they stood as immobile as the statues, the fierce potential for violence that beat within the breast of every Astartes warrior was evident in each of them.

'Even so,' agreed Julius, 'it would be impolitic to begin the campaign proper without consulting the other officers of the expedition, so the speartip will be presented as reconnaissance in force rather than as the opening strike of a campaign.'

Lycaon shrugged and shook his head. 'What do we care for the feelings of the expedition? The primarch commands and they are his to order as he sees fit. Such is only right and proper.'

Though he agreed with Lycaon, Julius didn't answer, chafing at not leading the warriors on the planet below. He had listened to the initial vox reports of Solomon and Marius, who were, even now, involved in heavy fighting to secure the floating land-mass known as Atoll 19, with growing anger as the casualty reports flooded in.

But his primarch had ordered his presence at the council of war that would announce the manner in which the 28th Expedition would make war upon this alien species and such orders were not to be denied.

Julius already knew what the Lord Fulgrim was to present to the senior commanders of the fleet, and the audacity and scale of it still took his breath away. You didn't need to be First Captain of the Emperor's Children to know what their reaction would be.

'Enough talking, Lycaon, we're here,' he said as he saw the great Phoenix Gate before them, a towering bronze portal that depicted the Emperor symbolically presenting Fulgrim with the Imperial eagle. The eagle was the Emperor's own symbol, and he had commanded that Fulgrim's Legion alone bear it upon their armour, as a mark of the regard in which they were held. The honour done to the Emperor's Children was immeasurable. As he saw the gate, Julius felt fierce pride swell within his breast, and he reached up to touch the carved eagle on his armour.

More guards stood before the Phoenix Gate, and they bowed deeply as he approached, clashing their spears into the ground as the great leaves of bronze smoothly parted before him, a slice of white light and the hubbub of voices drifting through from beyond.

He nodded respectfully to the warriors at the gate and passed through into the Heliopolis.

SOLOMON SPUN HIS bolter to face the creature that slashed through the air towards him, its claws outstretched to tear him in two. His finger squeezed the trigger and a hail of bolts spat from the barrel of his gun. Sparks and yellow blood spattered his purple and gold armour as the creature burst apart and collapsed in a torn heap beside him. More followed it, and soon the plaza was alive with whipping, sinuous bodies and struggling Astartes.

In appearance, each Laer could be wildly diverse, their bio-forms differing between war zones, and apparently engineered for each particular theatre of war. In his short time on the oceanic world of Laeran, Solomon had seen winged, aquatic and all manner of variations on the basic Laer form. Whether they were divergent strands of genetic mutation or deliberately engineered warrior creatures, Solomon didn't know, nor did he care.

These particular beasts were tall, sinuous monsters, with the snake-like lower body common to all Laer, and muscular thoraxes sheathed in silver armour, from which sprouted two pairs of limbs. The upper arms each bore long, lightning wreathed blades, their elegant forms curved like scimitars, while the lower arms each wielded crackling gauntlets that fired the lethal green energy bolts.

Their heads were insect-like and bulbous, with glossy, multi-faceted eyes and jutting mandibles that produced a grating screech when the Laer attacked. Solomon spun on the spot, firing his bolter at every slithering body that emerged from the alien structures carved from the hard coral of the atoll. The veterans who accompanied him formed a curving line with him at its centre, each warrior moving smoothly into his allotted place to push the Laer back towards the crackling plume of energy in the middle of the plaza with every marching step they took.

Bolter rounds filled the air, and explosions sent chunks of coral flying, as the unstoppable advance of the Emperor's Children pushed deeper into the screaming ruins of the floating city. With no inter-suit vox, Solomon had no idea how Caphen or Thelonius were doing, but trusted their expertise and courage to see them through. Solomon had person-ally approved both their commands and whatever fate befell them was his responsibility.

Green fire washed from a previously unseen bur-row entrance and a trio of Astartes warriors went down, their armour and flesh disintegrating beneath the electrochemical energies.

'Enemy to the flank!' shouted Solomon and his warriors reacted with smooth precision to meet the threat. As the Laer emerged from their hiding place, they were met by disciplined volleys of bolter fire, the first Emperor's Children to meet the threat shifting position to allow their comrades to fire while they reloaded.

Solomon watched with pride as they fought with a flawless martial discipline unmatched by any other Legion. The berserk rages of Russ's Wolves or the wild showmanship of the Khan's Riders were not the way of the Emperor's Children. Fulgrim's Legion fought with the cold, clinical application of perfect force and discipline.

A huge explosion mushroomed skyward from Solomon's right and he heard the crash of falling coral as a conch tower collapsed in a billowing cloud of dust and fire, its damnable horns silenced as it smashed to pieces. The Emperor's Children had pushed some forty metres into the plaza, their curving line of advance carrying them into the centre of its crater and rubble strewn openness.

The plume of energy was close enough for him to feel its heat and as he gave the order to surround it, the Laer renewed their assault, their writhing bodies slipping around the ruins of their homes with unnatural speed. Whipping bolts of green light and bolter rounds crisscrossed the plaza, flaring explosions rippling the air as the occasional pair of shots impacted on one another.

A boiling tide of aliens slid towards the Emperor's Children, their snake-like lower bodies powering them across the uneven ground with unnatural speed, and Solomon knew that the time for guns was over. He placed his bolter on the ground with reverent care and drew his chainblade from its sheath across his back.

Like his bolter, he had extensively modified his sword in the *Pride of the Emperor's* armouries under the stern gaze of Marius Vairosean. The blade and grip of the weapon had been lengthened to increase his reach and to allow him to wield the blade two handed. The quillons were fashioned in the form of upswept wings and the pommel bore a majestic eagle's head.

He thumbed the activation stud and shouted, 'Unsheath!'

A hundred blades glittered in the sunlight as the circle of Emperor's Children drew their swords in one smooth motion.

The Laer hit the Emperor's Children in a blur of silver armour and crackling blades, the Astartes stepping in to meet their enemies head to head. Mars-forged steel met alien blades in a clash of fire that echoed throughout the city.

Solomon ducked a blow aimed at his head and spun inside the stroke of the alien's second blade, driving his sword into the gap between his foe's armoured thorax and lower body. The teeth of his blade ground on its thick spine, but he forced the blade onwards, dropping the creature into two flopping halves.

His warriors fought with calm serenity, confident in their superiority and knowing that their leader was among them. Solomon tore his blade free from the alien he had killed and stepped onwards, his warriors following his example and grimly fighting with killing strokes.

The first warning of something amiss was when a violent tremor shook the ground with a rumbling vibration. Then suddenly the world shifted as the ground violently canted to the side. Solomon was pitched to the ground, rolling on the slanted plaza and tumbling into one of the many deep craters that dotted the battlefield.

He quickly righted himself and scanned his immediate area for threats, but could see nothing, hearing the sound of battle from above him and gunfire closing on the plaza from either side. If the suspicions of the Mechanicum were correct and the energy coils were what kept the atolls afloat in the sky, it seemed likely that one or more elsewhere on the atoll must have been destroyed.

Solomon rolled to his feet and sheathed his sword as he began clambering up the rocky slopes of the crater. As he neared the top, he felt the hairs on the back of his neck stand to attention, and looked up in time to see the silhouette of a Laer warrior over the lip of the crater.

He reached for his sword, but the Lear was on him before he could draw the weapon.

THOUGH JULIUS KAESORON had stood in the Heliopolis many hundreds of times, its beauty and majesty still had the power to render him speechless with its towering walls of pale stone and rank upon rank of marble statues on golden plinths that supported the vast domed room. Intricate mosaics, too high to make out the details, filled the coffers of the dome and long, silk banners of purple and gold hung between fluted pilasters of green marble.

A lustrous beam of focused starlight shone down from the centre of the dome, reflecting dazzlingly from the black terrazzo floor of the Heliopolis. Marble and quartz chips laid into the mortar and ground to a polished sheen turned the floor into a glittering, dark mirror that shone like the heavens beyond. Dust motes danced in the brightness, and the smoky aroma of scented oils filled the air.

Rows of marble benches ran around the circumference of Fulgrim's council chamber, rising in stepped tiers towards the walls in serried ranks, enough to seat two thousand men, though barely a quarter of that number were present for this council of war. A chair of polished black marble sat in the centre of the pillar of starlight and it was from here that Lord Fulgrim heard the petitions of his warriors and granted audiences. Though the primarch had not yet graced this assemblage with his arrival, the empty chair was a potent presence in the chamber.

Julius saw officers drawn from all the military arms of the 28th Expedition seated in the marble benches, and moved to take his place on the bench nearest the floor, nodding to men whose faces he knew and noticing wary glances at his red *lacerna* cloak. Those who had served with the Emperor's Children for any length of time knew that the wearing of such a cloak signified a warrior about to go into battle.

Julius ignored their stares and retrieved his sword and helmet from his bearers before taking his seat. He cast his eyes around the chamber, seeing silver and scarlet officers of the Imperial Army filling the lower tiers of the Heliopolis, their closeness to the floor indicative of their higher ranks.

Lord Commander Fayle sat at the centre of a gaggle of flunkies and aides. He was a stern man with a horribly scarred face, augmented with a steel plate that obscured the left side of his head. Julius had never spoken to the man, but knew him by reputation; a skilled general, a blunt speaker and a ruthless, unforgiving soldier.

Behind the officers of the army, occupying the mid-level of seating, were the adepts of the Mechanicum, looking uncomfortable in the bright light of the Heliopolis. Their hooded robes hid much of their features, and Julius could not remember if he had ever seen one with his hood down. He shook his head at the foolish veils of secrecy and ritual they surrounded themselves with.

Alongside the Mechanicum were the remembrancers, earnest men and women in beige robes that scrawled in battered notepads and data-slates or sketched on cartridge paper with charcoals. The greatest artists, writers and poets of the Imperium had spread through the expedition fleets in their thousands to document the monumental achievements of the Great Crusade, meeting varying degrees of welcome. Precious few of the Legions appreciated their efforts, but Fulgrim had declared their presence to be a great boon and had granted them unprecedented access to his most intimate and guarded ceremonies.

Following his gaze, Lycaon spat, 'Remembrancers. What purpose do scriveners and their ilk serve at a council of war? Look, one of them has even brought an easel!'

Julius smiled and said, 'Perhaps he is attempting to capture the glory of the Heliopolis for future generations, my friend.'

'Russ has the truth of it,' said Lycaon. 'We are warriors, not subjects for poetry or portraits.'

'The pursuit of perfection extends beyond the martial disciplines, Lycaon. It encompasses fine arts, literary works and music. Only recently, I was privileged to hear Bequa Kynska's recital and my heart soared to hear such sweet music.'

'You've been reading poetry again, haven't you?' asked Lycaon, shaking his head.

'When I have the chance, I delve into one of Ignace Karkasy's *Imperial Cantos*,' admitted Julius. 'You should try it sometime. A little culture would be no bad thing for you. Fulgrim himself has a sculpture in his chambers that he commissioned from Ostian Delafour, and it's said that Eidolon has a landscape of Chemos painted by Keland Roget hanging above his bed.'

'Never! Eidolon?'

'So they say,' nodded Julius

'Who'd have thought it?' mused Lycaon. 'Anyway, I'll stick to achieving perfection in war if it's all the same to you.'

'Your loss,' said Julius, as the benches in the upper reaches of the Heliopolis filled with people; the scribes, notaries and functionaries who served those nearer the centre of power.

'Big turnout,' noted Lycaon.

'The primarch is going to speak,' said Julius. 'That always brings the adorers out.'

As though speaking his name was the key to summoning him, the Phoenix Gate opened and the Primarch of the III Legion entered the Heliopolis.

Fulgrim was flanked by his senior lord commanders, and the assembled warriors, adepts and scribes immediately rose to their feet and bowed their heads in wonder at the magnificent, perfect warrior before them.

Julius rose with them, his earlier discomfort washed away in the rush of excitement at seeing his beloved primarch once again. A swell of rippling applause and cries of 'Phoenician!' filled the Heliopolis, a roaring gesture of affirmation that only halted when

Fulgrim raised his palms to quiet his reverent followers.

The primarch wore a long flowing toga of pale cream, and the dark iron hilt of his sword, *Fireblade*, was visible at his hip, the blade itself sheathed in a scabbard of gleaming purple leather. The flaring wings of an eagle were embroidered in gold thread across his chest and a slender band of lapis lazuli kept his silver hair from his face. Two of the Legion's greatest warriors, Lord Commander Vespasian and Lord Commander Eidolon came in behind the primarch. Both warriors were dressed in plain, white togas, unadorned save for a small eagle motif over the right breast. Their stern martial bearing was an inspiration for Julius, who held himself a little straighter at their presence.

Eidolon looked unimpressed at the gathered warriors, while Vespasian's humours were unreadable behind his flawless, classical features. Both lord commanders were armed, Vespasian's sword held sheathed at his side and Eidolon's hammer carried upon his shoulder.

Julius could feel the tension in the air as the expedition awaited Fulgrim's words.

'My friends,' began Fulgrim, taking his seat before the assembled warriors, his pale skin radiant in the glow from above, 'it gladdens my heart to see you gathered so. It has been too long since last we made war, but what a chance we have now to remedy that.'

Though he knew what was coming, Julius felt an unreasoning excitement build within him and saw that the normally sardonic Lycaon smiled broadly when he heard the primarch speak.

'We orbit the world of a fearsome species that calls itself the Laer,' continued Fulgrim, his voice having lost the Cthonic harshness he had picked up while the Emperor's Children had fought alongside the Warmaster's Luna Wolves. The cultured accent of Old Terra again flavoured every syllable, and Julius found himself beguiled by the timbre and cadence of the primarch's words. 'And such a world it is! One that the honoured representatives from the Mechanicum tell me would be of immeasurable value to the crusade of the Emperor, he who is beloved by all.'

'Beloved by all,' echoed the chamber.

Fulgrim nodded and said, 'Though a world such as this would be of immense value to us, its alien inhabitants do not wish to share what blind fortune has blessed them with. They refuse to see the manifest destiny that guides us through the stars and have made it abundantly clear that they hold us in nothing but contempt. Our peaceable advances have been rebuffed with violence, and honour demands we answer in kind!'

Angry shouts of threatened violence filled the Heliopolis. Fulgrim smiled, clasping his hands to his chest in thanks for their devotion. As the cheering and shouts died away, Julius saw Lord Commander Fayle stand and bow deeply to the primarch.

'If I may?' ventured the soldier, his voice deep and laden with experience.

'Of course, Thaddeus, you are my most favoured ally,' said Fulgrim, and Fayle's stern mask twitched in pleasure at being addressed by his first name.

Julius smiled as he remembered the skill with which Fulgrim flattered those he spoke to, knowing full well that he was soon to blindside Fayle with hard facts and uncomfortable truths.

'Thank you, my lord,' began Fayle, placing his gnarled hands on the wall that separated him from the dark floor of the Heliopolis. As Thaddeus Fayle spoke, microscopic motes of crystal floating in the column of light focused on the Army commander, wreathing him in a diffuse glow. 'Perhaps you can enlighten me as to something?'

Fulgrim smiled and his dark eyes were alive with mirth. 'I shall endeavour to bring illumination to your ignorance.'

Fayle bristled at the implied insult, but pressed on. 'You have called us here for a council of war regarding what is to be done with Twenty-Eight Three? Yes?'

'Indeed I have,' replied Fulgrim. 'For I could not conceive of undertaking such a decision without your counsel.'

'Then why have you already sent warriors to the planet's surface?' asked Fayle with impressive force of will. Most mortals were rendered imbecilic simply by standing in the presence of a primarch, but Thaddeus Fayle spoke as though to a member of his own staff, and Julius felt his choler rise at such boorish behaviour.

'I heard word that the Council of Terra had decided that subjugating the Laer would cost too many lives and would take too long. Ten years was the figure I heard,' continued Fayle without pause. 'Wasn't there even talk of making them a protectorate of the Imperium?'

Julius saw the faint, but unmistakable signs of Fulgrim's annoyance at being so questioned, though he must surely have known that virtually the entire expedition was aware of the assault on Atoll 19 and that he would face such interrogation.

Such was the price of cultivating openness within the expedition, Julius realised.

'There was indeed such talk,' said Fulgrim, 'but it was ill-founded and singularly failed to appreciate the value of this planet to the Imperium. The attack underway is an attempt to gather a more thorough appreciation of the war capability of the Laer.'

'Surely the destruction of our scout ships demonstrated that amply, my lord,' said Fayle. 'It seems to me that you already have your course set on war without consulting us.'

'And what of it, lord commander?' asked Fulgrim, his eyes flashing with dangerous anger. 'Would you back down from the effrontery of a xenos species? Would you have me compromise my honour by meekly avoiding this fight because it might be dangerous?'

Lord Commander Fayle blanched at Fulgrim's tone, realising that he had pushed too far, and said, 'No, my lord. My forces are at your disposal as always.'

Fulgrim's features settled from annoyance to conciliation in a moment, and Julius knew that his outburst had been carefully orchestrated to manipulate Fayle into ceasing his questions. Fulgrim had already drawn up his perfect plans for war and was not about to be dissuaded from his course by the doubts of mortals.

'My thanks, lord commander,' said Fulgrim, 'and I apologise for my abruptness. You are right to ask such things, for it is said that a man's character can be judged by his questions rather than by his answers.'

'There's no need to apologise to me,' protested Fayle, uncomfortable at the suggestion he had angered the primarch. 'I spoke out of turn.'

Fulgrim inclined his head in the direction of the lord commander, accepting his apology, and said, 'You are gracious, Thaddeus and the matter is already forgotten, but we are here to discuss matters of war are we not? I have devised a campaign that will see Laeran delivered to us, and while I appreciate the counsel you all give me, this is the kind of war for which the Astartes were forged. I will outline its particulars to you in a moment, but as time is critical, I hope you will forgive me if I unleash my war dogs first.'

The primarch turned his gaze towards him, and despite himself, Julius felt his pulse quicken as Fulgrim's inky black eyes bored into him. He knew what question would be asked and only hoped his men could deliver on what Fulgrim was to demand of them.

'First Captain Kaesoron, are your warriors ready to take the Imperial Truth to Twenty-Eight Three?'

Julius stood to attention, feeling the light from the dome's room bathe him in radiance. 'I swear by the fire, they are, my lord. We await only your word.'

'Then the word is given, Captain Kaesoron,' said Fulgrim, casting off his robes to reveal his magnificently polished battle plate. 'In one month's time, the eagle will rule Laeran!'

THE LAER'S ARMS tore at Solomon's armour, dragging great gouges from its immaculate surfaces, the talons tearing through the gold eagle on his breastplate. The two warriors fell to the base of the crater as the ground shifted again and Solomon found himself pinned beneath the weight of the creature. Its mandibles opened wide and it screeched deafeningly in his face, spraying him with hot spittle and mucus.

Solomon shook his vision clear and punched upwards, his fist cracking bone beneath the ruddy red flesh of the alien warrior. It screeched once more and a burst of green light exploded from its fists as it stabbed one of its lower arms towards him. He rolled aside as the silver gauntlet sheared through the rock, as though it were no more solid than sand.

Solomon scrambled away from the creature, his back against the walls of the crater. The Laer howled, the power of its scream a physical force that sent Solomon staggering backwards, his ears ringing and his vision blurred. He tried to draw his sword, but the Laer was on him again before the weapon was halfway from its sheath. The combatants crashed to the ground in a maelstrom of thrashing armoured limbs and segmented claws.

The horrific eyes of the Laer reflected his contorted face, and he felt his anger and frustration rise at the thought of being trapped down in this crater while his men fought on above without him. Hot pain lanced into his side as the Laer scored its glowing green weapon across his flank, but he twisted away before it could drive the weapon up into his guts. He had nowhere to move and his back was still to the wall.

A string of unintelligible screeches emerged from its mandibles, and though its language was utterly alien to Solomon, he could have sworn that the monster was taking pleasure in this struggle.

'Come on then,' he snarled, bracing himself against the rocky side of the crater. The Laer coiled its serpentine form beneath it and leapt for him, its arms and claws extended towards him.

He leapt to engage it and the two met with a clash of armoured plate, tumbling to the ground once more. As they fell, Solomon seized one of the Laer's glowing arms and smashed his elbow down hard on the junction of the limb and the creature's body.

The arm sheared from its body in a spray of stinking blood and Solomon spun on his heel, driving the energy sheathed weapon up into its middle. The glowing edge easily tore through the silver armour and the Laer collapsed in a coil of ruptured flesh. A howling shriek burst from its throat as it died, and again Solomon was repulsed by the pleasure he heard in its cry.

Disgusted, Solomon threw the Laer's severed arm down, the dim glow already fading from the foul weapon. Once again he scrambled up the side of the crater, hauling himself over the lip in time to see his warriors struggling against yet more of the Laer as they poured into the plaza.

Isolated from the fighting for a moment, Solomon saw that his warriors were trapped, desperately defending against this tide of aliens. His practiced eye saw that without reinforcements there could be no holding it against such numbers. Dozens of Astartes were already down, their bodies twitching as the alien weapons triggered involuntary nerve spasms in their wounded flesh.

His sense for the shape of a battle told him that his warriors knew they were on the verge of being overwhelmed, and his choler rose at the thought of these aliens defiling the bodies of the Second.

'Children of the Emperor!' he bellowed, marching from the crater into the lines of fighting Astartes. 'Hold the line! I swore in the fire to First Captain Kaesoron that we would capture this place and we will not be shamed by failing in that oath!'

He saw an almost invisible stiffening of backs and knew that his warriors would not shame him. The Second had never yet shown their backs to an enemy and he did not expect them to now.

In ancient times, when warriors had run from battle, their ranks had been decimated, one in every ten warriors beaten to death by their former battle-brothers as a bitter warning to the survivors. Such a punishment was, in Solomon's opinion, too lenient. Warriors that ran once would run again, and he was proud that none of his squads had ever needed such a brutal lesson in courage. They took their lead in all things from him, and he would rather die than dishonour his Legion with cowardice.

The clamour of battle was deafening, and though the line of Emperor's Children bent backwards under the onslaught of the Laer, it did not break. Solomon retrieved his bolter from the uneven ground and slid a fresh magazine into the weapon. He moved to the centre of the line and took his place in the thick of the fighting, killing with methodical precision until he ran out of ammunition and switched back to his sword.

He fought two-handed, cleaving his blade through alien flesh, and bellowing at his warriors to stand firm as a seething tide of Laer surrounded them.

THREE

The Cost of Victory/Up the Centre/Predator

STRIDING THROUGH THE shredded carcasses of the Laer, Marius Vairosean watched impassively as the warriors of Third Company gathered up their dead and wounded as they prepared to continue their advance. His stern face was lined with displeasure, though at who or what he couldn't say, for his men had fought as bravely as he would expect them to and Lord Fulgrim's plan had been followed to the letter.

With the landing zones and objective secured, all that remained was to link his forces with those of Solomon Demeter's Second Company, and Atoll 19 would be theirs. The cost of winning this victory had been damnably high: nine of his warriors would never fight again, their gene-seed harvested by Apothecary Fabius, and many others would require extensive augmetic surgery upon their return to the fleet.

The flaring pillar of energy that had been their objective was secure and he had split a detachment to hold it while they sought out Solomon's warriors, a hunt that might prove easier said than done. Explosions, gunfire and the blaring howls of the towers echoed strangely through the twisting coral streets of Atoll 19, and with the vox-network scrambled it was difficult to pinpoint exactly where the fighting was coming from.

'Solomon,' he said into the vox-bead at his throat. 'Solomon, can you hear me?'

Crackling static was his only answer and he swore silently to himself. It would be just like Solomon Demeter to have removed his helmet in the heat of battle to better experience the sensations of combat. Marius shook his head. What manner of fool would go into a firefight without all the protection he could muster?

The sounds of battle seemed to be coming from the west, though how to get there was going to be problematic, as the streets – if they could even be called that – snaked through the atoll in meandering paths that might take them kilometres out of their way.

The idea of setting off without a detailed plan rankled at Marius, a warrior for whom each advance and manoeuvre was planned with meticulous perfection and enacted without deviation. Julius Kaesoron had once joked that he should have been selected to join the Ultramarines, meaning it as a friendly jibe, but Marius had taken it as a compliment.

The Emperor's Children strove for perfection in all things and Marius Vairosean prized this striving above all things. The idea of not being the best made him feel physically sick. To be less than the best was unacceptable, and Marius had long ago decided that nothing was going to stop him from achieving his goal.

'Third Company,' he shouted, 'Move out on me!'

Instantly, his warriors were ready to move and formed up on him with parade ground precision, their weapons held at the ready. Marius led his men off with a ground-eating stride that Astartes warriors could maintain for days on end and still be ready to fight at the end of it.

The glistening coral walls of the city twisted and turned, fragments of crystal and stone crunching under their armoured boots as they made their way through the city. Marius kept following the path he thought best led to the sounds of fighting, encountering scattered bands of Laer warriors that fought with the desperation of a cornered foe. Each of these fights was easily won, for nothing could stand before the warriors of the Third on the advance and live.

He kept checking the vox for any word from Solomon, but eventually gave up on his fellow captain and switched channels. 'Caphen? Can you hear me. This is Vairosean. Answer if you can hear me!'

More static spat from the earpiece in his helmet, but it was swiftly followed by the sound of a voice, chopped and garbled, but a voice nonetheless.

'Caphen? Is that you?' asked Marius.

'Yes, captain,' said Gaius Caphen, his voice surging in the earpiece as Marius turned a corner into yet another twisting street of burrows and corpses.

'Where are you?' he demanded. 'We're trying to reach you, but these damned streets keep turning us around all over the place.

'The main arterial route towards our objective was strongly held, so Captain Demeter sent us and Thelonius to flank their position.'

'While he went up the centre, no doubt,' said Marius.

'Yes, sir,' said Caphen.

'We shall home in on your signal, but if there's something else you can do to mark your position, then do it! Vairosean out.'

Marius followed the blue dot projected onto the internal surface of his visor that represented Gaius Caphen's vox signal, though it faded with each turn they took through the maze of coral.

'Damn this place! No!' snarled Marius as the signal faded completely.

He raised his hand and called a halt, but as he did so a huge explosion erupted from nearby and a tall, curling tower of coral collapsed in flames not more than thirty metres to their left.

'That has to be it,' he said and searched for a way around the bristling lumps of coral. The streets wound away from the explosion, and he knew they would never reach Caphen by taking any of them. He looked over at the billowing black clouds and said, 'We're going over! Move out!'

Marius scrabbled up the face of a Laer burrow, easily finding hand- and foot-holds in the gnarled coral. He pulled himself higher and higher, the ground rapidly receding beneath him as he and the warriors of the Third made their way over the roofs of Atoll 19.

OSTIAN WATCHED THE first assault craft launch from the *Pride of the Emperor* with a mixture of awe and irritation. Awe, for it was a truly magnificent thing to watch the martial power of the Legion unleashed on an enemy world, and irritation because it had taken him away from the unblemished marble in his studio. First Captain Julius Kaesoron had sent advance word of the launch to Serena and she had immediately come to fetch him from his studio to a prime spot on the observation deck.

He'd tried to refuse, saying he was busy, but Serena had been adamant, claiming that all he was doing was sitting looking at the marble, and nothing he could say would persuade her otherwise. Now, standing before the armoured glass of the observation deck, he was heartily glad she had dragged him away.

'It's rather wonderful, don't you think?' asked Serena, glancing up from her sketchbook as her hand dashed across its surface, capturing the moment with astounding skill.

'It's amazing,' agreed Ostian, staring at her profile as a second wave of ships wreathed in the blue fire of their launch caught the sunlight on their steel flanks. The observation deck was hundreds of metres above the launch rails, but Ostian fancied he could still feel the vibrations of their release in his bones.

A final wave of Stormbirds launched from the other vessels of the Emperor's Children and he turned from Serena to watch them fly, birds of prey shooting into space like great darts of fire. Kaesoron had said that this was to be a full-scale assault and, seeing the sheer number of craft being launched, Ostian could well believe it.

'I wonder what it would be like,' said Ostian, 'the entire surface of a world covered by one enormous ocean. I can barely conceive of such a thing.'

'Who knows?' replied Serena, flicking a tendril of dark hair from her eyes as she continued furiously sketching. 'I imagine it would be like any other sea.'

'It looks wonderful from here.'

Serena gave him a sidelong glance and said, 'Did you not see Twenty-Eight Two?'

Ostian shook his head. 'I got here just as the fleet left for Laeran. This is the first world other than Terra I've seen from space.'

'Then you've never seen the sea?'

'I've never seen the sea,' agreed Ostian, feeling foolish for admitting such a thing.

'Oh, my dear boy!' said Serena, looking up from her sketchpad. 'We shall have to see about getting you down to the surface once the fighting is done!'

'Do you think that would be allowed?'

'I should bloody well hope so,' said Serena, ripping the page from her sketchpad and throwing it angrily to the floor. 'A very select few of us were allowed down to the surface of Twenty-Eight Two, and it was a magnificent place: snow covered mountains, continents of forests, and lakes the colour of a summer's morning, and the sky... oh the sky! It was a wondrous shade of cerulean blue. I think I loved it so much because it was how I imagined Old Earth might once have looked. I took some picts, but they didn't really capture it. Shame, really, as I'd have loved to have been able to mix it, but I couldn't manage it.'

As Serena spoke of her failure to mix the colour, Ostian saw her surreptitiously pressing the tip of her quill into the flesh of her wrist, leaving a tiny weal of ink and blood on her pale skin.

'I just couldn't get it to work,' she said absently, and Ostian wished he knew how to stop Serena from hurting herself, and to see the value in what she did.

'I'd like you to show me the surface of the planet if possible,' he said.

She blinked and smiled at him, reaching up to press her fingertips against his cheek.

✠ ✠ ✠

GAIUS CAPHEN DUCKED below the screeching attack of
a Laer warrior and drove his chainsword into its guts,
ripping the weapon free in a spray of blood and bone.
Fire billowed around them from the shattered
remains of a pair of Stormbirds that lay smouldering
in the ruins of a Laer burrow complex.

The crew and passengers had died in the crash and
the violence of the impact had almost toppled a rearing spire of twisted coral. It had only taken a handful
of grenades lobbed into the shattered base of the
tower to complete its destruction and bring it thundering to the ground. Marius Vairosean wanted them
to mark their position, and if he couldn't see that
then they were as good as dead.

He and his squad had fought through the Laer burrow complexes as Captain Demeter had ordered, but
the aliens had anticipated the flanking manoeuvre.
Every burrow held a pair of monstrous alien warriors
poised to slither from hiding to kill in a frenzy of
flashing blades and energy bolts.

The fighting had been close and brutal, no room for
skill or artistry, and each screeching snake-like warrior
had pounced into their midst, where all that separated the living from the dead was luck. Caphen bled
from a score of wounds, his breathing ragged and
uneven, though he was determined not to let his captain down.

Sounds of desperate fighting came from all around
him, and even as he watched, more Laer warriors spat
from their burrows like coiled springs, deadly bolts of
energy slicing through the air towards them. Coral
and fragments of armour ricocheted around him.

'Squad, make ready!' he shouted, as another trio of
Laer appeared behind them, weapons spitting fire
and light. Screams sounded from nearby and he

raised his bolter to fire on this new threat when the ground shifted violently underfoot and the entire atoll took a sickening lurch downwards.

Gaius dropped to one knee, grabbing onto a nearby spur of coral as more Laer emerged from burrow holes. A spray of bolter fire from above him cut one practically in two, and it thrashed in pain as it fell. Deafening reports echoed, and the Laer that had been set to overrun them were obliterated in volleys of precisely aimed gunfire.

He looked up to see where the shots had come from and laughed in relief as he saw a host of Astartes dropping from above, the trims of their shoulder guards marking them as warriors of Marius Vairosean's Third Company.

The captain himself dropped down next to Caphen, the muzzle of his bolter flaring as he gunned down a Laer warrior that had somehow survived the initial volleys.

'On your feet, sergeant!' shouted Vairosean. 'Which way is Captain Demeter?'

Caphen pushed himself erect and pointed towards the end of the street. 'That way!'

Vairosean nodded as his warriors cut down the last of the Laer defenders with grim efficiency.

'Then let's go and link up with him as ordered,' said Vairosean.

Caphen nodded and followed the captain of the Third.

ANOTHER SIX OF his warriors were down, torn apart by the energised blades of the Laer or with whole segments of their bodies rendered molten in the furnace heat of their ranged weapons. Solomon was beginning to regret casting off his helmet with such a

cavalier disregard for communication, knowing that
now more than ever he needed to know what was
happening elsewhere on the atoll.

He had seen no sign of Sergeant Thelonius or
Gaius Caphen's flanking forces and though the warriors of Goldoara had attempted to punch through to
them, they were not equipped with the weapons to
fight in such brutal close quarters and had been
forced back by the Laer.

They were on their own.

Solomon drove his sword through the stretched
mandibles of a Laer warrior, the blade punching out
through the back of its skull, and felt himself being
dragged down by its weight. He fought to withdraw
the blade, but its madly whirring teeth were lodged
in the dense bone of the alien's skull.

A screeching cry of pleasure sounded nearby and
he dropped flat as a searing bolt of light flashed over
him and gouged a furrow in the ground. Solomon
rolled as the Laer slithered over the bodies of its fellows with horrifying speed and launched itself
towards him. He rolled onto his back and hammered
his feet into its face, feeling is mandibles snap with
the impact.

The alien reeled, its whipping tail thrashing on the
ground and a cry of pain gurgling from its ruined
mouth. The sound of bolter fire echoed through the
plaza as Solomon scrambled over the uneven ground
and smashed his fist into the Laer's face. The force of
the blow burst one of its eyeballs and drew another
screech of pain from it. His other fist slammed into
its armoured chest, the bloodstained metal buckling
under the assault. It spat a froth of hot blood and
mucus into his face and he roared in anger, a red
mist of fury descending on him as he grabbed its

glistening flesh in both hands and slammed its head into the ground.

The creature kept up its keening screech and Solomon slammed its head into the ground again and again. Even when he was sure the creature was dead, he kept pounding its skull until there was nothing left but a ragged mess of sodden skull and brain matter.

He laughed with savage joy as he picked himself up from the ground, his armour covered from head to toe in the dark blood of the Laer. He staggered over to the first alien he'd killed and wrenched his sword clear as the noise of bolter fire intensified. It took a moment before the fact that he and his warriors had run out of ammunition could penetrate the red fog that had engulfed him as he fought the Laer.

He turned to the source of the gunfire and punched the air as he saw the unmistakable form of Marius Vairosean leading the warriors of the Third into the plaza with merciless perfection. Gaius Caphen fought alongside him and the Laer reeled from this fresh assault, their ranks thrown into disarray as Marius's warriors cut them down.

Seeing their fellows, the Second redoubled their efforts, and tired limbs fought on with fresh strength. The Laer attack faltered and even though their features were utterly alien, Solomon could see the paralysis of indecision tear at them as they realised that they were surrounded.

'Second, with me!' he shouted and set off in the direction of his fellow captain. His Astartes needed no further encouragement or orders, falling in behind him to form a fighting wedge that carved through the stunned Laer like a bloody knife.

None of the Emperor's Children were in the mood to offer mercy and within minutes it was all over. As the last of the alien warriors was slain by the overwhelming force of Vairosean's veterans, the atonal howling of the rearing coral towers finally ceased and a blessed silence fell over the battlefield.

Cries of welcome passed between the Astartes who had survived as Solomon sheathed his sword and bent to retrieve his bolter from the carnage of the plaza. His limbs were stiff and aching from numerous wounds he didn't remember receiving.

'You went up the centre again, didn't you?' asked a familiar voice as he straightened.

'I did, Marius,' replied Solomon without turning around. 'Are you going to tell me that was wrong?'

'Maybe, I don't know yet.'

Solomon turned as Marius Vairosean removed his helmet and shook his head to clear the momentary disorientation of returning to the employment of his own senses as opposed to those of his Mark IV plate. His friend wore a stern expression, but then he always did, and his salt and pepper hair was slick with oily sweat.

Unlike many of the Astartes, Marius Vairosean had a narrow face, its features sharp and inquisitive, his skin dark and lined like old wood.

'Well met, brother,' said Solomon, reaching out and gripping his battle-brother's hand.

Marius nodded and said, 'A hard fight by the looks of it.'

'Aye, it was that,' agreed Solomon, wiping some blood from the fascia plates of his bolter. 'They're tough bastards, these Laer.'

'Indeed they are,' said Marius. 'Maybe you should have thought of that before you went up the centre.'

'If there was another way to have done it, I would have tried it, Marius. Don't think I wouldn't have. They plugged the middle and I sent men around the flanks. I couldn't have let someone else lead the attack up the centre, it had to be me.'

'Luckily for you Sergeant Caphen seems to agree with your assessment of the battle.'

'He's got a good eye on him, that one,' said Solomon. 'He'll go far, maybe even make captain someday.'

'Maybe, though he has the look of a line officer about him.'

'We need good line officers,' noted Solomon.

'Maybe so, but a line officer does not seek to better himself. He will never attain perfection by simply doing his job and no more.'

'Not everyone can be captain, Marius,' said Solomon. 'We need warriors as well as leaders. Men like you, Julius and I will lead this Legion to greatness. We take our strength and honour from the primarch and the lord commanders, and it is up to us to pass on what we learn from them to those below us. Line officers are part of that, they take their lead from us and communicate our will to the men.'

Marius stopped and placed his hand on Solomon's shoulder guard. 'Even though I have known you for decades, you still have the power to surprise me, my friend. Just when I think I need to reprimand you for cavalier tactics, you give me a lesson on how it behoves us to lead our warriors.'

'What can I say? Julius and his books must be having an effect on me.'

'Speaking of Julius,' said Marius, pointing into the sky. 'It looks as if he has secured the order to commence the campaign.'

Solomon looked up into the crystal sky and saw hundreds of gunships descending from the upper atmosphere.

WITH THE CAPTURE of Atoll 19, the opening stage of the campaign had been won, though the ferocity of the fighting and the brittle knife-edge upon which it had been won would never be known except by those whose words would one day be reviled.

Interceptors descended alongside the gunships and circled in figure of eight patrol circuits above Atoll 19 in case the Laer counter-attacked, while fat army transporters brought anti-aircraft guns and detachments of Lord Commander Fayle's Archite Palatines, who spread through the atoll in their crimson tunics and silver breastplates.

Wide bodied Mechanicum loaders landed in screaming clouds of grit, disgorging silent, red-robed adepts who hurried to study the blazing energy plumes that kept the atoll aloft. Massive earth moving machines and teams of cutters and drillers rumbled onto the atoll, their sole purpose to level entire swathes of it before laying honeycombed sheets of metal to serve as runways for assault and supply craft.

Atoll 19 would be the first of many bridgeheads established before the Emperor's Children were finished with Laeran.

SERENA HAD RETURNED to her quarters, claiming tiredness, but Ostian had decided to remain on the observation deck to watch the planet below. The beauty of Laeran was entrancing and Serena's talk of the landscapes of alien worlds had kindled a desire in him he had not known existed. To stand on the surface of an alien world beneath a strange sun and feel the wind blown from far-off continents, never before seen by man, would be an intoxicating thrill, and he longed, ached even, to see the surface of Laeran.

He tried to imagine the sweep of its horizon, a featureless curve of endless blue that swelled with enormous tides and clung to the surface of the world by the slenderest of margins. What manner of life might thrive in the depths of its oceans? What calamity had befallen its lost civilisation that had seen it submerged beneath thousands of metres of dark water?

As a native of Terra, a world whose oceans had long since boiled away in ancient wars or environmental catastrophes, Ostian found the idea of a world without land hard to picture.

'What are you looking at?' asked a voice at his ear.

Ostian hid his surprise and turned to see Bequa Kynska standing behind him, her blue hair pulled tight in an elaborate weave on the top of her head that Ostian guessed must have taken many hours to achieve.

She smiled at him with a predator's grin. Ostian guessed that her scarlet corset gown was supposed to be more casual than her recital dress, but the overall effect suggested that she had just stepped from one of the Merican ballrooms.

'Hello Ms Kynska,' he said as neutrally as he could.

'Oh please, call me Beq, all my dear friends do,' said Bequa, linking her arm through his and turning him back to face the thick glass of the observation deck. The fragrance of her scent was overpowering and the cloying aroma of apples caught in the back of his throat. The front of her dress was scandalously low, and Ostian found himself sweating as he felt his eyes drawn to the barely contained curve of her breasts.

He looked up and saw Bequa staring right at him, and a fierce heat built in his cheeks as he knew she must have noticed exactly where he was looking.

'I'm… uh, sorry, I was…'

'Hush, my dear, it's quite all right,' soothed Bequa, with a playful grin that reassured him not at all. 'No harm in it, is there? We're all grown ups.'

He fixed his gaze on the gently spinning world below, trying to keep his mind on the swirls of ocean and atmospheric storms as she leaned close to him and said, 'I must admit that I find the prospect of war quite stirring, don't you? Gets the blood pounding and sets the loins afire with the sheer "maleness" of it all. Don't you find that, Ostian?'

'Um… I can't say I'd thought of it that way.'

'Nonsense, of course you have,' scolded Bequa. 'You're not a man if the thought of war doesn't wake the animal within you. What kind of person doesn't feel the blood fill their extremities at the thought of such things? I'm not ashamed to admit that the thought of the thunder of guns and the crash of fighting gets me all hot and bothered, if you know what I mean.'

'I'm not sure I do,' whispered Ostian, though he had a very good idea of exactly what she meant.

Bequa playfully punched his arm with her free hand and said, 'Don't be obtuse, Ostian, I shan't stand for it. You're a dreadful boy to tease me so.'

'Tease you?' he said. 'I don't know–'

'You know exactly what I mean,' said Bequa, releasing his arm and turning on her heel to face him. 'I want you, right here, right now.'

'What?'

'Oh don't be so prudish, have you no sense for the sensual? Haven't you heard my music?'

'Yes, but –'

'But nothing, Ostian,' said Bequa, jabbing him in the chest with a long, painted fingernail and pushing him back against the glass. 'The body is the soul's prison unless all five senses are fully developed and open. Open your senses and the windows to your soul fly open. I've always found that when sex involves all five senses it's a quite mystical experience.'

'No!' cried Ostian, squirming free of her grip.

Bequa took a step towards him, but he backed away with his hands held out before him. His body palpitated at the thought of being Bequa Kynska's plaything and he shook his head as she advanced towards him.

'Oh stop being such a silly boy, Ostian,' she said. 'It's not as if I'm going to hurt you. Well, not unless you want me to.'

'No, it's not that,' gasped Ostian. 'It's just…'

'Just what?' asked Bequa, and he could see she was genuinely confused. Perhaps no one had ever refused her advances before and he struggled to think of an answer to her question that wouldn't offend her, but his mind was as blank as the marble in his studio.

'It's just… that I have to go,' he said, inwardly cringing at such a pathetic answer and hating the wretched, snivelling creature he was. 'I have to meet Serena. She and I have… an appointment.'

'The painter woman? You and she are lovers?'

'No, no, no!' said Ostian hurriedly. 'I mean… yes. We're very much in love.'

Bequa pouted and folded her arms, her entire body telling him that he was now less than sump scum to her.

He started to say something else, but she cut him off, saying, 'No, you can go away now, I'm quite finished talking to you.'

Not knowing what else to say, he meekly obeyed her and all but fled from the observation deck.

FOUR

The Speed of War/A Longer Road/Brotherhood of the Phoenix

IN MANY WAYS, the cleansing of Laeran represented the epitome of Fulgrim's quest for perfection. The battles waged on the ocean planet were savage and merciless, each victory won only after fighting that was as bloody as any in the Legion's history, but won with a speed of war that bordered on the miraculous. The extermination of the Laer and the bringing to its knees of their entire world was being bought with the dead of the Emperor's Children.

Each atoll that was captured was swiftly transformed into a base of operations to be held by the Archite Palatines, while the Space Marines prosecuted their primarch's relentless campaign. Though the Laer were a technologically advanced species, they had never fought a foe as dedicated to their utter destruction as Fulgrim's Legion. Such was the primarch's exquisite planning and prescient thoroughness, that nothing the Laer could do was enough to halt or even delay their inevitable fate.

Living and dead specimens of Laer warriors were brought aboard the *Pride of the Emperor* for study under strict quarantine protocols, and were dissected by Legion Apothecaries to glean as much information about the foe as was possible. Specimens varied from the warrior breed that had defended Atoll 19, to avian creatures with barbed wings and poisonous bites, and aquatic monsters with genetically modified lungs and harpoon like barbs instead of tails. To see such varieties in one species was fascinating, and more and more were brought on board for study.

With each victory, the renown earned by the Legion's captains and warriors grew, and Fulgrim commissioned hundreds of new works of art in their honour. The vessels of the fleet soon resembled immense galleries, with exquisite paintings hanging on their walls and sculpted marble sitting on pedestals of gleaming onyx. Libraries-worth of poetry and entire symphonies were written, and it was even whispered that Bequa Kynska had begun a new opera to commemorate the imminent victory.

First Captain Julius Kaesoron, denied a place in the initial assaults of Atoll 19, was granted the honour of leading the front line troops under the overall command of Lord Commander Vespasian. Though Eidolon held seniority of rank, he had led the forces that had rendered Twenty-Eight Two compliant and thus the honour fell to Vespasian.

The war for Laeran was fought across many varied battlefields, the warriors of the Emperor's Children fighting on floating atolls and through the ruins of ancient structures that reared from the oceans, while foaming breakers crashed against walls that had once stood thousands of metres in the air.

Underwater cites were discovered within days of the campaign's opening and detachments of Astartes took the fight to the abyssal darkness of undersea trenches, smashing into structures that had never known the touch of sunlight, in specially modified boarding torpedoes fired from cruisers hovering above the sea.

Solomon Demeter led the Second against the first of these cities, subjugating it within six hours, his plan of attack garnering praise from the primarch. Marius Vairosean fought numerous actions against Laer orbitals that had previously escaped detection, fighting boarding actions on alien vessels, controlled by pilots telepathically linked to their ships in a loathsome parasitic manner.

Julius Kaesoron coordinated the attacks on the Laer atolls, discerning a pattern in their movements that had hitherto been perceived as random. At first, the atolls had been thought of as independent entities that forged their own destinies through the skies of the planet, but as he analysed the patterns, Julius had seen that each travelled within the orbit of one particular atoll.

It was neither the biggest, nor most impressive of the atolls that had been identified, but the more the pattern was studied, the more obvious its importance became. Strategic advisors theorised that it was perhaps a seat of what passed for government on Laeran, but when the pattern was revealed to the primarch, he immediately saw its true purpose.

It was not a place of governance: it was a place of worship.

ICY FLUORESCENT LIGHTS bathed the apothecarion of the *Pride of the Emperor* in a bright glare that reflected dazzlingly from glass cabinets and gleaming, steel bowls containing surgical instruments or bloody organs. Apothecary Fabius directed his menials as they wheeled a heavy gurney bearing the corpse of a Laer warrior from the chill of the temperature controlled mortuary cabinets.

Fabius kept his long white hair, the mirror of the primarch's, tied in a severe scalp lock, accentuating the sharpness of his features and the coldness of his dark eyes. His movements were curt, their exactness reflecting his intensity and the precision of his methodology. His armour stood upon a rack in his arming chamber and thus he was dressed in his red surgical robes and a heavy rubberised apron smeared with dark alien blood.

Wisps of cold air rose from the body, and he nodded in satisfaction as the menials halted the gurney next to the stone autopsy slab upon which lay another Laer warrior, fresh from the battlefield. This specimen had been killed by a shot to the head and so the majority of its body was largely undamaged – at least from the fighting. Its flesh was still warm to the touch and it stank with the oily stench of its secretions. Reams of data scrolled on hololithic panes suspended on thin cables from the ceiling, projecting ghostly, crawling images around the bare, antiseptic walls.

Fabius had been working on this warm body for the last few hours and the fruits of his labours had been singular. He had removed the alien's innards, its organs displayed like trophies on silver trays that surrounded the mortuary slab. The suspicion that had been forming in his mind since the assault on Atoll 19 had been confirmed and, armed with this information, he had sent word to Lord Fulgrim of his findings.

The primarch stood at the entrance to the apothecarion, the halberd-armed Phoenix Guard standing a respectful distance behind the lord of the Emperor's Children. Though the white-tiled apothecarion was spacious and high-ceilinged, it felt cramped with the primarch here, such was his presence. Fulgrim had come directly from the fighting, still clad in his purple battle plate, the blood still singing in his veins from the fierce mêlée. The war was entering its third week and there had been no let up in the fighting, each battle pushing the Laer from their various atolls towards the one the primarch had identified as a place of worship.

'This had better be good, Apothecary' said Fulgrim. 'I have a world to win.'

Fabius nodded and leaned over the cooled corpse, a scalpel blade sliding from his narthecium gauntlet and slicing through the stitching that held the incisions on its chest closed. He pulled the thick flaps of skin and muscle back to reveal its interior, affixing clamps to hold them open. Fabius smiled as he saw the insides of the Laer warrior, again admiring the perfect arrangement of organs that had made it such a fearsome killing machine.

'It is, my lord,' promised Fabius. 'I've never imagined anything like it, and nor, I suspect, has anyone else for that matter, save the more extreme genetic theorists of Terra.'

'Anything like what?' demanded Fulgrim. 'Do not try my patience with riddles, Apothecary.'

'It's fascinating, my lord, quite fascinating,' said Fabius, standing between the two Laer corpses. 'I have performed genetic analyses of both these specimens and have found much that may be of interest.'

'All that interests me about these creatures is how they die,' said Fulgrim, and Fabius knew that he had better reach his point quickly. The pressures of leading such an intensive campaign personally were demanding, even for a primarch.

'Indeed, my lord, indeed,' said Fabius, 'but I believe you may be interested in how these specimens lived. From the researches I have undertaken, it appears that the Laer are not so dissimilar to us in their approaches to perfection.'

Fabius indicated the opened chest cavities of the Laer warriors and said, 'Take these two specimens. They are genetically identical in the sense that they are from the same gene-strand, but their internal workings have been modified.'

'Modified?' asked Fulgrim. 'For what purpose?'

'To better adapt them for the role they were to fulfil in Laer society, I should imagine,' replied Fabius. 'They are quite marvellous specimens, genetically and chemically altered from birth to perfectly fulfil a pre-determined role. This one, for example, is clearly a warrior, its central nervous system designed to operate at a much higher level of functionality than the envoys we captured at the outset of the war, and do you see these glands here?'

Fulgrim leaned close to the corpse, his nose wrinkling in disgust at the alien stench of it. 'What do they do?'

'These are designed to release a compound onto the Laer's carapace, which forms a toughened "scab" over areas damaged in combat. In effect, these organs are a biological self-repairing function that can patch up damage within moments of it occurring. We are lucky that Captain Demeter was able to kill it so cleanly with a head shot.'

'Do all the Laer have these organs?' asked Fulgrim.

Fabius shook his head, indicating the scrolling data on the hololithic plates. Images of dissected Laer flashed up, and flickering projections of various alien organs rotated in the air above the corpses.

'No, they do not,' explained Fabius, 'and that is what makes them so fascinating. Each Laer is altered from birth to perfectly achieve the purpose for which it is designed, be it a warrior, a scout, a diplomat or even an artist. Some of the earliest envoys we apprehended had enlarged ocular cavities to better capture light, others had enhanced speech centres of the brain, while yet others had been designed for strength and endurance, perhaps to better function as labourers.'

Fulgrim watched the data on the plates, absorbing the information at a speed beyond that of any mortal man. 'They move towards their own perfection.'

'Indeed, my lord,' said Fabius. 'To the Laer, altering their physical makeup is simply the first step on the road to perfection.'

'You believe the Laer to be perfect, Fabius?' asked Fulgrim, a note of warning in his voice. 'Be careful what you say. To compare these xeno creatures to the work of the Emperor would be unwise.'

'No, no,' said Fabius hurriedly. 'What the Emperor has made of us is incredible, but what if it was but the first step on a longer road? We are the Emperor's Children, and like children, we must learn to walk on our own and take our own steps forward. What if we were to look upon our flesh and find new ways to improve upon it and bring it closer to perfection?'

'Improve upon it!' said Fulgrim, towering over Fabius. 'I could have you killed for saying such things, Apothecary!'

'My lord,' said Fabius quickly, 'our purpose for living is to find perfection in all things, and that means we must put aside any notions of squeamishness or reverence that limit us in finding it.'

'What the Emperor crafted in us *is* perfect,' stated Fulgrim.

'Is it really?' asked Fabius, amazed at his own hubris in questioning the miraculous work that had gone into his own enhancement. 'Our beloved Legion was almost destroyed at its very birth, remember? An accident destroyed nearly all the gene-seed that went into our creation, but what if it was imperfection rather than an accident that brought about such a terrible thing?'

'I remember my own history,' snapped Fulgrim. 'By the time my father first brought me to Terra, barely two hundred warriors were all the Legion could muster.'

'And do you remember what the Emperor told you when you learned of the accident?'

'I do, Apothecary,' said Fulgrim. 'My father said that it was best to have failure happen early in life, for it would awake the phoenix bird within me so that I would rise from the ashes.'

Fulgrim stared at him, and he felt the power and anger in his lord's eyes as he remembered the anguish of those long ago days, knowing that he played a dangerous game. He may very well have signed his death warrant by speaking so frankly, but the possibilities that might be opened up were worth any risk. To attempt to unlock the secrets of the Emperor's work in creating the Astartes would be the greatest undertaking of his life. If such a thing was not worth a little risk, then what was?

Fulgrim turned to the warriors of the Phoenix Guard and said, 'Leave us. Wait outside for me and do not return until I summon you.'

Even though their master was aboard his flagship, Fabius could see that the primarch's bodyguards were uneasy about leaving their charge without their protection, but they nodded and made their way from the apothecarion.

When they had gone and the door had shut behind them, Fulgrim turned to Fabius. The primarch's eyes were thoughtful and he glanced between the corpses and Fabius, though what thoughts filled his head were as alien to Fabius as those of the Laer.

'You believe you can enhance the gene-seed of the Astartes?' asked Fulgrim.

'I do not know for certain,' said Fabius, struggling to contain his elation, 'but I believe we have to at least try. It may be that it will prove to be fruitless, but if it is not…'

'We would move closer to perfection,' said Fulgrim.

'And only by imperfection can we fail the Emperor,' said Fabius.

Fulgrim nodded and said, 'You may proceed, Apothecary. Do what must be done.'

THE BROTHERHOOD OF the Phoenix met by firelight in the Heliopolis, arriving in ones and twos as they passed through the great bronze portal and took their seats around a wide, circular table placed at the centre of the dark floor. Reflected light from the ceiling bathed the table in light and crackling orange flames burned in a brazier set into the surface of the table's centre. The high-backed chairs of black wood were equally spaced around the table, half of them occupied by cloaked warriors of the Emperor's Children. Their armour shone, but each plate was battered and had clearly seen better days.

Solomon Demeter watched Julius Kaesoron and Marius Vairosean pass the Phoenix Gate, and the remainder of the Legion's captains that were not currently in battle filed in after them. Solomon could feel their weariness and nodded to them as they sat to either side of him, grateful to see that his friends had returned safely from yet another gruelling tour of duty on the planet below.

The cleansing of Laeran had been tough on them all. Fully three-quarters of the Legion's strength was in the field at any one time and there was little chance for respite in such a demanding war. No sooner had each company's warriors returned to the fleet for re-supply than they were sent into battle once more.

Lord Fulgrim's plan was audacious and brilliant, but left little room for rest and recuperation. Even the normally indefatigable Marius looked exhausted.

'How many?' asked Solomon, already fearing the answer.

'Eleven dead,' said Marius. 'Though I fear another may die before the day is out.'

'Seven,' sighed Julius. 'What about you?'

'Eight,' said Solomon. 'By the fire, this is brutal. And the others will have suffered a similar fate.'

'If not worse,' said Julius. 'Our companies are the best.'

Solomon nodded, knowing that Julius was not boasting, for such a thing was unknown to him, but simply stating a fact.

'New blood too,' he said, seeing two faces around the table that were new to the Brotherhood of the Phoenix. They bore the rank insignia of captain on their shoulder guards, the paint probably not even dry yet.

'Casualties are not confined to the rank and file warriors of the Legion,' said Marius. 'Good leaders must necessarily put themselves in harm's way to inspire the men they lead.'

'You don't need to quote the book to me, Marius,' said Solomon. 'I was there when they wrote that part. I practically invented going up the centre.'

'Did you also invent the concept of being the luckiest bastard alive?' cut in Julius. 'I've lost count of the number of times you ought to have been killed.'

Solomon smiled, pleased to see that the war on Laeran had not crushed everyone's spirits. 'Ah, Julius, the gods of battle love me and they wouldn't see me dead on this piss-poor excuse for a planet.'

'Don't say such things,' cautioned Marius.

'What things?'

'Talking of gods and the like,' said the captain of the Third. 'It is not seemly.'

'Ah, don't get upset, Marius,' smiled Solomon, clapping a hand on his friend's shoulder guard. 'There's only one god of battle around this table and I'm sitting next to him.'

Marius shrugged off his hand and said, 'Don't mock me, Solomon. I'm serious.'

'Don't I know it,' said Solomon, a hurt look on his face. 'You need to lighten up a little, my friend. We can't go around with grim faces all the time, can we?'

'War is a grim business, Solomon,' said Marius. 'Good men die and we are responsible for bringing them back alive. Each death lessens us and you would make jokes about it?'

'I don't think that's what Solomon meant,' began Julius, but Marius cut him off.

'Don't defend him, Julius, he knows what he said and I am heartsick of hearing him run his mouth while brave warriors are dying.'

Solomon was stung by Marius's words, and he felt his choler rising at the insult in his friend's words. He leaned close to Marius and said, 'I would never dream of making light of the fact that men are dying, but I know that a great many more would not come back alive if not for me. We all deal with war in different ways and if my way offends you then I am sorry, but I am who I am and I will change for no man.'

Solomon stared at Marius, practically daring him to prolong the unexpected argument, but his fellow captain shook his head and said, 'I am sorry, my friend. All this fighting has left me bellicose and I seek to find cause to vent my anger.'

'It's fine,' said Solomon, his anger draining away in an instant. 'You're so by the book that I can't help needling you from time to time, even when I know I shouldn't. I'm sorry.'

Marius offered his hand, which Solomon took, and said, 'War makes fools of us all, when never more are we required to maintain our standards.'

Solomon nodded and said, 'You're right, but I don't know any other way to be. I let Julius take care of the culture side of things. Speaking of which, how is that little stable of remembrancers you've been cultivating? Any new busts or portraits of you yet? I swear, Marius, soon you won't be able to turn a corner without seeing his face in a painting or carved in marble.'

'Just because you're too ugly to be immortalised in art doesn't mean that I shouldn't be,' grinned Julius, well used to Solomon's friendly barbs. 'And it's hardly a stable. Mistress Kynska's music is wondrous and yes, I hope to be the subject of a painting by Serena d'Angelus. Perfection exists in all things, my friends, not just war.'

'Ego this big...' chuckled Solomon, spreading his arms wide as the Phoenix Gate opened once more and Fulgrim entered, fully armoured and robed in a great cloak of feathers the colour of fire. The effect was magnificent, all conversation around the table ceasing in an instant as the Astartes gazed in awe at their beloved leader.

The assembled warriors stood and bowed their heads as the Primarch of the Emperor's Children took his place at the table. As always, Eidolon and Vespasian flanked the primarch, their armour similarly wreathed in cloaks of feathers. Each carried a staff topped with a small brazier of black iron that burned with a red flame.

Though the circular table was, in theory, supposed to do away with rank and position, there was no doubting who the master of this gathering was. Other Legions might have a more informal setting for their warrior lodges, but the Emperor's Children thrived on tradition and ritual, for in repetition came perfection.

'Brothers of the Phoenix,' said Fulgrim, 'in the fire I welcome you.'

BEQUA KYNSKA SAT at the wide desk of her stateroom aboard the *Pride of the Emperor* and stared at the blue world below her through the brass rimmed viewport. Though the scene was beautiful, she hardly saw it, still fuming over the blank pages of music before her and the rejection of Ostian Delafour.

Though the boy was plain and unassuming, with no great physical attributes to recommend him over the lovers she had taken over the years, he was young, and Bequa craved the adoration of the young above all else. They had such innocence, and to corrupt that with the bitterness of age and experience was one of the few pleasures left to her. Since her earliest years, Bequa had been able to have any man or woman she desired. Nothing had been beyond her. To be denied something now, when she had the opportunity to achieve the incredible, was supremely frustrating.

Her anger at Ostian's refusal of her advances gnawed at her and she swore a silent oath that he would pay for such effrontery.

No one rejected Bequa Kynska!

She placed her fingertips on her temple and gently circled them in an attempt to ease the headache she could feel building behind her eyes. The smooth, artificial texture of the skin felt cold to her and she dropped her hands to the desk. Surgical augmentations had kept the worst effects of her age from becoming visible, but although she was still considered beautiful, it was only a matter of time before human artifice would not be able to disguise the ravages of ageing.

She picked up the quill from the desk and her hand hovered over the page of musical staves, though each line was infuriatingly blank. She had spread the word that she was to compose a new triumphal symphony for the Lord Fulgrim, but thus far she had not put so much as a single note in the ledger.

Being selected to join the Remembrancer Order had been a great, if altogether expected honour, for who else could compete with Bequa Kynska's musical talents? It was a natural progression from her time at the Conservatoire de Musique, and the potential for new horizons and new conquests seemed limitless. In truth the spires of Terra had grown stale for Bequa, the same faces and the same platitudes heaped upon her, now ashen and tasteless after so long. What was new for her on Terra now that she had sampled every

carnal and narcotic pleasure that her money could
buy? What new sensations did a bleak, empty world
like Terra have to offer a libertine of her epicurean
palate?

Perhaps, she had thought, a galaxy, reawakening to
the manifest destiny of humanity, to rule would provide new and undreamed raptures and enchantments.

And for a time it had; the newly emergent worlds
providing a surfeit of wonders. To be around others of
talent had been intoxicating at first and the music had
poured from her fingertips onto the sheet music as it
had before she had won the Argent Mercurio robes for
her *Symphony of Banished Night*.

Now the music had stopped, for there was nothing
left to inspire her.

The world below spun gently on its axis and she fervently hoped that its beauty would move her to
compose once more.

SOLOMON STOOD AS he and his assembled battle-
brothers rose to answer their primarch's greeting. As
great an honour as it was just to be in the presence of
Lord Fulgrim, being included in such rarefied
company was another level of pleasure entirely.

'We welcome you, our lord and master,' he said with
the others.

Solomon watched as Eidolon and Vespasian moved
to either side of Fulgrim and planted their staffs in
stirrup cups attached to their chairs before taking their
seats. Immediately, Solomon could see the tension
between the two lord commanders and wondered
what had passed between them before their arrival.

The Brotherhood of the Phoenix was a more exclu-
sive warrior lodge than those within many of the
other Legions. While the Emperor's Children had

fought alongside the Luna Wolves, they had formed great bonds of friendship with the warriors of Horus, and in the times between the fighting, a few loose tongues had spoken of their warrior lodge.

The Luna Wolves lodge was, in theory, open to any warrior who desired to be a member, an informal place of lively debate where rank held no sway and a man could speak his mind freely without fear of reprisals. Eventually Solomon and Marius had been permitted to attend one such meeting, a pleasant evening of honourable camaraderie under the titular leadership of a warrior named Serghar Targost. Solomon had enjoyed the evening, despite the cloak and dagger theatrics of their masked arrival, but he could tell that Marius had been uncomfortable with the informality and mingling of ranks. In the traditionally hierarchical core of the Emperor's Children only warriors of rank could join this confraternity.

Fulgrim had issued the summons to this meeting of the Brotherhood, and Solomon was intrigued as to what the primarch had to say.

'The cleansing of Laeran is almost complete, my brothers,' said Fulgrim, and a great cheer went up from the warriors of the Emperor's Children. One last xenos bastion awaits our fury and I shall lead the attack, for did I not promise that I would plant our standard in the ruins of the Laer's heartland?'

'You did!' cried Marius, and Solomon shared a glance with Julius as they both heard the tone of sycophancy in his words. Others hammered their fists on the table at the Captain of the Third's words, and Fulgrim raised a palm to quiet their adulation.

'The fighting on Laeran has been hard and we have all lost brothers in arms,' said Fulgrim, his tone solemn and redolent with the grief they all felt, 'but much honour has been won and when men look back and read what we achieved here, they will believe the chroniclers lie, for surely no Legion could conquer an entire race in such a short time. But the Emperor's Children are not just any Legion; we are the chosen of the Emperor, the only warriors perfect enough to bear his eagle upon their breasts.'

Each warrior gathered around the table slammed his palm into his breastplate, acknowledging the honour the Emperor had done them as Fulgrim continued.

'Your courage and sacrifices have not gone unnoticed and the Colonnade of Heroes will forever bear the names and deeds of the dead. I honour their memory in my heart as will those who come after them.'

Fulgrim rose from his seat and moved around the table to stand behind the two new warriors. One had the look of the eagle about him, a born warrior with a swaggering expression that Solomon immediately liked, while the other seemed ill at ease with the attention soon to be lavished upon him. Solomon could well understand the warrior's discomfort, remembering his own presentation to the Brotherhood of the Phoenix.

'Though some die, their deaths allow others to move closer to achieving perfection through war by taking their place. Welcome them, brothers, welcome them to your ranks!'

The two warriors stood and Solomon joined with the others in applauding mightily as they bowed to the warrior lodge. Fulgrim placed his hands on the shoulders of the more modest of the pair and said, 'This is Captain Saul Tarvitz, a warrior who has fought with great courage on the atolls of Laeran. He will be a fine addition to our ranks.'

Fulgrim moved to stand behind the cockier of the two, 'And this, my brothers, is Lucius, a swordsman of great skill who embodies what it means to be one of the Emperor's Children.'

Solomon recognised the names, knowing the warriors by reputation only. He liked the look of Lucius, seeing something of his own wildness in the man, but Tarvitz had what Marius would call the look of a line officer.

Tarvitz clearly sensed the scrutiny and inclined his head respectfully in Solomon's direction. He returned the gesture, understanding in a moment that there was no greatness to the warrior and that he would never amount to much.

Both Astartes sat back down as Fulgrim circled the table, his cloak of feathers trailing on the smooth floor behind him. Solomon turned to face Marius as he sensed that the primarch was reluctant to speak. Marius shrugged imperceptibly.

'The war below us is almost over and when we seize the final atoll, it will be time to plan for our next venture into the darkness. I have received word from Ferrus Manus that his Iron Hands are soon to embark on a new crusade and he requests the honour of our assistance to deal with a most vexing enemy. He is to begin a mass advance into the Lesser Bifold Cluster to engage the enemies of mankind, and this will be a fine chance to demonstrate the principles of perfection upon which our honour rests. We will rendezvous with my brother at the Carollis Star when the destruction of the Laer is complete and assist the 52nd Expedition before continuing as planned to the Perdus Anomaly.'

Solomon felt his heart beat wildly in his chest and found himself cheering along with the rest of his fellows at the thought of once again going into battle alongside the X Legion. The brotherhood between Ferrus Manus and Fulgrim was legendary, their friendship closer than any of the other primarchs, even that of Fulgrim and the Warmaster – a brother he had fought alongside for decades.

'Now tell them the rest,' said a bitter voice from the other side of the table, and Solomon was shocked rigid that anyone would dare use such a tone to address the primarch. Angry stares were directed at the speaker until they realised that it was Lord Commander Eidolon that had spoken.

'Thank you, Eidolon,' said Fulgrim, and Solomon could see that he was struggling to hold his temper in check at such a breach of protocol. 'I was just getting to that.'

An unsettled mood descended upon the gathering, Eidolon's uncharacteristic outburst putting everyone off-balance. Solomon felt an odd sensation in his gut, not knowing what it was, but not liking it one bit.

Fulgrim returned to his seat and said, 'Unfortunately, not all of us will take part in this campaign, for there are demands of conquest we must obey. The galaxy does not remain compliant without effort and determination, and the Warmaster has decreed that a portion of our strength must be employed in ensuring that those territories already won do not slip from our grasp through inattention.'

Cries of disappointment and denial raced around the table, and Solomon felt his chest tighten at the possibility of not fighting alongside two of the greatest warriors of the age.

'Lord Eidolon will take a company-sized force aboard the *Proudheart* to the Satyr Lanxus Belt, where he will ensure that the Imperial governors are maintaining the lawful rule of the Emperor. Captains Lucius and Tarvitz, you will ready your men for immediate transit to the *Proudheart*. This will be your first action as members of the Brotherhood of the Phoenix, so I expect nothing less than perfection from you both. I know you will not disappoint me.'

Both the newly elevated warriors saluted, and though Solomon could see their regret at being denied the chance to travel with the rest of the Legion, Fulgrim's faith in them filled their hearts with joy.

Solomon saw that no such joy filled Eidolon's heart and knew that the lord commander must feel shame at his exclusion, though to honour the Warmaster's command, the force had to be led by a commander of such stature. While Vespasian commanded the forces at Laeran, there was no other choice. He realised that Eidolon must know this, but the knowledge would have been no comfort to Solomon had he been in the lord commander's position.

'We will sing songs of your bravery upon your return, but for now, let us drink and feast to the doom of the Laer,' said Fulgrim. The Phoenix Gate was flung open as servants and menials entered, bringing platters of hot meat and case after case of victory wine.

'We shall toast the victory to come!' shouted Fulgrim.

FIVE

Downed/Follow the Firebird/The Fane of Excess

THE FORCE OF Stormbirds and Thunderhawks that took to the air against the final Laer atoll was amongst the greatest aerial armadas yet launched in the Great Crusade. Nine hundred craft took off from a score of captured atolls as the last of the daylight faded, the timing of their launches and approach vectors calculated by the primarch to ensure that each wave arrived precisely when he intended it to.

Howling interceptors and gunships took off in clouds of jet wash and gritty coral, followed by scores of Stormbirds and Thunderhawks. Within minutes the skies above each atoll were filled with dark, predatory shapes that circled like flocks of screeching crows set to embark on a mission of murder. At a signal from orbit, the flocks of craft angled their courses, streaking through the cloudless skies on plumes of blue fire towards their prey.

Fulgrim launched from the *Pride of the Emperor* in the *Firebird*, a gunship he had personally designed and constructed in the armourium decks of his flagship. Its wings had a greater span than a Stormbird, curved in a graceful backward sweep, and its hooked prow gave it a fearsome war visage that struck terror into the hearts of the primarch's foes.

The *Firebird* streaked through the atmosphere of Laeran, its fiery re-entry wreathing its wings and body in ghostly flames that lit up the night sky like a glittering comet.

THE METAL FIXTURES of Solomon Demeter's Stormbird were gilded and the internal facings decorated with mosaics depicting the Legion's conquests won alongside the Luna Wolves. Grey-armoured warriors fought alongside the purple of the Emperor's Children, and Solomon felt a sudden pang of regret that they no longer fought alongside the Warmaster's Wolves as he stared at the scenes that bounced and shuddered before him.

'It's only going to get worse,' said Gaius Caphen, seeing Solomon's unease.

'Thanks,' he shouted back. 'I'm trying not to think of the wall of flak we have to fly through to reach this damn place.'

Even though the roaring of the engines was muffled by his helmet's auto-senses it was still deafening. The crack of explosions sounded dull and unthreatening beyond the Stormbird's armoured walls, though he knew exactly how deadly they were.

'I don't like this,' Solomon shouted. 'I hate the surrender to the fates that comes with being delivered to a warzone in a manner that's beyond my control.'

'You say that every time,' noted Caphen, 'whether we go in by Stormbird, drop-pod or Rhino. The only other way is to this battle is to walk on water.'

Solomon said, 'And look what happened to our speartip on Atoll 19, the bird barely made it to the damned rock! Too many good men will die in this fire before they have the chance to earn their warrior's fate.'

'Warrior's fate?' laughed Caphen, shaking his head. 'Sometimes I swear I ought to report you to Chaplain Charmosian with all your talk of fates and gods of battle. I don't like it any better than you do, but we're as protected as we can be, yes?'

Solomon nodded, knowing that Gaius was right. Understanding that the rest of the fleet had to share in the honour of conquering Twenty-Eight Three, Lord Fulgrim had permitted the fleet interceptors to launch several raids to knock out the worst of the Laer air defences.

Much of the Laer's defensive capabilities had been rendered to rubble, though there was still a fearsome amount to endure. Solomon glanced down the length of the crew compartment to see what effect their violent journey was having on his men, pleased to see that they appeared as calm as though they were on a training mission.

His warriors might be calm, but he was not, and despite Caphen's reassurances, he knew he wouldn't be happy until he was at last watching the pilots guide them in. Solomon was trained to fly a Stormbird, and even had some time in the newer Thunderhawks, but he was the first to admit that he was only a fair pilot at best.

Others with greater skill were to fly them into battle, and since the primarch's plan required absolute, perfect precision for this assault to work, he had kept his concerns to himself until it was too late to do anything about them.

He slammed a palm into the restraint of his grav-harness and pushed himself to his feet, gripping the brass handrail that ran the length of the ceiling.

'I'm going to the flight deck,' he said.

'You going to fly us in?' asked Caphen. 'I feel safer already.'

'No, I just want to see what's going on.'

Caphen didn't reply, and Solomon turned towards the cockpit as the aircraft bucked in the air and he felt the hammering of a nearby explosion. He made his way along the companionway and pulled open the door to the flight compartment.

'How long till we reach the landing zone?' he shouted over the din.

The co-pilot spared him a glance and shouted, 'Two minutes!'

Solomon nodded, anxious to speak, but not wanting to distract the pilots from their duties. The night sky beyond the armoured glass of the cockpit was lit up as bright as day with traceries of gunfire and flak, the fleet's interceptors duelling with the remaining airborne units of the Laer to clear a path for the Legion's warriors. Ahead, Solomon could see a bright island of light floating in the sky, the temple atoll like a beacon in the darkness.

'Foolish,' he said to himself. 'I would have enforced a blackout.'

The compartment was filled with an eerie red light, and Solomon suddenly found himself thinking of blood. He wondered if it was an omen for the battle to come; then shook off such a gloomy thought. Omens and portents were for weak minds that did not know the truth of the galaxy and feral barbarians who needed a reason for the sun to rise or the rains to fall.

Solomon was beyond such petty superstitions, but he smiled as he realised that his obsessive habit of modifying his battle gear and entreating it to keep him safe before going into battle might be considered superstitious. No, he decided, honouring your battle gear was just sensible, not superstitious.

He crouched down in the doorway, unwilling to return to his seat and perversely fascinated by the web of light and explosions painted on the sky. Even as he watched the intricate ballet of fire into which they flew, a blazing light filled the cockpit as the *Firebird* passed overhead, its greater speed meaning it would be amongst the first of the assault craft to reach the atoll.

Flames still trailed from its wings, and Solomon smiled, knowing it was no accident that the primarch had decreed that this attack should be launched at night. The flickering red glow of the flames was reflected in the crew's faces, and Solomon was once again seized by the certainty that something terrible was going to happen.

Not just to him, but to his entire Legion.

Solomon's gut tightened as the Stormbird suddenly veered to one side and he heard the pilots swear. A thudding impact struck the side of the Stormbird, and Solomon felt a sickening lurch as the mighty craft dropped through the sky.

His mind filled with thoughts of the yawning abyss of the world sea below, remembering the battles he had fought beneath its empty darkness and having no wish to revisit that cold, subterranean world.

'Port engine's on fire!' shouted the pilot. 'Increase power to the starboard engine.'

'Stabilisers are gone! Compensating!'

'Cut off the fuel feeds from the wing and get us level!'

Solomon gripped the edge of the door as the Stormbird swung wildly to the side. The crew issued orders to one another and attempted to stabilise their flight. Emergency lights flashed across the command console, and Solomon could hear the warning klaxon of the altimeter. Though he could hear the strain in the pilots' voices, Solomon also heard their training and discipline as they went through the emergency procedures with determined efficiency.

Eventually the gunship began to level out, though angry lights still blinked and the altimeter klaxon still sounded.

A palpable sense of relief filled the flight compartment and Solomon began to ease his grip on the edge of the door.

'Well done, people,' said the pilot, 'we're still flying.'

Barely a moment later, the entire left side of the Stormbird erupted in flames. Solomon was hurled to the deck and a seething wall of flame lit up the sky. The glass of the cockpit disintegrated and flames boiled into the gunship.

He felt the heat on his armour, but it could do him no harm, though scads of burning fuel dribbled from the plates of his legs and arms. The roaring of the wind filled his senses as the gunship spun, cold air roaring through the stricken Stormbird and howling in his ears.

Miraculously, the co-pilot was still alive, though his flesh was horribly burned and his skin was on fire. Solomon knew there was nothing to be done for him, and the wounded man's cries of pain mingled with the wind as they spiralled downwards to destruction.

Solomon saw the black wall of the ocean rushing up to meet him and cold, wet darkness swallowed him as the Stormbird smashed into the water.

SCREAMING FROM THE coral towers filled the air, more strident than Julius remembered, and he was struck by the notion that the atoll was shrieking in anger. The last of the Laer defended this place, but if there was any desperation or fear in them, they didn't show it. These alien warriors fought as hard as any they had killed in this campaign.

The Stormbird had barely touched down when Julius and Lycaon had led the warriors of the First onto the atoll, the monstrously thick plates of their Terminator armour reflecting the firelight of battle.

The sound of screams and gunfire and explosions filled his senses, though his armour protected him from the worst of it. Emperor's Children spread out around him without needing any orders, and he knew that the exact same scene was being played out at hundreds of other locations throughout the atoll.

Alien gunfire reached out to them, but what had carved through Mark IV plate barely scratched Terminator armour.

If only we had more of these, this war would have been won long ago, thought Julius, but the general issue of Tactical Dreadnought armour had only just begun and only a very few units had the correct training to make use of them.

'Forward,' ordered Julius, as his warriors fell into position behind him. The Terminators moved off in a phalanx, bolters and inbuilt heavy weapon systems ripping apart any Laer that stood in their way in a flurry of broken bodies and pulverised coral.

The forces of the Emperor's Children had surrounded the temple like a closing fist, and would now
crush the last of its defenders.

Flames leapt skyward as strafing gunships sawed
towers apart with high explosive shells and provided
support for the ground troops. Heavier transports
were even now inbound with armoured units: Land
Raiders, Predators and Vindicators.

Heavy footfalls pounded through the battle, and
Julius saw Ancient Rylanor smash through a wall of
coral that had served as a barricade to a group of Laer
warriors armed with a high-powered energy weapon.
A lance of green energy speared into the Dreadnought's sarcophagus, and Julius cried out as he saw
the damage, but the mighty war machine shrugged
off the impact. Rylanor picked up the nearest Laer
warrior and broke it in two in his monstrous fists as
gouts of yellow fire from his underslung weapon
burned them from their cover.

Julius and his warriors finished the job, sending a
hail of shells tearing through the burning corpses of
the aliens.

'My thanks for your assistance,' said the Dreadnought. 'Though it was not needed.'

Sudden orange light bathed the battlefield in a
hellish glow as the *Firebird* screamed overhead,
Fulgrim's attack ship taking him to the very heart of
the battle, to the temple of the Laer.

'Come on, Lycaon!' shouted Julius exultantly. 'We
follow the *Firebird*!'

ON THE SOUTHERN spurs of the atoll, Marius Vairosean
was finding things much tougher than the captain of
the First. Too many of his gunships had been shot
down and he knew he was dangerously below the

strength the primarch had decreed necessary to seize his objectives. The Laer fought with a hitherto unseen ferocity, their slithering bodies coiling over one another as they rushed to engage his warriors.

A musky fog enveloped the far reaches of coral burrows, and Marius thought he detected a faint reddish tinge to it. Was this some form of gas weapon? If so, it was wasted against the Astartes, for their armour was proof against such primitive weapons.

The screaming of the towers was quieter in this part of the atoll, for which Marius was profoundly grateful. How the Laer could live under such conditions, surrounded by an excess of noise and colour, thankfully confounded him. To understand the ways of the alien was a dark path that he had no intention of following.

'Support squads forward!' he ordered. 'We need to forge a path quickly. Our brothers are depending on us and I won't have the Third found wanting!'

Astartes carrying heavy weapons took up positions in the ruins of coral towers and a heavy barrage snatched at the fog, the thumping of heavy-calibre shells forming a dense roar in Marius's skull.

With suppressing fire laid down, he knew it was time to launch an assault while the enemies' heads were down. Though he disapproved of Solomon's reckless ways, sometimes you had no choice but to go up the centre.

'Kollanus squad! Euidicus squad! Front and centre!'

JULIUS SMASHED A Laer warrior to the ground, the energy field wreathing his massive gauntlet ripping through its silver armour and snapping its snake-like body virtually in two. He and his Terminators were punching a hole clean through the defences of the Laer, having only left a single warrior in the care of the Apothecaries. Though the fighting had been hard, the protection offered by Terminator armour was prodigious, and Julius had revelled in the sensation of power it conferred. To walk through the fire unscathed was what it must be like to be a god, though he chided himself for such a ridiculous thought.

The *Firebird* had touched down a kilometre ahead of them, but from the reports he was hearing over the vox, it sounded as though the resistance of the aliens guarding the temple was fierce. The warriors of the First were not fast, but their pace was relentless and with the support of Ancient Rylanor, they were able to push their way through without difficulty.

Indeed, it felt like the Laer resistance was melting away a little too easily the closer they came to the centre of the atoll. The ground had become rockier and steeper, the perfect terrain to defend against an attacker, so why weren't the Laer making use of it?

'Lycaon, what does this feel like to you?' asked Julius, pausing as he clambered over the steep coral and tried to discern a way onwards. The slopes of coral reared above him in an impenetrable barrier, but the Laer ahead of them had somehow retreated, so there must be a way through.

'It feels like they aren't trying very hard to stop us,' answered Lycaon. 'I haven't fired my weapon in minutes.'

'Exactly.'

'Not that I'm complaining, though.'

'There's something not right about this,' said Julius. 'It feels wrong.'

'Then what are your orders, sir?'

The sound of the screaming towers had grown
louder the closer they came to the centre of the atoll,
and Julius could see that the curving passages that
wound their way upwards through the coral to their
objective were growing narrower and narrower.

More suited to a being with a serpentine body, he
realised.

The sounds of hissing, screaming and battle were
close, and melded into such a cacophony that he
wondered that the Laer were not driven mad by them.

'The *Firebird* has to be around here somewhere,' said
Julius. 'Spread out and find a way through the coral.
Our primarch needs us!'

The sounds of battle were like those described in
the old poems of ancient Terra: hyperbolic works
filled with florid descriptions of combat that were
obviously penned by someone who had never seen a
war.

Even amid the chaos of a battle, Julius was thinking
of poetry and works of literature, and he resolved to
keep a tighter rein on his thoughts. Perhaps Solomon
was right and he *was* spending too much time with
the remembrancers.

'Captain!' shouted Lycaon. 'Over here!'

Julius turned his attention to his equerry, seeing he
had found a previously concealed burrow hole that
appeared to lead through the porous mass of coral.
The passageway beyond was wide, though it would
still be cramped for a warrior clad in Terminator
armour, and Julius hoped that it led to their objective.

'Let's go, First,' ordered Julius, setting off at the
fastest pace his armour would allow.

Keeping his bolter raised, Julius led his men along
the darkened pathway through the coral. Echoes of
battle distorted weirdly through the passageway and

there was a glistening moistness to the tunnel that made Julius think that they were crawling through the innards of some vast beast.

The unbidden thought suddenly worried him. Were the atolls of the Laer alive? Had anyone thought to check?

He pushed the thought from his mind as he realised it was too late to do anything about it anyway, and he pressed onwards, guided by the sounds of fighting and the light of flames.

Eventually, he saw a dark patch ahead that was crisscrossed by tracer fire and knew they had found the exit. He just hoped it was where they were meant to be. The tunnel narrowed and Julius was forced to use the bulk of his armour and the energy of his power fist to break through into the interior of the atoll.

Julius emerged into the end of a wide valley of pink coral with a monstrous, twin-spired temple that penetrated the clouds at its furthest end. The valley's edge was fringed with hundreds of screaming, jagged spires that curved inwards so that the valley resembled a toothed wound in the coral.

Clouds of flying Laer warriors flocked around the temple's upper reaches, and in the centre of the valley Julius could see the heroic form of the primarch battling his way forwards with great sweeps of the golden sword, *Fireblade*. Fulgrim's eagle-winged helmet shone in the darkness, and Julius felt enormous pride at the sight of his lord.

The crackling blades of the Phoenix Guard surrounded Fulgrim, their long halberds keeping the Laer at bay as they forged their way towards the temple at the far end of the valley. He could see the massive form of Brother Thestis at the primarch's

side, holding the great Legion standard of the
Emperor's Children high. The eagle atop the pole
blazed with a white gold light in the glow of the
moon, and the purple cloth of the banner rippled like
silk in the wind.

Julius saw at once that his primarch was surrounded and shouted, 'Warriors of the First, to the
Phoenician!'

THE LORD OF the Emperor's Children struck out at his
foes with mighty strokes of his sword, each terrible
blow slaying one of the Laer. None could stand
against him and live, so when the traitorous thought
arose that this fight was not going according to plan,
it came like an assassin in the night.

His Phoenix Guard fought like the heroes they
were, golden blades killing anything that dared come
within range of their deadly halberds, and brave
Thestis valiantly held the Legion standard high, chop-
ping apart any enemies that came near him with his
long blade. All around them, Laer were dying, cut
down by deadly sword strikes or gunned down by disciplined, precisely aimed bolter fire. A strange pink
musk drifted across the battlefield and clung to his
ankles, its scent fragrant and not at all unpleasant.
The screams of the towers drowned out the screeches
of the Laer, and Fulgrim could not remember a more
frenetic battlefield.

He had never before experienced such a riot of
colour and noise, and what purpose it served, he
could not fathom. The rearing temple appeared to be
the centre of the cacophony. Tears in its fabric, like
windows, were the source of the loudest screaming,
and from them more of the pink musk seeped into
the air. The structure was perhaps three hundred

metres in front of him, but without more of his warriors, he saw that it might as well have been three hundred light years.

Another treacherous thought came to him as his sword clove a Laer warrior from head to tail, that perhaps they had been drawn into this hellish valley deliberately. The pink coral of its walls and the jagged spires that lined the ridges of its summit reminded him of a plant he had seen in the humid swamps of Twenty-Eight Two that feasted on the great buzzing insects of the jungles by luring them into its leafy jaws before snapping shut and digesting them.

Only the warriors who had accompanied him on the *Firebird* fought with him, and though they fought bravely, they were being dragged down one by one, and such a rate of attrition could have only one outcome. He scanned the slopes of the valley for any sign of his battle companies. He punched the air as he saw Julius Kaesoron and the warriors of the First fighting their way through the press of slithering, screeching Laer warriors towards him.

Terminator armour gave each warrior the strength and power of a tank, and though Fulgrim had loathed these inelegant suits of armour at first sight, his heart leapt to see them now.

'See now the mighty First!' shouted Fulgrim. 'Push on my brothers, push on!'

Brother Thestis surged forward, holding the Legion standard with one hand and cutting his way through the Laer with his sword. Fulgrim leapt to join him, protecting his faithful standard bearer's flank as the Phoenix Guard rallied to the banner.

'Follow the Phoenician!' Julius Kaesoron shouted, behind him, and Fulgrim laughed with the sheer joy and artistry of the fighting as the warriors of the First smashed into the Laer. Apothecary Fabius had said that the Laer were chemically modified to move towards perfection, but they were a poor shadow of the perfection embodied by his Legion.

As he punched his fist through a Laer warrior's skull, Fulgrim tried to imagine what heights he and his warriors could scale were they to embark on a similar path, and how proud his father would be when he saw what wonders and marvels they had wrought.

A hissing Laer warrior hacked its weapon into the shoulder guard of his armour, the blade sliding clear and its tip scoring a line across his golden helm. Fulgrim cried out, more in surprise than pain, and thrust his sword through the alien's jaws.

He forced himself to concentrate on the fighting and not the glories the future held, seeing that yet more of his warriors were pushing into the valley through burrow holes in the coral. He frowned at their lateness, for his plan had called for an over-whelming strike delivered to this temple in perfect concert. Somewhere things had gone awry and many of his warriors had been delayed. The sudden thought troubled him greatly and his mood darkened.

As more and more Emperor's Children poured into the valley, Fulgrim and the Legion banner pushed deeper into the frenzied ranks of the Laer, the temple now tantalisingly close. A flaring sheet of green fire shot out and Fulgrim threw himself to the side. He felt the heat of the alien weapon, but shrugged off the pain where it had caught him, and turned to face the threat. The Phoenix Guard had already slaughtered his attacker.

'The banner falls!' shouted a voice, and Fulgrim saw Brother Thestis on his knees, his body a flaming statue as the deadly alien fire consumed him. The Legion standard slipped from Thestis's dead hand and toppled towards the ground, the cloth of the banner blazing where it had caught light.

Fulgrim leapt towards Thestis and snatched up the banner before it landed, raising it high with one hand so that all the Legion might see that it still flew. Fire rippled across the fabric, destroying what a hundred weeping women had created for the beautiful Primarch of the III Legion, in its unthinking hunger. The eagle's claw heraldry emblazoned upon the banner vanished in the flames, and Fulgrim felt his fury rise at this fresh insult to his honour. Burning scraps of cloth fluttered around him, but he saw that the eagle atop the banner pole remained untouched by the fire, as though some greater power protected it from harm.

'The eagle still flies!' he shouted. 'The eagle will never fall!'

Fulgrim's warriors roared in anger at this violation done to their banner and redoubled their efforts to destroy their enemies. Hard bangs of bolter fire sounded beside Fulgrim, and he turned to see Julius Kaesoron gunning down a pair of winged Laer warriors that swooped towards the blackened banner. The Phoenix Guard formed a protective cordon around him as Fulgrim marched over to the Terminator captain, the glittering eagle still held high.

'Captain Kaesoron!' cried Fulgrim. 'You are late.'

'I apologise, my lord,' said Kaesoron contritely. 'Finding a path through the coral proved to be more difficult than we imagined.'

'Difficulty is no excuse,' warned Fulgrim. 'Perfection must overcome difficulty.'

'It must, my lord,' agreed Kaesoron. 'It will never happen again.'

Fulgrim nodded and said, 'Where are Captain Demeter's Second?'

'I do not know, my lord. He has not answered any of my vox hails.'

Fulgrim turned from Kaesoron and returned his attention to the battle. 'I shall need you and your warriors to break open that temple. Follow me in.'

Without waiting for acknowledgement, Fulgrim set off at a brisk jog through his Phoenix Guard, who formed up around him as he took the eagle once more into the fight. Missiles and shells slammed into the temple and massive chunks of coral smashed down into the valley, crushing the Laer that gathered around its base.

With Fulgrim at their head, the Emperor's Children formed a fighting wedge that speared through the Laer. Closer to the temple, the aliens fought with a violence that bordered on the insane, the pink musk wreathing their bodies in a filmy gauze, and their screeching cries like those of the banshees of ancient myth. They attacked with no thought to their own defence, and Fulgrim swore that some were simply hurling themselves onto his blade. Dark blood and howls of what he would later swear were pleasure ripped from their bodies with every stroke.

The gnarled spires of the screaming temple towered above him, the wide arched entrance like the mouth of an undersea cave. Huge chunks of blasted coral lay scattered around, and scores of snaking Laer bodies slithered around them, their multiple arms bearing curved blades, which crackled with blue flames that shone brightly in the mist that poured from the shattered temple.

The Emperor's Children hammered into them, and the battle was as bloody as it was brief, the Laer fighting with inhumanly quick strikes of their lethal blades. Even the armour of the Terminators was not proof against such weapons, and more than one of Kaesoron's First lost a limb or his life to their unnatural energies.

With more and more Emperor's Children pushing into the valley, there could be no stopping their advance, and they slashed through the alien warriors that stood between them and the yawning cave mouth of the temple.

'We have them now, my children!' shouted Fulgrim.

Holding the shining eagle banner in one hand and his golden sword in the other, Fulgrim fought his way into the temple of the Laer.

Julius Kaesoron had killed with the fury of one of Angron's warriors, the shame of the primarch's rebuke driving him to undreamt of heights of reckless courage to once again prove his mettle. He had lost count of the Laer he had killed, and now the darkness of the temple enfolded him as he followed the golden eagle borne by his primarch into the heart of the black coral structure.

The darkness was like a living thing, swallowing light and sound as though jealously guarding it. Beyond the temple, Julius could still hear the crump of explosions, the rattle of gunfire, the clash of blades and the nerve shredding screams of the towers, but with each step he took, the sounds diminished as though he were descending into an infinitely deep pit.

Ahead of him, Fulgrim strode onwards, unaware or uncaring of the effect the darkness of the temple was having on his warriors. Julius could see that even the normally implacable Phoenix Guard were uneasy in this place, and no wonder, for the primarch himself had declared that it was a place of worship.

The idea of such things was as repugnant to Julius as the idea of failure, and the thought that he stood in a fane where loathsome aliens had offered praise to false gods stoked the fires of his hatred. The warriors who had fought their way into the temple spread out as they followed their leader, swords raised or bolters at the ready in case some new threat lay within the place that the Laer had fought so hard to defend.

'There is power here,' said Fulgrim, his voice sounding impossibly distant. 'I can feel it.'

The Phoenix Guard closed ranks around the primarch, but he waved them away, sheathing *Fireblade* and reaching up to remove his eagle-winged helmet before handing it to the closest of his bodyguards. Though the Phoenix Guard retained their helmets, a great many other warriors reached up and followed their primarch's example.

Julius did likewise and released the catches at his gorget, lifting the close-fitting helmet clear of his head. His skin was clammy with sweat, and he took a deep breath of air to clear his lungs of the stale, recycled oxygen of his armour. The air was hot and scented, a cloying musk drifting from holes in the walls, and he was surprised to feel a little light-headed.

The darkness of the temple began to lift as they penetrated deeper, and Julius could hear what sounded like frantic music from up ahead, as though a million demented orchestras were playing a million different tunes at once. A flickering, multi-coloured glow pierced the gloom where Julius believed the source of the discordant music to lie. Even at this distance, Julius could feel the cold breath of air that spoke of a much larger space ahead, and he picked up his pace, marching in heavy, ponderous strides to draw level with his primarch.

As Julius entered the cavern, he felt as though a smothering blanket he had not known existed was suddenly pulled from his skull, and he clapped his hands to his ears as a cacophonous flood of sensations assaulted him with a surge of light and noise.

Blazing light filled the immense space within the temple, leaping from wall to wall, and riotous noise echoed in a deafening thunder of sounds. Fantastical colours wheeled in the air, as though the light were somehow caught in the humid, aromatic smoke that snaked through the chamber. Monstrous statues of what Julius assumed were the gods of the Laer ran around the circumference of the temple, massive bull-headed creatures with multiple arms and great horns curling from their skulls. Numerous barbed rings pierced their stone flesh and each god's chest was sheathed in layered armour plate that left the right breast bare.

Wild murals covered every centimetre of the walls, and Julius stiffened as he saw that hundreds of the Laer writhing on the chamber's floor, the horrid, dry susurration of their bodies the most hideous sound imaginable. He made to shout a warning, but saw there was no need, for the serpentine bodies were hideously intertwined in what looked like some form of grotesque sexual congress.

Clearly, whatever power had driven the Laer defending the temple into a manic frenzy did not extend to those within it. They sprawled in languorous repose, their glistening, multi-hued bodies pierced in the same manner as the statues, and their sluggish movements suggesting the effects of a powerful narcotic.

'What are they doing?' asked Julius over the din. 'Are they dying?'

'If they are, then it seems to be a very pleasurable death,' said Fulgrim, his eyes fixed hungrily on something in the centre of the chamber. Julius followed his gaze, seeing that the slithering Laer surrounded a circular block of veined black stone, embedded within which was a tall sword with a gently curved blade.

The handle was long and silver, its surface patterned like the scales of a snake, and its pommel was set with a winking purple stone that threw off dazzling reflections.

'They were protecting this,' said Fulgrim, his voice sounding distant and faint to Julius. His eyes stung with the smoke, and he could feel the beginnings of a powerful headache as the noise and light continued to batter at his senses.

'No,' whispered Julius, knowing, but not knowing how he knew, that the Laer had not offered praise in this temple, but had been in thrall to it. 'This is not a place of worship, it is a place of dominance.'

Still holding the eagle-topped banner pole, Fulgrim walked into the mass of writhing Laer. His Phoenix Guard moved to follow him, but Fulgrim held them back. Julius tried to cry out to his primarch that something was very wrong here, but the perfumed smoke seemed to rush to fill his lungs and he could not draw breath to shout as a strident whisperer hissed in his ear.

Let him take me, Julius.

The words slipped from his mind as soon as they were spoken and he felt a strange numbness suffuse him, the tips of his fingers tingling pleasantly as he watched Fulgrim march through the sprawled Laer.

With every step the primarch took, the Laer parted before him, clearing a pathway towards the block of stone, and as he reached the sword, Julius recalled Fulgrim's words as they had entered the temple: *There is power here.*

He could feel a charge in the air, a breath on the wind that howled around the temple's interior, a pulse in the living walls and... and... the cry of release as a blade slices open an eyeball, the caress of silk across bare skin, the scream torn from the mouth of violated flesh and the bliss of agony as it takes pleasure in its own mutilation.

Julius cried out as sensations of horror and ecstasy filled his head, a delirious laughter echoing through the chamber, though none but he appeared to hear it. He looked up from his agony to see Fulgrim's fingers slip easily around the sword's handle. A sigh, like the ancient winds of the emptiest deserts, filled the chamber. Julius felt a tremor run through the temple, a shudder of release and fulfilment, as he watched Fulgrim draw the blade from the block of stone.

The Primarch of the Emperor's Children admired the sword blade, a spectral glow thrown across his pale features by the dancing lights that filled the chamber. The Laer still writhed on the ground, their bodies undulating obscenely as the primarch raised the burned banner pole high and drove it into the stone he had just drawn the sword from.

The eagle caught the light and threw off hundreds of fractured reflections from its wings, and to Julius the sight was hideous, the light making the eagle appear to twist and writhe in pain.

Fulgrim spun the sword in his grip, testing it for balance, and he smiled as he cast his gaze out over the hundreds of Laer sprawled around him.

'Destroy them all,' he said. 'Leave none alive.'

PART TWO

THE PHOENIX &
THE GORGON

SIX

Diasporex/The Molten Heart/Young Gods

As MUCH AS he hated what they had become, Captain Balhaan of the Iron Hands couldn't help but admire the skill of the fleet masters of the Diasporex. For nearly five months they had managed to evade the ships of the X Legion around the Carollis system of the Lesser Bifold Cluster with an efficacy that was beyond even the longest serving captains of the Iron Hands.

That was set to change now that the *Ferrum* and her small company of escort ships had managed to calve a pair of vessels from the larger mass of the enemy fleet and drive them towards the gaseous rings of the Carollis Star from whence this endeavour had begun.

Ferrus Manus, Primarch of the Iron Hands, had noted bitterly that it was a tragedy of their own making that would see the Diasporex destroyed. They had come to the attention of the 52nd Expedition quite by accident when forward reconnaissance vessels had

traversed the western reaches of the cluster and
detected some unusual vox transmissions.

This region of space comprised three systems, two
of which contained a number of habitable worlds
that had been brought back into the Imperial fold
with a minimum of resistance. Remote probe ships
had revealed the existence of other systems deeper in
the cluster with the potential to support life and, at
first, it had been surmised that the signals had come
from this unconquered region of space. Prior to the
order for the mass advance, the unusual transmissions had once again been detected, this time in
Imperial space around the Carollis Star.

The Primarch of the Iron Hands had immediately
ordered the expedition's surveyor officers to locate
the source of the transmissions, whereupon it was
quickly deduced that an unknown fleet of some magnitude was at large in Imperial space. No other
expeditions were authorised to be operating close by,
and none of the newly compliant worlds had fleets of
any significance, thus Ferrus Manus had declared that
these interlopers must be found and eliminated
before any advance could begin.

And so the hunt had begun.

Balhaan stood behind the iron lectern that served
as his command post on the *Ferrum*, a mid-size strike
cruiser that had served faithfully in the 52nd Expedition's forces for almost a century and a half. For sixty
of those years it had been under Balhaan's command
and he prided himself that it was the best ship and
crew in the fleet, for anything less than the best was
weakness that he would not tolerate.

Named for the X Legion's primarch, Ferrus Manus,
the bridge of the *Ferrum* was stark and spartan, its
every surface gleaming and pristine. Though there

was ornamentation, it was kept to a bare minimum, and the ship looked much as it had when it first launched from its moorings in the Martian shipyards. She was fast, deadly and the perfect ship to serve as a hunter of this unknown fleet.

The hunt had proven to be problematic, for the fleet clearly did not want to be found. Eventually, however, the origin of the mysterious fleet was revealed when the battle-barge *Iron Will* had chanced upon an unidentified cluster of vessels and intercepted them before they could flee.

To the surprise and delight of the expedition's size-able Mechanicum contingent, the vessels had turned out to be of human origin, and interrogation of the surviving crew had been undertaken immediately. This revealed that the ships were part of a larger con-glomeration of vessels the captured crewmen had called the Diasporex, and belonged to an age of Terra long since passed.

Balhaan was a keen student of the history of ancient Earth, and had read extensively of the golden age of exploration, thousands of years before the darkness of Old Night had descended upon the galaxy, when humanity had travelled from Earth in vast colonisation fleets. The very purpose of the Great Crusade was to reclaim what had been won by the early pioneers and then lost in the anarchy of the Age of Strife. Such ancient fleets were the stuff of legend, for the ships of the earliest starfarers had taken the children of Terra to the furthest corners of the galaxy.

To stumble upon their descendants was declared providential by Ferrus Manus himself.

With information gleaned from the captured crew, contact was established with these brothers of antiq-uity, but much to the 52nd Expedition's disgust, the

Diasporex had incorporated many incongruent elements in its makeup over the long millennia. Ancient human vessels flew alongside starships belonging to a wide variety of alien races, and instead of rejecting such contamination, as the Emperor had dictated, the fleet masters of the Diasporex had welcomed them into their ranks, forming a co-operative armada that plied the darkness of space together.

In the spirit of forgiving brotherhood, Ferrus Manus had generously offered to repatriate the thousands of humans that made up the Diasporex to compliant worlds, if they would submit to the rule of the Emperor of Mankind.

The primarch's offer had been rejected out of hand and all communication broken off.

Faced with such an insult to the Emperor's will, Ferrus Manus had no choice but to lead the 52nd Expedition into a legitimate war against the Diasporex.

BALHAAN AND THE *Ferrum* were the forward vanguard of the primarch's war, and now he had the honour of striking back at the humans who dared turn their back on the Emperor and the emergent Imperium. Like the vessel he commanded, Balhaan was stark and unforgiving, as befitted a warrior of the Kaargul Clan. He had commanded a fleet of ships on the icy seas of Medusa by his fifteenth winter and knew the shifting temperaments of the sea better than any man. No man who served under him had ever dared question his orders and no man had ever failed him.

His Mark IV armour was polished a lustrous black, and a white, wool cloak embroidered with silver thread hung to his knees. A greenskin cleaver had taken his left arm three decades ago and a Deuthrite flenser his right barely a year later. Now both his arms were heavy augmetics of burnished iron, but Balhaan welcomed his new mechanised limbs, for flesh, even Astartes flesh, was weak and would eventually fail.

To receive the Blessing of Iron was a boon, not a curse.

An industrious hubbub filled the bridge with an excited hum, and Balhaan permitted the crew their excitement, for the *Ferrum* was to have the honour of the first kill. The main viewing bay was filled with the dark void of space, lit up by the brilliant yellow glow of the Carollis Star. A multitude of flickering lines looped across the display: flight trajectories, torpedo tracks, ranges and intercept vectors, each one designed to bring an end to the two vessels that lay a few thousand kilometres off his prow.

The irony of this hunt was not lost on Balhaan, for despite his rank as captain of a ship of war, he was not a man without sensibilities beyond his duties. These were human vessels and to attack them was to destroy a piece of history that fascinated him.

'Come about to new heading, zero two three,' he ordered, gripping the lectern tightly with his iron fingers. He did not dare betray any emotion as they closed on the two wallowing cruisers they had managed to shear from the Diasporex fleet, but he could not help a small smile of triumph as he watched his gunnery officer come towards him with a data-slate clutched in his eager hands.

'You have a solution for the forward batteries, Axarden?' demanded Balhaan.

'I do, sir.'

'Inform the ordnance decks,' said Balhaan, 'but close to optimum range before unmasking the guns.'

'Aye, sir,' replied Axarden, 'and the containers they ejected?'

Balhaan pulled up the feed from the starboard picters, watching as the enormous cargo containers that the cruisers had abandoned drifted away. In an attempt to gain more speed, the enemy cruisers had ditched whatever cargo they were hauling, but it hadn't been enough to prevent the Imperial ships from catching them.

'Ignore them,' ordered Balhaan. 'Concentrate on the cruisers. We will return for them later and examine what they were carrying.'

'Very good, sir.'

Balhaan watched the range to the two cruisers close with a practiced eye. They were following a curving trajectory around the star's corona, hoping to lose themselves in the electromagnetic clutter that spurted and foamed around its edges, but the *Ferrum* was too close to be thrown off by such a clumsy subterfuge.

Clumsy…

Balhaan frowned as he wondered at his prey's apparent foolishness. Everything he had learned of the Diasporex suggested that its captains were highly skilled, and for them to believe that such an obvious stratagem would throw him from their scent was inherently suspicious.

'Ordnance decks report all guns ready to fire,' reported Axarden.

'Very good,' nodded Balhaan, worried that there was something he wasn't seeing.

The two ships followed a divergent course, peeling away from one another, and Balhaan knew he should order his ship to all ahead full to pull into the gap and give both of them a good broadside, but he kept his counsel, knowing there was something wrong.

His worst fears were suddenly realised when his surveyor officer shouted, 'New contacts! Multiple signals!'

'Where in the name of Medusa did they come from?' shouted Balhaan, swinging his heavy body around to face the wide, waterfall displays of surveyor command. Red lights were winking into life on the display, and without asking Balhaan knew that they were behind his ships.

'I'm not sure,' said the surveyor officer, but even as he spoke, Balhaan knew where they had come from, and returned his gaze to the command lectern. He called up the external picters and watched in horror as the vast cargo containers abandoned by their quarry split open and disgorged scores of gleaming darts; bombers and fighters no doubt.

'All ahead full!' ordered Balhaan, though he knew it was already too late. 'Come to new heading, nine seven zero and launch interceptors. Activate close-in defence turrets. All escorts to perimeter protection duties.'

'What about the cruisers?' asked Axarden.

'Damn the cruisers!' shouted Balhaan, watching as they ceased their flight and began turning to face the *Ferrum*. 'They were nothing more than decoys, and like a fool I fell for it.'

He could hear the groaning metal of the deck shifting beneath his feet as the *Ferrum* desperately sought to turn to face this new foe.

'Torpedoes launched!' warned the defence officer. 'Impact in thirty seconds!'

Balhaan shouted, 'Countermeasures!' though he knew that any torpedo launched from such close range was practically guaranteed to hit. The *Ferrum* continued to turn, and Balhaan could feel the juddering fire of the defence turrets as they opened fire on the incoming ordnance. Some of the enemy torpedoes would be shot down, exploding soundlessly in the void, but not all of them.

'Twenty seconds to impact!'

'All stop,' ordered Balhaan. 'Reverse turn, that might throw some of them off.' It was a vain hope, but right now he would take a vain hope over no hope.

His interceptors would be leaping from their launch rails by now, and they would bring a few more torpedoes down before engaging the enemy forces. His vessel heeled hard to the side as the strike cruiser twisted her bulk faster than she was ever designed to and the creaks and groans of the vessel were painful to Balhaan's ears.

'*Ironheart* reports that it has engaged the enemy cruisers. Heavy damage.'

Balhaan returned his attention to the main view screen, watching the smaller *Ironheart* wreathed in flickering detonations. Pinpricks of light flickered between the vessel and its attackers, the silence and distance diminishing the ferocity of the conflict.

'We have our own problems,' said Balhaan. 'The *Ironheart* is on her own.' Then he gripped the lectern as he heard his defence officer shout once more.

'Impact in four, three, two, one...'

The *Ferrum* rocked hard to port, the deck lurching underfoot as the torpedoes impacted on her rear starboard quarter. Warning bells began chiming, and the display on the view screen faded briefly before vanishing completely. Fire burst from ruptured conduits, and hissing steam vented into the bridge.

'Damage control!' shouted Balhaan, cracking the command lectern with the force of his grip. Servitors and deck ratings struggled to contain the blaze, and

Balhaan watched as burnt crewmen were dragged
from shattered control stations, their flesh and uniforms blackened by fire. He leaned over to gunnery
control and shouted, 'All guns open fire, full defensive spread!'

'Sir!' cried Axarden. 'Some of our own craft will be
in the engagement zone.'

'Do it!' ordered Balhaan. 'Or there will be no ship
for them to return to and they will die anyway. Open
fire!'

Axarden nodded and staggered across the ruptured
deck to carry out his captain's orders.

The enemy fighters would soon find that the *Ferrum*
still had teeth.

THE PRIMARCH'S CHAMBERS aboard the battle-barge,
Fist of Iron, were constructed of stone and glass, as
cold and austere as the frozen tundra of Medusa, and
First Captain Santar could almost feel the chill of his
icy home world in the design. Blocks of shimmering
obsidian carved from the sides of undersea volcanoes
kept the chamber dark, and glass cabinets of war trophies and weapons stood as silent sentinels over the
primarch's most private moments.

Santar watched as Ferrus Manus stood nearly naked
before him, his servants washing his iron hard flesh
and applying oils before scraping him clean with
razor edged knives. As each gleaming, oiled limb was
finished, his armourers would apply the layers of his
battle armour, gleaming black plates of polished
ceramite that had been crafted by Master Adept
Malevolus of Mars.

'Tell me again, equerry Santar,' began the primarch,
his voice gruff and full of the molten fury of a Medusan volcano. 'How is it that an experienced captain

like Balhaan was able to lose three vessels and not manage to bring down one of our enemy's?'

'It appears he was lured into an ambush,' said Santar, straightening his back as he spoke. To serve as First Captain of the Iron Hands and equerry to the Primarch of the Iron Hands was the greatest honour of his life, and while he relished every moment spent with his beloved leader, there were moments when the potential of his anger was like the volatile core of their home, unpredictable and terrifying.

'An ambush?' snarled Ferrus Manus. 'Damn it, Santar, we are becoming sloppy! Months of chasing shadows have made us foolhardy and reckless. It will not stand.'

Ferrus Manus towered above his servants, his knotted flesh pale as though carved from the heart of a glacier. Scars crossed his skin from the wounds he had taken in battle, for the Primarch of the Iron Hands was never one to shirk from leading his warriors by example. His close cropped hair was jet black, his eyes like glittering silver coins, and his features were battered by centuries of war. Other primarchs might be considered beautiful creations, handsome men made godlike by their ascension to the ranks of the Astartes, but Ferrus Manus did not count himself amongst them.

Santar's eyes were drawn, as they always were, to the gleaming silver forearms of his primarch. The flesh of his arms and hands shimmered and rippled as though formed from liquid mercury that had flowed into the shape of mighty hands and somehow been trapped in that form forever. Santar had seen wondrous things fashioned by these hands, machines and weapons that never dulled or failed, all beaten into shape or crafted by the primarch's hands without need of forge or hammer.

'Captain Balhaan is already aboard to personally apologise for his failure, and he has offered to resign command of the *Ferrum*.'

'Apologise?' snapped the primarch. 'I should have his head just to make an example.'

'With respect, my lord,' said Santar, 'Balhaan is an experienced captain and perhaps something less severe might be in order. Perhaps you might simply remove his arms?'

'His arms? What use is he to me then?' demanded Ferrus Manus, causing the servant with his breast-plate to flinch.

'Very little,' agreed Santar, 'though probably more than if you remove his head.'

Ferrus Manus smiled, his anger vanishing as swiftly as it had arisen. 'You have a rare gift, my dear Santar. The molten heart of Medusa burns in my breast and sometimes it rises in my gullet before I can think.'

'I am your humble servant,' said Santar.

Ferrus Manus waved away his armourers and moved to stand before Santar. Though Santar was tall for an Astartes and was clad in his full armour, the primarch still towered over him, his silver eyes shining and without pupils. Santar suppressed a shiver, for those eyes were like chips of napped flint, hard, unforgiving and sharp. The scent of lapping powder and oil was strong on his flesh, and Santar felt his soul open up beneath that gaze, his every weakness and imperfection laid bare.

Santar was like unto Medusa himself, his craggy features like a cliff face shorn from the flanks of a mountain, his grey eyes like the great storms that tore the skies of his home world. Upon his induction into the Legion, many decades ago, his left hand had been removed and a bionic replacement grafted in its place. Since then, both his legs had been replaced, as had the remainder of his left arm.

'You are much more than that to me, Santar,' said Ferrus Manus, placing his hands on his equerry's shoulder guards. 'You are the ice that quenches my fire when it threatens to overwhelm the good sense the Emperor gave me. Very well, if you won't let me take his head, what punishment would you suggest?'

Santar took a deep breath as Ferrus Manus turned away from him and returned to his armourers, the dreadful respect the primarch instilled leaving his mouth dry.

Angrily, he pushed aside his momentary weakness and said, 'Captain Balhaan will have learned from this debacle, but I agree his weakness must be punished. To remove him as captain of the *Ferrum* would damage the morale of the crew, and if they are to restore their honour, they will need Balhaan's leadership.'

'So what do you suggest?' asked Ferrus.

'Something to make it clear that he has earned your ire, but which shows that you are merciful and willing to allow him and his crew the chance to earn back your trust.'

Ferrus Manus nodded as the armourers fitted his breastplate to his backplate, his silver arms extended either side of him as they dipped linen cloths into iron bowls of scented oils and applied them to his hands.

'Then I will appoint one of the Iron Fathers to joint command of the *Ferrum*,' said Ferrus Manus.

'He won't like that,' warned Santar.

'I'm not giving him a choice,' said the primarch.

THE ANVILARIUM OF the *Fist of Iron* resembled a mighty forge, huge, hissing pistons rising and falling at the edges of the audience chamber, and the distant clang of hammers echoing through the sheet metal of the floor. It was a cavernous space, with the pungent aromas of oil and hot metal heavy in the air, the space redolent of industry and machines.

Santar relished the chance to come to the Anvilarium, for mighty deeds were planned and unbreakable bonds of brotherhood were forged here. To be part of such a fraternity was an honour few would ever dream of, let alone achieve.

It had been two months since Captain Balhaan's disastrous encounter with the Diasporex ships, and the 52nd Expedition was no nearer to achieving the destruction of the enemy fleet. The new caution engendered by Balhaan's punishment ensured that no other vessels had been lost, but also meant that there had been few opportunities to engage in a decisive battle.

Santar and the rest of his warriors of the Avernii Clan stood at parade rest flanking the great gate that led into the Iron Forge, the primarch's most secret reclusiam. The Morlocks gathered at the far end of the Anvilarium, the glimmering steel of their Terminator armour reflecting the red flames of the torches that hung in iron sconces on the walls. Soldiers and senior officers of the Imperial Army stood together with the robed adepts of the Mechanicum, and Santar nodded respectfully as he caught the glowing eye of their senior representative, Adept Xanthus.

As captain of the First Company, the duty of acknowledging the primarch was his, and he strode to the centre of the Anvilarium, the Legion's standard bearers marching to stand beside him. One standard bore the primarch's personal banner, depicting his slaying of the great wyrm Asirnoth, while another carried the Iron Gauntlet of the Legion. The devices on the banners were stitched in gleaming silver thread on black velvet, their edges ragged and torn where bullets and blades had snatched at them. Though both had seen the hard edge of battle, neither one had yet fallen or faltered in a thousand victories.

As the gates opened fully with a hiss of escaping steam and a furnace heat, the primarch strode into the Anvilarium, his armour glistening with oil and his pale flesh ruddy from the heat. With the exception of the Terminators, the assembled warriors dropped to their knees in honour of the mighty primarch, who bore his mighty hammer, *Forgebreaker*, hefted across one huge, dog-toothed shoulder guard.

The primarch's armour was black, its every surface hand-forged, its every curve and angle perfect, its majesty matched only by the being that wore it. A high gorget of dark iron rose at the back of his neck and embossed rivets stood proud on the silver edge trims of every plate.

The primarch's face was as though carved from marble, his expression thunderous and his heavy brows furrowed in smouldering fury. When Ferrus Manus marched among his warriors, any joviality was sacrificed to his warrior persona, a ruthless war leader who demanded perfection and despised weakness in all things.

Behind Ferrus Manus came the tall figure of Cistor, the fleet's Master of Astropaths, swathed in a robe of cream and black that was edged with gold anthemion. His head was shaved, and ribbed cables snaked from the side and top of his skull, vanishing into the darkness of the metallic hood that rose stiffly above his head. The astropath's eyes glowed with a soft pink light and, in honour of his position with the Iron Hands, his right arm had been replaced with a mechanical augmetic. He clutched a staff topped with a single eye in his other arm, and a golden pistol, presented to him by the primarch, was holstered at his side.

Santar stood before the primarch and held his hands out to receive the primarch's hammer. Ferrus Manus nodded and placed the enormous weapon in Santar's outstretched hands, the weight enormous and unbearable for anyone but one of the Emperor's Astartes. Its haft was the colour of ebony, elaborately worked with threads of gold and silver that formed the shape of a lightning bolt, and the head was carved into the shape of a mighty eagle, its barbed beak forming the striking face and its tapered wings the claw. The honour of holding this weapon, forged on Terra by the hands of a primarch was incalculable.

He stood to one side, placing the hammer with its head between his feet, and the two banner bearers fell into step behind their great leader as he began circling the chamber. Not for Ferrus Manus the ritual of conferences or meetings, he held his councils of war in a room without chairs or formality, where debate and questions were encouraged.

'Brothers,' began Ferrus Manus, 'I bring word of my brother primarchs.'

The Iron Hands cheered, always grateful for news of their Astartes brothers throughout the galaxy. To celebrate the triumphs of other expeditions was only right and proper, but it also gave the Iron Hands the motivation to push harder and to achieve more, for their Legion would be second to none, perhaps save the Warmaster's Legion.

'It appears that the Imperial Fists of Rogal Dorn have been summoned back to Terra, where his warriors are to fortify the gates and walls of the Imperial Palace.'

Santar saw quizzical looks around the chamber and their confusion mirrored his own. The VII Legion was to quit the Crusade and return to the cradle of mankind? Theirs was a glorious Legion, with courage and strength the equal of the Iron Hands. To withdraw them from the fighting made no sense.

Ferrus Manus also saw the confusion on the faces of his warriors and said, 'I know not what prompts the Emperor's decision, for I know of no shame endured by the Imperial Fists that might occasion such a recall. They are to serve as his praetorians, and though such an honour, honestly given, is great, it is not for the likes of us when there are wars yet to win and foes yet to defeat!'

More cheering rang out over the din of hammers, and Ferrus Manus again circled the chamber, his silver hands and eyes shining in the perpetual gloom of the Anvilarium. 'The Wolves of Russ push ever outwards and their tally of victories grows daily, but we should expect no less from a Legion that hails from a world that beats with the same fire as our own.'

'Any word of the Emperor's Children?' asked a voice, and Santar smiled, knowing the primarch would enjoy speaking of his closest brother. The glacial mask slipped from Ferrus Manus's face and he smiled at his warriors.

'Indeed there is, my friends,' said the primarch. 'My brother Fulgrim journeys here even now with the best part of his expedition.'

Yet more cheers, louder than before, echoed from the metal walls of the chamber, for the Emperor's Children were the most beloved of Legions to the Iron Hands. The brotherhood shared by Fulgrim and Ferrus Manus was well known, the two demi gods having formed an instant connection upon their first meeting.

Santar knew the tale, his primarch having told it many times over the feast table, the details known so well to him it was as though he had been there himself.

It had been beneath Mount Narodnya, the greatest forge of the Urals, where the primarchs had first met, Ferrus Manus toiling with the forge-masters who had once served the Terrawatt Clan during the Unification Wars. The Primarch of the Iron Hands had been demonstrating his phenomenal skill and the miraculous powers of his liquid metal hands when Fulgrim and his Phoenix Guard had descended upon the sprawling forge complex.

Neither primarch had yet met the other, but each had felt the shared bonds of alchemy and science that had gone into their making. Both were like gods unto the terrified artisans, who prostrated themselves before these two mighty warriors as though fearing a terrible battle. Ferrus Manus would then tell Santar of how Fulgrim had declared that he had come to forge the most perfect weapon ever created, and that he would bear it in the coming Crusade.

Of course the Primarch of the Iron Hands could not let such a boast go unanswered, and he had laughed in Fulgrim's face, declaring that such pasty hands as his could never be the equal of his own metal ones. Fulgrim had accepted the challenge with regal grace, and both primarchs had stripped to the waist, working without pause for weeks on end, the forge ringing with the deafening pounding of hammers, the hiss of cooling metal, and the good natured insults of the two young gods as they sought to outdo one another.

At the end of three months unceasing toil, both warriors had finished their weapons, Fulgrim having forged an exquisite warhammer that could level a mountain with a single blow, and Ferrus Manus a golden bladed sword that forever burned with the fire of the forge. Both weapons were unmatched by any yet crafted by man, and upon seeing what the other had created, each primarch declared that his opponent's was the greater.

Fulgrim had declared the golden sword the equal of that borne by the legendary hero Nuada Silverhand, while Ferrus Manus had sworn that only the mighty thunder gods of Nordyc legend were fit to bear such a magnificent warhammer.

Without another word spoken, both primarchs had swapped weapons and sealed their eternal friendship with the craft of their hands.

Santar looked down at the weapon, feeling the power within it and knowing that more than just skill had gone into its forging. Love and honour, loyalty and friendship, death and vengeance... all were embodied within its majestic form, and the thought that his primarch's sworn honour brother had created this weapon made it truly legendary.

He looked up as Ferrus Manus continued his circuit of the Anvilarium, his face thunderous once more. 'Yes, my brothers, cheer, for it will be an honour to fight alongside Fulgrim's warriors, but he only comes to our aid because we have been weak!'

The cheering immediately died and the assembled warriors looked anxiously from one to another, none willing to meet the eye of the angry primarch as he spoke.

'The Diasporex continue to elude us, and there are worlds in the Lesser Bifold Cluster that require the illumination of the Emperor's Truth. How is it that a fleet of ships thousands of years older than ours, and led by mere mortals, can elude us? Answer me!'

None dared respond, and Santar felt the shame of their weakness in every fibre of his being. He gripped the haft of the hammer tightly, feeling the exquisite craftsmanship beneath the steel of his augmetic hand, and suddenly the answer was clear to him.

'It is because we cannot do this alone,' he said.

'Exactly!' said Ferrus Manus. 'We cannot do this alone. We have struggled for months to accomplish this task on our own when it should have been clear that we could not. In all things we strive to eradicate weakness, but it is not weakness to ask for help, my brothers. It is weakness to deny that help is needed. To fight on without hope when there are those who would gladly lend a hand is foolish, and I have been as blind as any to this, but no more.'

Ferrus Manus strode back to the entrance to the Anvilarium and put his arm around the shoulders of Astropath Cistor. The mighty primarch dwarfed the man and his very nearness seemed to cause the astropath pain.

Ferrus Manus extended his hand and Santar stepped forward, holding *Forgebreaker* out before him. The primarch took up his hammer and held it aloft as though its monstrous weight was nothing at all.

'We will not be fighting alone for much longer!' cried Ferrus Manus. 'Cistor tells me that his choirs sing of the arrival of my brother. Within a week the *Pride of the Emperor* and the 28th Expedition will be with us and we shall once again fight alongside our brothers of the Emperor's Children!'

SEVEN

There Will be Other Oceans/Recovery/
The Phoenix and the Gorgon

HE HAD BEGUN with small, tentative chips into the
marble, but as he had grown more confident in his
vision, and the bitterness towards Bequa Kynska had
risen once more, he found himself hacking at the marble with no more thought to his actions than a wild
beast. Ostian drew a stale breath through his mask
and took a step back from the marble block, leaning
against the metal scaffolding that surrounded it.

The thought of Bequa made him grip the metal of
his chisel tighter, and he felt his jaw clench at the
depth of her spite. The sculpture was not going as
smoothly as he would have liked, the lines more
jagged and harsh than would normally be the case,
but he couldn't help himself, the bitterness was too
great.

He thought back to the day he and Serena had
walked arm in arm to the embarkation deck, their
thoughts joyous and carefree at the idea of discovering

a new world together. The corridors of the *Pride of the Emperor* were abuzz with excited speculation in the wake of the Emperor's Children's victory on Laeran, or as it was formally, and correctly known, Twenty-Eight Three.

Serena had come to fetch him the moment the word had gone out, dressed in a fabulous gown that Ostian had felt sure was unfit for a journey to a world where the surface was composed entirely of water. They had laughed and joked as they made their way through the fabulous, high galleries of the ship, joining more remembrancers the closer they got to the embarkation deck.

The mood had been light, artists and sculptors mingling with writers, poets and composers in a happy throng as armoured Astartes escorted them towards their transports.

'We're so lucky, Ostian,' murmured Serena as they made their way towards a huge, gilded set of blast doors.

'How so?' he asked, too caught up in the festive atmosphere of the crowd to notice the baleful stare of Bequa Kynska at his back. He was finally going to see the ocean, and his heart leapt at the thought of such a wondrous thing. He calmed himself by remembering the writings of the Sumaturan philosopher, Sahlonum, who had said that the real voyage of discovery consisted not in finding new landscapes, but in having new eyes with which to see them.

'The Lord Fulgrim appreciates the value of what we're doing, dear heart,' explained Serena. 'I've heard that in some expeditions, the remembrancers are lucky to even see an Astartes warrior let alone get a trip to the surface of a compliant world.'

'Well, it's not as though Laeran's exactly hostile any-more,' said Ostian. 'There's nothing left of the Laer, they're all dead.'

'And good riddance too! I've heard it said that the Warmaster won't let any of his remembrancers down to the surface of Sixty-Three Nineteen yet.'

'I'm not surprised,' said Ostian. 'They say that there's still resistance, so I can see why the Warmaster's not letting anyone down.'

'Resistance,' scoffed Serena, 'the Astartes will soon have that quashed. What's the worst that could happen? Haven't you seen them? Like gods unto us they are! Invincible and immortal!'

'I don't know,' said Ostian, 'I've been hearing some rumours in *La Fenice* of some quite appalling casualty figures.'

'*La Fenice*,' tutted Serena. 'You should know better than to believe anything you hear in that nest of vipers, Ostian.'

That at least was true, reflected Ostian. *La Fenice* was the area of the ship the Emperor's Children had given over to the remembrancers, a great theatre in the high decks that served as a recreation space, eating hall, exhibition area and place of relaxation. During the course of the fighting, Ostian had taken to spending his evenings there, chatting, drinking and exchanging notes with fellow artistes. The currency of ideas was in full flow, and the thrill of being in an environment where designs were tossed into the air and swatted around with lively debate, each time acquiring some strange new form its originator had not yet conceived, was intoxicating.

Yes, *La Fenice* fostered ideas, but when the wine flowed, it was also a hotbed of scandal and intrigue. Ostian knew it was impossible to put so many people

of an artistic persuasion in one place without gener-
ating operas worth of salacious gossip, some of it
undoubtedly true, but some wildly inaccurate, slan-
derous and downright lunatic.

But the stories that had come back regarding the
ferocity of the fighting on Laeran had the ring of truth
to them. Three hundred dead Astartes was what some
people were saying, but others put the figure even
higher at seven hundred, with perhaps six times that
injured.

Such figures were nigh impossible to believe, but
Ostian could only wonder at the force of will that
would be required to destroy an entire civilisation in
a month. It was certainly true that the Astartes he had
seen around the ship were more sombre of late, but
could the casualties really have been that high?

All thoughts of dead Astartes had been washed
away as he and Serena entered the embarkation deck
through the mighty blast doors that sealed it from the
rest of the ship. Ostian's jaw fell open at the sheer
scale and noise of the space, its ceiling lost to darkness, and the servitors and craft at its far end rendered
miniscule by distance. The cold blackness of space
was visible through a flashing rectangle of red lights
that indicated the edge of the integrity field, and Ostian shivered, terrified of what might happen should
the field fail.

Menacing Stormbirds and Thunderhawks sat on
launch rails that ran the length of the massive deck,
their purple and gold hulls pristine and gleaming as
they were tended to like the finest studs of the stable.

Wheeled gurneys snaked through the deck, carrying
crates of shells and racks of missiles, fuel tankers rumbled, and brightly coloured crewmen directed the
chaos with a measure of calm control that Ostian

found amazing. Everywhere he looked, he could see activity, the bustle of a fleet that had recently been at war, the deafening industry of death rendered mechanical and prosaic by repetition.

'Close your mouth, Ostian,' said Serena, smiling at his amazement.

'Sorry,' he muttered, finding new marvels at every turn: huge lifters carrying armoured vehicles in mechanised claws as though they weighed nothing at all, and phalanxes of Astartes warriors marching in perfect step both on and off gunships.

Their escorts kept them in line, and Ostian soon recognised the intricate ballet of movement that operated in the embarkation deck, realising that, without it, this place would be a nightmare of collisions and anarchy. Where before there had been an irreverent atmosphere among the remembrancers, all levity ceased as they were herded through the embarkation deck towards a towering, handsome Astartes warrior and a pair of robed iterators standing on a podium draped with purple cloth. He recognised the Space Marine as First Captain Julius Kaesoron, the warrior who had attended Bequa Kynska's recital, but he had never seen the iterators before.

'Why are there iterators here?' hissed Ostian. 'Surely there's no populace left to sway?'

'They're not for the Laer,' said Serena. 'They're for us.'

'For us?'

'Indeed. Though the Lord Fulgrim appreciates us, I assume he still wants to make sure we see the right things and say the right things when we get back. I'm sure you remember Captain Julius, and the man on the left with the thinning hair, that's Ipolida Zigmanta, a decent enough sort. He loves the sound of his own voice a bit too much in my opinion, though I suppose that's an occupational hazard for an iterator.'

'And the woman?' asked Ostian, his interest piqued by the raven-haired woman's stunning countenance.

'That,' said Serena, 'is Coraline Aseneca. She's a harpy, that one: an actress, an iterator and a beautiful woman. Three reasons not to trust her.'

'What do you mean? Iterators are here to spread the word of the Imperial Truth.'

'Indeed they are, my dear, but there are some that only employ words for the purposes of disguising their thoughts.'

'Well, she looks pleasant enough.'

'My dear boy, you of all people should know that looks are not everything. One with the countenance of Hephaestus may have the most beautiful soul, while she with the comeliness of Cytherea can harbour the bitterest heart.'

'True,' agreed Ostian, glancing over at the blue-haired form of Bequa Kynska, and remembering her attempted seduction of him.

He turned back to Serena and said, 'If that's the case, Serena, how can I trust you, since you are also a beautiful woman?'

'Ah, you can trust me because I am an artist and therefore seek truth in all things, Ostian. An actress seeks to conceal her real face from her audience, to project only what she wants you to see.'

Ostian chuckled and returned his gaze to the platform as Captain Julius Kaesoron began to speak, his voice deeply musical, and worthy of an iterator.

'Honoured remembrancers, it gladdens my heart to see you here today, for your presence is a vindication of what my fellow warriors and I have achieved on Laeran. The fighting was hard, I won't deny it, and it tested us to the limits of our endurance, but such endeavours only help us in our quest for perfection. As Lord Commander Eidolon teaches us, we always need a rival to test us, and against whom we can measure our prowess. You have been selected as the pre-eminent documentarists and chroniclers of our expedition, to travel to the surface of this new world of the Imperium and tell others what you have seen.'

Ostian felt his chest swell with unaccustomed pride at the praise the Astartes had placed upon them, surprised at the eloquence with which the warrior had delivered his speech.

'Laeran is still a warzone, however, and as units from Lord Commander Fayle's Palatines secure the planet, it behoves me to tell you that you will see evidence of our war and the raw, bloody aftermath of killing. Be not afraid of this, for to speak the truth of war, you must see it all: the glory and the brutality. You must experience all the sensations of history for it to matter. Any who feel their sensibilities would be offended by such sights should make themselves known and will be excused.'

Not a single soul moved, nor had Ostian expected any to. To see the surface of a new world was too tempting for anyone to resist, and he saw that same knowledge on Kaesoron's face.

'Then we shall begin with the allocation of transports,' said Kaesoron, and the two iterators descended from the platform and moved among the assembled remembrancers with data-slates, checking names against those on their lists, and directing them to the designated transport that would take them to the planet's surface.

Coraline Aseneca moved towards him, and his pulse quickened as he appreciated the full impact of her beauty, sculpted, elegant and with hair so dark it was like an oil slick. Her full mouth was painted a luscious purple, and her eyes sparkled with an inner light that spoke of expensive augmetics.

'And what are your names?' she asked. Ostian found himself lost for words at the silky, liquid sound of her voice. Her words flowed over him like smoke, hot, and making him blink as he struggled to remember what his name was.

'His name is Ostian Delafour,' said Serena, haughtily, 'and mine is Serena d'Angelus.'

Coraline checked her list and nodded. 'Ah, yes, Mistress d'Angelus, you are to travel on *Perfection's Flight*, the Thunderhawk just over there.'

She turned to move on, but Serena caught the sleeve of her robe and asked, 'And my friend?'

'Delafour… yes,' said Coraline. 'I'm afraid your invitation to the surface was revoked.'

'Revoked?' asked Ostian. 'What are you talking about? Why?'

Coraline shook her head. 'I do not know. All I know is that you do not have permission to visit Twenty-Eight Three.'

Her words were seductively delivered, but cut like hot knives into his heart. 'I don't understand, who revoked my invitation?'

Coraline checked her list with an exasperated sigh. 'It says here that Captain Kaesoron revoked it under the advisement of Mistress Kynska. That's all I can tell you. Now, if you'll excuse me.'

The beautiful iterator went on her way, and Ostian was left stunned and speechless by the magnitude of Bequa Kynska's malice. He looked up from the deck in time to see her ascend the boarding ramp of a Stormbird and blow him a mocking kiss from her palm.

'That bitch!' he snapped, clenching his fists. 'I can't believe this.'

Serena placed her hand on his arm and said, 'This is ridiculous, my dear, but if you cannot go, then I shan't either. Seeing Laeran will mean nothing if you are not there beside me.'

Ostian shook his head. 'No, you go. I won't have that blue haired freak spoil this for both of us.'

'But I wanted to show you the ocean.'

'There will be other oceans,' said Ostian, struggling to keep his bitter disappointment in check. 'Now go, please.'

Serena nodded slowly and reached up to touch his cheek. On impulse, Ostian took her hand and leaned forward to kiss her, his lips brushing her powdered cheek. She smiled and said, 'I'll tell you all about it in nauseating detail when I get back, I promise.'

Ostian had watched her board the Thunderhawk before being escorted back to his studio by a pair of grim faced Army soldiers.

There, he began to attack the marble in his anger.

THE TILED WALLS and ceiling of the medical bay were bare and gleaming, their surfaces kept spotlessly clean by the menials and thralls of Apothecary Fabius. Staring at them day and night, Solomon felt that he was losing his mind just lying here while his bones healed, unable to look at anything but their utter whiteness. He couldn't remember exactly how long it had been since his Stormbird had gone into the ocean during the final attack of the Laer atoll, but it felt like a lifetime. He remembered only pain and darkness where, to keep himself alive, he had shut down the majority of his bodily functions until the rescue craft had pulled his shattered body from the wreckage.

By the time he had regained consciousness in the *Pride of the Emperor's* apothecarion, Laeran had long since been won, but the cost of that victory had been damnably high. Apothecaries and medical thralls bustled up and down the deck, attending to their charges with due diligence, and fighting to ensure that as many as possible returned to full service as quickly as possible.

Apothecary Fabius had personally tended to him, and he was grateful for the attention, knowing that he was amongst the Legion's best and most gifted chirurgeons. Row upon row of cot beds was filled with nearly fifty wounded Astartes warriors, and Solomon had never thought to see so many of his battle-brothers laid low.

No one would tell him how many of his brother Astartes filled the other medical decks.

The sight made him melancholy. He wanted to get out of this place as soon as possible, but his strength had not yet returned, and his entire body ached abominably.

'Apothecary Fabius tells me that you will be back in the training cages before you know it,' said Julius, guessing his thoughts. 'It's just a few bones after all.'

Julius Kaesoron had been sitting next to him on a steel stool since Solomon had woken this morning, his armour gleaming and polished, the scars of war repaired by the Legion's artificers. Fresh honours were secured to his shoulder guards by gobbets of red wax, his deeds of valour recorded on long strips of creamy vellum.

'Just a few bones, he says!' replied Solomon. 'The crash broke all my ribs, both my legs and arms, and fractured my skull. The Apothecaries say it's a miracle that I'm able to walk at all, and my armour was down to its last few minutes of air when the search and rescue birds finally found me.'

'You were never in any real danger,' said Julius as Solomon painfully propped himself up in the bed. 'What was it you said? That the gods of battle wouldn't let you die on a piss-poor excuse for a planet like Laeran? Well they didn't, did they?'

'No,' groused Solomon, 'I suppose not, but they didn't let me fight in the final battle either. I missed all the fun, while you got all the glory by the Phoenician's side.'

He saw a shadow pass over Julius's face and said, 'What is it?'

Julius shrugged. 'I'm not sure. I'm just… I'm just not sure you'd have wanted to be at the primarch's side at the end. It was… unnatural in that temple.'

'Unnatural? What does that mean?'

Julius looked around, as though checking for any who might be listening, and said, 'It's hard to describe, Sol, but it felt… it felt as though the temple itself was alive, or something in it was alive. It sounds stupid, I know.'

'The temple was alive? You're right, that does sound stupid. How can a temple be alive? It's just a building.'

'I have no idea,' admitted Julius, 'but that's what it felt like. I don't know how else to describe it. It was horrible, but at the same time it was magnificent: the colours, the noise and the smells. Even though I hated it at the time, I keep thinking back to it with longing. Every one of my senses was stimulated and I felt… energised by the experience.'

'Sounds like I should try it,' said Solomon. 'I could do with being energised.'

'I even went back with the remembrancers,' laughed Julius, though Solomon could hear the confusion in it. 'They thought it was such a great honour that I accompanied them, but it was not for them, it was for me. I had to see it again, and I don't know why.'

'What does Marius make of all this?'

'He never saw it,' said Julius. 'The Third never made it inside the temple. By the time they fought their way through, the battle was already over. He went straight back to the *Pride of the Emperor*.'

Solomon closed his eyes, knowing the anguish Marius must have felt upon reaching the field of battle and discovering that victory was already won. He had already heard that the Third had failed to reach the battlefield in accordance with the primarch's meticulous plan, and knew that his friend must be suffering unbearable torments at the thought that he had failed in his duty.

'How is Marius?' he asked at last. 'Have you spoken to him?'

'Not much, no,' said Julius. 'He's been keeping himself confined to the armament decks, working his company day and night so they will not fail again. He and his warriors were shamed, but Fulgrim forgave them.'

'Forgave him?' asked Solomon, suddenly angry. 'From what I hear, the southern spur was the most heavily defended part of the atoll, and too many of his assault force were shot down on the way in for him to have had any hope of reaching Fulgrim in time.'

Julius nodded. 'You know that and I know that, but try telling Marius. As far as he is concerned the Third failed in their duty, and must fight twice as hard to regain their honour.'

'He must know that there was no way he could have reached the primarch in time.'

'Maybe, but you know Marius,' pointed out Julius. 'He thinks they should have found a way to overcome impossible odds.'

'Speak to him, Julius,' said Solomon. 'I mean it, you know how he can get.'

'I'll speak to him later on,' said Julius, rising from the stool. 'He and I are part of the delegation that is to meet Ferrus Manus when he comes aboard the *Pride of the Emperor*.'

'Ferrus Manus?' exclaimed Solomon, sitting bolt upright and wincing in pain as his wounds pulled tight. 'He's coming here?'

Julius pressed a hand on his shoulder and said, 'We are due to rendezvous with the 52nd Expedition within six hours, and the Primarch of the Iron Hands is coming aboard. Fulgrim and Vespasian want some of the most senior captains to be part of the delegation.'

Solomon pushed himself upright once more and swung his legs from the bed. His vision swam and he held tight to the bed frame as the gleaming walls suddenly grew sickeningly bright. 'I should be there,' he said groggily.

'You are in no state to be anywhere except here, my friend,' said Julius. 'Caphen will represent the Second. He was lucky, he made it out of the crash with nothing but a few scrapes and bruises.'

'Caphen,' said Solomon, sinking back down into the bed. He was an Astartes, invincible and immortal, and this helplessness was utterly alien to him. 'Keep an eye on him. He's a good lad, but a bit wild sometimes.'

Julius laughed and said, 'Get some sleep, Solomon, you understand? Or did that crash scramble your brains too?'

'Sleep?' said Solomon, slumping back onto the bed. 'I'll sleep when I'm dead.'

THE UPPER EMBARKATION deck had been chosen as the location where the delegation from the Iron Hands would be met, and Julius felt a great excitement seize him at the thought of once again laying eyes upon Ferrus Manus. Not since the bloody fields of Tygriss had the Emperor's Children fought alongside the X Legion, and Julius remembered the cries of triumph and the victory pyres with great pride.

He wore an ivory cloak, its edges picked out with scarlet leaves and eagles, and a laurel wreath of gold upon his brow. He carried his helmet under the crook of his arm, as did his brothers who gathered with him to greet Ferrus Manus. Marius stood to his left, his austere features drawn in a sombre expression that stood out amongst the excited faces that awaited this reunion of the Emperor's sons. Solomon was right, he decided, he would need to keep an eye on his brother and attempt to lift him from the pit of self-loathing he had dug for himself.

In contrast, Gaius Caphen could barely contain his excitement. He shifted his weight from foot to foot, unable to believe his luck at having come through the crash that had so grievously wounded his captain, and then being selected to join this august assembly. Another four captains made up the rest of the gathering: Xiandor, Tyrion, Anteus and Hellespon. Julius knew Xiandor reasonably well, but knew the others only by reputation.

Lord Commander Vespasian talked quietly to the primarch, who stood resplendent in his full battle plate, the golden winged gorget sweeping up over his shoulder to the level of his high, shishak helmet, the lamellar aventail sweeping down across the shoulders of his armour in a glittering cascade.

The golden sword *Fireblade* was belted at the primarch's waist, and Julius was unaccountably glad to see it at Fulgrim's hip instead of the silver-handled blade he had taken from the Laer temple.

Behind them, the vicious, beaked prow of the *Firebird* watched over proceedings, the primarch's assault vessel sporting a fresh coat of paint after her fiery entry into the atmosphere of Laeran.

Vespasian nodded at whatever Fulgrim said and turned to march back towards the company captains, his face set in an expression of quiet amusement. Vespasian was everything Julius could ever desire to be as a warrior, controlled, graceful and utterly deadly. His golden hair was short and tightly curled, and his features were the very image of everything an Astartes ought to be, regal, angelic and stern. Julius had fought alongside Vespasian on countless battlefields, and the warriors he commanded would boast that his prowess was the equal of the primarch's. Though all knew that such a boast was made in jest, it served to push his warriors to greater heights of valour and strength to emulate the lord commander.

Vespasian was also immensely likeable, for his incredible abilities as a warrior and commander were tempered by a rare humility that made others warm to him immediately. In the manner of the Emperor's Children, warriors who followed Vespasian would take their lead from him in all things, his example serving as a model of how they might best achieve perfection through purity of purpose.

Vespasian moved down the line of captains, ensuring that everything was in order and that his captains would do the Legion honour. He stopped before Gaius Caphen and smiled.

'I bet you can't believe your luck, Gaius,' said Vespasian.

'No, sir,' replied Caphen.

'You won't let me down will you?'

'No, sir!' repeated Caphen, and Vespasian slapped a gauntlet on his shoulder guard. 'Good man. I've got my eye on you, Gaius. I expect you to achieve great things in the coming campaign.'

Caphen beamed with pride as the lord commander moved to stand between Julius and Marius. He nodded curtly to the captain of the Third, and leaned over to whisper to Julius as the red lights of the integrity field began to flash.

'Are you ready for this?' asked the lord commander.

'I am,' replied Julius.

Vespasian nodded and said, 'Good man. At least one of us is.'

'Are you trying to tell me you are not?' asked Julius with a smile.

'No,' grinned Vespasian, 'but it's not every day we get to stand in the presence of two such beings. I have a hard enough time being around Lord Fulgrim without looking like a slack jawed mortal, but put two of them in a room...'

Julius nodded in understanding. The sheer magnetism of the primarchs was something that took a great deal of getting used to, the force of their personalities and sheer physical charisma leaving men who had fought the darkest horrors of the galaxy trembling with paralysing fear. Julius well remembered his first meeting with Fulgrim, an embarrassing encounter where he found he couldn't even remember his own name when it was asked of him.

Fulgrim's presence humbled a man with its flaw-lessness and exposed his every imperfection, but as Fulgrim had said to him after that first meeting, 'This is the very perfection of man, to find out his own imperfections and eliminate them.'

'You have met the Primarch of the Iron Hands?' asked Julius.

'I have, yes,' said Vespasian. 'He reminds me of the Warmaster in many ways.'

'How so?'

'You have not met the Warmaster have you?'

'No,' said Julius, 'though I saw him when the Legion marched at Ullanor.'

'Then you'll understand when you do, lad,' said Vespasian. 'Both of them come from worlds that hammer the soul with fire. Their hearts are forged of flint and steel, and the blood of Medusa surges in the Gorgon's veins, molten, unpredictable and violent.'

'Why do you call Ferrus Manus the Gorgon?'

Vespasian chuckled as the immense form of a heav-ily modified Stormbird eased through the integrity field, its midnight-black hull glimmering with wisps of condensation. The engines growled as the craft turned, its increased bulk formed by racks of missiles and extra stowage compartments fitted at its rear.

'Some say it's a reference to an ancient legend of the Olympian Hegemony,' said Vespasian. 'The Gorgon was a beast of such incredible ugliness that its very gaze could turn a man to stone.'

Julius was outraged at the disrespect in such a term and said, 'And people are allowed to insult the pri-march in this way?'

'Don't fret, lad,' said Vespasian. 'I believe Ferrus Manus quite enjoys the name, but in any case, that's not where the name comes from.'

'So where does it come from?'

'It's an old nickname our primarch gave him many years ago,' said Vespasian. 'Unlike Fulgrim, Ferrus Manus has little time for art, music or any of the cultural pastimes our primarch enjoys. It's said that after the two of them met at Mount Narodnya, they returned to the Imperial Palace where Sanguinius had arrived bearing gifts for the Emperor, exquisite statues from the glowing rock of Baal, priceless gemstones and wondrous artefacts of aragonite, opal and tourmaline. The lord of the Blood Angels had brought enough to fill a dozen wings of the palace with the greatest wonders imaginable.'

Julius willed Vespasian to reach the conclusion of his tale as the Iron Hands Stormbird finally touched down on the deck with a heavy clang of landing skids.

'Of course, Fulgrim was enthralled, finding that another of his brothers shared his love of such incredible beauty, but Ferrus Manus was unimpressed and said that such things were a waste of their time when there was a galaxy to win back. I'm told that Fulgrim laughed and declared him a terrible gorgon, saying that if they did not value beauty, then they would never appreciate the stars they were to win back for their father.'

Julius smiled at Vespasian's tale, wondering how much of it was true and how much was apocryphal. It certainly suited what he had heard of the Primarch of the Iron Hands. All thoughts of gorgons and tales were dispelled when the frontal assault ramp of the Stormbird lowered, and the Primarch of the Iron Hands emerged, followed by a craggy featured warrior and a quartet of Terminators, their armour the colour of unpainted iron.

His first impression of Ferrus Manus was of sheer bulk. The Primarch of the Iron Hands was a brutally rugged giant, his width and height quite unimaginable next to Fulgrim's slender frame. His armour shone like the darkest onyx, the gauntlet upon his shoulder fashioned from beaten iron, and a cloak of glittering mail billowed behind him as he marched. A monstrous hammer was slung across his back, and Julius knew that this was the dreaded *Forgebreaker*, the weapon Fulgrim had forged for his brother.

Ferrus Manus wore no helmet and his battered face was like a slab of granite, scarred from the ravages of two centuries of war among the stars. As he caught sight of his brother primarch, his stern face broke apart in a warm grin of welcome, the sudden change almost unbelievable in the completeness of its reversal.

Julius risked a glance at Fulgrim, seeing that grin mirrored in his own primarch's face, and before he knew it, he too was smiling like a simpleton.

To see such honest brotherhood between these two incredible, god-like warriors made his heart sing. The Primarch of the Iron Hands extended his arms, and Julius found his gaze drawn to the shimmering hands that shone like rippling chrome under the harsh lights of the embarkation deck.

Fulgrim went to meet his brother, and the two warriors embraced like long lost friends suddenly and unexpectedly reunited. Both laughed in pleasure at the meeting, and Ferrus Manus slapped his hands hard on Fulgrim's back.

'It's good to see you, my brother!' roared Ferrus Manus. 'Throne, I've missed you!'

'And you are a sight for sore eyes, Gorgon!' returned Fulgrim.

Ferrus Manus stepped back from Fulgrim, still holding him by the shoulders, and looked over at those who had come to greet him. He released his grip on Fulgrim's shoulders, and together they marched over towards the captains of the Emperor's Children. Julius caught his breath at the nearness of Ferrus Manus, the primarch towering above him like a giant of legend.

'You wear the colours of the first captain,' said Ferrus Manus. 'What is your name?'

Julius was horribly reminded of the first time he had met Fulgrim face to face, fearing a repetition of that humiliating experience, but as he caught Fulgrim's amused expression, he forced some steel into his voice. 'I am Julius Kaesoron, Captain of the First, my lord.'

'Well met, captain,' said Ferrus Manus, taking his hand and pumping it enthusiastically while waving forward the craggy-faced warrior who had accompanied him from the Stormbird with his free hand. 'I have heard great things of you.'

'Thank you,' managed Julius, before remembering to add, 'my lord.'

Ferrus Manus laughed and said, 'This is Gabriel Santar, captain of my veterans and the man who has the misfortune to serve as my equerry. I think you and he should get to know one another. If you don't know a man, how can you trust your life to him, eh?'

'Well, quite,' said Julius, unused to such informality from his superiors.

'He's my very best, Julius, and I expect you will learn a lot from him.'

Julius bristled at the implied insult and said, 'As I am sure he will from me.'

'Of that I have no doubt,' said Ferrus Manus, and Julius felt suddenly foolish as he saw the glint of mischief in his strange silver eyes. His gaze slid from the primarch to Santar, seeing an unspoken respect there as they sized one another up in the manner of warriors who wonder which of them is the greater.

'Good to see you're still alive, Vespasian!' said Ferrus Manus as he moved on from Julius to take the lord commander in a crushing bear hug. 'And the *Firebird*! It has been too long since I saw the phoenix fly!'

'You shall see her fly ere long, my brother,' promised Fulgrim.

EIGHT

The Most Important Question/Warmaster/Progress

THE TWO PRIMARCHS wasted no time in convening the senior officers of the Legions in the Heliopolis to discuss strategy for the destruction of the Diasporex. The marble benches nearest the dark floor were filled with the purple and gold of the Emperor's Children, and the black and white of the Iron Hands. So far the council of war was not going well, and Julius could see the choler rising in Ferrus Manus as Fulgrim dismissed his latest idea as unworkable.

'Then what do you propose, brother? For I have no more stratagems to suggest,' said the Primarch of the Iron Hands. 'As soon as we threaten them, they flee.'

Fulgrim turned to face Ferrus Manus and said, 'Do not mistake what I say as criticism, brother. I am merely stating what I see as fundamental to the reason why you have not yet managed to bring the Diasporex to battle.'

'Which is?'

'That you are being too direct.'

'Too direct?' asked Ferrus Manus, but Fulgrim held
up a quieting hand to forestall any further outbursts.

'I know you, brother, and I know the way your
Legion fights, but sometimes chasing the comet's tail is
not the best way to catch it.'

'You would have us skulk around this sector like
thieves while we wait for them to come to us? The Iron
Hands do not make war that way.'

Fulgrim shook his head. 'Do not think for a moment
that I am unaware of the simple joy to be had in going
up the centre, but we must be prepared to accept that
other ways may advance our cause more perfectly.'

Fulgrim walked the circumference of the Heliopolis
as he spoke, directing his words to his fellow primarch
and the warriors who surrounded him. Reflected light
from the ceiling lit his face from below and his eyes, a
dark mirror of Ferrus Manus's silver ones, were alight
with passion as he spoke.

'You have become fixated on destroying the Diasporex, Ferrus, which is only right and proper given
their associations with vile aliens, but you have not
asked yourself the most important question regarding
this enemy.'

Ferrus Manus crossed his arms and said, 'And what
question would that be?'

Fulgrim smiled. 'Why are they here?'

'You wish to get into a philosophical debate?'
snapped Ferrus Manus. 'Then speak to the iterators,
I'm sure they can furnish you with a better, less direct,
answer than I.'

Fulgrim turned to address the warriors of the two
Legions and said, 'Ask yourselves this then. Knowing
that a powerful fleet of warships is hunting you and
seeks your destruction, why would you not simply

leave? Why would you not move on to somewhere safer?'

'I do not know, brother,' said Ferrus Manus. 'Why?'

Julius felt his primarch's gaze upon him and the weight of expectation crushed him to his seat. If the intellect of a primarch could not answer this question, what chance did he have?

He looked into Fulgrim's eyes, seeing his lord's faith, and the answer was suddenly clear.

Julius stood and said, 'Because they can't. They're trapped in this system.'

'Trapped?' asked Gabriel Santar from across the chamber. 'Trapped how?'

'I don't know,' said Julius. 'Perhaps they have no Navigator.'

'No,' said Fulgrim, 'that's not it. If they were without a Navigator then the 52nd Expedition would have caught them long ago. It's something else. What?'

Julius watched as the officers of both Legions contemplated the question, sure that his primarch already knew the answer.

Even as the answer came to him, Gabriel Santar stood and said, 'Fuel. They need fuel for their fleet.'

Though Julius knew it was foolish, he felt a stab of jealousy at being denied the chance to answer his primarch and glared angrily at the weathered face of Iron Hand's first captain.

'Exactly!' said Fulgrim. 'Fuel. A fleet the size of the Diasporex must consume a phenomenal amount of energy every day, and to make a jump of any distance they will need a great deal of it. The fleet masters of this sector's compliant worlds do not report any significant losses of tankers or convoys, so we must assume the Diasporex are getting their fuel from another source.'

'The Carollis Star,' said Julius. 'They must have solar collectors hidden somewhere in the sun's corona. They're waiting to gather enough fuel before moving on.'

Fulgrim turned back to the centre of the chamber and said, 'That is how we will bring the Diasporex to battle, by discovering these collectors and threatening them. We will draw our enemies to a battle of our choosing and then we will destroy them.'

LATER, AFTER THE war council had disbanded, Fulgrim and Ferrus Manus retired to the lord of the Emperor's Children's private staterooms aboard the *Pride of the Emperor*. Fulgrim's chambers were the envy of Terra's master of antiquities; every wall hung with elegantly framed pictures of vibrant alien landscapes or extra-ordinary picts of the Astartes and mortals of the Crusade.

Antechambers filled with marble busts and the spoils of war radiated from the central stateroom, and everywhere the eye fell, it alighted on a work of unimaginable artistic beauty. Only the far end of the room was bare of ornamentation, the space filled with part carved blocks of marble, and easels of unfinished artwork.

Fulgrim reclined on a chaise longue, stripped out of his armour and dressed in a simple toga of cream and purple. He drank wine from a crystal goblet and rested his hand on a table upon which lay the silver hilted sword he had taken from the Laer temple. The sword was a truly magnificent weapon, hardly the equal of *Fireblade*, but exquisite nonetheless. Its balance was flawless, as though it had been designed for his hand alone, and its keen edge had the power to cut through Astartes plate with ease.

The purple gem at the pommel was of crude workmanship, but had a certain primitive charm to it that was quite at odds with the quality of the blade and hilt. Perhaps he would replace the gem with something more appropriate.

Even as the thought arose he dismissed it, feeling suddenly as though such an exchange would be the basest act of vandalism. With a shake of his head, Fulgrim put the sword from his mind and ran a hand through his unbound white hair. Ferrus Manus paced the room like a caged lion, and though scout ships were even now hunting the Diasporex fuel collectors, he still chafed at this enforced inaction.

'Oh, sit down, Ferrus,' said Fulgrim. 'You will wear a groove in the marble. Take some wine.'

'Sometimes, Fulgrim, I swear this isn't a ship of war anymore, it's a flying gallery,' said Ferrus Manus, examining the works hung on the walls. 'Although, these picts are good; who took them?'

'An imagist named Euphrati Keeler. I'm told she travels with the 63rd Expedition.'

'She has a fine eye,' noted Ferrus. 'These are good picts.'

'Yes,' said Fulgrim. 'I suspect that her name will be known throughout the expedition fleets soon.'

'Although I'm not sure about these paintings,' said Ferrus, pointing at a series of abstract acrylics of riotous colour and passionate brushstrokes.

'You have no appreciation of the finer things, my brother,' sighed Fulgrim. 'Those are works by Serena d'Angelus. Noble families of Terra would pay a small fortune to own such a piece.'

'Really?' said Ferrus, tilting his head to one side. 'What are they supposed to be?'

'They are...' began Fulgrim, struggling to put into words the sensations and emotions evoked by the colours and shapes within the picture. He looked closely at the picture and smiled.

'They are recreations of reality formed according to the artist's metaphysical value judgments,' he said, the words leaping unbidden to his lips. 'An artist recreates those aspects of reality that represent the fundamental truth of man's nature. To understand that is to understand the truth of the galaxy. Mistress d'Angelus is aboard *The Pride of the Emperor*, I should introduce you to her.'

Ferrus grunted and asked, 'Why do you insist on keeping such things around? They are a distraction from our duty to the Emperor and Horus.'

Fulgrim shook his head. 'These works will be the Emperor's Children's lasting contribution to a compliant galaxy. Yes, there are planets yet to conquer and enemies yet to defeat, but what manner of galaxy will it be if there are none to appreciate what has been won? The Imperium will be a hollow place if it is to be denied art, poetry and music, and those with the wit to appreciate them. Art and beauty are as close to the divine as we find in this godless age. People should, in their daily lives, aspire to create art and beauty. That will be what the Imperium comes to stand for in time, and it will make us immortal.'

'I still think it's a distraction,' said Ferrus Manus.

'Not at all, Ferrus, for the foundations of the Imperium are art and science. Remove them or degrade them and the Imperium is no more. It is said that empire follows art and not vice versa as those of a more prosaic nature might suppose, and I would rather go without food or water for weeks than go without art.'

Ferrus looked unconvinced and pointed to the unfinished works that lay at the far end of the state-room. 'So what are these ones then? They're not very good. What do they recreate?'

Fulgrim felt a flush of anger, but suppressed it before it could show.

'I was indulging my creative side, but it is nothing serious,' he said, a traitorous kernel within him seething at his handiwork being dismissed so lightly.

Ferrus Manus shrugged and sat on a tall wooden chair before pouring himself a chalice of wine from a silver amphora.

'Ah, it's good to be back amongst friends,' said Ferrus Manus, raising his chalice.

'That it is,' agreed Fulgrim. 'We see too little of one another now that the Emperor has returned to Terra.'

'And taken the Fists with him,' said Ferrus.

'I had heard,' said Fulgrim. 'Has Dorn done something to offend our father?'

Ferrus Manus shook his head. 'Not that I'm aware of, but who knows. Perhaps Horus was told.'

'You should really try to get into the habit of calling him the Warmaster now.'

'I know, I know,' said Ferrus, 'but I still find it hard to think of Horus that way, you understand?'

'I do, but it is the way of things, brother,' pointed out Fulgrim. 'Horus is Warmaster and we are his generals. Warmaster Horus commands and we obey.'

'You're right of course. He's earned it, I'll give him that,' said Ferrus, raising his chalice. 'No one has a greater tally of victories than the Luna Wolves. Horus deserves our loyalty.'

'Spoken like a true follower,' smiled Fulgrim, an inner voice goading him into baiting his brother primarch.

'What's that supposed to mean?'

'Nothing,' said Fulgrim with a shake of his hand. 'Come on, didn't you hope it would be you? Didn't you wish with all your heart that the Emperor would name you his regent?'

Ferrus shook his head emphatically. 'No.'

'No?'

'I can honestly say that I didn't,' said Ferrus, draining his chalice and pouring another. 'Can you imagine the weight of the responsibility? We've come this far with the Emperor at our head, but I can't even begin to conceive of the ambition that it must have taken to lead a crusade in conquest of the galaxy.'

'So you don't think Horus is up to it?' asked Fulgrim.

'Not at all,' chuckled Ferrus, 'and don't put words in my mouth, brother. I won't be branded a traitor for failing to support Horus. If any of us can be Warmaster, I'd expect it to be Horus.'

'Not everyone thinks so.'

'You've been talking to Perturabo and Angron haven't you?'

'Amongst others,' admitted Fulgrim. 'They communicated their... disquiet at the Emperor's decision.'

'No matter who was chosen, they would have raged against it,' said Ferrus.

'Probably,' agreed Fulgrim, 'but I am glad it was Horus. He will achieve great things.'

'I'll drink to that,' said Ferrus, draining his chalice.

He is a sycophant and easily swayed... said a voice in his head, and Fulgrim blinked at the force of it.

With the end of the war on Laeran, the steady stream of wounded and dead to the apothecarion had slowed, leaving Fabius more time to devote to his researches. To ensure the secrecy his experiments demanded, he had relocated to a little-used research facility aboard the *Andronius*, a strike cruiser under the authority of Lord Commander Eidolon. Its facilities had been basic at first, but with Eidolon's blessing, he had gathered a bewildering array of specialist equipment.

Eidolon himself had escorted him to the facility, marching along the length of the Gallery of Swords to the forward starboard apothecarion, its brushed steel walls gleaming and sterile. Without pause, Eidolon had led him through the circular hub of the main laboratory and along a tiled corridor to a gilded vestibule where two corridors branched left and right. The wall before them was blank, though there were indications that there was soon to be something placed upon it, a mosaic or bas-relief.

'Why are we here?' Fabius had asked.

'You will see,' said Eidolon, reaching out to press a portion of the wall, whereupon it had arced upwards to reveal a glowing passageway and a spiral staircase. They had descended into a research facility: surgical tables covered with white sheets and incubation tanks lying dormant and empty.

'This is where you will work,' declared Eidolon. 'The primarch has placed a heavy burden on you, Apothecary, and you will not fail.'

'I will not,' agreed Fabius. 'But tell me, lord commander, why do you take such a personal interest in my labours?'

Eidolon's eyes had narrowed and he had fixed Fabius with a baleful glare. 'I am to take the *Proudheart* to the Satyr Lanxus Belt on a "peacekeeping" mission.'

'An inglorious, but necessary duty to ensure that the Imperial governors are maintaining the lawful rule of the Emperor,' said Fabius, though he had known full well that Eidolon would not see it that way.

'It is shameful!' snapped Eidolon. 'It is a waste of my skill and courage that I should be sent away from the fleet like this.'

'Perhaps, but what is it you require of me?' asked Fabius. 'You did not escort me here personally without reason.'

'Correct, Apothecary,' said Eidolon, placing his hand on Fabius's shoulder guard and leading him deeper into the secret laboratory. 'Fulgrim has told me the scale of what you are to attempt, and though I do not approve of your methods, I will obey my primarch in all things.'

'Even in undertaking peacekeeping missions?' asked Fabius.

'Even so,' agreed Eidolon, 'but I shall not be put in a position where I shall be made to suffer such indignities again. The work you are doing will enhance the physiology of the Astartes will it not?'

'I believe so. I have only just begun to unlock the mystery of the gene-seed, but when I do… I will know all its secrets.'

'Then upon my return to the fleet, you will begin with me,' said Eidolon. 'I shall become your greatest success, faster, stronger and more deadly than ever before, and I shall become the indispensable right hand of our primarch. Begin your work here, Apothecary and I shall see to it that you have everything you need brought to you.'

Fabius smiled at the memory, knowing that Eidolon would be pleased with his results when he rejoined the fleet once again.

He leaned over the corpse of an Astartes warrior, his surgical robes stained with the cadaver's blood and his portable chirurgeon kit fitted to a servo harness at his waist. Clicking steel arms like metal spider legs reached over his shoulders, each bearing syringes, scalpels and bone saws that assisted with the dissection and organ removal. The stench of blood and cauterised flesh filled his nostrils, but such things did not repulse Fabius, for they spoke of thrilling discoveries and journeys into the unknown reaches of forbidden knowledge.

The cold lights of the apothecarion bleached the corpse's skin and reflected from the incubation tanks he had set up to mature the altered gene-seed through chemical stimulation, genetic manipulation and controlled irradiation.

The warrior on the slab had been on the brink of death when he had been brought to the apothecarion, but he had died in bliss with his cerebral cortex exposed as Fabius had taken advantage of his imminent demise to work within its pulpy, grey mass in order to better understand the workings of a living Astartes brain. Inadvertently, Fabius had uncovered the means of linking the nervous system with the pleasure centres of the brain, thus rendering each, painful incision a joyous sensation of unalloyed delight.

Quite what this discovery might mean to his researches, he wasn't sure, but it was yet another fascinating nugget of information to store away for future experiments.

Thus far, Fabius had met with more failures than successes, though the balance was gradually shifting towards the positive now that the war on Laeran had provided him with a ready source of gene-seed upon which to experiment. The furnaces of the apothecarion had burned day and night disposing of the waste of his failed experiments, but these blows to progress were necessary for his and the Emperor's Children's pursuit of perfection.

He knew there were those in the Legion who would recoil from the work he was doing, but they were without vision and could not see the great things he would achieve, the necessary evils that must be endured to reach perfection.

By taking the next step in the Astartes evolutionary journey, Fulgrim's Legion would become the greatest warriors of the Emperor's armies, and the name of Fabius would be celebrated the length and breadth of the Imperium as the chief architect of this elevation.

Even now the apothecarion's incubation tanks held the nascent fruits of his experiments, tiny, budding organs floating in a nutrient rich suspension. The tissue samples were from Astartes who had fallen on Laeran, and Fabius predicted that his enhancements should double their efficiency. Already he was growing a superior Ossmodula that would increase the strength of the epiphiseal fusion and ossification of a warrior's skeleton, resulting in bones that were virtually unbreakable. Next to the enhanced Ossmodula was a test organ that combined elements of Laer hormones, which if successful, would alter the fundamental nature of the Betcher's gland, allowing an Astartes to replicate the sonic shriek of the Laer with devastating results.

Work on refining other organs was only just beginning, but Fabius had high hopes for his work on enhancing the Biscopea to stimulate muscle growth beyond the norms and produce warriors as strong as Dreadnoughts who could punch through the side of a tank with their bare fists. The multi-spectral eyes of the Laer had provided a great deal of information he hoped to incorporate into the experiments he had begun on the Occulobe. Scores of eyeballs were pinned like butterflies in the sterile cabinets beside him, chemical stimulants working to enhance the capabilities of the optic nerves.

With some modification, Fabius believed he could create visual organs that would function at peak efficiency in total darkness, bright light or stroboscopic conditions, rendering an Astartes effectively immune to being blinded or disorientated.

His first success sat behind him on steel shelves in thousands of vials of blue liquid, a drug he had synthesised from a genetic splice between a gland taken from the Laer that replicated the functions of the thyroid gland and the Biscopea.

In the test subjects – those warriors wounded too badly to survive – Fabius had found that their metabolism and strength had increased markedly before their deaths. Refinement of the drug had kept the increases from overloading the recipient's heart, and now it was ready for distribution to the Legion en masse.

Fulgrim had authorised the use of the drug and within days it would be coursing through the blood of every warrior who chose to take it.

Fabius straightened from the dead body before him and smiled at the thought of the wonders he could create now that he had a free hand in turning his genius to improving the physical stature of the Emperor's Children.

'Yes,' he hissed, his dark eyes alight with the prospect of unlocking the secrets of the Emperor's work. 'I *will* know your secrets.'

THE COLOURS ON the palette swirled before Serena's eyes, and the blandness of them infuriated her beyond measure. She had spent the best part of the morning attempting to create the red of the sunset she had seen on Laeran, but the emptied pots of paint and broken brushes scattered around her bore mute testament to her failure. The canvas before her was a mess of frantic pencil strokes, the outline of a painting that she was sure would be her greatest work… if only she could get this red to mix properly!

'Damn you!' she shouted and hurled the palette away with such force that it smashed to splinters on the wall.

Her breath came in short, painful gasps as the frustration built within her. Serena put her head in her hands and tears came on the heels of hard, wracking sobs that hurt her chest.

The anger at her failure surged through her body, and she snatched up the broken stem of a paintbrush and pressed the jagged edge of wood into the soft skin of her upper arm. The pain was intense, but at least she could feel it. The skin broke and blood welled around the splintered wood, bringing her a measure of relief. Only the pain made anything real, and Serena ground the wood deeper into her flesh, watching as the blood ran down her arm over the pale ridges of her older scars.

Long, dark hair hung in lank ribbons to Serena's waist, stained with spots of colour, and her skin had the unhealthy pallor of one who had not slept in days. Her eyes were bloodshot and grainy, her fingernails cracked and encrusted with paint.

Her studio had been turned upside down since she had returned from the surface of Laeran. It was not vandalism that had brought about such a transformation, but a frenzied passion to create that had reduced her once immaculate studio to something that resembled the aftermath of a battle.

The desire to paint had been like an elemental force within her that could not be denied. It had been thrilling and a little bit frightening… the burning need to create art of passion and sensuality. Serena had filled three canvases with colour and light, painting like a woman possessed before exhaustion had claimed her and she had fallen asleep in the ruin of her studio.

When she had awoken she had looked at what she had painted with a critical eye, seeing the crudity of the work, and the primitive colours that had none of the life and urgency she remembered from the temple. Serena had dug through the disarray of her studio for the picts she had taken of the temple and the mighty coral city, its gloriously masculine towers and wondrously hued skies and ocean.

For days she had tried to rekindle the rapturous sensations that had filled her on Laeran, but no matter what proportions she mixed her paints in, she could not achieve the tonal qualities she sought.

Serena cast her mind back to Laeran, remembering the sorrow she had felt when Ostian had been denied a place in the craft travelling to the planet's surface. Guiltily, that sorrow had vanished when they had broken the cloud cover, and she had seen the vast blue expanse of the oceans of Laeran spread before her.

She had never seen such a glorious, vivid blue and had snapped a dozen picts before they had even begun their descent towards the Laer atoll. Circling the floating city had stirred feelings within her that she hadn't known existed, and Serena had ached to set foot on its alien structure more than anything.

Upon landing they had been escorted through the broken ruins of the city, every one of the remembrancers staring open mouthed at the wonderful otherness of it all. Captain Julius had explained that the tall conch towers had screamed all through the war, though all but a handful were now silenced, brought down by explosives to render them mute. The few ululating screams Serena could hear sounded impossibly distant, achingly lonely and infinitely sad.

Serena had taken pict after pict as they were led through the wreckage of battle, and even the torn corpses of the Laer could not detract from the thrill of walking on a city that floated above the ocean. The sights and colours were so vibrant that she couldn't take it all in, her senses stimulated to the point of overload.

Then she had seen the temple.

All thoughts other than achieving entry to its mysterious interior were banished from her mind as Captain Julius and the iterators had led the way towards the towering structure. A hungry, intense determination had seized the remembrancers, and they made their way towards the temple with unseemly haste.

Picking their way through the rubble, she had smelled the strange, smoky aroma of what she had at first thought to be incense, burnt by the Army units to mask the stench of blood and death. Then she saw the ghostly wisps of pink mist seeping from the porous walls of the temple and realised that it was something of alien origin. A delicious, momentary panic filled her until she smelled more of the strange musk and decided that it was quite pleasant.

Arc lights had been set up inside the cave-like entrance of the temple, and the brilliant glow illuminated wondrous colours and murals of such lifelike imagery that they took her breath away. Gasps of astonishment came from all around her as artists attempted to capture the scale of the murals, and imagists took panoramic picts of the scene.

From somewhere inside, Serena could hear music, wild, passionate music that lodged like a splinter in her heart. She turned from the murals, following the blue hair of Bequa as the siren song of the music grew louder and drew them both onwards.

From nowhere, her anger at Bequa suddenly pounded hot in her veins, and she felt her lip curl back in a snarl. Serena set off after Bequa, the music of the temple swelling within her the deeper she went. Though she was conscious of people around her, Serena paid them no mind, her thoughts filled with the sensations flooding her system. Music, light and colour were all around her, and she put a hand out to steady herself as the sheer excessiveness of it all threatened to overwhelm her.

Serena pushed herself onwards, rounded a corner into the temple's interior… and dropped to her knees as she saw terrifying beauty and awesome energy in the lights and noise of the temple.

Bequa Kynska stood in the middle of the great space, her arms raised in a 'V' as she held up the wands of a vox-thief and the music poured over her.

Serena thought she'd never seen anything so beautiful in all her life.

Her eyes burned with colour and it had been all she could do not to weep at its perfection.

Now, back in her studio, she had spent all her energies trying to recapture that brief, shining moment of perfect colour without success. Straightening her back and wiping her tears on her sleeve, she picked up another palette from the detritus strewn around her and began mixing her paints to try, once again, to capture it.

She mixed cadmium red with quinacridone crimson, leavening the red with some perylene maroon, but already she could see that the colours weren't quite right, the tone off by a fraction.

Even as her anger built again, a droplet of blood fell from her arm into the paint as she was mixing it, and suddenly there it was. The colour was perfect and she smiled, understanding what she had to do.

Serena picked up the small knife she used for cutting the nibs of her quills and drew the blade across her skin, cutting into the soft flesh above her elbow.

Droplets of blood fell from the cut and she held the palette beneath it, smiling as she saw the colours forming.

Now she could begin painting.

SOLOMON DUCKED BENEATH the swinging cut of a sword, bringing his own weapon up in time to block the reverse cut to his chest. The blow rang up the length of his arm, and he gritted his teeth as his freshly healed bones protested at the rigours he was putting them through. He backed away from Marius as the captain of the Third came at him again with his sword aimed at his heart.

'You are slow, Solomon,' said Marius.

Solomon swept his sword down, pushing aside the clumsy thrust, and spun to deliver the deathblow to his opponent, but pulled up short as Marius's blade clove towards him. He twisted out of the way, his body feeling as if it was coming apart at the seams.

'Fast enough to see you coming, old man,' laughed Solomon, though he knew it was only a matter of time before Marius wore him down.

'You're lying,' noted Marius, throwing his sword down to the mat. He backed towards the racks of

FULGRIM   169

weapons that lined the walls of the training hall and
selected a pair of Sun and Moon spear blades. The
double-headed daggers were impractical in a real
fight, but made for a deadly training weapon.
Solomon threw aside his own sword and picked up a
pair of Wind and Fire wheels.

Like his opponent's weapons, these too were
largely decorative, the circular blade held by a tex-
tured grip and embellished with curved punch spikes
around its circumference, but Solomon enjoyed
training with weapons that were beyond his normal
range. He faced Marius and extended his left arm,
while keeping his right hooked at his side.

'Maybe I am, maybe I'm not,' grinned Solomon.
'There's only one way to find out.'

Marius nodded and stormed towards him, the twin
bladed daggers spinning before him in a web of glittering steel. Solomon blocked first one strike then
another, each ringing clang forcing him back towards
the wall.

He swayed aside from a high, slashing cut and sent
a low, sweeping blow towards Marius's legs. Marius
stabbed one of his daggers down, the tip lancing
through the centre of the circular weapon and pin-
ning it to the floor. Solomon jumped back, forced to
leave it behind as the second blade was thrust
towards him.

'Have you heard the news?' gasped Solomon, desperate to distract Marius and buy himself some
space.

'What news?' asked Marius.

'That we're to be issued some new chemical stimulant for testing,' said Solomon.

'I'd heard, yes,' nodded Marius. 'The primarch
believes it will make us stronger and faster than ever.'

Solomon frowned at his friend's tone, the words sounding as though he was speaking them by rote, but didn't really believe them. Solomon paused in his retreat and said, 'Aren't you a little bit concerned at where it came from?'

'It comes from the primarch,' said Marius, putting up his dagger.

'No, I mean the drug. It hasn't come from Terra, I know that much,' said Solomon. 'In fact, I think it was made right here. I heard Apothecary Fabius saying something about it before he transferred to the *Andronius*.'

'What difference does it make where it comes from?' asked Marius. 'The primarch has authorised its use for those that wish it.'

'I'm not sure,' admitted Solomon as Marius began to circle him. 'Perhaps none at all, but I just don't like the idea of some new chemical being pumped into me when I don't know where it came from.'

Marius laughed and said, 'All the genetic enhancements done to your flesh in the laboratory and you choose now to worry about chemicals in your body?'

'It's not the same thing, Marius. We were created in the image of the Emperor as his perfect warriors, so why do we need more?'

Marius shrugged and lunged with his dagger. Solomon swatted it away with his remaining weapon and groaned in pain as he felt something tear inside. The bout was over.

Deciding that his mind would break before his body would heal, he had removed himself from the apothecarion and returned to his company's arming chambers. Gaius Caphen had been pleased to see him, but Solomon could tell that his subordinate

had enjoyed the brief taste of command and knew
that he would need to see about getting him his
own company.

As the days passed with no sign of the Diasporex,
he had trained fiercely to rebuild his strength, and
had taken to visiting Marius Vairosean for gruelling
sparring matches, none of which he had the
strength to win.

'Fulgrim has said we should do so,' said Marius, as
if that were an end to the matter.

'He has, but I still don't like it,' gasped Solomon.
'I just can't see why it's needed.'

'What you see or don't see is irrelevant,' said Marius. 'The word has been given, and we are duty
bound to obey. Our ideal of perfection and purity
comes from Fulgrim, and it passes down through
the lord commanders to us, the company captains,
whereupon it is beholden to us to enact the primarch's will amongst our warriors.'

'I know all that, but this just feels wrong,' said
Solomon, breathing heavily and tossing his dagger
to the floor. 'Enough, I'm done. You win.'

Marius nodded and said, 'You are getting stronger
every day, Solomon.'

'Not strong enough,' said Solomon, slumping to
his haunches on the training mat.

'No, not yet, but your strength will return soon
enough and then perhaps you'll give me a decent
fight,' replied Marius, sitting down next to him.

'Don't you worry about that,' promised Solomon.
'I'll have you beaten soon enough.'

'You won't,' replied Marius without irony. 'I've
been training the Third harder than ever before and
we're at our very best. I'm at my very best, and with
this new chemical I'll be even faster and stronger.'

Solomon looked into his friend's eyes and saw the desperate yearning to atone for his failure on the atoll. He reached out and placed his hand on Marius's arm.

'Listen, I know you know this already, but I'm going to say it anyway,' he said.

'No,' said Marius, shaking his head, 'don't. The Third were shamed and you will only make it worse if you try and excuse our failure.'

'It wasn't a failure,' said Solomon.

'Yes, it was,' nodded Marius. 'If you can't see that, then perhaps you were lucky to have been shot down before you got there.'

Solomon felt his choler rise and said, 'Lucky? I almost died.'

'It would be easier if I had died,' whispered Marius.

'You don't mean that.'

'Perhaps not, but the fact remains that the Third failed in its appointed task, and until we atone for that, I will ensure that my company follows the primarch's orders without question.'

'No matter what they are?' asked Solomon.

'Exactly,' said Marius. 'No matter what they are.'

NINE

Discovered/Blayke/An Honest Counsellor

THE FERRUM SLIPPED through the bright corona of the
Carollis Star, her shields keeping the worst of the electromagnetic hash from scrambling her systems as the
crew hunted for the solar collectors of the Diasporex.
Her hull had been patched and the ruptured elements
of her superstructure repaired, though she would still
need some time in docks to undo all the damage that
had been inflicted upon her.

Captain Balhaan stood at his command lectern, the
frustrating routine of disappointment his menial
command consisted of having long grown stale. Iron
Father Diederik stood at surveyor control next to
Axarden, and though Balhaan knew that he deserved
no less for his failure to protect his ship, the fact that
he had to share command of the *Ferrum* with another
still rankled.

Diederik oversaw every command decision and had
glared pointedly at every order he issued, but Balhaan

knew that his presence was a necessary reminder of
the dangers of complacency. The Iron Father's body
was largely augmetic, his organic parts having been
replaced long ago to bring him closer to mechanised
perfection and the eventual interment in the sarcophagus of an ancient Dreadnought.

'Is your surveyor sweep finished yet?' asked
Balhaan.

'Just about, sir,' replied Axarden.

'How is it looking?'

'Not hopeful, sir. There is so much interference that
we could be right on top of them and not know it,'
explained Axarden, as much for the Iron Father's ben-
efit as his captain's.

'Very good, Axarden. Let me know if there is any
change,' ordered Balhaan.

He leant on the lectern, trying to remember periods
of history where the great men of the age had been
forced to endure such tedious duties. None sprang to
mind, though he knew that history tended to leave
out the parts between the heroics, and concentrated
on the battles and drama of the passage of time. He
wondered what the remembrancers of the 52nd Expedition would write of this portion of the Great
Crusade, knowing that in all likelihood, it would not
even be recorded. After all, where was the glory in
scores of ships scouring the outer edges of a sun for
solar collectors?

He remembered reading a passage in his Herodotus
that spoke of a battle on the coast of an ancient land
known as Artemision in northern Euboea, between
two mighty fleets of ocean-going vessels. The battle
was said to have lasted three days, though Balhaan
could not conceive of such a thing and wondered how
much of that battle had actually been spent fighting.

Very little, he suspected. In Balhaan's experience, battles at sea tended to be short, bloody affairs where one war galley would quickly gain the advantage and ram the other, sending its crew to an icy death at the bottom of the ocean.

Even as he formed such gloomy thoughts, Axarden said, 'Captain, I think we might have something!'

He looked up from his melancholy reverie and all thoughts of the long, empty stretches of history were banished at the excited tone he heard in his surveyor officer's voice. His fingers swept across the command console, and the viewing bay lit up with the brightness of the star beyond.

Immediately, he saw what Axarden had seen, the shimmering gleam of reflected starlight winking on the giant, rippling sails of a solar collector.

'All stop,' ordered Balhaan. 'No sense in letting them know we are here.'

'We should attack,' said Diederik, and Balhaan forced himself to mask his annoyance at the Iron Father's impetuous interruption. Hadn't the *Ferrum* fallen foul of just similar thinking?

'No,' said Balhaan, 'not until we have alerted the expedition fleets.'

'How many collectors are there?' asked Diederik, turning to Axarden.

The surveyor officer leaned in close to his plotter, and Balhaan waited anxious seconds as Axarden sought to answer the Iron Father.

'At least ten, but there are probably more I can't yet pinpoint,' said Axarden. 'The star's radioactive output appears to be highly concentrated here.'

Balhaan moved from behind his lectern, descended the steps that led to surveyor control and said, 'It does not matter how many there are, Iron Father. We cannot attack.'

'And why not, captain?' sneered Diederik. 'We have discovered the source of the enemy's fuel as Lord Manus ordered.'

'I am aware of our orders, but without the warships of the fleets to back us up, the Diasporex will vanish once more.'

Diederik appeared to consider this and said, 'Then what do you suggest, captain?'

Grateful that the Iron Father had deferred to his authority, Balhaan said, 'We wait. We send word back to the fleets and gather as much information as we can without giving away our position.'

'And then?' asked Diederik, clearly uncomfortable with the idea of waiting.

'Then we destroy them,' said Balhaan, 'and regain our honour.'

THE ARCHIVE CHAMBERS of the *Pride of the Emperor* were spread over three long decks, the gilded shelves stacked high with texts from Old Earth. The manuscripts of this magnificent collection had been painstakingly collated by the 28th Expedition's archivist, a meticulous man by the name of Evander Tobias. Over many years of study, Julius had come to know Tobias very well, and now made his way towards the old man's sanctum in the vaulted nave of the upper archive decks.

The marble columned stacks stretched out before him, a reverential hush filling the wide aisles with a solemnity befitting such a vast repository of knowledge. Tall pillars of green marble marched into the distance, and the shelves of dark wood bowed under the weight of scrolls, books and data crystals that filled the spaces between them.

Julius made his way along the polished marble floor, floating glow-globes throwing his shadow out before him. He had stripped out of his armour, and wore combat fatigues, over which he had thrown a mail shirt emblazoned with the eagle of the Emperor's Children.

He saw the beige robes of remembrancers down many of the sub-aisles, and barefoot servitors carrying oversized panniers of books passed him without so much as a glance.

In one of the open spaces of the archive chambers, he saw the distinctive blue hair of Bequa Kynska, and briefly considered pausing to speak with her. She sat at a wide desk strewn with music paper, her unbound hair wild and unkempt, and the headphones of a portable vox-thief clamped over her ears. Even from a distance, Julius could make out the strange music that had filled the Laer temple, the blaring sound rendered tinny and distant, though he knew it must surely be deafening in Bequa Kynska's ears. Her hands alternated between scrawling frantically across the paper and flitting like birds as she appeared to conduct some invisible orchestra. She smiled as she worked, but there was something manic to her movements, as though the music within her might consume her were it not poured onto the page.

So that is how genius works, thought Julius, deciding not to interrupt Mistress Kynska, and pressing onwards.

It had been some time since he had come to the archive chambers, his duties and the cleansing of Laeran leaving him little time to indulge in reading, and he felt the absence keenly. He had come to reacquaint himself with this place, though he had left instructions with Lycaon to contact him should anything arise that required his attention.

Numerous scribes and notaries passed him, each bowing deferentially to him as they went. He recognised some from his time spent here, most he did not, but just being back in the archive chambers gave him an enormous sense of wellbeing.

He smiled as he saw the familiar form of Evander Tobias ahead of him, the venerable archivist haranguing a sheepish group of remembrancers for some infraction of his strict rules.

The old man paused in his diatribe and looked up to see Julius approaching. He smiled warmly, and dismissed the wayward remembrancers with an imperious sweep of his hand. Dressed in a sober, dark robe of heavy cloth, Evander Tobias exuded an air of knowledge and respect that even the Astartes recognised. His bearing was regal, and Julius held a great affection for the venerable scholar.

Evander Tobias had once been the greatest public speaker of Terra and had trained the first Imperial iterators. His role as the Primary Iterator of the Warmaster's fleet had been assured, but the tragic onset of laryngeal cancer had paralysed his vocal chords and led to his retirement from the School of Iterators. In his place, Evander had recommended that his brightest and most able pupil, Kyril Sindermann, be sent to the Warmaster's 63rd Expedition.

It had been said that the Emperor himself had come to Evander Tobias's sickbed and instructed his finest chirurgeons and cyberneticists to attend him, though the truth of this was known only to a few. Though capricious fate had taken his natural talents for oratory and enunciation from him, his throat and vocal chords had been reconstructed, and now Evander spoke with a soft, mechanical burr that had fooled many unsuspecting remembrancers into thinking of him as a grandfatherly old man without a vicious bite.

'My boy,' said Evander, reaching out to take Julius's hands, 'it has been too long.'

'It has indeed, Evander,' smiled Julius, nodding at the retreating remembrancers. 'Are the children misbehaving again?'

'Them? Pah, foolish youngsters,' said Evander. 'One would think that selection to become a remembrancer implies a certain robustness of character and level of intellect beyond that of a common greenskin. But these fools seem incapable of navigating their way around a perfectly simple system for the retrieval of data. It confounds me, and I fear for the quality of work that will be this expedition's legacy with such simpletons to record the mighty deeds of the Crusade.'

Julius nodded, though having seen Evander's byzantine system of archiving, he could well understand the potential for confusion, having spent many a fruitless hour trying to unearth some nugget of information. Wisely, he decided to keep his own council on the subject, and said, 'With you here to collate it, my friend, I am sure that our legacy is in safe hands.'

'You are kind to say so, my boy,' said Evander, tiny puffs of air soughing from the silver prosthetic at his throat.

Julius smiled at his friend's continued use of the phrase 'my boy', despite the fact that he was many years older than Evander. Thanks to the surgeries and enhancements that had been wrought upon Julius's chassis of meat and bone to elevate him to the ranks of the Astartes, his physiology was functionally immortal, though it gave him great comfort to think of Evander as the fatherly figure he had never known on Chemos.

'I am sure you did not come here to observe the quality or otherwise of the fleet's remembrancers, did you?' asked Tobias.

'No,' said Julius, as Tobias turned and made his way down the stacks of shelves.

'Walk with me, my boy, it helps me think when I walk,' he called over his shoulder.

Julius followed the scholar, quickly catching up to him and then reducing his own strides in order not to outpace him.

'I am guessing that there is something specific you are after, am I right?'

Julius hesitated, still unsure of what he was looking for. The presence of what he had seen and felt in the temple of the Laer still squatted in his mind like a contagion, and he had decided that he must attempt to gain some understanding of it for, even though it had been vile and alien, there had been a horrific attraction to it all.

'Perhaps,' began Julius, 'but I'm not sure exactly where I might find it, or even what to look for in the first place.'

'Intriguing,' said Tobias, 'though if I am to assist you I will, obviously, require more to go on.'

'You have heard about the Laer temple I assume?' asked Julius.

'I have indeed and it sounds like a terribly vile place, much too lurid for my sensibilities.'

'Yes, it was like nothing I have ever seen before. I wanted to know more about such things, for I feel my thoughts returning to it time and time again.'

'Why? What is it that so enamoured you of it?'

'Enamoured me? No, that's not what I meant at all,' protested Julius, though the words sounded hollow, even to him, and he could see that Tobias saw the lie in them.

'Maybe it is, then,' admitted Julius. 'I don't think I've felt anything similar, except when I have been enraptured by great art or poetry. My every sense was stimulated. Since then everything is grey and ashen to me. I take no joy in the things that once set my soul afire. I walk the halls of this ship, halls that are filled with the works of the greatest artists in the Imperium, and I feel nothing.'

Tobias smiled and nodded. 'Truly this temple must have been wondrous to have jaded people so.'

'What do you mean?'

'You are not the first to come to my archives seeking knowledge of such things.'

'No?'

Tobias shook his head, and Julius saw the quiet amusement in his weathered features as he said, 'A great many of those who saw the temple have come here seeking illumination as to what it was they felt within its walls: remembrancers, Army officers, Astartes. It seems to have made quite an impression. I almost wish I had taken the time to see it myself.'

Julius shook his head, though the elderly archivist failed to see the gesture as he halted beside a shelf of leather-bound books with gold edging. The spines of the books were faded, and clearly none of them had been read since their placement on the shelf.

'What are these?' asked Julius.

'These, my dear boy, are the collected writings of a priest who lived in an age before the coming of Old Night. He was called Cornelius Blayke; a man who

was labelled a genius, a mystic, a heretic and a visionary, often all in the same day.'

'He must have lived a colourful life,' said Julius.
'What did he write about?'

'Everything I believe you are looking to understand, my dear boy,' said Tobias. 'Blayke believed that
only through an abundance of experience could a
man understand the infinite, and receive the great
wisdom that came from following the road of excess.
His works contain a rich mythology in which he
worked to encode his spiritual ideas into a model for
a new, unbridled age of experience and sensation.
Some say he was a sensualist who depicted the struggle between indulgence of the senses and the
restrictive morals of the authoritarian regime under
which he lived. Others, of course, simply denounced
him as a fallen priest and a libertine with delusions
of grandeur.'

Tobias reached up, pulled one of the books from
the shelf and said, 'In this book, Blayke speaks of his
belief that humanity had to indulge in all things in
order to evolve to a new state of harmony that would
be more perfect than the original state of innocence
from which he believed our race had sprung.'

'And what do you think?'

'I think his belief that humanity could overcome
the limitation of its five senses to perceive the infinite
is wonderfully imaginative, though, of course, his
philosophies were often thought of as degenerate.
They involved... enthusiasms that were considered
quite scandalous for the times. Blayke believed that
those who restrained their desires did so only
because they were weak enough to be restrained. He
himself had no such compunctions.'

'I can see why he was labelled a heretic.'

'Indeed,' said Tobias, 'though such a word has more or less fallen out of usage in the Imperium, thanks to the great works of the Emperor. Its etymological roots lie in the ancient languages of the Olympian Hegemony and it simply means a "choice" of beliefs. In the tract, *Contra Haereses*, the scholar Irenaeus describes his beliefs as a devout follower of a long dead god, beliefs that were later to became the orthodoxy of his cult and the cornerstone of a great many religions.'

'How does that make it a misunderstood word?' asked Julius.

'Come, my dear boy, I thought I had taught you better than that,' said Tobias. 'By following the logic of Irenaeus, you must surely perceive that heresy has no purely objective meaning. The category exists only from the point of view of a position within any society that has previously defined itself as orthodox. Anyone who espouses views or actions that do not conform to that point of view can be perceived as heretics by others within those societies who are convinced that their view is orthodox. In other words, heresy is a value judgment, the expression of a view from within an established belief system. For instance, during the Wars of Unification, the Pan-Europan Adventists held the secular belief of the Emperor as a heresy, while the ancestor worshippers of the Yndonesic Bloc considered the rise to power of the despot Kalagann as a great apostasy.

'So you see, Julius, for a heresy to exist there must be an authoritative system of dogma or belief designated as orthodox.'

'So you're saying there can never be heresy now, since the Emperor has shown the lie in the belief in false gods and corpse worshipers?'

'Not at all; dogma and belief are not reliant on the predisposed belief in a godhead or the cloak of religion. They might simply be a regime or set of social values, such as we are bringing to the galaxy even now. To resist or rebel against that could easily be considered heresy, I suppose.'

'Then why should I wish to read this man's books? They sound dangerous.'

Tobias waved his hands dismissively. 'Not at all; as I often told my pupils at the School of Iterators, a truth that is told with bad intent will triumph over all the lies that can be invented, so it behoves us to know all truths and separate the good from the bad. When an iterator speaks the truth, it is not only for the sake of convincing those who do not know it, but also to defend those that do.'

Julius was about to ask more when the vox-bead crackled at his ear and he heard Lycaon's excited voice.

'Captain,' said Lycaon, 'you need to get back here'.

Julius raised the vox-cuff to his mouth and said, 'I'm on my way. What's happened?'

'We've found them,' said Lycaon, 'the Diasporex. You need to get back here right now.'

'I will,' said Julius, sensing something amiss in Lycaon's words, even over the distortion of the vox. 'Is there anything I should know?'

'Best you come and see for yourself,' replied Lycaon.

FULGRIM ANGRILY PACED the length of his stateroom to the deafening sound of a dozen phonocasters. Each broadcast a different tune: booming orchestral scores, the thumping music of the low hive cavern tribes and, greater than them all, the music of the Laer temple.

Each tune screamed in discord with the others, the sound filling his senses with wild imaginings and the promise of undreamt of possibilities.

His temper simmered just below the surface at his brother's actions, but there was nothing to do but wait to catch up with the 52nd Expedition. For Ferrus to have acted alone displayed a lack of respect that infuriated Fulgrim and threw his carefully laid plans for the Diasporex into disarray.

The plan had been perfect and Ferrus was ruining everything.

The thought surfaced swiftly and with such venom behind it that Fulgrim was shocked at its intensity. Yes, his beloved brother had acted impetuously, but he should have suspected that Ferrus would be unable to contain the Medusan rage that lay at his core.

No, you did all you could to contain his rage. His impetuosity will be his undoing.

Fulgrim felt a chill travel the length of his spine as the thought, one surely dragged from the darkest reaches of his being, surfaced in his head. Ferrus Manus was his brother primarch and, while there were those amongst their number that Fulgrim counted as close friends, there was no closer brotherhood than the bond between him and Ferrus.

Ever since the victory on Laeran, Fulgrim's thoughts had turned inwards to claw the furthest depths of his consciousness, dragging out an acid resentment he had not known existed. Each night as he lay on his silk bed, a voice whispered in his ear and ensnared him with dreams he never recalled and nightmares he could not forget. At first he had thought he was going mad, that some last, deceitful trick of the Laer had begun to unravel his sanity, but he had discounted such a notion as preposterous, for what could lay a perfect being such as a primarch low?

Then he had wondered if he was receiving some astrotelepathic message from afar, though he knew of no psychic potential he possessed. Magnus of Prospero had inherited their father's gift of foresight and psychic potential, though it was a gift that had distanced him from his brothers, for none truly trusted that such a power was without price or consequence.

At last he had come to accept that the voice was in fact a manifestation of his subconscious, a facet of his own mindscape that articulated the things he could not, and stripped away deceits the conscious mind created to protect it from the barriers society placed upon it.

How many others could lay claim to such an honest counsellor as their own mind?

Fulgrim knew he should make his way to the bridge, that his captains needed his direction and wisdom to guide them, for they looked to him in all things, and from him would come the direction and character of his Legion.

Which is as it should be; what is this Legion but a manifestation of your will?

Fulgrim smiled at the thought, reaching over to increase the volume on the phonocaster that played the music recorded within the Laer temple. The music reached deep inside him, its sound without tune or melody, but primal in its intensity. It awoke a longing for better things, for newer things, for greater things.

He remembered returning to the surface of Laeran and seeing Bequa Kynska in the temple with her hands raised to the roof, her face wet with tears as she recorded the music of the temple. She had turned to face him as he entered, falling to her knees as the passion of the alien music washed through her.

'I shall write this for you!' she shouted. 'I shall compose something marvellous. It will be the *Maraviglia* in your honour!'

He smiled at the memory, knowing the marvels she would compose for him were sure to be wondrous beyond belief. *La Fenice* was already undergoing great renovations, with exquisite paintings and mighty sculptures already commissioned from those who had also visited the surface of Laeran.

If there had been any conscious thought as to why only they should receive commissions, he had since forgotten it, but the appropriateness of the decision still pleased him.

The greatest of these works would be a mighty picture of him, a magnificently ambitious piece he had commissioned from Serena d'Angelus after seeing the work she had begun to produce in the wake of the victory on Laeran: work so full of vibrancy and emotion that it made his heart ache to see such beauty.

He had sat for Serena d'Angelus several times since then, but he would need to find the time to engage with her properly when the Diasporex were annihilated.

Yes, he thought, soon the *Pride of the Emperor* will echo to the music of creation, and his warriors will carry it to every corner of the galaxy so that all might have a chance to hear such beauty.

His mood soured as he cast his gaze towards the end of his staterooms and the pile of smashed marble that had been his attempt to create a thing of beauty. Each stroke of the chisel had been delivered with precise skill. The lines of the figure's anatomy were perfect, and yet... there was something indefinably wrong

with the sculpture, something that eluded his understanding. The frustration of it had driven him to inflict
violence upon his work, and he had reduced it to rubble with three blows from his silver sword.

Perhaps Ostian Delafour could instruct him as to
what mistakes he was making, though it galled him
that he, a primarch, should have to consult a mortal.
Wasn't he created to be the greatest in all things? His
other brothers had inherited aspects of their father,
but the gnawing doubt that perhaps the accident that
had almost destroyed the Emperor's Children at birth
had encoded some hidden defect into his genetic
makeup returned to haunt him in the dark watches of
the night.

Was his nature a sham, a thinning veneer of perfection that hid a hitherto unknown core of failure and
imperfection? Such doubt was alien to him, yet the
horror of it had lodged like a canker in his chest.
Already he felt as though events were slipping away
from him. The battles on Laer had been vanity, he
knew that now, but they had been won and that was
what the remembrancers would tell. They would gloss
over the appalling casualty figures he had suppressed,
but which haunted his dreams with images of the
fallen, warriors whose names he knew and memories
he cherished. Now Ferrus, rushing off impetuously to
engage the Diasporex fleet his scout ships had discovered, was closing in on the solar collectors.

The familiar anger towards his brother surfaced
once again, all thoughts of love and centuries of
friendship stained with this latest betrayal.

He shames you with this display and must be punished.

JULIUS HEARD THE reports through the vox as they
crackled over the speakers and watched the surveyor

officers chart the unfolding shape of the battle on the plotter table in lines of glowing green.

Without consulting the Primarch of the Emperor's Children, Ferrus Manus had ordered the 52nd Expedition to make all speed for the Carollis Star in response to the *Ferrum's* discovery of the solar collectors. The Diasporex had reacted to his rash advance by rushing to recover them. Unlike previous encounters, this was to be no hit and run ambush, but it seemed clear to Julius that without timely aid from the 28th Expedition the ships of the 52nd could not prevent the escape of the Diasporex once more.

The bridge of the *Pride of the Emperor* was hushed, the quiet industry of the crew and the chatter of machines the only sound. Julius wished for some noise, something out of the ordinary to highlight to everyone that without Fulgrim's presence, things were not as they should be. There was a gaping void in the bridge that Fulgrim's towering leadership normally filled, but the routine of the bridge crew continued as it always did, and he found their insensibility to the primarch's absence infuriating.

The captain of the *Pride of the Emperor*, Lemuel Aizel, a warrior so used to following the orders of his primarch that he had none of his own, had simply sent the ships of the Emperor's Children after the Iron Hands. Julius could see that he was foundering without the reassuring presence of his lord and master at his side.

Even his other captains seemed oblivious, and he fought to control his temper at their unappreciative senses. Solomon, only recently returned to full duties, stared intently at the surveyor plot, though he was gratified to see that Marius wore an expression of angry disgust. Julius was becoming unaccountably angry,

wishing for something to break the silence and monot-
ony of the bridge, and found himself clenching his fists.
He fought the urge to smash those fists into the face of
one of the bridge crew, just to feel something beyond
the blandness his senses were feeding him.

'Are you all right?' asked Solomon, who stood at his
elbow. 'You look tense.'

'Well of course I'm bloody tense!' snapped Julius, the
sound of his voice a welcome relief from the stress, its
very loudness soothing his burgeoning anger. 'Ferrus
Manus has launched his fleet directly at the Diasporex,
and we have to catch up and fight a battle without a
plan of any perfection.'

Heads turned at his outburst, and Julius felt a curious
elation surge through his body at the feeling. He could
see he had shocked Solomon, and felt a delicious thrill
at allowing his thoughts to slip the leash of control.

'Calm your jets,' said Solomon, gripping his arm
tightly. 'Yes, the Iron Hands started without us, but that
may work to our advantage if they draw the Diasporex
in. We will be the hammer that smashes them on the
anvil of the Iron Hands.'

The thought of battle extinguished his earlier anger,
and the thought that it was to be fought without shape
or form sent a thrill of anticipation through him.

'You're right,' he said. 'This is exactly what we came
here for.'

Solomon stared quizzically at him for a second
before turning his attention back to the plotter table. 'It
won't be long now,' he said after a moment's delibera-
tion.

'What won't?' asked Marius.

'Bloodshed,' said Solomon, and Julius felt his pulse
quicken.

TEN

The Battle of Carollis Star/Going up the
Centre/New Heights of Experience

FILLED WITH THE collected energy of a sun, the explosion of the solar collector bloomed like the birth of a new star. Fiery clouds of debris and released potential spread over hundreds of kilometres, shattering warships that had risked passing close to the collector in an attempt to gain some advantage in the battle raging in the star's corona.

Nearly a thousand starships jockeyed and manoeuvred above the Carollis Star, each moving in its own intricate ballet as blinding streaks of lance fire and the looping contrails of torpedoes crisscrossed the space between them.

Finally brought to battle by the Iron Hands, the Diasporex fleet had turned like a beast at bay protecting its young. Heavily armed warships of ancient design formed a cordon around the solar collectors while smaller, faster escorts attempted to run the blockade of Imperial vessels and remove their invaluable charges from the battle.

Some slipped past, but many more were bracketed by relentless bombardments and reduced to so much scrap metal within moments of being acquired by the gunners of the 52nd Expedition. Fiery explosions flared, blooming brightly as the fires of their deaths ignited the clouds of flammable gasses that filled the space around the star.

The *Fist of Iron* led the charge of the Iron Hands, bludgeoning a path through the centre of the Diasporex fleet, and battering the enemy ships with devastating broadsides. Mass drivers and battery after battery hammered the Diasporex ships, and plumes of venting oxygen bled into space from the wounded vessels.

Spurts of nuclear fire speared up from the surface of the star, clouds of radioactive material following in their wake and wreathing the battle in streaks of light. Smaller fighters and bombers were ripped apart by these random acts of the star's violence, their ordnance erupting in flames and sending them spinning through space like tumbling meteors.

An alien warship duelled with the Iron Hands, unknown weapons hurling bolts of energy that melted through the hulls of the Imperial ships, scrambled their weapon systems, or slaved them to the enemy fleet. Confusion reigned as vessels of the Imperial fleet turned their weapons on allied ships, until Ferrus Manus understood what was happening and led the *Fist of Iron* once more into the thick of the fighting to destroy the enemy ship with a devastating close range torpedo volley.

The alien vessel broke apart in a rippling flurry of explosions, torn asunder from within as each torpedo smashed through bulkhead after bulkhead before detonating in the heart of its target.

Despite the best efforts of the Diasporex fleet masters, the cordon of ships thrown out before the solar collectors could not hold back the force of the Iron Hands. Trapped against the furnace of the Carollis Star, the democratic, multi-part confederacy of the Diasporex was proving to be its undoing. Set against the iron leadership of Ferrus Manus, their many captains could not co-ordinate quickly or ingeniously enough to outwit the tactical ferocity of a primarch.

The fiery halo surrounding the star became the grave of thousands of aliens and humans of the Diasporex as the 52nd Expedition tore through them, venting the anger and fury of the last few months in an unstoppable flurry of battery fire and missiles. Ships of both sides burned, and if it was indeed the end of the Diasporex, then it would be an end worthy of epic tales yet to be written.

The *Ferrum* fought at the heart of the battle, Captain Balhaan avenging his earlier failure in the fury of combat. More nimble than many of the warships of the Diasporex, he masterfully worked with the *Armourum Ferrus* to manoeuvre his vessel to outflank enemy ships and attack them from their vulnerable rear. Devastating battery fire crippled the engines of his prey, and as the Diasporex ships wallowed helplessly, the *Armourum Ferrus* swept in and tore the defenceless vessels apart with point blank broadsides.

Not that the Diasporex were not reaping a fearsome tally. Although their ships fought as individuals in this battle as opposed to a fleet, it did not take long before a great warship in the centre of the Diasporex fleet began to take charge, a hybridised vessel that bore the hallmarks of human design and embellishments of a grotesque alien nature.

Even as Ferrus Manus recognised the moment the hybrid vessel took command, the Diasporex fleet again displayed its teeth. Co-ordinated waves of bombers crippled *Medusa's Glory* and improbably destroyed the *Heart of Gold*. A daring boarding action upon the *Iron Dream* was barely repulsed, though the ship was left helpless and was ultimately destroyed by an almost casual broadside from the hybrid command ship.

The greatest loss to the Imperial fleet came when the battle-barge *Metallus* was destroyed by an enemy lance that tore through its reactor core and vaporised it in an explosion that rivalled that of the first solar collector.

Dozens of nearby ships were caught in the terrifying violence of its destruction, tumbling to their deaths in the star's fiery embrace. As the nuclear fire of the ship's demise faded, a gap of empty space was all that remained. The fleet masters of the Diasporex were not slow to see the opportunity this presented.

Within minutes, the escorts began changing course to lead the precious solar collectors through the gap.

It was a bold move, and the heavier warships of the Diasporex began to disengage from the fleet of the Iron Hands. It was a bold move indeed, and might have worked, had not the ships of the Emperor's Children chosen that moment to unmask their presence and begin their own destructive work amongst the ships of the Diasporex.

THE BOARDING TORPEDO shook with the violence of its delivery, a thundering metal tube hurled through space in a journey that would end either in death or a rush of battle. Though his body still ached, Solomon relished the chance to take the fight to the enemy once more, despite the great unease with which he had greeted Fulgrim's order that they were to be unleashed on the Diasporex via boarding torpedo.

Normal Astartes practice for starship assaults called for specialist troops to make lightning hit and run attacks on critical systems, such as the gun decks or engines, before making a rapid withdrawal, but this mission was to capture the command deck and end the battle in one fell swoop.

Such actions were dangerous at the best of times, but to cross the gulf of space between fighting vessels in the midst of such a furious conflict seemed foolhardy to Solomon.

Fulgrim had surprised everyone when he had marched onto the bridge at the commencement of the fighting, clad in the full panoply of battle instead of the cloak of a ship's captain, and surrounded by his Phoenix Guard.

His armour had been magnificently polished, and Solomon saw many new embellishments worked into the gleaming plates of his greaves. The golden eagle on his breastplate shone with a dazzling brilliance, and his pale features were alight with the prospect of battle. Solomon noticed that, instead of the golden *Fireblade*, the silver hilted sword he had taken from Laeran was belted at his side.

'Ferrus Manus may have instigated this fight without us,' Fulgrim had shouted, 'but by Chemos, he's not going to finish it without us!'

A fierce energy had suddenly seized the bridge of the *Pride of the Emperor*, and Solomon felt it surge from warrior to warrior like an electric current. Julius especially had leapt to obey the primarch's orders, as had Marius, though with a dogged determination rather than with genuine enthusiasm.

Rather than complete the destruction of the Diasporex from afar as the tactical position, as far as Solomon could see, would dictate, Fulgrim had elected to take the fight to the Diasporex directly, and ordered the ships of the 28th Expedition to surge forward to engage them at close range.

Information from the *Fist of Iron* had revealed the presence and location of the enemy command ship, and Fulgrim had immediately hurled the *Pride of the Emperor* towards it. Ferrus Manus may have started the fight prematurely, but the Emperor's Children would win the lion's share of the glory by ripping the heart from the Diasporex.

Not only that, but Fulgrim would once again lead them.

Though at first such a strategy seemed vainglorious to Solomon, he couldn't deny the thrill he felt as he led his men into harm's way, despite his loathing of travelling in a boarding torpedo. Gaius Caphen sat opposite him, his eyes fixed on the rudimentary controls that guided their headlong rush through space, and his mind on the battle to come.

Solomon and the warriors of the Second were to smash into the hybrid vessel first and secure the perimeter, before Fulgrim and the First reinforced their position and pushed through the enemy ship towards the bridge, in order to destroy it with demolition charges. In theory, what little tactical structure remained of the Diasporex fleet would be shattered by the loss of the command ship, and the remainder picked off at the Imperial fleet's leisure.

'Impact in ten seconds,' said Caphen.

'Everyone brace!' ordered Solomon. 'As soon as the entrance is clear, spread out and kill anything you find. Good hunting!'

Solomon closed his eyes and hunched down into the brace position as the torpedo slammed into the side of the enemy vessel, the inertial compensators reducing the impact from lethal to merely bone-jarring. He heard the booming thuds as the shaped charges on the torpedo's nose detonated in sequence, blasting a path through the thick superstructure of the ship.

The force of the detonations and the howling screech of metal juddered down the length of the torpedo. Solomon felt his vision blur and his freshly healed body protest at the force of their arrival and deceleration. It felt like an age, though it was surely no more than a few seconds, before they stopped, and the last charge on the nose cone blew the front of the torpedo clear. The assault ramp clanged down into a fiery inferno of twisted, blackened metal and ruptured corpses.

'Go!' bellowed Solomon, slamming the release on his grav harness and surging to his feet. 'Everyone out! Go!'

He snatched up his hand-crafted bolter, knowing that this was the most vulnerable portion of any torpedo-borne assault. The shock and horror of their arrival had to be exploited to prevent any resistance from materialising.

Solomon charged down the ramp into a tall, high vaulted chamber of blackened columns and walls of dark wooden panelling. The wood blazed, and several of the columns groaned under the weight of the roof, many of the other columns having been destroyed by the impact of the boarding torpedo. Smoke and flames billowed, though the auto-senses of Solomon's armour easily compensated for the low visibility.

Charred corpses filled the chamber, torn to shreds by the impact, and other bodies writhed and screamed in agony as flames consumed them. Solomon ignored them, already hearing distant crashes that told him the rest of his company were smashing through the hull of the vessel.

The warriors of the Second spread out as he saw movement at either end of the chamber, enemy warriors coming to repulse their attack. Solomon grinned as he saw that they were already too late. Flat bangs of bolter fire tore the defenders to their right apart, but an answering volley scythed from the opposite side, punching one of his warriors from his feet with a smoking crater in his chest.

Solomon turned his own bolter to face the new threat, and fired off a rapid burst of shots that sent a bizarre quadruped creature slumping to the ground. More shots and screams sounded, and within moments, the chamber was alive with booming gunfire and explosions.

'Gaius, take the right and secure it,' he said, moving off to the other end of the chamber as more of the ship's crew rushed to plug the breach in their vessel's defences. Solomon killed another enemy, this time seeing his target properly for the first time, as his warriors forced the enemy back in a crackling hail of bolter rounds.

Controlled bursts of gunfire cleared the entrances to the chamber of enemies as Solomon examined the corpse of one of the aliens. Gaius Caphen organised the Astartes to secure the chamber from counter-attack, and ready it for the arrival of reinforcements.

The dead alien was a heavily muscled quadruped with ochre skin, scaled like a snake's, but harder and more chitinous. Portions of its limbs had been augmented with mechanised prosthetics, and its head was elongated. It appeared to be eyeless, its mouth a dark tooth-ringed circle filled with waving feelers. A bizarre armature was affixed to its back, connected via a series of looping cables to its spine and many fingered forelimbs.

The other dead creatures were of the same species, but others amongst the chamber's defenders were clearly human, their twisted bodies immediately recognisable despite the mutilations done to them by the breaching charges of the torpedo. That humans could fight alongside aliens was incomprehensible to Solomon. The very idea of such bizarre creatures working, living and fighting alongside pureblood humans, descended from the people of Old Earth, was repugnant.

'We're ready,' said Caphen, appearing at his shoulder.

'Good,' said Solomon. 'I don't understand how they could have done it.'

'Done what?' asked Caphen.

'Fought alongside xenos.'

Caphen shrugged, the movement awkward in battle plate. 'Does it matter?'

'Of course it matters,' said Solomon. 'If we understand what motivates someone to turn from the Emperor, then we can stop it happening again.'

'I doubt any of this lot has even heard of the Emperor,' said Caphen, tapping his boot against the charred body of a human soldier. 'Can you turn from someone you've never heard of?'

'They may not have heard of the Emperor, but that doesn't excuse this,' said Solomon. 'It should be self-evident that associations with alien filth like this can only end badly. It was our manifesto when we joined the crusade: suffer not the alien to live.'

Solomon knelt beside the dead man and lifted his limp head from the deck. His skin was bloody and his midsection had been burst open from the inside. His armour was an elaborate weave of kinetotropic mesh and energy reflective plates that had singularly failed to stop the brutality of a bolter round.

'Take this man,' said Solomon, 'the blood of Old Earth pours from his veins, and but for his associations with aliens we might have been allies in furthering the cause of the Great Crusade. All this killing is a terrible waste of what might have been, of the brotherhood we might have forged with these people. But there can be no equivocation in the fight for survival, there is only right and wrong.'

'And he chose wrongly?'

'His commanders chose wrongly, and that is why he is dead.'

'So are you saying that it's his commanders who are to blame, and that we might have been friends with this man if circumstances had been different?'

Solomon shook his head. 'No. Such evil can only succeed when good men stand by and allow it to. I do not know how the Diasporex came to be integrated with aliens, but if enough people had stood against the decision it could never have happened. Their fate is their own and I feel no remorse in killing them. All warriors who follow their leaders' orders must carry the weight of it also.'

Gaius Caphen said, 'And I thought Captain Vairosean was the thinker.'

Solomon smiled and said, 'I have my moments.'

Before he could say anything further, a voice in his helmet said, 'Captain Demeter, is the landing zone secure?' and he straightened as he recognised the voice of his primarch.

'It is, my lord,' said Solomon.

'Stand ready, I shall be with you directly,' replied Fulgrim.

THOUGH THE DIASPOREX were trapped between the Carollis Star and the combined Imperial fleets, there was yet the will to fight, and while the command ship still lived, there would be no easy victory.

More and more of the solar collectors were exploding as their escorts were stripped away, crippled and sent spinning down into the star. Some smaller vessels slipped past the Imperial cordon, but they were an irrelevance next to the larger battleships that still fought with undimmed fury.

The *Pride of the Emperor* did battle with tactics straight from a naval strategy textbook, Captain Lemuel Aizel commanding with methodical precision if not flair. The rest of the Emperor's Children fleet followed his example and engaged the foe in perfect attack patterns, destroying the enemy in efficient, elegant dissections.

In contrast, the ships of the Iron Hands fought like the Iron Wolves of Medusa, tearing their enemy apart in daring hit and run attacks that saw them destroy many more vessels than the ships of the Emperor's Children.

Through the heart of the firestorm, the *Firebird* soared like the most graceful of birds, its fiery wings leaving vortices of flaring gasses in its wake. Like a twisting comet trailing streamers of flame behind it, the assault craft seemed to glide easily through the explosions and streaking lines of deadly gunfire that painted the raging inferno of the star's corona.

As though realising the danger the fiery assault craft represented, a pair of Diasporex cruisers altered course to intercept it, and as the web of guns and lasers tightened around the *Firebird*, its doom seemed assured. The primarch's craft twisted desperately to avoid the storm of fire, but it was running out of room, and each explosion burst ever closer to it.

Even as the cruisers closed in to unleash the coup de grace, a monstrous shadow enveloped them, and the *Fist of Iron* sailed between them, a series of ruinous broadsides rippling from its dozens of gun decks. At such close range the results were devastating. The first cruiser was torn apart as a chain reaction of explosions bloated its superstructure from within, and it broke up in a shower of burning plasma and foaming oxygen. The second ship survived long enough to return fire at the *Fist of Iron*, killing hundreds of its crew and inflicting terrible damage on Ferrus Manus's flagship, before it was crippled by a second broadside that obliterated it in a huge explosion.

Saved from destruction, the *Firebird* hurtled through the crucible of battle towards the hybrid command vessel that Solomon Demeter's warriors had secured. Close in defence turrets desperately tried to engage the *Firebird*, as though the vessel's crew sensed that their doom came towards them on these wings of fire, but none came close to Fulgrim's craft, such was its deadly grace and manoeuvrability.

Like a great bird of prey settling on its quarry, the *Firebird* swooped in over the bridge section of the hybrid vessel and its landing claws descended to clamp firmly onto the upper hull of the ship. Searing blasts of melta fire bored through the outer hulls of the enemy vessel, and clouds of crystalline oxygen billowed from the ship's inner skins.

No sooner had the armoured plates of the outer hull been penetrated than a docking umbilical punched through the softer inner hull of the ship, creating a pressurised passageway that would allow the Primarch of the Emperor's Children to wreak bloody havoc on the Diasporex.

JULIUS FOLLOWED HIS primarch and hammered down onto the deck of the enemy vessel in time to see Fulgrim draw his shimmering silver blade. His commander rose to his full height, as a hundred or more enemy soldiers, humans and loping beasts that went on all fours, rushed towards them. Julius felt his heart surge with excitement and battle lust as weapons blazed, but Fulgrim threw up his sword to send the bolts of energy skidding across the walls and ceiling.

Lycaon and more of Julius's warriors dropped from the belly of the *Firebird*, and he watched in awe as the living avatar of battle that was his primarch charged into his enemies. Fulgrim's magnificence still had the power to make him catch his breath, and the honour of going into battle with such a god-like figure was beyond measure.

Fulgrim raised his pistol, a weapon with the power of a caged sun, which had been crafted in the forges of the Urals, to unleash a hail of molten bolts. Blazing light filled the hallway, the gleaming silver of its structure reflecting the brilliance of his shots as they tore through meat, bone and armour.

Men and aliens screamed as the primarch's shots tore through them.

'Spread out! Open fire!' he shouted, though his warriors needed no orders.

The first volleys of bolter fire were unleashed, sawing through the ranks of the aliens. Return fire felled one of the First, but by then it was already too late, as yet more of the Astartes poured from the *Firebird* and began the slaughter.

'Captain Demeter!' cried Fulgrim over the vox, laughing at the sheer joy of being in battle once more. 'You have my position. Join me! This will be my finest hour!'

SOLOMON LED HIS warriors from the cavernous space the boarding torpedo had punched into, setting a brisk pace through the halls of the enemy ship to join his primarch. He could hear the sounds of gunfire from all around, as the other members of his company fought their way to link up with him. Sporadic battles erupted as the ship's defenders attempted to prevent the assaulters from gathering their strength, but it was a hopeless task. The torpedoes had struck widely enough, so that they could not contain the threat without spreading themselves dangerously thin.

Warriors of the Second punched through enemy defensive positions, and the more Astartes that joined the fighting wedge he had aimed at the ship's bridge, the more inevitable the victory became.

He could see the blue glows on his visor that represented Fulgrim and Julius, knowing they would also be heading for the bridge. In any assault where warriors had to board an enemy ship, the key was to get in and out quickly, before any counter-attack could be launched. Solomon knew that missions to attack the bridge of a starship were always the bloodiest, for such an objective was always the most heavily defended.

Whether it was blind luck or the skill of Gaius Caphen at the torpedo's controls, he didn't know, but they had boarded much closer to the bridge than he would have believed possible, circumventing the bulk of the ship's defensive architecture. More troops would be racing to intercept them, but with the force led by the primarch and Julius converging on the bridge as well, it would be too late to stop them.

Solomon slowed his advance as he approached a four way junction and saw yet more Astartes in the colours of the Second coming from the passageway opposite.

Until now, he hadn't realised how much it had rankled missing the final fight on Laeran.

If there really were gods of battle, then they had offered him an incredible opportunity for glory. Solomon laughed as he sent them a playful nod of thanks. He reached the edge of the crossroads and ducked his head around the corner, seeing a defensive position at the end of the narrow passageway. Perhaps a dozen or so enemy soldiers held a strongpoint formed from white steel barriers, though there were sure to be more men out of sight. An automated gun turret was fixed to the ceiling and the barrel of a heavy rotary cannon protruded through a firing slit in the barricade.

Solomon ducked back as a deafening hail of shots roared down the corridor, and blazing traceries of fire ripped into the steel next to him. Sparks and shards of metal flew.

'Well,' he said, 'they're ready for us.'

He turned and waved Caphen forward, handing him his bolter as he said, 'Gaius, someone's going to have to go up the centre.'

Even though both warriors were helmeted, Solomon could sense Caphen's reaction.

'Let me guess,' said Caphen. 'You?'

Solomon nodded and said, 'I'll need cover.'

'You're serious?' asked Caphen, pointing to the torn metal at the corner of the junction. 'Didn't you see what happened?'

'Don't worry,' Solomon said, 'it'll be fine if I have all of you covering me. Just tell me when you're going to fire, eh?'

Caphen nodded wearily and said, 'I know I want command, but not through you getting yourself killed to prove a point.'

Solomon drew his sword, flexing his shoulders in preparation for the brutal ferocity of close quarters combat. 'You'll get command,' he promised, 'but I'm not planning on dying here.'

'Can we at least use grenades first?' asked Caphen.

'If it will keep you happy, then yes.'

Seconds later a trio of grenades arced up the corridor. Solomon waited until he heard the clatter of them landing. Defensive corridors that led to the bridge of a starship were designed to be too long to hurl grenades the length of, but this vessel had been designed in an age before the advent of Space Marines, and all three were hurled with a strength easily able to reach the barricades. The grenades detonated simultaneously with powerful concussive booms that engulfed the defenders in smoke and flame.

Even as the sound registered, Solomon ducked around the corner and ran as fast as he could towards the maelstrom of smoke and screams that boiled at the end of the corridor. His superior senses made out the whirring of the automated gun as it prepared to open fire, and he pistoned his arms to get as far along the corridor as he could before it tore him apart.

'Down!' shouted Caphen behind him, and he hurled himself forward onto his front, skidding along the floor and slamming into the steel barricade.

Bolter fire echoed from the narrow walls, and he felt the whip of the passing shells as the air above him was filled with lethal gunfire. He heard the explosions of their detonations and the screams of dying men. Caphen shouted for another volley, and this time Solomon heard the crack and clang of splintering metal as the automated gun was torn from its mount.

Solomon pushed himself to his feet and activated the blade of his sword in a roar of whirring teeth. The screams of injured men sounded over the crackle of flames and the echo of the bolter rounds. Solomon placed his free hand on the scarred barricade and vaulted over it. A burned soldier ran through the smoke as he landed, and Solomon swept his sword down, cleaving the man from collarbone to pelvis.

He roared in fury as he chopped the blade through the torso of another man, giving his enemy no time to regroup or recover from the shock of his sudden appearance in their midst.

His blade was a cleaver, hacking through his enemy's flesh and primitive armour, the teeth of his weapon shrieking as he killed. Shots fired at point blank range ricocheted from his armour, and a press of bodies surrounded him, the Diasporex soldiers' ignorance of an Astartes' lethality empowering them with doomed courage. Solomon struck out with his elbows and fist as well as his sword, smashing skulls from shoulders, and crushing ribcages with every blow.

In seconds it was over and Solomon lowered his bloody sword as the rest of his warriors advanced along the corridor towards him. His armour was streaked with blood, and the bodies of nearly fifty soldiers lay strewn around him, torn and bludgeoned to destruction in his fury.

'You're alive then,' said Caphen, waving warriors forward to secure their advance.

'Told you I didn't plan on dying here,' he said.

'What now?' asked Caphen.

'We push on. We're nearly at the bridge.'

'I knew you were going to say that.'

'We're so close, Gaius,' said Solomon. 'After getting shot down on Laeran don't you feel the need to win back some glory? If we can take the bridge before anyone else, then that will be what everyone will remember, not that we missed out on Laeran.'

Caphen nodded, and Solomon knew that his lieutenant was as hungry for glory as he was.

Solomon laughed and shouted, 'We move on!'

JULIUS STUMBLED AS a silver bolt of energy, like liquid mercury, struck his shoulder guard and ripped through the ceramite. The creature before him reared up on its hind legs, its powerfully muscled forearms reaching out to him as it fired its wrist mounted weapon once more. He spun away from the shot, feeling the icy cold of it slash past him.

Its yellowed skin pulsed a ruddy red on its underbelly, and Julius thrust his blade towards the alien's body as it attacked. Its speed was phenomenal and its clawed forearm smashed into his helmet, cracking it open from chin to temple. His vision dissolved into static, and he rolled away from the blow, ripping his helmet off as he rose to his feet with his sword extended before him.

The beast before Julius slashed at him again, and he grinned in pleasure at the thrill of fighting an opponent that truly tested his skills. The sounds of battle rang in his ears, and he could hear the blood pounding in his veins as he danced away from the beast's lethal talons. He spun around another slash of the alien's claws and brought his sword down on its neck, shearing its head from its body.

A spray of bright, arterial blood drenched Julius as the creature toppled to the deck. The blood was hot on his lips, the alien reek of it thick in his nostrils, and even the ache in his head felt wondrously real, as though he was experiencing pain for the first time.

All around him, the warriors of the First struggled with the loathsome aliens as they fought through the silver halls of the ship to reach the bridge. He saw Lycaon struggling with another of the mighty quadrupeds, and cried out as his equerry was smashed to the ground, his back clearly snapped in two at the impact.

Julius forged his way through the battle towards Lycaon, already knowing it was too late for him as he saw how limply he lay. He dropped to his knees beside his equerry, allowing the grief to come as he removed Lycaon's helmet. His warriors finished the slaughter of the ship's defenders.

Their surgical strike had been blunted by the counter-attack of the eyeless alien beasts, but with Fulgrim at their head, there could be no stopping the Astartes. Fulgrim killed aliens by the dozen, his white hair whipping madly around his head like smoke as he fought, but they cared not for losses, surrounding the primarch and his Phoenix Guard in an attempt to overwhelm them through sheer mass.

Such a feat was impossible, and Fulgrim laughed as he clove through the aliens with his shimmering silver sword without difficulty, slaying them as easily as a man might crush an insect. The primarch forged a path through the alien defenders for his warriors to follow and their advance continued.

Though Julius had felt great pride in his abilities as a warrior before, he had never felt such a physical joy in combat, such a vivid sensation of the brutality and the artistry of it all.

Nor had he felt such excitement in grief.

He had lost friends before, but the grief had been tempered by the knowledge that they had died warriors' deaths at the hands of a worthy foe. As he looked into Lycaon's dead eyes, he felt loss and guilt churning within him as he realised that, as much as he would miss his friend, he revelled in the sensations his death had stirred within him.

Perhaps this awareness was a side effect of the new chemical that had been issued to the warriors of the Emperor's Children, or perhaps his experience in the Laer temple had awakened hitherto unknown senses that allowed him to reach such dizzying heights of experience.

Whatever the reason, Julius was glad of it.

THE HATCH THAT led to the bridge blew out with a hollow boom, the shaped charges taking a large portion of the superstructure with it. Smoke billowed like blood from a wound as Solomon plunged through the gaping tear in the fabric of the ship. He had retrieved his bolter, and fired from the hip as he charged. His warriors followed, fanning out behind him as a desultory volley of gunfire reached out to them.

A stray bullet caught him on the shin, and he dropped to his knee as he lost his balance for a second. The bridge of the hybrid ship resembled the bridge of the *Pride of the Emperor* insomuch as it retained the basic ergonomics of a starship's command centre, but where Fulgrim's ship was a perfect marriage of functionality and aesthetic, the Diasporex flagship was clearly from a time when such considerations were deemed irrelevant. Dark arches of iron comprised a series of domed enclosures in which the ship's crew worked and from where the captain commanded his vessel. The glow of the Carollis Star and the flares of the ongoing space battle could be seen through the armoured glass of the domes, sporadic flashes lighting up the bridge like a fireworks display.

Ancient consoles winked with a multitude of warning lights, and Solomon could see that such technology was crude in comparison to that employed by the Imperium.

A mix of deck crew and soldiers in mesh armour fired from behind hastily assembled barricades, but Solomon's warriors were already overwhelming them, pistol shots and bolter rounds slaughtering the last of their resistance. Solomon stood as the noise of battle faded and his warriors spread out to secure the bridge.

The remainder of the crew stood helplessly by their consoles, hands raised in surrender, though their faces bore expressions of resigned defiance. Most were unarmoured, though Solomon saw that the officers wore what looked like ceremonial breastplates, and were unarmed save for ornamental foils and light pistols.

'Take them,' ordered Solomon, and Gaius Caphen formed details to secure the prisoners.

The bridge had been taken and the ship was theirs. *His*, he thought with a mischievous smile as he lowered his bolter and took a moment to explore this strange ship, a vessel that had left Old Earth thousands of years before his birth.

A great, high-backed command chair sat on a raised platform below the central dome, and Solomon stepped onto it, seeing one of the strange quadruped creatures they had fought earlier strapped into the chair. Hundreds of cables, wires and needles pierced the creature's body, and as its eyeless face turned to look at him, he felt a creeping revulsion steal over him.

Blood coated its upper body, and Solomon saw that a stray round had taken off the top of its skull. Blood oozed from its shattered cranium, and he was amazed that it could still be alive.

Had this… thing been the ship's captain? Its pilot? Its Navigator?

The alien creature let out a low moan, and Solomon leaned in close to hear its valediction, though he had no idea whether he would be able to understand it.

Its mouth moved, and though no sound issued from its gullet, Solomon could hear its words as clearly as if they had been planted directly into his brain.

All we wished was to be left alone.

'Step away from that xeno creature, Captain Demeter,' said a cold voice behind him.

Solomon turned and saw the towering form of Fulgrim standing in the smoke wreathed hole he had blown in the bridge wall. Behind the primarch, he saw Julius, his face a mask of blood, and Solomon felt a shiver of unease at the expressions of glacial anger he saw in both their eyes.

Fulgrim strode onto the bridge, his sword and armour drenched in alien gore, and his eyes wild with the fury of battle. He surveyed the captured bridge, and then looked up at the domed ceiling, where the fires of battle reflected dully on his opaque, dark eyes.

Solomon stepped down from the platform and said, 'The ship is ours, my lord.'

Fulgrim ignored him and spun on his heel, marching from the bridge without a word.

FULGRIM FOUGHT TO control his fury as he marched away from the bridge, the blood pounding in his skull with such force that he feared it might burst through at any moment. His warriors parted before him, seeing his fists clenched and the veins in his face pulsing darkly against his alabaster skin.

An amethyst fire built in his eyes, and a trickle of blood dripped from his nose as he gripped the hilt of his silver sword tightly.

This was to have been his greatest triumph!

Now it is ruined! First by Ferrus Manus, and then by Solomon Demeter.

'No!' he shouted, and nearby Astartes flinched at his sudden outburst to the air. 'The *Fist of Iron* saved us from destruction, and Captain Demeter fought with courage to win the honour of reaching the bridge!'

Saved us? No, it was for his own self-aggrandisement that Ferrus Manus prevented the destruction of the Fire-bird, not for altruism, and Demeter... he hungers for glory that ought to be yours.

Fulgrim shook his head and dropped to his knees.

'No,' he whispered. 'I can't believe it.'

It is the truth, Fulgrim, and you know it. In your heart of hearts you know it.

PART THREE

VISIONS OF TREACHERY

ELEVEN

The Seer/The Perdus Anomaly/The Book of Urizen

AMID THE EMPTY reaches of space, a pinprick of light shone like a jewel upon a pall of velvet, a mournful glow lost in the wilderness it travelled through. It was a ship, though not a ship that would be recognised by any but the most diligent remembrancer who had scoured the depths of the Emperor's Librarium Sanctus on Terra for references to the lost eldar civilisation.

The mighty ship was a craftworld, and it possessed a grace that human shipwrights could only dream of. Its colossal length was fashioned from a substance that resembled yellowed bone, and its form was more akin to something that had grown rather than been built. Gemlike domes reflected the weak starlight, and an inner radiance glistened like phosphorus through their semi-transparent surfaces.

Graceful minarets rose in scattered ivory clusters, their tapered tops shining gold and silver, and wide spires of bone swept from the vessel's flanks where a fleet of elegant ships like ancient sea galleons was docked. Vast conglomerations of wondrously designed habitations clung to the surface of the mighty craftworld, and a host of twinkling lights described beautiful traceries through the cities.

A great sail of gold and black soared above the mighty vessel's body, rippling in the stellar wind as it plied its lonely course. The craftworld travelled alone, its stately progress through the stars like the last peregrination of an elderly thespian before his final curtain.

Lost in the vastness of space, the craftworld floated in utter isolation. No star-shine illuminated its sleek towers, and distant from the warmth of sun or planet, its domes stared into the darkness of empty space.

Few outside of those who lived long and melancholy lives aboard the graceful space-city could know that it was home to the few survivors of planets abandoned aeons ago amidst terrifying destruction. Upon this craftworld dwelled the eldar, a race all but extinct, the last remnants of a people that had once ruled the galaxy and whose mere dreams had overturned worlds and quenched suns.

THE INTERIOR OF the greatest dome upon the craftworld's surface shimmered with a pallid glow, its translucency enclosing a multitude of crystal trees that stood beneath the light of long dead stars. Smooth pathways wove through the glittering forest, their courses unknown to even those who trod them. A silent song echoed through the dome, unheard and invisible, but achingly yearned for upon its absence. The ghosts of ages past and ages yet to come filled the dome, for it was a place of death and, perversely, a place of immortality.

A lonely figure sat cross-legged in the centre of the forest, a spot of darkness amongst the glowing crystal trees.

Eldrad Ulthran, Farseer of Craftworld Ulthwé smiled wistfully as the songs of long dead seers filled his heart with joy and sadness in equal measure. His smooth features were long and angular, his bright eyes narrow and oval. Dark hair swept over his tapered, graceful ears, gathered at the nape of his neck in a long scalp lock.

He wore a long, cream-coloured cloak and a tunic of flowing black cloth, gathered at the waist by a golden belt studded with gems and fashioned with complex runes.

Eldrad's right hand rested on the trunk of a crystal tree, its structure veined with darting lights, the suggestion of peaceful faces swimming in its depths. His other hand held a long seer staff of the same material as the ship, its gem encrusted surface redolent with dangerous power.

The visions were coming again, stronger than before, and his dreams were troubled with their meaning. Since the horror of the Fall, a dark, bloody age when the eldar had paid the price for their complacency and wild indulgences, Eldrad had guided his race through times of great crisis and desperation, but none had come close to the great calamity he felt as a gathering storm at the edge of his vision.

A time of chaos was set to descend on the galaxy, as calamitous as the Fall and just as momentous.

Yet he could not see it clearly.

Yes, his journey along the Path of the Seer had seen his race saved from danger a hundred times and more over the centuries, but his sight had faded in recent days, the gift gone from him as he sought to penetrate the veil that had been drawn over the warp. He had begun to fear that his gift had deserted him, but the song of the ancient seers had called him to the dome, calming his spirit and showing him the true path, as they had led him through the forest to this place.

Eldrad let his mind float free of his body, feeling the shackles of flesh left behind as he rose higher and faster. He passed through the pulsing wraithbone of the dome and out into the cold darkness of space, though his spirit felt neither warmth nor cold. Stars flashed past him as he travelled the great void of the warp, seeing the echoes of ancient races lost to legend, the seeds of future empires and the great vigour of the latest race to forge a destiny among the stars.

Humanity they called themselves, though Eldrad knew them as the mon-keigh, a brutal, short-lived race that was spreading across the heavens like a virus. From the cradle of their birth they had conquered their solar system, and then exploded across the galaxy in a vast crusade that absorbed the lost fragments of their earlier empire and destroyed those that stood in their way without mercy. The sheer bellicosity and hubris of this endeavour astounded Eldrad, and he could already see the seeds of humanity's destruction lodged in their hearts.

How such a primitive species could achieve so much and not be driven insane by their sheer insignificance in the grand scheme of the cosmos defied understanding, but they were possessed of such rampant self-belief that their own mortality and insignificance did not penetrate their conscious minds until it was too late.

Already, Eldrad had seen the death of their race, the blood soaked fields of the world named for the end of days, and the final victory of the dark saviour.

Would their course be altered by the knowledge of their inevitable doom? Of course it would not, for a race such as the mon-keigh would never accept the inevitable, and would always seek to change that which could not be changed.

He saw the rise of warriors, the treachery of kings, and the great eye opening to release the mighty heroes of legend trapped there to return to their warriors' sides for the final battle. Their future was war and death, blood and horror, yet still they would push ever onwards, convinced of their own superiority and immortality.

And yet… perhaps their doom was not inevitable.

Despite the bloodshed and despair, there was still hope. The flickering ember of an unwritten future guttered in the darkness, its light surrounded by amorphous warp-spawned monsters with great, yellowed fangs and talons. Eldrad saw that they hoped to extinguish this light by their very presence, and as he looked into the fading dream of the future, he saw what might yet come to pass.

He saw a great warrior of regal countenance, a towering giant in sea-green armour with a great amber eye at the centre of his breastplate. This mighty figure fought through a host of the dead on a sickly planet of decay, his sword cleaving a score of corpses with every blow. Warp light filled the rotted eye sockets of the dead, and the energies of the Lord of Pestilence gave their limbs fierce animation. The calamitous doom of his race hung around this warrior like a shroud, though he knew it not.

Eldrad's spirit flew close to the light, trying to discern the identity of the warrior. The warp beasts roared and gnashed their teeth, flailing in idiot blindness at his spirit form. The warp seethed around

him, and Eldrad knew that the monstrous gods of the
warp would not stand for his presence, as the currents
of the warp sought to cast his spirit back to his body.

Eldrad fought to hold onto the vision, extending
his warp sight as far as he dared. Images flooded his
mind: a cavernous throne room, a great god-like
figure in gleaming armour of gold and silver, a sterile
chamber deep beneath a mountain, and a betrayal of
such magnitude that his soul burned with the
enormity of it.

Cries of anguish echoed all around him, and he
fought to hold on to some sense of them as the power
of the warp hurled him away from this jealously
guarded secret. Words formed from the cries, but few
offered any meaning or understanding, their essence
burning in his mind with a fierce light.

Crusade... Hero... Saviour... Destroyer.

But above them all, blazing brighter than all
others... *Warmaster*.

FROM THE STILLNESS and darkness, came light. A rippling plume of fire like the tip of a comet appeared
in the darkness of the system's edge, growing steadily
bigger as it increased in brightness and intensity.
Without warning, the light suddenly expanded with
the speed and violence of an explosion, and where
once there had been nothing but empty space, there
was now a mighty starship, its purple and gold hull
still battle scarred.

Glistening streamers of fading energy, like fronds
of seaweed caught on the hull of an ocean-going
vessel, trailed behind the *Pride of the Emperor*, and her
hull groaned with the suddenness of the translation
from warp space to real space. A host of smaller
vessels appeared in the wake of the mighty warship,

winking into existence with bright flashes and
whorls of strangely coloured light flaring around
them.

Over the course of the next six hours, the remainder of the 28th Expedition completed the translation
to real space and formed up around the *Pride of the
Emperor*. One vessel amongst the fleet, the *Proudheart*,
bore no scars earned at the Battle of the Carollis Star.
The vessel was the flagship of Lord Commander
Eidolon. It had recently returned from a peace keeping tour of the Satyr Lanxus Belt, and unexpected war
alongside the Warmaster's 63rd Expedition on a
world known as Murder.

The 28th Expedition had taken its leave of the Iron
Hands following the great victory over the Diasporex
with much sadness, for old brotherhoods had been
renewed and new ones forged in the crucible of combat in ways that could not be achieved in times of
peace.

The human prisoners of the Diasporex had been
transported to the nearest compliant world and
handed over to the Imperial governor to be
employed as slave labour. The aliens had been exterminated and their vessels pounded to destruction by
close range broadsides from the *Fist of Iron* and the
Pride of the Emperor. A detachment of the Mechanicum had remained behind to study what remained
of the ancient human technologies of the Diasporex,
and Fulgrim had given them leave to rejoin the 28th
Expedition upon the completion of their researches.

Thus, with duty and honour to the 52nd Expedition discharged, Fulgrim had led his expedition to a
region of space known to Imperial Cartographae as
the Perdus Anomaly, their original objective following the defeat of the Laer.

Little was known of this area of the galaxy. Its reputation amongst starfarers was one of dark legend, for vessels that sailed this region of space were never seen again. Navigators shunned the Perdus Region, as dangerous currents and freak tides within the immaterium made it an incredibly hazardous region to traverse, and astropaths spoke of an impenetrable veil that shielded it from their warp sight.

All that was known had come from a single surviving probe that had been launched at the outset of the Great Crusade, and which had returned a faint signal that indicated that the local systems of the Perdus region contained many habitable worlds ripe for compliance.

Most other expeditions had chosen not to venture into this ill-fated region, but Fulgrim had long ago declared that no region of space would remain unknown to the forces of the Emperor.

That the Perdus Anomaly was uncharted was simply another way for the Emperor's Children to once again prove their superiority and perfection.

THE TRAINING HALLS of the First Company echoed to the clash of weapons and the grunts of fighting Astartes. The six-week journey to the Perdus region had allowed Julius time to grieve for Lycaon and the honoured dead of the First as well as train a great many of the warriors elevated from the novitiates and Scout Auxilia to the status of full Astartes. Though they were yet to be blooded, he had instructed them in the ways of the Emperor's Children, passing down his experience and newly awakened sense of pleasure in the fury of combat. Eager to learn from their commander, all the warriors of the First had embraced his new teachings with an enthusiasm that pleased him greatly.

The time had also allowed him to reacquaint himself with his reading, and the hours he had not spent with the warriors of his company, he had passed in the Archive Chambers. He had devoured the works of Cornelius Blayke, and though he had found much that illuminated him, he was certain that there was yet more still to learn.

Stripped to the waist, he stood in one of the training cages with a trio of mechanised fighting armatures, their armed limbs inert as he savoured the anticipation of the coming fight.

Without warning, all three machines leapt into life, ball joints and rotating gimbals on their ceiling mounts allowing them a full range of motion around him. A sword blade licked out, and Julius swayed aside, ducking as a spiked ball slashed towards his head and a pistoning spike thrust towards his belly.

The nearest armature launched a savage series of clubbing blows, but Julius laughed as he blocked them with his forearms, the pain making him grin as he kicked out behind him and sent the armature that had been coming in to attack spinning back. The third machine sent a hooking blow towards his head. He rolled with the impact as it snapped his head around.

He tasted blood and laughed, spitting it at the first machine as it darted in to deliver a killing blow. Its blade slashed out and caught him a glancing blow to his side. He welcomed the pain, stepping in to deliver a thunderous series of hammer blows to the machine.

Metal split and the armature was wrenched from its mount on the ceiling. Even as he savoured its destruction, a powerful blow smashed into the side of his head, and he dropped to one knee, feeling the new chemicals in his blood pumping fresh strength into his body in response.

He leapt to his feet as a blade scythed towards him, and slammed his palm down hard onto the flat of the blade, snapping it from the machine. With the weapon gone, Julius stepped in close and enveloped the machine in a crushing bear hug, hauling it round to face the final armature as it let rip with a volley of iron spikes.

All three pierced the body of the armature he held, and it sputtered with sparks as it died. He pushed it aside and rounded on the final machine, feeling more alive than ever before. His body sang with the pleasure of destruction, and even the pain of his wounds was like a tonic flowing in his veins.

The machine circled him warily, as though appreciating on some mechanical level that it was on its own. Julius feinted a blow to it with his fist. The armature darted to the side, and Julius delivered a powerful roundhouse kick that crumpled the machine's side and rendered it motionless.

He shook his head, dancing back and forth on the balls of his feet as he waited for the machine to restart, but it remained inert and he realised that he had destroyed it.

Suddenly disappointed, he opened the sphere of the training cage and stepped back down into the hall. He had not even broken sweat, and the excitement he'd felt as he'd faced the three machines seemed like a distant memory.

Julius closed the training cage, knowing a servitor would already have been despatched to repair the damaged armatures, and made his way back to his personal arming chamber. Scores of Astartes warriors trained in the halls, either in feats of arms or simple physical exercise to maintain the perfection of their physiques. A strict regime of chemical enhancers and genetic superiority kept an Astartes body in peak physical condition, but many of the new drugs being introduced to the dispensers in Mark IV plate required physical stimulation to begin the reaction in the recipient's metabolism.

He opened the door of his arming chamber, the smell of oil and his armour's lapping powder filling his nostrils. The walls were of bare iron, and a simple cot bed ran the length of one wall. His armour hung on a rack next to a small sink, his sword and bolter in a footlocker at the end of the bed.

The blood drawn by the training machines had already clotted, and he picked up a towel from a rail beside the sink to wipe it from his body before slumping on the bed and wondering what to do next.

A metal-framed shelf unit beside his bed held Ignace Karkasy's *Reflections and Odes*, *Meditations on the Elegiac Hero* and *Fanfare to Unity*, books that had, until recently, filled him with joy whenever he read them. Now they seemed hollow and empty. Beside Karkasy's works were three volumes of Cornelius Blayke that he had borrowed from Evander Tobias. He reached up to read more of the fallen priest's words.

This particular volume was entitled *The Book of Urizen* and was the least impenetrable of Blayke's books he had read thus far. In addition, it was prefaced by an anonymously written biography of the man, the reading of which greatly illuminated the text that followed.

Julius now knew that Cornelius Blayke had been many things in his life, an artist, a poet, a thinker and a soldier, before finally deciding to enter the priesthood. A visionary from childhood, Blayke had, it appeared, been afflicted with visions of an ideal world where every dream and desire could be realised, though he struggled to reproduce them in paintings, prose and hand coloured etchings with poetic text.

Blayke's younger brother had died while fighting in the many wars that raged in the Nordafrik Conclaves, an event the biographer credited with driving him into the priesthood. In later life, Blayke attributed his revolutionary techniques of illuminated printing to his long dead brother, claiming that he had been shown the technique in a dream.

Even as a priest, a life Julius suspected he had chosen as a means of refuge, the visions of forbidden desires and his powers as a mystic returned to haunt him. Indeed, it was said that when the high priest of another order first laid eyes upon Blayke, the sight of him caused the man to drop dead on the spot.

Cloistered in a church within one of the nameless cities of Ursh, Blayke became convinced that mankind would profit from his efforts, and bent his will to perfecting the means by which he could best convey his beliefs.

Julius had read much of Blayke's poetry and, while he was no scholar, even he knew that much of it had no clear plot, rhyme or meter. What did make sense to Julius was Blayke's belief in the futility of denying any desire, no matter how fantastical. One of his chief revelations had been the understanding that the power of sensual experience was necessary for creativity and spiritual progress. No experience was to be denied, no passion was to be restrained, no horror to be turned from and no vice to remain unexplored. Without such experience there could be no progression towards perfection.

Attraction and repulsion, love and hate: all were necessary to further human existence. From these conflicting energies sprang what the priests of his order called good and evil, words that Blayke had quickly realised were meaningless concepts when set beside the promise for advancement that could be achieved by indulging every human desire.

Julius chuckled as he read this, knowing that Blayke had later been cast from his religious order for practising his beliefs vigorously in the back streets and bordellos of the city. No vice was beneath him and no virtue beyond him.

Blayke believed that the inner world of his visions was of a higher order than that of physical reality, and that mankind should fashion its ideals from that inner world rather than from the crude world of matter. His work spoke over and over of how reason and authority constrained and inhibited mankind's spiritual growth, though Julius suspected that this was a reflection of his feelings towards the ruler of the client state of Ursh, a warrior king named Shang Khal, who sought to dominate the nations of the Earth through brutal oppression.

To have openly espoused such philosophies in such a time reeked of madness, but Julius was reluctant to dismiss Blayke as a madman; after all, his pronouncements had attracted a great many followers who hailed him as a great mystic, set to usher in a new age of passion and liberty.

Julius remembered reading the aphorisms of Pandorus Zheng, a philosopher who had served in the court of one of the Autarchs of the Yndonesic Bloc. He had spoken in support of mystics and how they exaggerated truths that truly existed. By Zheng's definition, the mystic could not exaggerate a truth that was imperfect. He had further defended such men by saying, 'To call a man mad because he has seen ghosts and visions denies him his full dignity, since he cannot be neatly categorised into a rational theory of the cosmos.'

Julius had always enjoyed the works of Zheng and his teaching that the mystic did not bring doubts or riddles, for the doubts and riddles existed already. The mystic was not the man who made mysteries, but the man who destroyed them through his works.

The mysteries Blayke sought to destroy were those that held mankind back from achieving its full potential and the understanding of the hope for a better future. All of which placed him in opposition to the despairing philosophies of men like Shang Khal and the despot, Kalagann, tyrants who preached an inevitable descent into Chaos, a terrifying realm that had once been the womb of creation, and which would inevitably be its grave.

Blayke used beauty as a window to this wondrously imagined future, and from contemporary thinkers, he had been drawn to ideas of alchemical symbolism, coming to believe, as the Hermetists did, that mankind was the microcosm of the Divine. His reading became voracious, and he became well versed in the Orphic and Pythagorean tradition, Neo-Platonism, the Hermetic, Kabbalistic, and the alchemical writings of scholars such as Erigena, Paracelsus and Boehme. Julius knew none of these names, but felt sure that Evander Tobias could help him find their works should he desire it.

Armed with such weighty knowledge, the gigantic framework of Blayke's mythology took shape in his greatest poem, *The Book of Urizen*.

This epic work began the narrative of the Fall of the Heavenly Man into the maelstrom of experience, what Blayke called, 'the dark valleys of self-hood'. Over the course of the book, mankind struggled with the task of transmuting his worldly passions into the purity of what Blayke called the Eternal. To help this cosmic process along, Blayke personified the essence of revolution and renewal in a fiery awakener, a being he named ork, and Julius laughed at the aptness of the name, wondering if Blayke had foreseen the scourge of the greenskin that infested the galaxy.

According to the poem, mankind's fall from grace had divided him from his divinity, and through the ages he was forced to struggle to reunite himself with the Divine. In the poem, mankind's soul was disintegrated and had to reconcile every element of its being on the road back to the Eternal, echoing a myth he had read of the Gyptian tombs. This legend spoke of the dismemberment of an ancient god known as Osiris at the beginning of time, and man's obligation to gather together the dismembered parts in order to arrive once more at spiritual wholeness.

In the works of Blayke, Julius recognised an original voice in a conventional age unsuited for such libertarian philosophies. Pitted against forces of oppression that could not be swayed by reason, he had resorted to violent imagery and the force of his powers as a mystic.

He had become what forces of order do not welcome, a disturbing spiritual force that urged men to awaken their passions in order to change and grow.

'Knowledge is merely sense perception,' said Julius, smiling as he read aloud from the book. 'Indulgence is the wellspring of all things in Man, and reason the only curb upon nature. The attainment of ultimate pleasure and the experience of pain are the end and aim of all life.'

TWELVE

No Purity in Pride/Paradise/Never be Finished

ONCE AGAIN EVERY seat around the round table in the Heliopolis was occupied. The tiered chamber was lit only by the flames burning in the brazier at the centre of the table and torches that hung from the golden plinths of the statues. This was only the second time Saul Tarvitz had set foot in the Heliopolis, though he knew he had changed a great deal since the first time he had sat in this brotherhood.

Lord Fulgrim stood by the Phoenix Gate, dressed in a purple toga embroidered with gold thread and emblazoned with a phoenix motif. His long hair was crowned in a wreath of golden leaves, and a new sword with a silver hilt was belted at his side. The primarch personally welcomed his captains back to the quiet order, and the effect on each warrior as Fulgrim offered his greeting was incredible. Tarvitz still felt the tangible excitement

and pleasure that came from being personally
acknowledged by such a beautifully perfect warrior.

Solomon Demeter of the Second sat opposite him
and had given him a quiet nod of acknowledgement
when he, Lucius and Lord Commander Eidolon had
passed through the Phoenix Gate. Marius Vairosean
sat sullenly beside Captain Demeter, and Julius Kaesoron laughed and told wild tales of his exploits in
fighting the xenos creatures of the Diasporex, complete with gestures and hand motions to demonstrate
a particularly delicious blow.

Tarvitz caught the glint of annoyance in Solomon
Demeter's eyes as Captain Kaesoron described how
he and the primarch had fought their way to the
bridge of the hybrid command ship, though Tarvitz
had already heard that it had been Captain Demeter's
warriors who had the honour of first reaching the
bridge.

Lord Commander Vespasian sat in the seat next to
the primarch's, and his eyes sparkled with good
humour at seeing their safe return from their mission.
Tarvitz returned the lord commander's smile, though
in truth he was weary and glad to be back amongst
his brothers, for the experience on Murder had been
a draining one. The megarachnid had been a terrible
foe and the raw vigour of the Luna Wolves was, in its
own way, exhausting.

He glanced over at Eidolon, remembering the tense
standoff between the lord commander and Captain
Torgaddon on the surface of Murder after the Luna
Wolves speartip had arrived. Though Tarvitz was honour bound to serve Eidolon, he couldn't deny the
satisfaction he had taken from seeing the lord commander put in his place by the irrepressible Tarik
Torgaddon. Although Eidolon had later managed to

work his way back into the good graces of the Warmaster, he still smarted from his mistakes on Murder
and the insolence Torgaddon had shown him.

Nor had Lucius come back from the time spent
with the Luna Wolves without scars. A duel in the
training cages with Garviel Loken had given him a
much-needed lesson in humility and seen his nose
broken. Despite the ministrations of the Apothecaries, the bone had not set properly, and Lucius's
perfect profile was, in his eyes, ruined forever.

At last the Phoenix Gate closed and Fulgrim took
his seat at the table, extending his hand towards the
brazier.

'Brothers,' he said, 'in the fire I welcome you all
back to the Brotherhood of the Phoenix.'

The assembled warriors mirrored the primarch's
gesture and said, 'In the fire we return.'

'Ah, it is good to see you all again, my sons,' said
Fulgrim, favouring each of them with a radiant smile
that lit up each warrior's soul. 'It has been some time
since our order met to tell tales of courage and honour, but we are once again whole and set upon the
discovery of new wonders in an unknown region of
space. Our astropaths can tell us little of the region of
space we find ourselves in, but we are not cowed by
such mysteries, rather we welcome them as a chance
to further our pursuit of perfection.'

Tarvitz saw the fierce excitement in Fulgrim's eyes,
and felt it transmitted to him like a fire in his blood.
Even in his most eloquent moments, the primarch
had never seemed this energised, his entire body
looking as though charged with the enjoyment of
every word.

'Our beloved brothers are returned from their
peacekeeping duties, and though I know they feared

for the glory they would miss while we fought with our brothers in the Iron Hands, they have won laurels of their own, and were fortunate enough to fight alongside the Warmaster's warriors against a vile alien foe.'

Tarvitz recalled the war on Murder, how there had been little honour in the initial drop to the planet's surface, and the death and frantic nature of the combat against the loathsomely quick megarachnid warriors. It had been brutal, intense and bloody work, and many good warriors had met their end beneath its raging, bruised skies. Thanks to Eidolon's mistakes, there had been precious little glory won until the Luna Wolves had arrived and brought their strength to bear.

Then Sanguinius had come, and Tarvitz smiled as he once again pictured the awesome sight of the Warmaster and the Lord of the Angels fighting side by side, bestriding the horrific battlefields of Murder like gods of war unbound. *That* had been glorious, and the victories they had gone on to win had redeemed their honour.

'Perhaps Lord Commander Eidolon will favour us with a tale of battle,' said Vespasian.

Tarvitz looked over to his lord commander as he stood with a curt bow. 'I shall, if you desire to hear it.'

A chorus of cheers responded in the affirmative, and Eidolon smiled. 'As Lord Fulgrim said, we won great glories upon Murder, and I humbly thank you, my lord, for allowing us to go to the rescue of our brothers of the Blood Angels.'

Tarvitz blinked in surprise at Eidolon's words, for he remembered well the fact that no one had dared use the word "rescue" at the time, for it had been deemed improper to openly suggest that the Blood

Angels had needed rescuing. 'Reinforcement' was the word they had been encouraged to use.

'Upon arrival at One-Forty Twenty, it was clear that the master of the 140th Expedition, a man named Mathanual August, had not the vision to command the action. Upon learning of the imminent arrival of the Warmaster, I led our forces to the surface of Murder to secure landing sites and begin the rescue of the Blood Angels forces, August had unwisely committed in piecemeal actions.'

Tarvitz had been surprised at Eidolon's earlier words, but was shocked rigid at this blatant twisting of the facts. Yes, Mathanual August had drip-fed his expeditionary forces into a danger zone until they were all gone, but it had been no notion of nobility that had motivated Eidolon's decision to drop onto Murder before the arrival of the Luna Wolves, rather a desire not to share the glory with the Warmaster's elite.

Eidolon went on to tell of the initial battles and the subsequent destruction of the megarachnid, taking great pains to emphasise the Emperor's Children's role in the final victory, while minimising the parts played by the Luna Wolves and the Blood Angels.

When he had finished it was to rapturous applause and pounding of the table as the assembled warriors lauded the honourable victory and feats of arms of Eidolon's command. Tarvitz looked over to Lucius to try and discern some reaction to Eidolon's blatant reinvention, but the cool features of his friend were unreadable.

'A fine tale,' acknowledged Vespasian. 'Perhaps later we might hear of the heroism of your warriors?'

'Perhaps,' said Eidolon grudgingly, but Tarvitz already knew that such tales would never be heard in this company. The lord commander would never allow anything that might contradict his version of the events on Murder.

Fulgrim said, 'You do our Legion proud, Eidolon, and all your warriors will be lauded for the part they played. The names of your dead will be engraved upon the walls of the processional way beyond the Phoenix Gate.'

'You honour us, Lord Fulgrim,' said Eidolon, once again taking his seat.

Fulgrim nodded in agreement and said, 'Lord Commander Eidolon's courage in the face of adversity is an example to us all, and I urge you to pass on his words to your warriors. However, we are here to plan future glories, for a Legion must never rest on its laurels and live off past glories. We must always push onwards towards new challenges and new foes against which we may once again prove our superiority.

'We find ourselves in a region of space where little is known, and we pierce the darkness with the light of the Emperor. There are worlds here that crave the illumination of Imperial Truth and it is our manifest destiny to provide it. We draw near to one such world, and I hereby designate it Twenty-Eight Four in honour of the conquest to come. We will talk more of what I expect from every one of you later, but for now, enjoy the victory wine!'

With those words, the Phoenix Gate was flung open and an army of menials in simple chitons of pale cream entered the Heliopolis bearing amphorae of rich wine and heaped trays of exotic meats, fresh fruits, soft bread, sweetmeats and extravagant pastries.

Tarvitz watched in amazement as the procession of exquisite food and wine was set out on trestles around the edge of the Heliopolis. It was traditional for the Emperor's Children to toast a victory before it was won, such was the surety of their way of war, but such a lavish feast seemed an excessive display of hubris.

He joined the other captains as they made their way over to the trestles and poured a goblet of wine, keeping his gaze averted from Eidolon for fear of revealing his misgivings at his retelling of the War on Murder. Lucius moved alongside him, a sly grin creasing his handsome features.

'Trust the lord commander to put a spin on Murder, eh, Saul?'

Tarvitz nodded and checked to make sure that no one could overhear his reply. 'It was certainly an… interesting take on events.'

'Ah, who cares anyway?' said Lucius. 'If there's glory to be had, better it comes to us than the damned Luna Wolves.'

'You're just bitter after Loken beat you in the training cages.'

Lucius's face darkened and he snapped. 'He did not beat me.'

'Seems like I remember you flat on your back at the end of it,' pointed out Tarvitz.

'He cheated when he punched me,' said Lucius. 'It was supposed to be an honourable duel of swords, but the next time we cross blades I will have the best of him.'

'Assuming he doesn't learn any new tricks along the way.'

'He won't,' sneered Lucius. Tarvitz was again struck by the sheer arrogance of the swordsman, feeling the balance of their friendship tipping further away from him. 'After all, Loken's a base born cur, just like the rest of the Luna Wolves.'

'Even the Warmaster?'

'Well, no, of course not,' said Lucius hurriedly, 'but the rest of them are little better than Russ's barbarians, uncouth and without the poise and perfection of our Legion. If anything, Murder proved our superiority to the Luna Wolves.'

'Our superiority?' said a voice. Tarvitz turned to see Captain Solomon Demeter standing behind them.

'Captain Demeter,' said Tarvitz, bowing his head. 'It is an honour to see you again. My congratulations on capturing the bridge of the Diasporex command ship.'

Solomon smiled and leaned in close. 'My thanks, but I'd keep such sentiments quiet if I were you. I don't think Lord Fulgrim was too pleased the Second stole his thunder, but that's by the by, I didn't come over here to hear how wonderful I am.'

'Then why did you?' asked Lucius.

Solomon ignored the insulting tone of Lucius's question and said, 'I was watching you, Captain Tarvitz, as Eidolon told the tale of Murder, and I get the feeling there might be more to it than we heard. I think I'd like to hear your version of what happened, if you take my meaning.'

'Lord Eidolon described our campaign as he perceived it,' said Tarvitz neutrally.

'Come on, Saul, you don't mind if I call you Saul do you?' asked Solomon. 'You can be honest with me.'

'I'd be honoured,' said Tarvitz honestly.

'You and I both know Eidolon's a blowhard,' said Solomon, and Tarvitz was taken aback by his fellow captain's bluntness.

'Lord Commander Eidolon,' said Lucius, 'is your superior officer. You would do well to remember that.'

'I know the chain of command,' snapped
Solomon, 'and as ranking captain, I am *your* superior officer. You would do well to remember that.'

Lucius nodded hurriedly as Solomon continued.
'So what really happened on Murder?'

'Exactly what Lord Commander Eidolon said happened,' said Lucius.

'Is that true, Captain Tarvitz?' asked Solomon.

'You dare call me a liar?' demanded Lucius, his
hand twitching towards his sword, a weapon forged
in the Urals by the Terrawatt Clan during the Unification Wars.

Solomon saw the gesture and turned to face
Lucius, squaring his shoulders as though in expectation of a fight. Where Captain Demeter was taller
than Lucius, broader in the beam and undoubtedly
stronger, Lucius was the more slender of the pair and
was certainly faster. Tarvitz briefly wondered who
would prevail in such a conflict, but was thankful
that such a thing would never be tested.

'I remember the first time you came here, Lucius,'
said Solomon. 'I thought you had the makings of a
great officer and a fine warrior.'

Lucius beamed at being so remembered until
Solomon said, 'But I see now that I was wrong.
You're nothing but a lickspittle and a sycophant who
has failed to grasp the difference between perfection
and superiority.'

Tarvitz could see Lucius's face turn purple with
anger, but Solomon wasn't done yet. 'Our Legion
strives for purity of purpose by modelling itself on
the Emperor, beloved by all, but we should not
strive to be like unto him, for he is singular and
above all others. Its true our doctrines sometimes
make us seem aloof and haughty to others, but there

is no purity in pride. Never forget that, Lucius. Lesson over.'

Lucius nodded curtly, and Tarvitz could see that it was taking all of his self-control not to let his temper get the better of him. The colour drained from his face and Lucius said, 'Thank you for the lesson, captain. I only hope I can give you a similar lesson someday.'

Solomon smiled as Lucius bowed curtly, and turned on his heel to join Eidolon.

Tarvitz tried to hide a smile.

'He won't forget this, you know,' he warned.

'Good,' said Solomon. 'Perhaps he might learn from it.'

'I wouldn't count on it,' said Tarvitz. 'He's not a fast learner.'

'But you are, eh?'

'I serve to the best of my abilities.'

Solomon laughed. 'You're a tactful one, Saul, I'll give you that. You know, I had you down as a career line officer when I first saw you, but now I think you may go on to do great things.'

'Thank you, Captain Demeter.'

'Solomon. And once this meeting is over, I think you and I should have a talk.'

THE SURFACE OF Twenty-Eight Four was the most beautiful sight Solomon had ever seen. From orbit, the planet's surface appeared peaceful; the land plentiful, the oceans a clear blue and the atmosphere flecked with spiral patterns of clouds. Atmospheric readings showed the planet had a breathable atmosphere, untouched by the pollution that choked so many Imperial worlds, turning them into nightmarish visions of an industrial hell, and electromagnetic surveyors reported no signs of intelligent life.

Detailed surveys would need to wait for the planet's official compliance, but aside from what looked like the ruins of a long vanished civilisation, the planet appeared to be completely deserted.

In short, it was perfect.

Four Stormbirds had touched down high on the rocky cliffs at the mouth of a wide valley. A majestic range of mountains towered above them, their soaring peaks capped with snow despite the temperate climate. As the gritty dust of their landing dispersed, Fulgrim had led his warriors onto the surface of the next world to be brought into the fold of the Imperium.

Solomon stepped down from his Stormbird and looked around this new world with great hope as Julius and Marius disembarked from their aircraft. Lord Fulgrim marched alongside Julius, and Saul Tarvitz followed behind Marius. Astartes spread out to secure the perimeter of the position, but Solomon already knew that such measures weren't necessary. There was no enemy to fight here, no threat to overcome. This world was as good as theirs already.

As soon as his auto-senses confirmed that the atmosphere was breathable, he removed his helmet and took a deep breath, closing his eyes at the simple pleasure of breathing air that hadn't been through a multitude of filters and air scrubbers.

'You should keep your helmet on,' said Marius. 'We don't know for certain that the air is breathable.'

'According to my armour's sensors it's fine.'

'The Lord Fulgrim hasn't taken his helmet off yet.'

'So?'

'So you should wait until he does.'

'I don't need Lord Fulgrim to tell me the air's breathable, Marius,' said Solomon, 'and since when did you become such a worrier?'

Marius did not reply, but turned away as the rest of the warriors disembarked from the growling Storm-birds. Solomon shook his head and tucked his helmet into the crook of his arm, as he strode over the rocks to stand at the edge of the cliffs that over-looked the land far below.

Beyond the mountains, the landscape swept out before him in a vast swathe of green. Thick forests blanketed the lower slopes of the mountains, and a startlingly blue river flowed lazily along the bottom of the valley towards a far distant coast. Across the valley, he could see one of the tall ruins the orbital cartographer had indicated rising from a cluster of overgrown ferns. From here, it looked like one half of a great archway, but there was no sign of the structure it had once been part of.

From his vantage point, Solomon could see for hundreds of kilometres, the glitter of far-away lakes rippling on the horizon and wild beasts grazing on the plains far below. The wondrously fertile land of Twenty-Eight Four undulated into the mist shrouded distance and birds circled in the clear sky above.

How long had it been since they had seen a world as unspoiled as this?

Like many of the Emperor's Children, Solomon had grown to manhood on Chemos, a world that knew neither day nor night, thanks to a nebular dust cloud that isolated the planet from its distant suns. A perpetual grey twilight through which the stars never shone was all he had known, and his heart leapt to see such a beautiful, cloudless sky.

It was a shame that the coming of the Imperium would forever change this world, but such change was inevitable, for it was a matter of record that it had been claimed by the 28th Expedition in the name of the Emperor. Within days, Mechanicum pioneer teams and prospecting rigs would descend to the surface to begin the colonisation process, and exploitation of its natural resources. Solomon knew he was just a simple warrior, but as he looked into the eye of the world, he dearly wished there was some way for mankind to avoid such wanton destruction of the landscape.

With the light of science and reason they brought with them, could the Mechanicum not find some way to harness the resources of a planet without bringing the inevitable fallout of such industry: pollution, over-crowding and the rape of a world's beauty?

Such concerns were beyond Solomon and made no difference to him, for if this planet was as deserted as it appeared then they would move on soon, leaving a garrison of Lord Commander Fayle's Archite Palatines to protect the soon to be developed world of the Imperium.

'Solomon,' shouted Julius from the side of the Stormbirds.

He turned away from the stunning vista and made his way back to the assault craft.

'What's up?'

'Get your men ready,' said Julius. 'We're going down to take a look at that ruin.'

THE INTERIOR OF *La Fenice* had changed markedly over the last two months, reflected Ostian as he nursed another glass of cheap wine. Where once the place had possessed a faded bohemian chic, it now resembled some monstrously overblown theatre from a more decadent age. Gold leaf covered the walls and every sculptor on board had been commissioned to produce dozens of pieces for the multitude of newly erected plinths... almost every sculptor.

Artists painted frenziedly, colouring mighty frescoes on the walls and ceiling, and an army of seamstresses worked on the creation of a mighty embroidered theatre curtain. A vast space above the stage had been left for a great work that Serena d'Angelus was supposedly working on, but Ostian had seen nothing of his friend for weeks to verify this fact.

The last time he had seen Serena had been over a month ago and she had looked terrible, a far cry from the fastidious woman he had, if he was honest, begun to fall a little in love with. They had exchanged only a few words of greeting, before Serena had hurriedly and clumsily excused herself.

'I have to go and see her,' he said to himself, as though the act of saying the words aloud would make their realisation more likely.

A troupe of dancers and singers cavorted on the stage to a cacophonous racket that Ostian hoped wasn't supposed to be music. Coraline Aseneca, the beautiful remembrancer and actress who had denied him the chance to visit the surface of Laeran, stood centre stage. The true architect of that misfortune strutted like a martinet before the stage, screaming and yelling at the dancers and choral singers. Bequa Kynska's blue hair waved around her head like alien seaweed, and her dress flailed as she raged at the incompetence of those around her.

To Ostian's eye, the effect of what was being done to *La Fenice* was grotesque, the excess of the design rendering the overall aesthetic into a confused jumble of sensations. At least the bar area was still intact, the crazed interior designers not yet having the courage to try and shift several hundred surly remembrancers from their perches for fear of inciting a full scale riot.

A great many of those remembrancers gathered around the huge figure of an Astartes named Lucius. The pale-faced warrior regaled his audience with tales of a planet he called Murder, telling improbable tales of the Warmaster and Sanguinius, and of his own mighty deeds. Ostian thought it rather wretched that a mighty warrior such as an Astartes should seek so obviously to impress the likes of those that filled *La Fenice*, but he kept such thoughts to himself.

In the past, *La Fenice* had served as a place of relaxation, but the constant hammering, blaring 'music' and caterwauling from the stage had transformed it into a place where people simply came to complain and curse the fates that had seen them excluded from the process of its renovation.

'You notice it's all the folks that went down to Laeran that got to work on this place?' said a voice at his elbow. The speaker was a bad poet by the name of Leopold Cadmus. Ostian had spoken to him on a few occasions, but he had, thankfully, managed to avoid reading any of his poetry.

'I had, yes,' said Ostian as a shouting team of labourers tried to guide a lifter servitor in the placement of a libidinous statue of a naked cherub.

'Bloody disgrace is what it is,' said Leopold.

'That it is,' agreed Ostian, though he wondered what part someone like Leopold had expected to play in the work going on.

'I'd have thought someone like you would have been a definite to do something,' said Leopold, and Ostian couldn't miss the jealous edge to his statement.

He shook his head and said, 'I'd have thought so too, but looking at what they're doing to the place, I think I'm well out of it.'

'What do you mean?' slurred Leopold and Ostian realised the man was drunk.

'Well I mean, look at it,' he said, pointing towards the paintings along the nearest wall. 'The colours look as though a blind man has chosen them, and as for their subject matter, well, I'd expect some nudes in a theatre, but most of these are virtually pornographic.'

'I know,' smiled Leopold. 'It's wonderful isn't it?'

Ostian ignored the remark and said, 'Listen to that bloody music. I loved Bequa Kynska's work when I first heard it, but this is like a cat hung up by its tail outside a window and trying to stick to the panes of glass with its claws. As for the sculptures, I don't know where to start? They're crude, obscene and there's not one of them I'd consider finished.'

'Well, you are the expert,' said Leopold.

'Yes,' said Ostian, shivering as he remembered hearing that same sentiment recently.

It had been an ordinary day, the high-pitched tapping of his hammer and chisel filling the studio as he sought to render his vision into the stone. The statue was slowly coming to life, the armoured body of the warrior taking shape within the marble as Ostian had chipped away all that wasn't part of the form he had seen in his mind. His silver hands roamed the marble, the metriculators within his fingertips reading the stone to unlock the secret fault lines and stress points hidden within its mass.

Each stroke of the hammer was finely judged, delivered with an instinctive feel for the shape he was creating and a love and respect for the marble he worked with. From a slow beginning, where anger had been motivating his hammer blows, a new calmness and respect for his vision had softened his attacks on the marble, and he found the serenity that came with the satisfaction of seeing something beautiful emerge.

As he stepped back from the marble, he became aware of a presence within his chaotic studio. He turned to see a giant warrior in purple and gold plate armour, carrying a great, golden-bladed halberd. His armour was ornate, much more so than was common for an Astartes. The warrior's helm was winged and the frontal visor had been fashioned to resemble the countenance of a great bird of prey.

Ostian pulled down his dust-mask as another five identical warriors entered his shuttered studio, followed by a lifter servitor bearing a wide pallet upon which were three irregularly shaped objects draped in white cloth. Ostian immediately recognised the warriors as belonging to the Phoenix Guard, the elite praetorians of...

Fulgrim entered his studio and Ostian was stunned rigid at the towering presence of the primarch. The master of the Emperor's Children wore a simple robe of deepest red, woven with subtle purple and silver threads. His pale features were powdered, his eyes rimmed with copper ink and his silver hair was pulled back in an elaborate pattern of plaits.

Ostian had dropped to his knees and bowed his head. To be in such close proximity to a being of perfect beauty was like nothing Ostian had ever experienced. Yes, he had seen the Primarch of the Emperor's Children before, but to be in a confined space and have his dark eyes fixed upon him was akin to being rendered dumb and idiotic in the space of a moment.

'My lord, I...' began Ostian.

'Please stand, Master Delafour,' said Fulgrim, walking towards him. Ostian could smell the pungent aroma of the scented oils that had been rubbed into his skin. 'Genius such as yours need never kneel before me.'

Ostian slowly rose to his feet and tried to raise his head to look the primarch in the eye, but found his body unwilling to obey.

'You may look upon me,' said Fulgrim. Ostian suddenly felt as though his muscles were under the control of the primarch, and his head came up without any apparent command from his brain. Fulgrim's voice was like music, each syllable pronounced with perfect pitch and tone as though no other sound could have filled the air so appropriately.

'I see your work progresses,' said Fulgrim, walking around the shorn block of marble and admiring his work. 'I look forward to its completion. Tell me, will it be a representation of any particular warrior?'

Ostian nodded, trying and failing to find the right words to express his thoughts to this magnificent being.

'Who?' asked Fulgrim.

'It is to be the Emperor, beloved of all,' said Ostian.

'The Emperor,' said Fulgrim, 'a fine subject.'

'I thought it fitting,' said Ostian, 'given the perfection of the marble.'

Fulgrim nodded as he circled the statue with his eyes closed, running his hands over the marble much as Ostian had done only moments before. 'You have a rare gift, Master Delafour. You bring such life to the stone. Would that I could do similar.'

'I am told that you have a great gift for sculpture, my lord.'

Fulgrim smiled and shook his head fractionally. 'I can craft pleasing shapes, yes, but to bring it to life… that is something that frustrates me and with which I would ask your help.'

'My help?' gasped Ostian. 'I don't understand.'

Fulgrim waved his hand towards the lifter servitor, and one of the Phoenix Guard pulled back the cloths covering the objects on the pallet to reveal three statues carved in pale marble.

Fulgrim took him by the shoulder and guided him towards the three statues. All were of armoured warriors, and, by the markings carved on their shoulder guards, each was a company captain.

'I set out to sculpt the likeness of each of my captains,' explained Fulgrim, 'but as I finished the Captain of the Third, I began to feel that something was wrong, as though some essential truth was missing.'

Ostian looked at the sculptures, seeing the clean lines and exquisite detailing, even down to the perfectly captured expressions of the three captains. Every line of carving was immaculate and not a single trace of the sculptor's chisel was left upon the marble, as though each image had been pressed from a mould.

Even as he appreciated the perfection of the statues, Ostian felt no passion stirring within him as he would expect to feel from great art. Yes, the sculptures were perfect, but therein lay their flaw, for something of such technical splendour had nothing of the creator in it, no humanity that spoke to the viewer and allowed him a rare glimpse inside the artist's soul.

'They are wonderful,' he said at last.

'Do not lie to me, remembrancer,' said Fulgrim, and Ostian heard a curtness in the words that caused him to look up into the primarch's icy features. Fulgrim stared down at Ostian, and the expression the sculptor saw there chilled him to the bone.

'What would you have me say, my lord?' he asked. 'They are perfect.'

'I would have the truth,' said Fulgrim. 'Truth, like surgery, may hurt, but it cures.'

Ostian struggled to think of words that would not offend the primarch, for to do so seemed like the basest behaviour imaginable. Who could conceive of giving insult to someone of such beauty?

Seeing Ostian's dilemma, Fulgrim placed a reassuring hand on his shoulder and said, 'A good friend who points out mistakes and imperfections, and rebukes evil is to be respected as if he reveals a secret of hidden treasure. I give you leave to speak freely.'

The primarch's words were spoken softly, but they acted like a key to a locked room within Ostian, opening the door to thoughts that he would not have dared give voice to before.

'It's as if... they are too perfect,' he said, 'as though they have been carved with the head rather than the heart.'

'Can it be possible for a thing be *too* perfect?' asked Fulgrim. 'Surely everything that is beautiful and noble is the product of reason and calculation.'

'Great art isn't about reason, it's about what comes from the heart,' said Ostian. 'You can work with all the technical perfection in the galaxy, but if there's no passion, then it is wasted effort.'

'There is such a thing as perfection,' snapped Fulgrim, 'and our purpose for living is to find that perfection and show it forth. Everything that limits us we have to put aside.'

Ostian shook his head, too caught up in his words to notice the primarch's growing anger. 'No, my lord, for the artist who aims at perfection in everything achieves it in nothing. It is the essence of being human that one does not seek perfection.'

'And what of your own work?' asked Fulgrim. 'Do you not seek perfection in it?'

'People throw away what they could have by insisting on perfection, which they cannot have, and looking for it where they will never find it,' replied Ostian. 'Were I to await perfection, my work would never be finished.'

'Well, you are the expert,' growled Fulgrim.

Ostian suddenly, horribly, became aware of the primarch's displeasure. Fulgrim's eyes were like gleaming black pearls, the veins on his cheeks pulsing with suppressed anger, and Ostian was filled with terror at the depths of yearning he saw within them.

He saw past the primarch's desire to render beauty in marble or painting to the obsessive compulsion to achieve the impossibility of perfection, a desire that would allow nothing to stand in its way. Too late, Ostian saw that despite asking for honesty, Fulgrim had not wanted honesty, he had wanted validation of his work and honeyed lies to prop up his towering ego.

'My lord…' he whispered.

'It is of no matter,' said Fulgrim acidly. 'I see that I was right to have spoken to you. I shall never lay chisel to marble again, for I am clearly wasting my time.'

'No, my lord, that's not what–'

Fulgrim raised a hand to cut him off and said, 'I thank you for your time, Master Delafour, and I will leave you to continue your imperfect work.'

Surrounded by his Phoenix Guard, the Primarch of the Emperor's Children had left his studio, leaving Ostian trembling with the horror of seeing inside Fulgrim's head.

Ostian shook off the memory of Fulgrim's visit to his studio as he realised that he was being spoken to. He looked up and saw the pale-skinned Astartes looking down at him.

'I am Lucius,' said the warrior.

Ostian nodded and drained his glass. 'I know who you are.'

Lucius smiled, pleased at the recognition. 'I'm told that you are a friend of Serena d'Angelus. Is that true?'

'I suppose so,' said Ostian.

'Then might you direct me to her studio?' asked Lucius.

'Why?'

'I wish her to paint me, of course,' smiled Lucius.

THIRTEEN

New Model/Maiden World/Mama Juana

DRESSED ONLY IN his surgical robes, Apothecary Fabius loomed over the operating slab where his subject lay and nodded to the apothecarion servitors. They lifted the chirurgeon device so that it slotted neatly into the interface unit mounted at his waist, and plugged in the connectors that meshed his own senses with the workings of the chirurgeon.

In effect, the device would give him multiple, independent arms that would all work in concert with his own thoughts, responding to his needs far quicker and more skilfully than any orderly or nurse could ever hope to. In any case, the surgery he was about to perform was best kept from the eyes of those who might baulk at what he must do for it to succeed.

'Are you comfortable, my lord?' asked Fabius.

'Never mind about my comfort, damn you,' snapped Eidolon, clearly ill at ease and feeling vulnerable on the surgical table. The lord commander was stripped out of his armour and fatigues, lying naked upon the cold metal slab as he prepared to go under the Apothecary's knife.

Hissing, gurgling machines surrounded him, and the flesh of his neck and throat was covered in counterseptic gel. A cold blue fluorescence bathed his skin in a dead light, and the glass jars around the apothecarion were filled with all manner of abominable, fleshy growths, the purpose of which defied understanding.

'Very well,' nodded Fabius. 'I take it you have spoken to the captains under your command regarding their volunteering for augmentative surgery?'

'I have,' confirmed Eidolon. 'I expect most of them to report to you within the next few weeks.'

'Excellent,' hissed Fabius. 'I have such things to offer them.'

'Never mind about them,' said Eidolon, the powerful soporifics rendering his voice quiet and a little slurred. Fabius checked the machine monitoring the speed of the lord commander's metabolism and adjusted the flow of drugs into his system, mixing the composition with some chemicals of his own devising.

Eidolon's eyes darted nervously over to the spiking lines on the monitor's screen, and Fabius could see a light sheen of sweat on his subject's brow.

'I am sensing a certain reluctance on your part to relax, my lord,' said Fabius, the cold light gleaming from the multiple scalpel blades he held poised above Eidolon.

Eidolon's face twisted in anger. 'Are you surprised, Apothecary? You are about to cut my throat open and implant an organ the purpose of which you still haven't told me.'

'It is a modified tracheal implant that will bond with your vocal chords and should allow you to produce a nerve paralysing shriek similar to that employed by certain warrior breeds of the Laer.'

'You are implanting me with xenos organs?' asked Eidolon, horrified.

'Not as such,' said Fabius with a toothy grin, 'though there are strands taken from the alien genome I chose to mesh with Astartes gene-seed mutated under controlled conditions. Essentially, I will be adding a new organ to your makeup, one that you will be able to trigger at will in battle.'

'No!' cried Eidolon. 'I do not wish this, not if it requires xenos filth to be implanted in me.'

Fabius shook his head. 'I am afraid it is too late to back out now, my lord. Fulgrim has authorised my work and you demanded that I work on you upon your return. What was it you wanted? Oh, yes, to be my greatest success, faster, stronger and more deadly than ever before.'

'Not like this, Apothecary!' shouted Eidolon. 'Cease what you are doing now!'

'I can't do that, Eidolon,' said Fabius, matter-of-factly. 'The soporifics are rendering you immobile and the samples I am to implant will not survive if they are not grafted to a host body. Why struggle? You'll feel so much better when I'm finished.'

'I will kill you!' snapped Eidolon. Fabius smiled as he saw the lord commander attempt to free himself. Such efforts were wasted, for the drugs being pumped around his system, and the metal restraints, held him fast to the table.

'No, Eidolon,' said Fabius. 'You won't kill me, for I will deliver on my promise to you. You will be more deadly than ever before. You should also remember that a warrior's life is a dangerous life, and that you will be under my knife many more times before this crusade reaches its climax, so do you really want to threaten me? Let the drugs take you, and when you wake you will be the model for how our beloved Legion is to take the next evolutionary leap forward!'

Fabius smiled and the scalpels descended.

EVEN BEFORE THEY reached the ruin on the other side of the valley, Solomon could tell that it was not a ruin after all, its structure intact and showing no signs of having been part of a larger building. However, having no better idea of what the unusual structure was, Solomon decided that 'ruin' was as good a word for it as any.

Shaped like the upper half of a bow stave, the curving structure reached to around twelve metres in height, its base set into an oval platform formed from the same smooth, porcelain-like substance as the ruin itself. The arch it described was graceful and alien, though it displayed none of the disturbingly excessive qualities of the Laer architecture.

In fact, thought Solomon, it was beautiful in its own way.

Once again, the Astartes spread out to surround their leaders as they approached the alien ruin. Solomon felt a curious apprehension at the sight of the structure, for it did not look like a building that had been abandoned for millennia.

For one thing, its surface was unblemished by so much as a single stain, moss or weathering, and the smooth stones that dotted its surface gleamed as though freshly polished.

'What is it?' asked Marius.

'I don't know,' replied Solomon, 'a marker perhaps?'

'A marker for what?'

'A boundary, maybe?' suggested Saul Tarvitz to general nods. 'But between whom?'

Solomon turned to see what Fulgrim made of it, and was shocked to see tears running down his primarch's face. Julius stood next to the primarch, his own face also streaked with tears. He looked around to see what his fellow captain's made of this, seeing that they were similarly stunned to see such a sight.

'My lord?' said Solomon. 'Is... is something the matter?'

Fulgrim shook his head and said, 'No, my son. Do not be alarmed, for I do not weep out of pain or anguish, but for beauty.'

'For beauty?'

'Yes, for beauty,' said Fulgrim, turning and extending his arms to encompass the wondrous landscape around them. 'This world is incomparable to anything we have thus far seen in our travels, is it not? Where else have we seen marvels laid out before us with such perfection? Nothing of this world is wanting and, were such things possible, I would believe that such a place could not come about by accident.'

Solomon followed his primarch's gaze, seeing the same natural marvels laid out before him, but unable to feel as moved as his commander. Julius nodded in time with Fulgrim's words, but of the four captains present, he alone appeared to have been affected in the same manner as the primarch.

Perhaps Marius had been correct to insist on the wearing of helmets, for surely there must be some undetected agent within the planet's atmosphere that had affected them so. But any agent capable of affecting a primarch would have long since affected him.

'My lord, perhaps we should return to the *Pride of the Emperor*?' he suggested.

'In time,' nodded Fulgrim. 'I wish to remain a little longer, for we shall not return here. We will enter the planet in our records and move on, leaving it untouched, for to despoil a place such as this would be a crime.'

'My lord,' said Solomon. 'Move on?'

'Indeed, my son,' smiled Fulgrim. 'We shall take our leave of this place and never return.'

'But you have already designated this world as Twenty-Eight Four,' Solomon pointed out. 'It is a world of the Emperor and is subject to Imperial laws given to us by him to uphold without equivocation. To abandon it without leaving armed forces to impose compliance and defend it against enemies is contrary to our mission amongst the stars.'

Fulgrim rounded on Solomon and said, 'I know our mission, Captain Demeter. You should not presume that I do not.'

'No, my lord, but the fact remains that to leave this world unoccupied would be contrary to the word of the Emperor.'

'And you have spoken with the Emperor on this?' snapped Fulgrim, and Solomon felt his objections withering under the intensity of the primarch's gaze. 'You claim to know his will better than one of his sons? I stood with the Emperor and Horus on the surface of Altaneum as its inhabitants destroyed the planet's ice caps and flooded their world beneath the oceans to destroy natural beauty that had taken billions of years to form, rather than allow us to take it from them. The Emperor told me that we must not make such mistakes again, for the galaxy will be worthless if we win it as a wasteland.'

'The Lord Fulgrim is correct,' said Julius. 'We should leave this place.'

Solomon felt his resolve harden in the face of Julius's support of the primarch, for he heard the tone of the sycophant in his friend's words.

'I agree with Captain Demeter,' added Saul Tarvitz, and Solomon had never been so glad to hear another's voice. 'A planet's beauty should have no bearing on whether or not we render it compliant.'

'Whether you agree or not is irrelevant,' growled Marius. 'Lord Fulgrim has spoken and we must obey his will. That is our chain of command.'

Julius nodded, but Solomon couldn't believe how easily they were going along with what was tantamount to disobeying the word of the Emperor.

OVER THE COURSE of the next two weeks, the 28th Expedition came upon another five worlds of a similar nature to Twenty-Eight Four, but each time, the fleet moved on without claiming it in the name of the Emperor. Solomon Demeter's frustration grew daily at the expedition's apparent unwillingness to enforce the Emperor's will upon these empty worlds, and no one other than he and Saul Tarvitz appeared to find it unusual to find such paradisiacal worlds unoccupied.

Indeed, the longer the expedition spent in the Perdus Region, the greater Solomon's conviction became that these worlds had not been abandoned but were, in fact *awaiting* their inhabitants. He had no facts upon which to base this supposition, save a feeling that the worlds they had seen thus far were too perfect, as though they had been deliberately fashioned rather than allowed to develop on a natural path.

He spoke less and less to Julius over the course of their travels through the Perdus Region, the Captain of the First spending much of his time either in the archive chambers or with the primarch. Marius appeared to have earned back his favour in the eyes of Fulgrim, for more and more, it was the warriors of the First and Third who accompanied him to the surface of each newly discovered world.

Saul Tarvitz had become a newfound ally, and Solomon had spent a great deal of time in the training halls with him. The man believed himself to be a line officer through and through, but Solomon could see the seed of greatness within him, even if he could not. Throughout their training sessions, he would encourage him to see his potential and stoke the fires of his ambition. Saul Tarvitz could be a great leader of men, given the chance, but Eidolon was his lord commander, and it was for him to say whether Tarvitz would advance beyond his current station. Solomon had despatched numerous communications to Eidolon on Tarvitz's behalf, but thus far the lord commander had replied to none of his messages.

After the fourth world had been passed by without an Imperial presence despatched or a planetary governor put in place, Solomon had sought out Lord Commander Vespasian. They had met in the Gallery of Swords, a mighty processional hallway where marble likenesses of long dead heroes of the Legion looked down upon their successors.

The Gallery formed part of the central spine of the *Andronius*, a strike cruiser that Fulgrim favoured as his second flagship, and was a place where a warrior could find solitude and inspiration from the presence of the dead heroes of his Legion.

Vespasian stood before the graven image of Lord Commander Illios, a warrior who had fought with Fulgrim against rival tribes of Chemos, and who

helped in the transformation of their home from a
hellish world of death and misery to one of culture
and learning.

The two warriors clasped hands, and Solomon said,
'It is good to see a friendly face.'

Vespasian nodded and said, 'You've been making
waves, my friend.'

'I've been honest,' countered Solomon.

'Not always the best way these days,' said Vespasian.

'What do you mean?'

'You know what I mean,' said Vespasian, 'so let us
not fence with words, but simply share the truth, eh?'

'Suits me,' said Solomon. 'I never did have much
time for fancy words.'

'Then I will speak plainly and believe that you are a
warrior I can trust, for I fear that something terrible
has happened to our Legion. It has become decadent
and arrogant.'

Solomon nodded and said, 'I agree. There's a new
superiority come over the Legion. It's a word I've
heard from too many throats not to notice. I've
already heard some of what happened on Murder
from Saul Tarvitz, and if what he tells me is even half
true, then we are already earning enmity among the
other Legions for our high handedness.'

'Do you have any idea what might have begun this?'

Solomon shrugged. 'I'm not sure, but it was after
the Laeran campaign that things changed.'

'Yes,' agreed Vespasian, turning and walking along
the length of the gallery and passing a grand staircase
that led to one of the ship's apothecarions. 'I believe
that to be the case, though I do not know what could
have engendered such a dramatic transformation.'

'I've heard a lot of talk about that temple Lord Fulgrim
captured,' said Solomon. 'Perhaps there was something

inside that affected those who entered, some sickness or weapon that altered their minds. What if the Laer had some unknown power in that temple, some collective corruption in their consciousness that was passed to the Legion?'

'That sounds farfetched to me, Solomon.'

'Maybe it is and maybe it isn't, but have you seen the renovations Lord Fulgrim has ordered to be carried out in *La Fenice*?'

'No.'

'Well, I never saw the inside of the Laer temple, but from what I've heard, it sounds as though *La Fenice* is being turned into a replica of it.'

'Why would Lord Fulgrim replicate an alien temple on board the *Pride of the Emperor*?'

'Why don't you ask him?' said Solomon. 'You are a lord commander, it is your right to speak to Fulgrim.'

'I will indeed, Solomon, though I still don't understand what relevance the Laer temple has.'

'Perhaps that it's a temple is what's relevant.'

Vespasian looked sceptical. 'Are you suggesting that the power of their gods somehow affected our warriors? I won't suffer any talk of unclean spirits in this place of heroes.'

'No,' said Solomon hurriedly, 'not gods as such, but we know that there are foul things that can pour through the gates of the empyrean from the warp, do we not? Perhaps the temple was a place where such things could more easily pass between worlds. What if the power that filled the Laer came with us when we left?'

The two warriors stared at one another for long seconds before Vespasian said, 'If you are right then what can we do about it?'

'I don't know,' admitted Solomon. 'You should talk to Lord Fulgrim.'

'I will try to,' replied Vespasian. 'What will you do?'

Solomon chuckled and said, 'Stand firm and act with honour in all things.'

'That isn't much of a plan.'

'It's all I have,' said Solomon.

SERENA D'ANGELUS WATCHED with amazement as the work on *La Fenice* continued with wondrous speed and boundless creativity. Colours leapt off the walls, and music that felt as though it knew her very heart filled the once drab and seedy theatre. Artists of all description had worked on the décor, and the splendour all but took her breath away.

To be surrounded by such an embarrassment of talent made her realise just how much she still had to work on her own paintings, and how worthless her pathetic skills were. The mighty portraits of the Lord Fulgrim and Lucius still sat mockingly unfinished in her studio, both canvases torturing her with their incompleteness. To have beings of such wondrous, unimaginable beauty sitting before her, and yet be unable to blend the precise tones she needed had driven her to fresh heights of self-loathing and mutilation. The flesh of her arms and legs was scarred with cuts from a sharpened palette knife, her blood mixing with her paints to enrich the colours.

But it hadn't been enough.

Each droplet of blood held its vibrancy for only a short time, and Serena's mind had filled with dark terrors of what would befall her if she didn't finish her work or if it was ridiculed for being found wanting or somehow lacking in sensation.

She closed her eyes as she tried to picture the light and colour that had filled the temple on the floating atoll, but the memory flitted beyond her, elusive and forever out of sight. Her blood had enhanced the colours of her paints, and she had turned to ever more esoteric fluids and substances of her own flesh to improve it yet further.

Her tears rendered her whites luminous, her blood, the reds to fire, while her waste gave her shades of deep darkness she had not previously imagined possible. Each colour had awakened new sensations and passions she had, until now, been unaware of. That such things would have repulsed her only a few months previously never entered her head, for her all-consuming passion was in reaching the next high, the next level of sensation, for as each one was experienced it was soon forgotten like an ephemeral dream.

Weeping with frustration, Serena had smashed yet another painting, the crack of timber, the tear of the canvas and the pain of the jarring impact giving her a moment's pleasure, but even that had faded within seconds.

She had nothing more to give, her flesh was spent and had exhausted the limit of sensation it could give, but even as the realisation came to her, so too did the solution.

Serena made her way through *La Fenice* towards the bar area, which, though it was late, was still home to a great many remembrancers without the wit to retire for the night. She recognised a few souls, but avoided them, seeking out one who would be least likely to object to her attentions.

Serena ran a hand through her long hair, unkempt compared to its normal shine, but she had at least brushed it and tied it back in an effort to look halfway presentable. Her eyes scanned the patrons of the bar, smiling as she saw Leopold Cadmus sitting alone in a booth nursing a bottle of dark spirit.

She made her way through the bar towards his table and slid into the booth next to him. He looked up suspiciously, but brightened up as he saw a woman joining him. Serena had worn her most revealing dress and a low pendant that drew the eye to her breasts. Leopold did not disappoint her, his red-rimmed eyes immediately darting to her cleavage.

'Hello, Leopold,' she said. 'My name's Serena d'Angelus.'

'I know,' said Leopold. 'You're Delafour's friend.'

'That's right,' she said brightly, 'but let's not talk about him. Let's talk about you.'

'Me?' he asked. 'Why?'

'Because I've read some of your poetry,' she said.

'Oh,' said Leopold, suddenly crestfallen. 'Well, if you've come to be a critic, save your breath. I don't have the energy for another bloody review.'

'I'm not a critic,' she said, placing her hand over his. 'I liked it.'

'Really?'

'Really.'

His eyes lit up and his expression changed from that of a mean-spirited drunk to one of pathetic desperation, where suspicion is suddenly ousted at the faint hope of praise.

'I'd like you to read some to me,' she said.

He took a drink from the bottle and said, 'I don't have any of my books with me, but–'

'That's all right,' interrupted Serena. 'I have one in my studio.'

'You LIKE TO work in a mess,' said Leopold, wrinkling his nose at the aroma that filled her studio. 'How do you find anything?'

He ambled around the edges of her workspace, warily stepping over discarded pots of paint and smashed pieces of timber and canvas. He examined the few pictures that still hung on the wall with a critical eye, though she could tell that the images there meant nothing to him.

'I imagine all artistic types work in such disarray,' said Serena. 'Don't you?'

'Me? No,' replied Leopold, 'I work in a small cubicle with a data-slate and a stylus that only works half the time. Only the important remembrancers get to work in studios.'

She heard the bitterness in his voice and it thrilled her.

The blood was singing in her skull and she had to fight to control her breathing. She poured a deep red liquid into a pair of glasses from a bottle she had obtained from a sutler on the lower decks of the ship for just this occasion.

'I suppose I am lucky,' she said, picking her way through the detritus of her work. 'Although I know I really should do something about this mess. I hadn't known I was going to have company tonight, but when I saw you in *La Fenice*, I knew I just had to talk to you.'

He smiled at the flattery and took the offered glass, looking inquisitively at the viscous liquid within it.

'I... I hadn't expected anyone to want to hear my work,' he said. 'I was only able to come out to the 28th Expedition when the shuttle carrying the poets selected from the Merican Hive crashed.'

'Don't be foolish,' said Serena, raising her glass. 'A toast.'

'What are we drinking to?'

'To a fortuitous crash,' smiled Serena. 'Without which we might never have met.'

Leopold nodded and took a cautious mouthful of his drink, smiling in return as he found the taste to his liking. 'What is this?' he asked.

'It's called Mama Juana,' explained Serena. 'It's a mix of rum, red wine and honey combined with the soaked bark of the Eurycoma tree.'

'Exotic,' said Leopold.

'They say it's a powerful aphrodisiac,' she purred, draining her glass in one long swallow and hurling it across the room. He jumped as the glass shattered, leaving a red stain on the wall as the dregs of the liquid dribbled down.

Emboldened by the directness of her desire, Leopold drained his own glass and dropped it to the floor with the nervous laugh of one who cannot believe his luck.

Serena leaned forwards and wrapped her arms around his neck, pulling him in for a passionate kiss. He was stiff in her arms for a moment, startled by the sudden move, but slowly relaxed into the kiss. He put his hands on her hips as she eased herself into the curve of his body.

They stood locked together for as long as she could bear it, before she dragged him to the floor, where she tore at his clothes in a frenzy, scattering paint and overturning her easels. The sensation of Leopold's hands on her body was repulsive, but even that made her want to cry with pleasure.

At one point he broke the kiss, blood dripping from his lip where she had bitten it, a look of bemused concern plastered across his idiot features. She pulled him tight to her body and rolled on top of him as they coupled like wild animals in the wreckage of her studio.

At last his eyes widened and his hips spasmed. She reached down to the floor to snatch up her sharpened palette knife.

'What...?' was all he managed before she slashed the blade across his throat. His blood sprayed in an arcing jet as he thrashed in his death throes.

Sticky red fluid covered her as Leopold convulsed, and this time she laughed at the wash of sensation that flooded her body. He gurgled beneath her as his lifeblood pumped out of him and his hands clawed at her in desperation. Blood pooled in a vast lake beneath Leopold, and Serena stabbed her knife into his neck again and again. His struggles grew weaker and weaker, while her pleasure heightened to an explosive climax.

Serena remained on top of Leopold's body until his convulsions ceased and his flailing arms fell to the floor. She rolled away, her flesh heaving and her heart thudding against the inside of her chest in a wild drumbeat.

She heard a last rattle of breath escape his ruined throat, and smiled to herself as she smelled his bowels and bladder voiding in death. Serena lay still for some moments, savouring the sensation of the kill, and taking pleasure in the thunder of her blood and the warmth within her.

What wonders might she work upon the canvas with such materials?

On THE THIRTIETH day after the 28th Expedition's arrival in the Perdus Region, a great many of the questions that had arisen following the discovery of the uninhabited paradise worlds were finally answered. Travelling in the vanguard of the expedition, the *Proudheart* was the first to pick up signs of the intruders.

Word flashed back to the fleet, and within moments, every ship was at battle readiness, gun ports unmasked and torpedoes loaded into their tubes. The alien vessel made no overtly hostile moves, and the *Pride of the Emperor* surged forward to join the *Proudheart* over the objections of Captain Lemuel Aizel.

At last the flagship of the Emperor's Children detected the presence of the enemy vessel, though its surveyor officers fought to keep the signal constant, for it kept fading in and out of the display.

Repeated hails were met with walls of static, though the fleet's astropaths reported a curious deadening of their warp vision, similar to that which had long shielded the region from the sight of Navigators and telepaths.

At last the forward elements of the fleet came into visual range of the lone vessel and it appeared on screen as a faint, slightly blurred outline.

Its true size was impossible to determine with any accuracy, but ship logisters estimated its length at between nine and fourteen kilometres. A vast triangular slice curved above the hull like a billowing sail, and even as the image resolved in the centre of the viewing bay, a voice sounded over the ship's vox system, crystal clear and speaking in perfect Imperial Gothic.

'My name is Eldrad Ulthran,' said the voice. 'In the name of Craftworld Ulthwé, I bid you welcome.'

FOURTEEN

To Tarsus/The Nature of Genius/Warning

SOLOMON KEPT A close eye on the assault warriors of the eldar delegation, their movements fluidly lethal in a way his could never be. A curving sword was sheathed across each of their backs, and they all carried delicate pistols holstered at their waists. Pale helmets of fearsome warrior aspects and scarlet plumes obscured their faces, and their smooth, segmented armour was formed of the same substance as the ruin they had seen on Twenty-Eight Four.

'They don't look much,' whispered Marius. 'A strong wind would break them in two.'

'Don't underestimate them,' warned Solomon. 'They are deadly warriors and their weapons are lethal.'

Marius looked unconvinced, but nodded in response to his fellow captain's wisdom for Solomon had faced the warriors of the eldar before.

He remembered fighting through the wind-lashed forests of Tza-Chao, where the Luna Wolves and the Emperor's Children had battled side by side against a piratical force of eldar reavers. What had started as a fairly straight up and down fight had degenerated into a bloody brawl in the depths of a storm, with weapons useless and brute strength and ferocity the only tools of destruction. He remembered the shrieking horror of blades that had charged from the trees with howls that chilled the blood, and he remembered watching as one Luna Wolf had garrotted a nameless eldar champion with a length of dirty, rusted wire in the rain.

Solomon remembered the walking monstrosities, taller than a Dreadnought, which had stalked the dark forest, like giants of legend, crushing Astartes in their mighty fists and destroying armoured vehicles with shoulder mounted cannons of unimaginable power.

No, thought Solomon, the eldar were not to be underestimated.

The encounter with the craftworld had come as a great surprise to the 28th Expedition, and had been greeted with guarded hostility until it became clear that the eldar had no apparent aggressive intent. Fulgrim himself had spoken to this Eldrad Ulthran, an individual who claimed to guide the craftworld, though he had fallen short of claiming to be its leader.

Thus began an elaborate ballet of proposal and counterproposal, with neither side willing to allow the other upon its ships. The calls for war were strident, with Solomon's loudest of all as he, Julius, Marius, Vespasian and Eidolon gathered in the primarch's staterooms to hear why they had not yet attacked the eldar, as their mandate of conquest demanded.

Fulgrim's quarters were a riot of paintings and sculpture, and Solomon had been quietly disconcerted to see a statue bearing his own features at the far end of the stateroom, standing next to ones of Julius and Marius.

'They are aliens!' he had said. 'What more reason do we need to make war upon them?'

'You heard what Lord Fulgrim said, Solomon,' said Julius. 'There is much we can learn from the eldar.'

'I know you don't believe that, Julius. I fought alongside you on Tza-Chao and you know exactly what they're capable of.'

'Enough!' Fulgrim had shouted. 'I have made my decision. I do not believe the eldar come with hostile intent, for they are but one vessel and we are many. They offer us friendship and I will honour that friendship as honest, unless proven otherwise.'

'When a sinister person means to be your enemy, they always start by trying to become your friend,' said Solomon. 'This is a sham and they mean us ill, I know it.'

'My son,' said Fulgrim, taking him by the arm, 'there is no man, however wise, who has not at some time in his youth said or done things that are so unpleasant to him in later life that he would gladly expunge them from his memory if he could. In years to come, I will not be haunted by the guilt of all the good I didn't do.'

The discussion, such as it was, had ended, and all but Eidolon and Julius had been dismissed to return to their companies. Further communication with the eldar had yielded no further unlocking of the impasse to a conference, until Eldrad Ulthran had offered a meeting on a world named Tarsus.

Such a solution had been deemed acceptable, and the ships of the 28th Expedition had followed the craftworld on a stately voyage through the Perdus Region towards yet another verdant world of beauty that was as empty of life as all the others had been before it. Co-ordinates had been transmitted to the *Pride of the Emperor*, and after yet more wrangling, the size of both group's deputations were agreed upon.

A Thunderhawk had brought them to the surface of Tarsus as the sun dropped towards the horizon. They had landed atop a rounded hillock, on the edge of a large forest, amid the ruins of what must at one time have been a stately dwelling of some description. As the clouds of their landing had dissipated, Solomon saw the eldar were already waiting for them, though the expedition fleet had detected no shuttles or landers detaching from the craftworld.

Solomon felt nothing but apprehension as he stared down at the eldar deputation. Lord Commanders Vespasian and Eidolon flanked Fulgrim, with Solomon, Julius, Marius, Saul Tarvitz and Lucius bringing up the rear.

The eldar gathered around an arched structure identical to the one they had seen on Twenty-Eight Four. A group of warriors in bone-coloured armour and high crests stood around the arch, each of them carrying a pair of long-bladed swords across their backs. Behind them, tall figures in dark plate stood sentinel with long barrelled weapons, while a pair of hovering tanks with jutting prows circled the perimeter. The air shimmered beneath the gracefully skimming vehicles and clouds of dust were kicked up by the mechanism that kept them in the air.

At the centre of the group of eldar, a slender figure robed in a dark tunic and wearing a high helm of bronze sat cross-legged at a low table of polished dark wood. He carried a long staff and beside him stood one of the giant walking war machines that Solomon had dreaded ever since the battle on Tza-Chao. It carried a sword as long as an Astartes warrior was tall, and its graceful limbs belied the fearsome power and strength within it. Though the golden sweep of its curved head was completely featureless, Solomon felt sure that it was looking right at him with nothing but scorn.

'Quite a gathering,' whispered Julius, and Solomon heard an eager edge to his voice.

Solomon said nothing, too intent on watching for the slightest hint of danger.

You BELIEVE HE *is the one?*

'I do not know,' said Eldrad as the voice of Khiraen Goldhelm echoed in his mind, 'and that troubles me.'

The fates are not clear?

Eldrad shook his head, knowing the mighty wraithlord was uneasy at this meeting Eldrad had urged with the mon-keigh. The long dead warrior's counsel had been to attack the humans as soon as they had violated eldar space, destroying them before they even knew the eldar were there, but Eldrad had sensed there would be something different in this encounter.

'I know that this one will be a great player in the bloody drama set to unfold, but I cannot see whether it will be for good or ill. His thoughts and future are hidden from me.'

Hidden? How is such a thing possible?

'I do not know for sure, but I believe that whatever dark forces his Emperor employed in the creation of these primarchs renders many of them as little more than spectres in the warp. I cannot read this one, nor sense anything of his future.'

He is mon-keigh; he has no future but war and death.

Eldrad could sense the contempt the dead warrior had for the humans, for it had been a human blade that had ended his life and left him a ghost in the shell of a mighty war machine. He tried not to let the wraithlord's anger cloud his judgement of the humans, but it was difficult not to agree with him, given the evidence of their blood-soaked history.

Yes, the mon-keigh were a brutal race that lived for conquest, but these humans had behaved in a manner unlike any he had witnessed before, and he fervently hoped that this Fulgrim might be the one with the wit to bear his warning to the ruler of his race.

You know I speak true, urged Khiraen. *You have seen it haven't you, the great war that set them at one another's throats?*

'I have seen it, great one,' nodded Eldrad,

Then why seek to prevent it? Why should we care whether the mon-keigh destroy one another in fire and blood? I say let them, for the life of one eldar is worth ten thousand of theirs!

'I agree,' said Eldrad, 'but I see a time in the grim darkness of the far future when our failure to act will be our undoing.'

I hope you are right, farseer and that this is not simply arrogance.

Eldrad looked up at the armoured warriors gathered on the hillside and felt a shiver within his soul as he hoped the same thing.

✠ ✠ ✠

FULGRIM LED THE way down the hillside without pre-amble, resplendent in his battle armour and a cloak of bright gold that shone dazzlingly in the fading light. His silver hair was pulled into a number of elaborate plaits and he wore a glittering golden wreath about his brow. Powder had been applied to his skin, rendering it even paler than normal and coloured inks had then been applied to his cheeks and eyes in elegant swirls.

Fulgrim had come armed, the silver sword belted at his waist, and to Solomon's eyes his master was dressed in a manner more akin to some theatrical impresario's vision of a primarch rather than the reality.

He kept his own counsel, however, as the Emperor's Children reached the bottom of the hill, and the eldar robed in black rose smoothly from the ground and bowed before Fulgrim. The faint hint of a smile ghosted across the alien's features, and Solomon tensed as he removed his bronze helmet.

'Welcome to Tarsus,' said the eldar, bending at the waist in a formal bow.

'You are Eldrad Ulthran?' asked Fulgrim, returning the bow.

'I am,' said Eldrad, turning to face the towering war machine. 'And this is Wraithlord Khiraen Gold-helm, one of Craftworld Ulthwé's most revered ancients.'

Solomon shivered as the towering war machine inclined its head curtly, the gesture of welcome ren-dered as one of hostility.

Fulgrim looked up at the giant wraithlord and returned the gesture, a nod of respect between war-riors, as Eldrad spoke again, 'And from your stature you must be Fulgrim.'

'Lord Fulgrim of the Emperor's Children,' put in Eidolon.

Again Solomon saw the ghost of a smile, and his jaw clenched at the insult he felt sure was implicit in such a gesture.

'I apologise,' said Eldrad. 'No disrespect or offence was intended. I simply sought to establish a dialogue based on virtue rather than rank.'

'No offence is taken,' assured Fulgrim. 'Your point is well made, for it is not birth or rank, but virtue that makes the difference between men. My lord commanders are simply anxious that my station be recognised. Although it will make no difference to our parlay, it is still unclear to me what rank you hold among your people.'

'I am what is called a farseer,' said Eldrad. 'I guide my people through the challenges of whatever the future might hold and offer guidance as to how best to meet those challenges.'

'Far*seer*…' said Fulgrim. 'You are a witch?'

Solomon's hand itched to reach for his sword, but he fought the impulse. The primarch had expressly forbidden them to draw their weapons unless he did so first.

Eldrad appeared unmoved by Fulgrim's provocative word, but shook his head slightly.

'It is an ancient term, one that perhaps does not translate well into your language.'

'I understand,' said Fulgrim, 'and I apologise for speaking without thought.'

Solomon knew his primarch better than that, and saw that Fulgrim had very deliberately chosen the word to gauge Eldrad's reaction to it.

Against a human counterpart such a ploy might have worked, but the farseer's features gave nothing away.

'So as a farseer, you are the craftworld's leader?'

'Craftworld Ulthwé has no formal leader as such, more a… council I suppose you would call it.'

'Then do you and Khiraen Goldhelm represent that council?' pressed Fulgrim. 'I desire very much to know with whom I deal.'

'Deal with me,' promised Eldrad, 'and you deal with Ulthwé.'

ONCE AGAIN OSTIAN rapped on the shuttered door to Serena's studio, telling himself he would give her five more minutes to answer before heading back to his own studio. The statue of the Emperor was coming on in leaps and bounds, as though some inner muse guided his hands, though there was still much to be done and this visit to Serena's was taking up much needed time.

He sighed as he realised that Serena wasn't going to answer. Then he heard shuffling behind the shutter and the faint, but unmistakable smell of an unwashed body.

'Serena? Is that you?' he asked.

'Who's that?' said a ragged and hoarse voice.

'It's me, Ostian. Open the shutter.'

Silence was his only answer and he feared that whoever the voice belonged to was simply going to ignore him. He raised his hand to knock once more when the shutter began to rattle upwards. Ostian stood back, suddenly nervous about who he might come face to face with.

Eventually the shutter rose enough for him to see who had opened it.

It was a woman, but one he would have expected to see hawking for loose change from the gutters of a downhive sump. Her long hair was greasy and unkempt, her features gaunt and wasted, and her clothes ragged and stained.

'Who are...?' he began, but the words died in his throat as he realised that this decrepit excuse for a human being was Serena d'Angelus.

'Throne alive!' cried Ostian, rushing forward to take her by the shoulders. 'What's happened to you, Serena?'

He looked down at her arms, seeing scores of cuts and scars crisscrossing her flesh. Dried blood was still crusted on the more recent wounds, and even he could tell that many were infected.

She looked at him with dull eyes, and he all but dragged her back into the studio, shocked at the disaster area it had become. What had happened to the meticulously neat artist who had kept every part of her life organised and compartmentalised? Paint pots were strewn all over the floor, and broken canvases lay around like so much garbage. A pair of easels still stood in the middle of the studio, but he could not see what had been painted on them for they were facing away from him.

Red stains streaked the walls and a large plastic barrel sat in one corner of the room. Even from here, Ostian could smell the rotten, acidic reek from it.

'Serena, what in the name of all that's sane has happened here?'

She looked up at him, as though seeing him for the first time and said, 'Nothing.'

'Well clearly something has happened,' he said, his anger growing in proportion to her indifference. 'I mean, look at this place: paint everywhere, smashed paintings... and that stench? Throne, what *is* that? It smells like something died in here.'

Serena shrugged and said, 'I've been too busy to clean.'

'Well that's just nonsense,' he said. 'I was always far messier than you and my studio's not this bad. Really, what's been going on here?'

He wandered through the smashed wreckage that filled Serena's studio, avoiding a large pool of reddish brown paint in the middle of the floor, and making his way towards the large barrel in the corner of her studio.

Before he reached it he felt a presence behind him and turned to see Serena right behind him, one hand held poised to reach out to him, the other tucked in the folds of her dress as though holding something.

'Don't,' said Serena. 'Please, I don't want to...'

'Don't want to what?' asked Ostian.

'Just don't,' she said, and he could see the tears welling up in her eyes.

'What have you got in that barrel?' asked Ostian.

'It's engraver's acid,' she said. 'I'm... I'm trying something new.'

'Something new?' repeated Ostian. 'Switching from acrylics to oils is something new. This is... well, I don't know what this is, but it's something insane if you ask me.'

'Please, Ostian,' she sobbed. 'Please go.'

'Go? Not until I find out what's been happening with you.'

'Ostian, you have to go,' begged Serena. 'I don't know what I might do.'

'What are you talking about, Serena?' asked Ostian, grabbing her by the shoulders. 'I don't know what's the matter with you, but I want you to know that I'm here for you. I'm an idiot and should have said something before now, but I didn't know how to. I knew you were hurting yourself because you didn't think your talent was worth anything, but you're wrong, it is. It so is. You have a rare gift and you have to realise it, because this... this is not healthy.'

She sagged into his arms, and he felt tears pricking his eyes as her body was convulsed by wracking sobs. His heart went out to her, though the wiring of his male brain could not understand the strangeness of her affliction. Serena d'Angelus was one of the most talented artists he had ever seen and yet she was tormented by delusions of her own inadequacy.

He pulled her tight and kissed the top of her head. 'It's all right, Serena.'

Without warning she pushed him away with a shriek of rage and shouted, 'No! No, it's not alright! Nothing lasts! No matter what I do it won't last. I think it was because he was inferior, no good. His talent wasn't able to sustain it.'

Ostian recoiled from her rage, not knowing who or what she was talking about, or what she meant. 'Serena, please, I'm trying to help.'

'I don't want your help,' she cried. 'I don't want anyone's help. I want to be left alone!'

Utterly confused, he backed away from her, sensing on some instinctive level that he was in danger just by being there. 'I don't know what's wrong with you, Serena, but it's not too late to come back from whatever's eating away at you inside. Please let me help you.'

'You don't know what you're talking about, Ostian. It's always been so easy for you, hasn't it? You're a genius and inspiration comes naturally to you. I've seen you do great things without even thinking about it, but what about the rest of us? What about those of us that aren't geniuses? What do we do?'

'Is that what you think?' he asked, outraged at her dismissal of his skill, as if it was the inevitable result of some intangible force within him spilling from him in a torrent. 'You think it's easy for me? Let me tell you this, Serena, inspiration comes of working every day. People think that my talent rises each morning, rested and refreshed like the sun, but what they don't appreciate is that, like everything else, it waxes and wanes. It always seems so easy for those without talent to look on those who have it and say that it's easy for us, but it isn't. I work every day to be as good as I am, and it annoys the hell out of me when mediocre people assume an air of knowing better than I do what makes good art. Appreciation of others work is a wonderful thing, Serena, it makes what is excellent in others belong to you as well.'

She backed away from him as he spoke, and he realised that he'd let his anger get the better of him.

Disgusted with himself, he stormed away as she reached for him, passing through the shutter and into the corridor beyond.

'Please, Ostian!' wailed Serena as he walked away. 'Come back! I'm sorry, I'm sorry! I need your help. Please!'

But he walked on.

THROUGHOUT THE JOCKEYING exchanges of greeting, Solomon had watched the motionless wraithlord behind the farseer. Its slender limbs seemed incapable of supporting its body and elongated golden head and curving crest. Solomon felt his skin crawl just looking at it, for though he knew such things could move with fearsome speed and agility, he felt no sense of life from the machine, as he did from a Dreadnought.

Even though nothing remained of the Old One within a Dreadnought's sarcophagus, save a ruined body hung in amniotic suspension, there was still a beating heart and living brain at its core. All he could sense from this monstrous creation was death, as though whatever dwelled within was little more than a ghost somehow bound to a lifeless shell.

Fulgrim nodded towards Eldrad and said, 'Very well, Eldrad Ulthran of Craftworld Ulthwé, you may deal with me as a representative of the Emperor of Mankind.'

Eldrad nodded graciously and gestured towards the low table. 'Sit, please, and let us talk and eat as travellers who find themselves on the same road.'

'That would be pleasant,' said Fulgrim, gracefully lowering himself to the ground and indicating that his captains should do the same, introducing each of them as they sat. Solomon adjusted his sword and sat at the table as the skimming tanks pivoted smoothly in the air and a ramp lowered gently to the ground from their rears.

Solomon sensed the tension in his fellow Astartes. He could almost feel the Phoenix Guard tighten their grips on their halberds. But no assault came from the interior of the vehicles, only a group of white-robed eldar bearing platters of food. They moved with such amazing poise and grace that their feet seemed to glide across the grass towards the table.

The platters were deposited, and Solomon saw that a feast had been laid before them: choice cuts of the most tender meat, fresh fruit and pungent cheese.

'Eat,' said Eldrad.

Fulgrim helped himself to meat and fruit as did Lord Commander Vespasian, but Eidolon refrained from eating. Julius and Marius likewise helped themselves, but for once, Solomon found himself in accordance with Eidolon and took nothing from the platters.

He noticed that Eldrad did not touch the meat, but ate only sparingly from a bowl of fruit.

'Does your kind not eat meat?' asked Solomon.

Eldrad turned his large oval eyes upon him, and Solomon felt as though he were a butterfly pinned to a wall. He saw great sadness in the farseer's eyes and, reflected in their ageless depths, he saw echoes of the great deeds he might yet achieve.

'I do not eat meat, Captain Demeter' said Eldrad. 'It is too rich for my palate, but you should try some, I am told it is very good.'

Solomon shook his head. 'No. What interests me more is why you choose now to reveal yourself to us. It is my belief that you have been shadowing us ever since we arrived here.'

Fulgrim shot him an irritated glance, but Eldrad pretended not to see it.

'Since you ask, Captain Demeter, yes, we have been shadowing you, for it is a curious thing to see your ships abroad in this region of space,' said Eldrad. 'We had thought that it was shrouded from your kind. How is it that you managed to reach it?'

Fulgrim put down his food and said, 'You have been shadowing us?'

'Merely a precaution,' said Eldrad, 'for the worlds you have encountered in your travels belong to the eldar race.'

'They do?'

'Indeed,' confirmed Eldrad. 'When first we realised you were traversing our territory, we thought to attack, but when we saw that you simply passed onwards without attempting to settle worlds that were not yours, I desired to know why.'

'I knew that to despoil such beautiful worlds would be wrong,' said Fulgrim.

'It *would* have been wrong,' agreed Eldrad. 'These maiden worlds have been awaiting the coming of my people for aeons. To try and take them from us would have been a grave mistake.'

'Is that a threat?' asked Fulgrim.

'A promise,' warned Eldrad. 'You have displayed a restraint we have not come to expect from your race, Lord Fulgrim. After all, you are led by a warrior known as the Warmaster and your aim is to conquer the galaxy for your own kind, regardless of the sovereignty or desires of the races with which you share it. I do not mean to antagonise you when I say that this is monstrously arrogant.'

Solomon expected Fulgrim's anger to be incandescent, but the primarch merely smiled and said, 'I am no expert on history, but did your race not once claim to have ruled the galaxy?'

'Claim? We did rule it once, and it was thanks to our arrogance and complacence that we lost it. But do not ask of such things again, for I will speak no more of those lost days.'

'Fair enough,' said Fulgrim, 'Empires rise and fall, civilisations come and go. For each it is tragic, but it is the way of things. One dynasty must die for another to rise and take its place. You cannot deny the human race its manifest destiny to rule the stars as you once did.'

'Manifest destiny,' laughed Eldrad. 'What does your race know of destiny? When things transpire in your favour you believe it to be destiny, but when you suffer disaster is that not also destiny? Who says destiny must be a good thing? I have seen sights that would make you curse destiny, and I know secrets that would shred your sanity were you to know but a fraction of them.'

Solomon felt the rising tension between the two leaders and knew that sooner or later this must end in blood. Clearly the Phoenix Guard were readying themselves for battle, and Solomon could see in the minute movements of the sword-armed eldar that they too sensed the escalation of words.

Instead of violence, Fulgrim simply laughed at Eldrad's words, as though he were enjoying the confrontation.

'We are a pair are we not? Needling at one another and fencing around the real issue.'

'And what is the real issue?' asked Eldrad.

'Why we are even speaking at all. You claim the worlds in this region are yours, but you have not settled them. Why? Your race fades, yet you cling to life aboard a starship when there are paradises awaiting you. You want more from us than simply to shepherd us away from your territories, so let us be honest with one another, Eldrad Ulthran of Craftworld Ulthwé. Why are we sitting opposite one another?'

'Very well, Fulgrim of the Emperor's Children, but I tell you now that you will not want to hear the real reason I desired to speak with you.'

'No?'

Eldrad shook his head sadly. 'No, for it will anger you greatly.'

'You know this do you?' asked Fulgrim. 'I thought you said you were no witch.'

'I need no powers of foresight to know my warning will anger you.'

'Tell me your warning and I will consider it objectively,' promised Fulgrim.

'Very well,' said Eldrad. 'At this very moment, the one you call Warmaster lies in death's shadow and there are forces beyond your comprehension battling for his soul.'

'Horus?' cried Fulgrim. 'He is injured?'

'He is dying,' nodded Eldrad.

'How? Where?' demanded Fulgrim.

'On the world of Davin,' said Eldrad. 'A trusted counsellor betrayed him, and now the powers of Chaos whisper lies wrapped in truth into his ears. They feed his vanity and ambition with a distorted vision of things yet to come.'

'Will he live?' cried Fulgrim, and Solomon heard anguish like nothing he had heard before.

'He will, but it would be better for the galaxy were he to perish,' said Eldrad.

Fulgrim slammed his fist down on the table, smashing it in two, and surged to his feet. His pale features blazed with anger. The Phoenix Guard lowered their halberds as the armoured eldar warriors flinched at his sudden rage.

'You dare wish the death of my dearest friend?' roared Fulgrim. 'Why?'

'Because he will betray you all and lead his armies against your Emperor!' said Eldrad. 'In one fell swoop, he will condemn the galaxy to thousands of years of war and suffering.'

FIFTEEN

The Worm at the Heart of the Apple/
War Calls/Kaela Mensha Khaine

AT FIRST, FULGRIM thought he'd misheard. Surely this alien could not be suggesting that Horus, most loyal son of the Emperor, would betray their father and lead his armies into civil war? The very idea was ludicrous, for the Emperor would never have appointed Horus to the position of Warmaster if he had not been utterly sure of his loyalty.

He searched Eldrad Ulthran's face for any sign of a jest or that this was all some hideous mistake, for there was no way such an insult could stand unchallenged. Even as he sought to find reason in this exchange, the voice in his head roared in anger.

This xeno filth means to sow the seeds of dissent among you!

'This is madness!' roared Fulgrim, his anger flaring. 'Why would Horus do such a thing?'

Eldrad rose from the ground as the giant wraithlord behind him widened its stance, and the

bone-armoured warriors reached for their swords.
Eldrad held up his staff to halt their warlike motions.
'His soul is being tempted with visions of power and
glory by the gods of Chaos. It is a battle he will not
win.'

Lies, lies, lies, lies, lies, lies, lies, lies, lies, lies, lies!

'Gods of Chaos?' cried Fulgrim, as a red mist of hate
fuelled power raced throughout his body. 'What in
the name of Terra are you talking about?'

Eldrad's implacable mask slipped and his face was
transformed in horror. 'You travel the warp and yet
you know not of Chaos? Khaine's blood! I see now
why they chose your race to strike at.'

'You speak in riddles, xenos,' said Fulgrim. 'I won't
stand for this.'

'You must listen,' pleaded Eldrad. 'The warp, as you
call it, is home to the most malign beings imaginable,
terrible energies that are elemental and ferocious.
They are gods that have existed since the dawn of
time and will outlast this guttering flame of a universe. Chaos is the worm at the heart of the apple and
the canker in the soul that devours from within. It is
the mortal enemy of all living things.'

'Then Horus will turn from such evil,' said Fulgrim,
his hand drawn towards his silver-hilted sword, the
purple crystal on the pommel winking with an alluring shimmer. The voice of his unspoken will
screamed at him.

Kill him! He will infect you with lies! Kill him!

'No,' said Eldrad, 'Horus will not turn from it, for it
promises him exactly what he wants to hear. He will
believe he does what is best for humanity, but he has
been blinded to the realities of what he is doing. The
gods of Chaos have woven falsehoods around him,

but these are mere fripperies that lesser minds will use to explain his betrayal. The truth is more prosaic. The fire of the Warmaster's ambition has been stoked from a steady flame to a roaring inferno, and it will damn the galaxy to an age of war and blood.'

'I should kill you for these words,' snarled Fulgrim.

'I am not trying to anger you, I am trying to warn you,' cried Eldrad. 'You have to listen to me. It is not too late to stop this, but you must act now. Warn your Emperor that he is betrayed and you will save billions of lives! The future of the galaxy is in your hands!'

'I will not listen to you!' roared Fulgrim, drawing his sword. Eldrad staggered as though a sudden force assailed him. The farseer's dark eyes flashed to the blade and his features twisted in an expression of horror and anguish.

'No!' cried Eldrad, as a great wind that seemed to rise from nowhere howled around the stunned observers. Fulgrim's blade swept out towards Eldrad's neck, cleaving the air in a sweeping, silver arc.

A fraction of a second before the sword took the farseer's head an enormous blade flashed and intercepted its deadly edge. An explosion of sparks burst before Eldrad and he staggered away from Fulgrim as the wraithlord stood erect, its huge sword drawing back to strike at the primarch.

Eldrad shouted, 'They are corrupted! Kill them!'

Fulgrim felt a massive swell of power fill him as he drew the sword, its blade rippling with after-images of vibrant purple energy. His Phoenix Guard and captains surged to their feet as he struck his blow against the farseer, and guns blazed as a vicious, short range firefight erupted.

The bone-armoured warriors charged with an ear-splitting shriek that tore at the nerves, and a hail of bolter fire cut down a handful before they hit home. Fulgrim left the warriors to his captains, as the Phoenix Guard charged the mighty, golden-helmed wraithlord.

You must kill him! The farseer must die before he ruins everything!

Fulgrim roared as he leapt after the farseer, the wraithlord's monstrous sword arcing towards him as the Phoenix Guard slashed at it with their golden blades. He rolled beneath the blow, rising to pursue the architect of this bloodshed. Eldrad Ulthran and the grim-faced warriors in black armour backed away from him towards the curving structure, as a pale nimbus of light began to gather at its base.

'I tried to save you,' said Eldrad, 'but you are already the unwitting tool of Chaos.'

The Primarch of the Emperor's Children swung his sword at the farseer, but his enemy vanished in a flare of light and his weapon clove only air. He roared in frustration as he realised that the structures were in fact teleportation devices.

He turned back to the battle raging behind him as a hail of energised bolts spat from the barrels of the nearest skimmer tank's guns. Its first shots had been hesitantly aimed, thanks to the presence of the farseer, but Fulgrim saw that no such caution restrained them now. The prow of the tank skimmed the grass as its pilot brought it around in a tight turn, expecting his quarry to flee, but Fulgrim had never run from an enemy in his life and wasn't about to start now.

Fulgrim leapt into the air just as the eldar pilot saw the danger and tried to gain height. It was already too late. The primarch's sword hacked through the side of the vehicle and tore downwards, ripping through its hull as he gave a bellow of hatred.

The tank's pronged front section dropped to the ground and the vehicle slewed around, the bevelled edge carving into the ground, flipping the vehicle over onto its side with a terrific crack of what sounded like splintering bone.

Bright energy exploded from the wreck in a huge plume of light, and Fulgrim laughed in triumph. He spun his sword and returned his attention to the clash of weapons, watching as the terrifying wraithlord reached down and crushed one of the Phoenix Guard in a massive fist. Armour cracked asunder and blood fell in a crimson rain as the warrior died. Fulgrim snarled in anger as he saw three of his elite praetorians lying twisted and broken at the machine's feet.

His captains fought with the warriors in bone armour, their swords a blur as shrieking war shouts filled the air over the ring of steel on bone. Fulgrim moved away from the blazing wreckage of the tank, his sword aimed at the gold-helmed war machine.

As if sensing his presence, the wraithlord turned its head towards him and hurled aside the dead warrior in its grip. Fulgrim could sense the ghost within the machine as a blazing hunger for vengeance and knew this thing wanted him dead as much as he desired to see it destroyed.

With a speed that shocked him, the wraithlord loped towards him, its agility terrifying. He stepped to meet it and ducked beneath a scything blow of its crackling blade, rising again to hack his sword into its slender arm. The blade bit a fingerbreadth before sliding clear, and Fulgrim felt the jarring vibration of the impact along the entire length of his body. The wraithlord's fist slammed into his chest and punched him from his feet, the eagle stamped breastplate cracking under the thunderous blow. Fulgrim grunted in pain, tasting blood on his lips.

The pain was enormous, but instead of laying him low it energised him, and he leapt to his feet with a wild cry of exultation. His wreath hung broken over his face and he ripped it clear, tearing out his plaits and smearing the powder and oils across his face.

Looking more like a feral savage than the Primarch of the Emperor's Children, Fulgrim once again launched himself at the wraithlord. Its huge sword slashed towards him, but he raised his own blade and the two met in a ferocious thunder of metal and fire. The purple gem in the pommel of Fulgrim's sword flared, and the wraithlord's blade exploded in a shower of bone fragments.

Fulgrim pressed his attack as the wraithlord reeled, and swung his sword in a murderous, two-handed swing at its legs. He roared as the blade smashed into its knee and tore through the joint with a shrieking howl of pleasure. Rippling coils of energy whipped from the wound as the great war machine swayed for the briefest moment before crashing to the ground.

Now finish it! Destroy what lies within its head and it will suffer a fate beyond death!

Fulgrim leapt on top of the struggling machine, smashing his fist into the smooth sheen of its golden face with a deafening war cry. The surface cracked and split under the force of his blow and he felt blood spring from his hand. He ignored the pain and hammered his fist against its head again and again, feeling the surface of the machine's carapace-like skull yield to his furious assault. It tried to reach up and hurl him from its body, but he lashed out with his sword, the blade hacking off its huge fist with an ease that had seemed impossible only moments before.

At last the golden helm cracked and Fulgrim tore the wraithlord's head open, revealing a smooth ceramic faceplate, pierced and woven with gold wire and engraved with silver runes. Its surface was studded with gleaming gems, and at the centre of this arrangement sat a pulsing red stone. Fulgrim could sense the fear emanating from this stone and reached down to pluck it from its mounting, a rising shriek of panic felt in the soul rather than heard. The stone was hot to the touch, and fiery lines danced within its depths, haunted shapes and alien features writhing within it.

He felt its anger and hatred towards him, but most of all he felt its dreadful, all-consuming fear of oblivion.

Fulgrim laughed as he crushed the stone in his fist, hearing a shrieking howl of anguish flee its destruction. He felt his sword grow warm, and looked down to see the gem at its pommel burn like an amethyst star, as though feeding on the spirit released from the stone.

How he knew this he did not know, but next to the elation he felt in victory, it seemed a minor mystery, and no sooner had the realisation surfaced than it was gone.

As the wondrous feeling of power faded, Fulgrim turned his face towards the battle being fought by his captains. They struggled against the shrieking warriors in bone armour, their swords fencing in a deadly ballet with these supremely skilled warriors. Behind them, the remaining enemy tank waited to support its fellow eldar, its guns useless while the combat raged.

Fulgrim raised his sword and charged.

ELDRAD CRIED OUT as he felt the soul of Khiraen Goldhelm torn from its spirit stone and cast into the void, alone and unprotected. He felt the great and terrible hunger of the Great Enemy devour the mighty soul of the warrior, and wept bitter tears of recrimination at his folly in attempting to parlay with the barbarous mon-keigh. Never again would he trust that their intentions could be anything other than hostile, and he vowed to remember forever the lesson Khiraen Goldhelm's loss had taught him.

The air still shimmered around him after his transit through the webway portal from the surface of Tarsus, and he could feel the psychic roar of violence running through the naked ribs of the craftworld's wraithbone skeleton. He could feel the lust for aggression from every eldar aboard and the racing, molten heartbeat of the Avatar of the Bloody-Handed God as it roused itself from the sealed wraithbone chamber at the heart of the craftworld.

How could he not have seen this? Fulgrim was already on a dark path, his soul embroiled in a secret war he did not even realise it was fighting. A dark and terrible force sought to dominate him, and though Fulgrim was resisting, Eldrad knew there was only one way such a battle could end. He knew now that this dark presence had been what shielded Fulgrim from his sight, jealously keeping its victim veiled so that none might unmask its designs.

The sword… he should have felt it the moment he laid eyes upon it, but the deceits of the Great Enemy had ensnared him with subtle illusions and rendered him blind to its presence. Eldrad knew that the essence of a powerful creature from beyond the gates of the empyrean lay bound within the sword, and that its influence was inexorably tainting the consciousness of the Primarch of the Emperor's Children.

Eldrad knew there was only one path open to him, and shouted, 'To battle!'

Fulgrim had to be destroyed before he could escape Tarsus.

An answering roar of war lust pulsed along the very bones of the craftworld.

Blood runs... anger rises... death wakes... war calls!

THE LAST OF the shrieking eldar were dead, hacked down by mighty sweeps of Fulgrim's sword, and Lucius felt the exhilaration of the fight still pounding within him like music. His sword hissed with alien blood and his muscles were alive with the skill it had taken to best them. The megarachnid had been terrifyingly swift, lethal killers who fought with blind, instinctual skill, but these howling warriors, many of whom Lucius now saw were female, were almost as skilful as he.

Their bladework had been exquisite. One of them, a female who had fought with axe and sword had actually managed to land several blows upon him. His armour was cut open in several places and but for his inhuman speed, he knew that he would be lying as dead as the warrior woman at his feet.

He reached down and lifted one of their swords, testing it for balance and weight. It was lighter than he'd expected and its grip was too small, but its edge was true and it was exquisitely made.

'Didn't you learn anything on Murder?' asked Saul Tarvitz. 'Get rid of that weapon before Eidolon sees you with it.'

Lucius turned and said, 'I was just looking at it, Saul. I'm not going to start using it.'

'Just as well,' said Tarvitz. Lucius saw that his fellow captain was almost spent, his breath ragged and his armour stained with his own and alien blood, but despite Saul's words, he held onto the alien woman's sword.

'Everyone still alive?' asked Fulgrim with a laugh. Blood caked the primarch's breastplate, where the wraithlord had struck him, and his appearance was a far cry from the regal splendour Lucius was used to seeing. Though ragged and filthy, Fulgrim had never looked more alive, his dark eyes shining with the excitement of the battle, his sword still clutched firmly in his fist.

Lucius looked around the battlefield, only now checking to see who else had survived. Both lord commanders were still alive, as were Julius Kaesoron, Marius Vairosean and that smug bastard, Solomon Demeter. Of the Phoenix Guard there were no survivors, their skill and strength no match for the power of the wraithlord.

'Looks like it,' said Vespasian, cleaning his sword on the helmet crest of one of the fallen eldar. 'We should get out of here before they return in greater numbers. That tank's keeping its distance after what happened to the other one, but it won't be long before the pilot finds his courage again.'

'Leave?' said Julius Kaesoron. 'I say we take the fight to that tank and destroy it! These aliens have betrayed the truce of a parlay, and honour demands we make them pay in blood!'

'You're not thinking, Julius,' said Solomon. 'We have no weapons to take out a tank and, after what happened to his friend, this one's unlikely to let us get close. We have to go.'

Lucius sneered. How like Solomon Demeter to run from a fight! He could see Eidolon was itching to stay and fight, but Marius Vairosean kept his counsel, awaiting the primarch's decision before undoubtedly supporting it. Silently he urged Fulgrim to order them to attack the tank.

Fulgrim's eyes homed in on him, as though sensing his need to inflict more violence. He smiled, his teeth bright against the smudged inks on his face.

'I think the decision has been taken out of our hands,' said Solomon as a bright light once again built at the base of the curved structure where the farseer had vanished.

'This can't be good,' said Tarvitz.

'Stormbird One!' shouted Vespasian into the vox. 'Spool up the engines, we're coming to you right now. My lord, we have to go.'

'Go,' said Fulgrim, his voice sounding as though he had just woken from a deep slumber. 'Go where?'

'Off this planet, my lord,' urged Vespasian. 'The eldar are returning and they would not do so unless they had overwhelming force.'

Fulgrim shook his head as if in pain and put a hand to his temple. The first eldar warriors emerged from a blazing ripple of light held suspended beneath the apex of the alien portal. The primarch looked up and saw the eldar sprint from the light, first in ones and twos, then in squads. Like the dead aliens at their feet, these eldar wore form-fitting armour of overlapping plates, though these warriors' armour was clear blue, and they sported yellow crests on their helms. Each carried a short-barrelled rifle, and they advanced with cautious grace towards the Astartes. Behind them came a pair of the dark armoured eldar with long bar-relled weapons aimed at the Stormbird above them.

Lucius twisted his neck and stretched his shoulder muscles in readiness for the fight, but Fulgrim shook his head once more and said, 'We go. Everyone back

to the Stormbird. We will return for our dead when
we destroy their craftworld and leave them nowhere
to retreat to.'

Lucius swallowed his disappointment and followed
his primarch as they fell back towards the screaming
aircraft, its engines building to a shrieking howl. He
kept hold of the alien sword as he jogged back up the
hill towards the vehicle.

Blinding streaks flashed overhead and Lucius was
slammed into the ground by the pressure wave of a
terrific explosion. More hissing streaks followed in
quick succession and secondary blasts filled the air
with debris and smoke. He spat dirt and looked up to
see the ruins at the hill's summit wreathed in fire. The
blazing wreck of the Stormbird lay slumped like a
downed bird, its wings smashed and a cluster of holes
punched in its side.

'Run!' shouted Vespasian.

ONCE MORE THE eldar were hurled back from the top
of the hill, leaving their dead piled at the foot of the
ruins. Whickering gunfire rattled from the cover of
the ruins with musical clangs, and slashing beams of
incandescent energy lit up the purpling sky in bright
streaks. The wreckage of the Stormbird still blazed
behind them, secondary explosions of onboard
ammunition popping and crackling in the heat.

Marius took a deep breath as he slotted another
magazine home into his bolter and waited for the
next assault. So far every one of them had come
through the violence of the eldar attacks alive, though
they all sported wounds from the hails of razor sharp
discs fired by the eldar weapons. One of the discs lay
on the ground next to him and he picked it up, turning it over in his hands. It seemed ridiculous that such

a thing could cause injury, but its edges were lethally
sharp and could penetrate even Mark IV plate if it
struck a weak area such as a joint.

It had been a bloody battle, one that had seen desperate heroics and incredible feats of arms. Marius
had watched Lucius fend off three of the howling
warrior women at once. Fighting with two weapons,
his own sword and an eldar blade, the swordsman
had killed them in a dazzling display of unimaginable skill.

Vespasian had fought like one of the heroes from
the Gallery of Swords, his perfection and purity shining like a beacon as he hurled back green armoured
eldar with bulbous helmets that spat blue fire.
Solomon and Julius had fought back-to-back, killing
with brutal vigour, while Saul Tarvitz fought with
mechanical precision, lending his sword arm to a
multitude of combats.

But Eidolon… how had he fought?

In the thick of the fighting, Marius had heard an
ululating howl of nerve shredding ferocity and
turned, expecting to see more of the warrior women
charging him. Instead, he had seen Lord Commander
Eidolon with a trio of shrieking enemies scattered
before him. Two were on their knees, clutching their
ruptured helmets, while a third staggered as though
in the grip of a powerful seizure. Eidolon stepped in
to finish them, and Marius had been left with the
impossible, but unshakeable sensation that the
scream had, in fact, come from Lord Commander
Eidolon.

'How long before the damn *Firebird* gets here?'
asked Julius, crawling through the smouldering
wreckage towards him, and shaking Marius from his
thoughts of the battle.

'I don't know,' he said. 'Lord Fulgrim has tried to call it down, but I think the eldar must be jamming our vox-system.'

'Filthy xenos bastards,' swore Julius. 'I knew we couldn't trust them.'

Marius didn't reply, remembering that Julius had been as vocal a supporter of the primarch's decision to come down to Tarsus as he had. Only Solomon had spoken in opposition, and it looked as though he might be proved right after all.

'We could all die down here,' said Marius sourly.

'Die?' said Julius. 'Don't be ridiculous. Even if we can't get through to the fleet, it won't be long before they send other ships. The eldar know that, it's why they're being so careless with their lives. A race on the edge of extinction are they? What say, you and I push them over that edge?'

Julius's enthusiasm was infectious, and it was hard not be inspired by his indefatigable confidence in victory. Marius smiled in return and said. 'All the way over.'

'Something's happening below!' shouted Saul Tarvitz. Marius scrambled to the edge of the ruins with Julius beside him and looked down at the strange alien gateway. Marius supposed it must lead onto the craftworld above, which explained why they had not detected any ships leaving the craftworld, and how the eldar had reached the surface of Tarsus first.

A gathering of warriors surrounded the light, which flickered and danced like a candle flame. Their weapons were upraised, and they chanted in a language that sounded more like song than communication.

'What do you suppose they're doing?' asked Tarvitz.

Julius shook his head. 'I don't know, but it can't be good for us.'

Suddenly the light flared and its edges erupted in flames, as though a mighty fire forced its way through it. A shape began to form in the light, massive and dark, its outline humanoid, but surely too large for an eldar warrior. Marius wondered if they would have to face another of the wraithlords.

A mighty speartip emerged first, blazing runic symbols writhing on its wide blade, followed by a brazen arm that bled molten light into the air. The limb groaned like hot iron as it flexed and the body it belonged to emerged from the gateway.

Solomon let out a breath at the primal horror of the giant warrior that stood at the base of the hill. Towering above the eldar warriors, the mighty creature's body was fashioned as if from dark iron, its veins rippling like rivers of lava across its surface. Curling horns of smoke and ash oozed from its skin and coiled about its head like a living crown of fire-pierced smoke.

Its head was a roaring, wailing terror, and its eyes blazed like ingots straight from the forge. The living avatar of bloody death bellowed its promise of carnage to the skies, and raised its mighty arms, a thick red gore oozing from between its fingers.

'Throne alive!' cried Lucius. 'What is it?'

Marius looked to Fulgrim for an answer, but the primarch simply watched the arrival of the monstrous being with apparent relish. Fulgrim unbuckled his golden cloak, which had been shredded by gunfire and blades, and drew his silver sword, the gem at its pommel winking in the twilight.

'My lord?' asked Vespasian.

'Yes, Vespasian?' replied Fulgrim, as though only half-hearing his lord commander.

'Do you know what that... thing is?'

'It is their heart and soul,' said Fulgrim, the words sounding as though they came from some distant place within him. 'Their lust for war and death beats within its chest.'

As the primarch spoke, Marius watched the brazen warrior take a thunderous step forward, the grass beneath its feet blackening and bursting into flame in its wake. The chanting of the eldar warriors grew more strident and they began a slow advance behind the blazing god, the rise and fall of their song in time with its every step. Dozens of the warrior women they had fought earlier ghosted through the night, and Marius could hear their piercing shrieks echoing from all around them.

'Stand ready,' warned Vespasian, silhouetted in the glow of the burning Stormbird.

Marius knew that, while ruins and the wreckage of the Stormbird were as good a defensive position as they could hope for , there was no way the eight of them could hold the eldar at bay for much longer, even if one of their number was a primarch.

The Bloody-Handed God picked up its pace. Marius looked at his fellow captains, seeing the same unreasoning dread of the monster across every face. The power of the dark, fiery idol spoke to their souls of the torments it would inflict and the blazing horror its wrath would unleash on those who defied it.

Fulgrim spun his sword and stepped from the cover of the ruins, a chorus of cries following him as he marched to meet the terrifying apparition. Though its features were of carved metal, Marius saw its mouth twist in a grimace of anticipation as the primarch came towards it.

Two mighty gods faced each other, and the world seemed to halt its progress, as though fearful of disturbing the drama being played out upon its surface.

With a mighty bellow of rage, the eldar god attacked.

FULGRIM SAW THE blazing spear hurtling towards him, and swayed aside as its fiery heat slashed past his head. He laughed as he saw that the eldar god had disarmed itself, but the laughter died in his throat as he heard the voice in his head scream a warning.

Fool! You think eldar trickery is so easily thwarted?

He turned to see the spear twisting in the air like a serpent, swooping back in a graceful arc towards him. It roared as it flew, the noise like the eruptions of a thousand volcanoes. He brought up his sword and deflected the flaming missile, the heat of its passing scorching the skin of his face and setting the plaits of his hair on fire.

Fulgrim beat his head with his free hand, extinguishing the flames in his hair, and raised his sword in challenge. 'Will you not fight me in honourable combat? Must you do your killing from afar?'

The monstrous iron creature plucked the flaming spear from the air, black smoke and spitting embers drifting from its eyes and mouth as it spun the weapon and aimed it at Fulgrim's heart.

Fulgrim grinned as he felt the thrill of combat pulsing through every fibre of his being. Here was a foe that would truly test his mettle, for what being had he ever fought that had truly challenged him? The Laer? The Diasporex? The greenskin?

No, this was a creature with a power to match his own, a terrible god-like being that bore the heart of its fading race within its iron breast. It would not be baited or riled with petty insults, it was a warrior creature with one purpose and one purpose alone: to kill.

Such a one-dimensional aspect made Fulgrim sick, for what was life and death but a series of sensations to be experienced one after another. Without sensation what was life?

A wild exultation filled him and his senses seemed to rise to the surface of his skin. He felt every tiny gust of wind as it wound past his body, the heat of the creature before him, the coolness of the planet's atmosphere and the softness of the grass beneath him.

He was truly alive and at the height of his powers!

'Come on then,' snarled Fulgrim. 'Come on and die.'

The two beings leapt towards each other, Fulgrim's sword slashing down to meet the mighty creature's blade, which he now saw resembled a great sword, where once it had been a spear. Both blades met with a tearing shriek that echoed in realms beyond those of the five senses and an explosion of unlight that left those who saw it blinded. The roaring eldar god recovered first and its molten sword arced for Fulgrim's head.

He ducked, and slammed his fist into its midriff, feeling the hard impact on iron and the blistering heat that seared the skin from his knuckles. Fulgrim laughed with the pain, and raised his sword to block a murderous slash towards his groin.

The eldar god attacked with wild, atavistic fury, its blows driven by racial hatred and the ferocious joy of unbound emotion. Flames wreathed its limbs, and dark tendrils of smoke enveloped the two combatants as they struggled. Silver sword and fiery blade sparked and clanged as they traded blows, neither able to penetrate the other's defences.

Fulgrim felt his anger at this blazing monstrosity surge in his veins, its inability to do more than simply fight and kill offending his refined sensibilities. Where was its appreciation of art and culture, beauty and grace? Such a thing did not deserve the boon of existence, and his limbs filled with renewed strength, as though a new-found power flowed from his sword arm and into his flesh.

He could hear the sounds of battle all around him: bolter fire, cries of pain, whickering razor-discs from alien weapons, and howling screams, like the cries of the banshees of legend. He paid them no heed, too focused on his own fight to the death. His sword pulsed with a silver glow, streamers of light and power rippling along its length as he swung it, every strike delivered with a roar of ecstasy. The gleam of purple light from the pommel stone was strong, and he could see that the fiery gaze of his foe's eyes was ever drawn to it.

A wild idea took root in his mind, and though a powerful surge of denial washed through him at the thought, he knew that it was the only way to defeat his enemy quickly. He stepped in close to the flaming eldar god and hurled his sword high into the air.

Instantly, its burning gaze snapped upwards, the coals of its eyes homing in on the spinning blade. It drew back its arm to hurl its spear at the sword, but before it could throw, Fulgrim leapt towards it and delivered a thunderous right hook to its face.

Every ounce of his power and rage powered the blow, and he let loose a bellowing cry of hate as he struck. Metal buckled and an eruption of red light exploded from the eldar monster's head. Fulgrim's fist hammered through its helmet and into the molten core of its skull, and he cried out in agony and plea-sure as he felt the blow smash from the back of its head.

The wounded creature staggered, its head a twisted ruin of metal and flame. Spears of red light streamed from its helmet, and the molten rivers of its blood blazed like phosphor against its iron skin. Fulgrim felt the pain of his maimed hand, but savagely suppressed it as he stepped in again and wrapped his hands around its neck.

The heat of its molten skin seared his flesh, but Fulgrim was oblivious to the pain, too intent on his foe's destruction. Plumes of red light streamed from the eldar god's face, the sound like a manifestation of the combined rage and heart of its creators. An age of regret and lust flowed from the creature, and Fulgrim felt the aching sadness of the necessity of its existence pour into him even as it poured out of the dying monster.

His hands blackened as he crushed the life from his enemy, the metal cracking with the sound of a dying soul. Fulgrim forced the creature to its knees, laughing insanely as the pain of his wounds vied with the powerful elation he felt in crushing the life from another being with his own bare hands and watching as the life fled from its eyes.

The sound of a great and terrible thunder built, and Fulgrim looked up from his murder to see a graceful bird of fire carve its way across the heavens. He released his hold on the dying eldar creature and punched the heavens as the *Firebird* streaked overhead, followed by a host of Stormbirds and Thunderhawks.

Fulgrim returned his gaze to his defeated foe as whipping light and noise poured from it like the nuclear fire blazing at the heart of a star. The light of the creature's death flared, and its body exploded in a thunder of hot iron and molten metal. Fulgrim was hurled through the air by the screaming explosion, and he felt the touch of its power sear his armour and skin.

The released essence of a god surrounded him. He saw a whirling cosmos of stars, the death of a race and the birth of a bright new god, a dark prince of pleasure and pain.

A name formed from the raw sound of ages past, a bloody paean of birth and a wordless shout of unbound sensation building into a mighty roar that was a name and a concept all at once... *Slaanesh!*

Slaanesh! Slaanesh! Slaanesh! Slaanesh! Slaanesh! Slaanesh! Slaanesh! Slaanesh!

Even as the name formed, Fulgrim slammed into the ground and laughed as the Emperor's Children descended to Tarsus on wings of fire. He lay still, broken and burnt, but alive, oh, how he was alive! He felt hands upon him and heard voices begging him to speak, but he ignored them, suddenly feeling an aching longing seize him as he realised he was unarmed.

Fulgrim pushed himself unsteadily to his feet, knowing that his warriors surrounded him, but not seeing them or hearing their words. His hands throbbed and he could smell the scorched ruin of his flesh, but all his attention was fixed on the silver glow that split the night.

His sword stood upright in the grass, its blade having come down point first after he had hurled it into the air. It shimmered in the darkness, the silver blade reflecting the light of the *Firebird* and the descending assault craft. Fulgrim's hands itched to reach out and grip the sword once more, but a screaming portion of his mind begged him not to.

He took a faltering step towards the weapon, his hand outstretched, though he could not remember consciously ordering it to do so. His blackened fingers trembled and his muscles strained as though forcing their way through an invisible barrier. The siren song of the sword was strong, but so was his will, and what remained of his vision of the dark god's birth stayed his hand for the moment.

Only through me will you achieve perfection!

The words thundered in his head, and memories of the battle surged powerfully in his mind, the fire and the hunger to kill, and the wondrous elation of a god's death by his own hands.

In that moment, the last vestige of his resistance collapsed and he slid his fingers around the hilt of the sword. Power flowed through him, and the pain of his wounds vanished as though from the most powerful healing balms.

Fulgrim stood straighter, his momentary weakness forgotten as though a wash of power suffused every atom of his body. He saw the eldar fleeing through their shimmering gateway until only the treacherous seer, Eldrad Ulthran remained, standing forlornly beside the arching structure.

The seer shook his head and stepped into the light, which vanished as suddenly as it had appeared.

'My lord,' said Vespasian, his face smeared with blood. 'What are your orders?'

Fulgrim's anger at the aliens' perfidy reached new, undreamed of heights, and he sheathed his sword, turning to face his gathering warriors.

He knew that there was only one way to ensure that the treachery of the eldar was burnt out forever.

'We return to the *Pride of the Emperor*,' he said. 'Order every ship to make ready to fire a spread of virus bombs.'

'Virus bombs?' asked Vespasian. 'But surely only the Warmaster–'

'Do it!' shouted Fulgrim. 'Now!'

Vespasian looked uneasy with such an order, but nodded stiffly and turned away.

Fulgrim cast his gaze out over the night shrouded planet before him and whispered, 'By the fire, I swear that every one of the eldar worlds will burn.'

PART FOUR

THRESHOLD

SIXTEEN

Called to Account/Scars/My Fear is to Fail

ORMOND BRAXTON CHAFED at being made to wait outside the golden doors of the primarch's chambers. He would have expected better manners from a primarch than to make a high-ranking emissary of the Administration of Terra wait for so long. He had boarded the *Pride of the Emperor* three days ago, and such delays were the kind of thing *he* inflicted on others to demonstrate his superior rank.

Finally his petition for an audience had been approved and his menials had bathed him before Fulgrim's servants arrived to apply perfumed oils to his skin, prior to bringing him before the primarch. The scent of the oils was pleasing enough, though somewhat powerful for his ascetic tendencies. Sweat glistened on his bald pate and mingled with the oils to produce stinging droplets that irritated his eyes and caught in the back of his throat.

A pair of elaborately armoured warriors stood to attention at the golden doors to Fulgrim's staterooms, beyond which Braxton could hear the deafening din of what he supposed was music, but sounded like an unmitigated racket to his ears. A pair of marble sculptures of wild curves and angles stood to either side of the guards, though what they were supposed to represent eluded Braxton's understanding.

He adjusted his administrator robes around his shoulders while letting his attention drift to the paintings that filled this great, terrazzo floored hallway. The golden frames were elaborate to the point of ridiculousness, and the garish colours that filled them quite defied any aesthetic appreciation, though he admitted that his understanding of art was limited.

Ormond Braxton had represented the Terran forces in the negotiations that had seen much of the solar system brought into compliance. He had been part of the delegation trained at the School of Iterators and Evander Tobias and Kyril Sindermann were his close acquaintances. His exceptional skills as a negotiator and civil servant in the Terran Administrative Corps had ensured his selection for this mission, as it called for delicate diplomacy and tact. Only one of such stature could petition a primarch, especially for such a task as was to be appointed him.

At last the doors to Fulgrim's staterooms were flung open and booming peals of music spilled into the hall before the primarch's chambers. The guards snapped to attention, and Braxton drew himself up to his full height as he prepared to enter into the presence of the Primarch of the Emperor's Children.

He awaited some signal that he was to go in, but nothing was forthcoming, and so he hesitantly stepped forward. The guards made no motion to stop him, so he carried on, his unease increasing as the doors swung closed behind him without apparent aid.

The music was deafening. Dozens of phonocasters were scattered around, blaring a multitude of what appeared to be different kinds of music. Paintings of all manner of vileness hung from the walls, some depicting acts of violent barbarity and others, of unspeakably vile conduct that was beyond pornography. Braxton felt his trepidation grow as he heard arguing voices from the central stateroom beyond.

'My Lord Fulgrim?' he inquired. 'Are you there? It is Administrator Ormond Braxton. I have come to see you from the Council of Terra.'

Instantly the voices ceased and the phonocasters fell silent.

Braxton glanced around him to see if he was alone, reckoning that the staterooms surrounding the central chamber were empty of life as far as he could see.

'You may enter!' called a powerful, musical voice from ahead. Braxton gingerly made his way towards the sound, fully expecting to see the primarch and one of his loyal captains, though the argumentative tone of the voices still puzzled him.

He stepped into the primarch's central stateroom and pulled up short at the sight confronting him.

Fulgrim, for the mighty physique could belong to none other, swept around his chambers, naked but for a purple loincloth, and brandishing a gleaming silver sword. His flesh was like hard marble, pale and veined with dark lines, and his face had a manic look to it, like that of a man in the grip of a chemical stimulant. The stateroom itself was a mess, with pieces of broken marble strewn around and the walls chipped and stained with paint. A giant canvas stood at the far end of the chamber, though its angle prevented Braxton from seeing what manner of image was painted upon it.

The odour of uneaten food hung heavy in the air, and not even the perfumed oils could mask the stench of rotten meat.

'Emissary Braxton!' cried Fulgrim. 'How good of you to come.'

Braxton covered his surprise at the state of the primarch and his stateroom, and inclined his head. 'It is my honour to attend upon you, my lord.'

'Nonsense,' exclaimed Fulgrim. 'I have been unforgivably rude in keeping you waiting, but I have been locked in counsel with my most trusted advisors in the weeks since our departure from the Perdus Region.'

The primarch towered over Braxton and he felt the sheer physical intimidation of such a magnificent being threaten to overwhelm him, but he dug deep into his reserves of calm and found his voice once more.

'I come with tidings from Terra, and would deliver them to you, my lord.'

'Of course, of course,' said Fulgrim, 'but first, my dear Braxton, would you do me an enormous favour?'

'I would be honoured to serve, my lord,' said Braxton, noticing that Fulgrim's hands were discoloured as though from a fire. What heat could wound such as a primarch, he wondered?

'What manner of favour would you have me do?'

Fulgrim spun his sword and put his hand on Braxton's shoulder, guiding him towards the vast canvas set up at the end of the stateroom. Fulgrim's pace practically forced Braxton to run, even though his generously fleshed form was unsuited to such a

speed. He mopped his brow with a scented handkerchief as Fulgrim proudly stood him before the canvas
and said, 'What do you think of this, then? The likeness is quite uncanny isn't it?'

Braxton stared in open mouthed horror at the
image slathered on the canvas, a truly repellent portrait of an armoured warrior, thickly painted with all
manner of garish colours, crude brushstrokes and
loathsome stench. The vastness of the image only
served to heighten the horror of what it portrayed, for
the subject was none other than the Primarch of the
Emperor's Children, so loathsomely delineated as to
be insulting and degrading to one so awe inspiring.

Though he was no student of art, even Braxton
recognised this as a vulgar atrocity, an affront to the
being it purported to represent. He glanced over at
Fulgrim to see if this was some elaborate jest, but the
primarch's face was rapt and unswerving in his adoration of the vile picture.

'You're lost for words, I can see,' said Fulgrim. 'I'm
not surprised. It is, after all, by Serena d'Angelus, and
only recently finished. You are honoured to see it
before its public unveiling at the first performance of
Mistress Kynska's *Maraviglia* in the newly refurbished
La Fenice. That will be a night to remember, I can tell
you!'

Braxton nodded, too afraid of what he might say
were he to open his mouth. The horror of the picture
was too much to bear, its colours nauseating in a way
that went beyond its simple crudity, and the stench of
its surface was making his gorge rise.

He moved away from the picture, pressing his
handkerchief to his mouth and nose, as Fulgrim
trailed behind him, idly swinging his sword in lazy
circles.

'My lord, if I may?' said Braxton.

'What? Oh, yes, of course,' said Fulgrim, as though listening to another voice entirely. 'You said something about news from Terra, didn't you?'

Recovering himself, Braxton said, 'Yes, my lord, from the mouth of the Sigillite himself.'

'So what does old Malcador have to say for himself?' asked Fulgrim, and Braxton was shocked at the informality and lack of respect inherent in the primarch's tone.

'Firstly, I bring word of Lord Magnus of Prospero. It has come to the attention of the Emperor, beloved by all, that, contrary to the dictates of the Council of Nikaea, Lord Magnus has continued his researches into the mysteries of the immaterium.'

Fulgrim nodded to himself as he began pacing once more and said, 'I knew he would, but the others were too blind to see it. Even with the new chaplains in place, I suspected Magnus would backslide. He does love his mysteries.'

'Quite,' agreed Braxton. 'The Sigillite has despatched the Wolves of Fenris to bring Magnus back to Terra to await the Emperor's judgement upon him.'

Fulgrim paused, turned to face the vile painting once more and shook his head as though disagreeing with some unseen interrogator.

'Then Magnus is to be… what? Charged with a crime?' asked Fulgrim heatedly, as though his anger at the messenger would somehow change the facts.

'I do not know any more, my lord,' replied Braxton, 'simply that he is to return to Terra with Leman Russ of the Space Wolves.'

Fulgrim nodded, though he was clearly unhappy at such a development, and said, 'You said "firstly". What other news do you bring?'

Braxton knew he would have to choose his words carefully, for there was more that would yet displease the primarch. 'I bring news concerning the conduct within one of your brother primarch's Legions.'

Fulgrim ceased his pacing and looked up in sudden interest. 'It is Horus's Legion?'

Braxton covered his irritation and nodded. 'It is. Have you already heard my news?'

Fulgrim shook his head. 'No, I was just guessing. Go on and tell me your news, but be aware that Horus is my sworn brother and I will brook no disrespect of him.'

'Of course not,' confirmed Braxton. 'At present, the 63rd Expedition makes war against a civilisation calling itself the Auretian Technocracy. Horus came in the name of peace, but the misguided–'

'The *Warmaster*,' put in Fulgrim, and Braxton cursed himself for making such an elementary error. The Astartes detested mortals showing a lack of respect for their position.

'My apologies,' continued Braxton smoothly. 'The rulers of these planets attempted to assassinate the Warmaster and thus he declared a legal war upon them to bring their worlds to compliance. In this matter he has been aided by Lord Angron of the VII Legion.'

Fulgrim laughed. 'Then I don't hold out much hope for there being much left of this Technocracy at the end of the war.'

'Quite,' said Braxton. 'Lord Angron's... excesses, shall we say, are not unknown to the Council of Terra, but we have received some unsettling reports from Lord Commander Hektor Varvarus, commander of the Army units within the 63rd Expedition.'

'Reports of what?' demanded Fulgrim. Braxton was unnerved to see that the primarch's previous manic distraction appeared to have quite vanished.

'Reports of a massacre perpetrated by Astartes against Imperial civilians, my lord.'

'Nonsense,' snapped Fulgrim. 'Angron may be many things, but massacring Imperial citizens seems a little out of character even for him, wouldn't you say?'

'Reports have reached Terra regarding Lord Angron's conduct in the war, it's true,' said Braxton, keeping his tone as neutral as possible. 'Though it is not of him that I speak.'

'Horus?' asked Fulgrim, his voice hoarse, and Braxton saw what in a mortal he would have regarded as fear in his dark eyes. 'What has happened?'

Braxton paused before continuing. He noted that there was no denial, as there had been when Fulgrim had thought if Angron accused.

'It appears that the Warmaster was grievously wounded on the planet of Davin, and some of his warriors were somewhat over-zealous when bringing him back on board the *Vengeful Spirit*.'

'Over-zealous?' barked Fulgrim. 'Speak plainly, man. What does that mean?'

'A sizeable crowd had gathered on the embarkation decks of the Warmaster's flagship, and when the Astartes came back on board they smote the crowd in their haste to reach the medicae decks. Some twenty-one people are dead and many more grievously injured.'

'And you blame Horus for this?'

'It is not my place to assign blame, my lord,' said Braxton. 'I am merely informing you of the facts.'

Fulgrim rounded on him suddenly. Braxton felt his bladder loosen, and a warmth trickle down his leg, as the wild-eyed Primarch of the Emperor's Children towered over him with his sword suddenly raised above his head as if to strike him down.

'Facts?' snarled Fulgrim. 'What does a foppish scribe such as you know of the facts of war? War is hard, fast and cruel. Horus knows this and he fights accordingly. If people are stupid enough to get in the way of that, then their own foolishness is to blame.'

Ormond Braxton had seen much in the way of egotism in his time within the civil administration of Terra, but he had never been faced with such barefaced arrogance and callous dismissal of human life.

'My lord,' gasped Braxton. 'People are dead, killed by the Astartes. Such things will not just go away. Those responsible must be called to account or the ideals of the Great Crusade will stand for nothing.'

Fulgrim lowered his sword, appearing only now to notice its presence. He shook his head and smiled, his ephemeral anger vanishing in the space of a moment 'You are right, of course, my dear Braxton. I apologise for my uncivil behaviour and beg of your pardon. I am much vexed by the pain of wounds suffered battling an alien monstrosity in our previous campaign, and my temper is a fragile thing as a result.'

'No pardon is necessary, my lord,' said Braxton slowly. 'I understand your brotherhood with the Warmaster and it is for that very reason that I am despatched to you. The Council of Terra wishes you to travel to Aureus and meet with the Warmaster to ensure that the principles that underpin the Great Crusade are being adhered to.'

Fulgrim snorted in derision and turned away. 'So now we must fight with an eye forever over our shoulder? Are we not trusted to make war? You civilians want your conquests, but you do not care for how they are won, do you? War is brutality, and the more brutal it is, the sooner it is over, but that's not good enough for you is it? In your eyes, wars must be fought according to an imperfect set of rules imposed by those who have never seen a shot fired in anger or risked their own blood alongside their brothers. Know this, Braxton, every petty, restrictive rule you civilians impose on our method of war means that more of my warriors die!'

Braxton was shocked by Fulgrim's bitterness, but hid his surprise. 'What response should I take back to the Council of Terra, my lord?'

Again Fulgrim's anger seemed to melt away in the face of reason, and the mighty primarch laughed humour-lessly. 'Tell them, Master Braxton, that I shall lead my warriors to join the 63rd Expedition, that I will examine how my brother makes war, and that I shall be sure to tell you all about it.'

The sarcasm was heavy in Fulgrim's tone, but Braxton ignored it and bowed. 'Then, my lord, if I may take my leave?'

Fulgrim waved his hand dismissively and nodded. 'Yes, go. Return to your courtiers and scriveners, and tell them that the Lord Fulgrim will do their bidding.'

Braxton bowed once more and backed away from the barely dressed primarch. When he had retreated a suffi-cient distance, he turned and made his way through the golden doors that led to normality.

Behind him, he could hear voices arguing, and he risked a glance over his shoulder in an attempt to iden-tify with whom Fulgrim spoke. He felt a shiver travel the length of his spine as he saw that Fulgrim was alone.

He was speaking to the loathsome painting.

✠ ✠ ✠

'WHAT ARE YOU doing?' asked a voice behind her and she froze. Serena clutched the knife to her breast as her mind raced to identify the questioner. In her fevered thoughts, she imagined that it was Ostian, come once again to save her, but when the question was asked again, she blinked and dropped the knife as she recognised that the speaker was the Astartes warrior, Lucius.

Her breathing was heavy and her blood was pounding as she looked down at the corpse lying next to the unfinished picture of the swordsman. She couldn't recall the dead man's name, an irony she found amusing given her official title as remembrancer, but he had been a talented composer once. Now he was raw material for her work, his blood pumping enthusiastically onto the floor from his opened throat.

The metallic smell of his blood filled her nostrils as she felt a hand grasp her shoulder and turn her around. She looked up into Lucius's boyish face, his handsome features marred forever by the crooked twist of his nose where it had been broken in some combat. She reached up with a bloodied hand to touch his face, and his eyes followed her fingers as they traced the line of his jaw.

'What happened here?' asked Lucius, nodding towards the corpse. 'That man is dead.'

'Yes,' said Serena, slumping to the floor. 'I killed him.'

'Why?' asked Lucius. Even in her fugue state Serena detected an interest beyond that which would normally be aroused by such a discovery. What remained of the rational part of her mind understood the precariousness of the situation and she covered her face with her hands and began to weep uncontrollably, hoping the onset of tears would trigger the male comfort reaction.

Lucius let her weep and she cried, 'He tried to rape me!'

'Rape you?' asked Lucius, aghast. 'What?'

'He tried to force himself upon me and I killed him... I... I fought him, but he was too strong. He... hit me and I reached out to grab the first thing I could find to use as a weapon... I suppose I must have picked up my knife and...'

'And you killed him,' finished Lucius.

Serena looked up through her tears, hearing no condemnation in Lucius's tone. 'Yes, I killed him.'

'Then the bastard got what he deserved,' said Lucius, pulling Serena to her feet. 'He tried to violate you and you defended yourself, yes?'

Serena nodded, the exhilaration of lying to this warrior who could snap her neck with his fingers sending warm rushes of pleasure through her entire body.

'I met him in *La Fenice*, and he said he wanted to see some of my work,' she gasped, already knowing that Lucius would not arrest her or otherwise call her to account for the killing. 'It was foolish, I know, but he seemed genuinely interested. When we returned to my studio...'

'He turned on you.'

'Yes,' nodded Serena, 'and now he's dead. Oh, Lucius, what am I to do?'

'Don't worry,' said Lucius, 'this won't need to go any further. I'll have some servitors dispose of his remains and this can all be forgotten about.'

Serena threw herself against Lucius in gratitude and let her tears come once more, feeling nothing but contempt for this man and his belief that such a traumatic event, had it been real, could be forgotten about so easily.

She pushed herself from his breastplate and bent to pick up her knife. The blade was still wet with blood and the cold steel glittered invitingly in the light.

Without conscious thought, she reached up and sliced the blade across her cheek, drawing a thin line of blood from her pallid skin.

Lucius watched her impassively and asked, 'What did you do that for?'

'So that I don't forget what happened,' she said, handing him the knife and rolling up her sleeves to show the many scars and fresh cuts in the flesh of her arms. 'Pain is my way of remembering all that has gone before. If I hold onto that pain, then I will never allow it to be forgotten.'

Lucius nodded and reached up to slowly run his fingertips over the crooked line of his nose. Serena could see the anger and hurt pride within him at the marring of his perfect features. A strange sensation of power filled her, as though her words carried more than meaning in their sounds, an influence beyond understanding. She felt this power flow through her and into the very air, filling the space between them with unknown potential.

'What happened to your face?' asked Serena, unwilling to lose this remarkable sensation.

'A barbaric son of a bitch named Loken broke it when he cheated in a fair fight.'

'He wounded you, didn't he?' she asked, the sound of her words flowing like honey in his ears. 'More than just physically, I mean?'

'Yes,' said Lucius, his voice hollow. 'He destroyed my perfection.'

'You'd want to hurt him, wouldn't you?'

'I'll see him dead soon,' swore Lucius.

Serena smiled, reaching out and placing her hands on his. 'Yes, I know you will.'

He gripped the knife tightly and she lifted his unresisting hand to his face.

'Yes,' she said with a nod, 'your perfect face is already gone forever. Do it.'

He returned her nod and with a quick flick of his wrist, cut deeply into the flawless skin of his cheek. He flinched at the pain, but lifted the dripping knife to cut an identical line across the opposite cheek.

'Now you will never forget this Loken,' she said.

FULGRIM PACED THE confines of his staterooms, marching from room to room as he pondered the words of Emissary Braxton. He had tried to conceal his unease at the news he had been brought, but he suspected that the man had seen through his façade of indifference. He swung the silver sword in a glittering arc, its blade cutting the air with a sound like ripping cloth.

Try as he might to forget them, the words of the eldar farseer kept returning, and though he had tried to purge the alien's lies from his head, they would not leave him alone. Braxton's news of the Council of Terra's desire for him to investigate Horus and Angron's conduct only heightened his fear that the farseer had spoken the truth.

'It cannot be true!' shouted Fulgrim. 'Horus would never betray the Emperor!'

Are you so sure? asked the voice, and Fulgrim felt the familiar jolt of unease as it spoke.

He could no longer delude himself that this was simply the voice of his own conscience, but was something else entirely. Since the portrait had been delivered to his stateroom, the honest counsellor in his head had by some unknown means relocated itself within the thick paints of the canvas, reshaping the image to suit its vocabulary.

Fulgrim marvelled at his ability to simply accept this development, and each time the hideousness of the notion surfaced in his mind, it was quashed by a feeling of elation and attraction that melted his concerns like snow before the spring sun.

He turned slowly towards the magnificent picture Serena d'Angelus had painted for him, its splendour matched only by his amazement at what it had become in the days since it had been delivered to his staterooms.

Fulgrim made his way through the ruin of his quarters and stared into the image of his own face on the canvas. The giant in purple armour stared at him from the picture, its features, refined and regal, the mirror of his own. The eyes sparkled as though recalling some long forgotten joke, the lips curled in the curved wrinkle of the hypocrite, and the brow furrowed as though plotting some scheme of great cunning.

Even as he stared into his own features the mouth twisted and pulled at the canvas as it formed new words.

What if the alien spoke true? If Horus has indeed forsaken the Emperor, where would you stand in such a contest?

Fulgrim felt clammy sweat coat his naked flesh, repulsed by the creeping horror of the picture, yet unaccountably drawn once again to hear its words, as though they possessed some silken, siren-like attraction to him. As much as he wanted to slice his blade through the painting, he could not bear to see it destroyed.

He is the most worthy of you, said the painting, its mouth contorting under the effort of speech. *If Horus were to turn his face from the Emperor, where would you stand?*

'The question is immaterial,' snapped Fulgrim. 'The situation would never arise.'

Think you so? laughed the painting. *Even now Horus plants the seeds of his rebellion.*

Fulgrim clenched his jaw and aimed his sword at the image of himself on the canvas. 'I will not believe you?' he shouted. 'You cannot know these things.'

But I do.

'How?' begged Fulgrim. 'You are not me, you cannot be me.'

No, agreed his twin, *I am not. Call me… the spirit of perfection that will guide you in the coming days.*

'Horus seeks war with the Emperor?' asked Fulgrim, almost unable to speak the words such was the horror of what they represented.

He does not seek it, but it is forced upon him. The Emperor plans to abandon you all, Fulgrim. His perfection is naught but a sham! He has used you all to conquer the galaxy for him, and now seeks to ascend to godhood on the blood you have shed.

'No!' cried Fulgrim. 'I won't believe this. The Emperor is human intelligence raised above all error and imperfection, and extended to all possible truth.'

Your belief is irrelevant. It is already happening. Grand things are necessarily obscure to weak men. That which can be made explicit to the idiot is not worth my care. If Horus, can see this, how is it that you, most perfect of primarchs, cannot?

'Because you are lying!' bellowed Fulgrim, smashing his fist into one of the green marble pillars that supported the domed roof of his staterooms. Powdered stone exploded from the column, and it collapsed in a cracked pile of splintered rock.

You waste time in denial, Fulgrim. You are already on the road to joining your brother.

'I will support Horus in all things,' gasped Fulgrim, 'but turn against the Emperor… that is too far!'

You will never know what is too far until you go beyond it. I know you, Fulgrim, and have tasted the forbidden desires you hold chained within the deepest, darkest recesses of your soul. Better to murder an infant in its cradle than nurse an unacted upon desire.

'No,' said Fulgrim, raising his bloodied hand to his temple. 'I won't listen to you.'

Expose yourself to your deepest fear, Fulgrim. After that, fear has no power and the fear of freedom shrinks and vanishes. You will be free.

'Free?' cried Fulgrim. 'Betrayal is not freedom, it is damnation.'

Damnation? No! It is liberty and unfettered freedom to explore all that is and all that can be! Horus has seen beyond the veil of this mortal flesh you call life and learnt the truth of your existence. He is privy to the secrets of the Ancients, and only he can help you towards perfection.

'Perfection?' whispered Fulgrim.

Yes, perfection. The Emperor is imperfect, for if he were perfect, then such things could not happen. Perfection is slow death. Only change is constant, the signal for rebirth, the egg of the phoenix from which you arise! Ask yourself this: what is it you fear?

Fulgrim stared into the eyes of the portrait, eyes that were his own but for the awful knowledge within them. With a clarity borne of perfect understanding, Fulgrim knew the answer to the question his reflection had posed him.

'My fear is to fail,' said Fulgrim.

THE COLD LIGHTS of the apothecarion were bright and hostile, staring down at Marius as he lay naked on the surgical slab. His limbs were immobile, held static by gleaming steel restraints and chemical inhibitors. The feeling of vulnerability was acute, but he had vowed to obey his primarch's orders, no matter what they were, and Lord Eidolon had assured him that this was what Lord Fulgrim desired.

'Are you ready?' asked Fabius, the silver steel arms of the Apothecary's chirurgeon machine looming over him like a great spider.

Marius tried to nod, but his muscles would not obey him.

'I am,' he said, fighting to say even that.

'Excellent,' said Fabius. His narrow dark eyes bored into Marius and examined his flesh, as a butcher might examine a choice cut of meat, or a sculptor a fresh block of virgin stone.

'Lord Commander Eidolon said you would make me better than before.'

'And so I shall, Captain Vairosean,' grinned Fabius. 'You will not believe the things I can do.'

SEVENTEEN

Nothing Against Your Conscience

THE SHIPS OF the 63rd Expedition floated like a school of silver fish above the twin worlds of the Auretian Technocracy. Sharing a common moon, the space above them was alive with electronic chatter as the Warmaster's forces prosecuted the war below. Wrecked communications satellites were debris in the upper atmosphere, and what remained of the Auretian monitors had long since plummeted as fiery meteors to the planet's surface.

Fulgrim watched the slow drift of the Warmaster's ships above the second planet, their attention fixed on the conflict raging below rather than their rear defences. He smiled as he realised that, if he was clever, he could catch his brother unawares.

'Slow to one-quarter flank speed,' ordered Fulgrim. 'All active systems to passive.'

The bridge of the *Pride of the Emperor* throbbed with activity as its crew hurried to obey his orders. He kept his eyes glued to the readouts and hololithic projections of the surveyor station, and issued fresh orders in response to each sensor sweep. Captain Aizel watched his every move with admiration. Fulgrim could just imagine the bitter envy that must fill any man who knew that he would never approach such genius.

The eight-week journey to the Auretian system had been one of enormous tedium for Fulgrim, with every diversion delighting him for only the briefest moment before becoming stale. He had even hoped for some catastrophe to occur in their warp translation, just for something to occupy his thoughts with some new sensation, but no such disaster had occurred.

In preparation for his meeting with his beloved brother, Fulgrim's armour had been polished to a mirror sheen, the great golden eagle's wing sweeping high over his left shoulder. His armour had been restored to its familiar brilliant purple, edged in bright gold, and inlaid with opalescent stones and gilded carvings. A long, scaled cloak was secured to his armour by silver brooches, and trailing parchments hung from his shoulder guards.

He bore no weapon, and his hands continually itched to reach for his absent sword, to feel the reassuring heat of its silver grip and the perversely comforting presence that spoke to him through Serena d'Angelus's masterpiece. Though he had not wielded *Fireblade* in many months, he missed even its balance and fiery edge. Without a weapon, especially the one torn from the Laer temple, his thoughts were clearer, uncluttered by intrusive voices and treacherous thoughts, but try as he might, he could not bring himself to forsake the weapon.

The wounds he had suffered on Tarsus had healed, such that no observer would ever suspect the seriousness of them, and to commemorate his defeat of the eldar god, a fresh mosaic had been created, and hung in the central apothecarion of the *Andronius*.

'Issue orders to all ships to disperse into attack formation at my order,' whispered Fulgrim, as though the glinting specks of light before him might hear his words were he to speak too loudly.

'Yes, my lord,' said Captain Aizel with a smile, though Fulgrim could see past his apparently genuine pleasure to the jealousy beyond. He returned his attention to the viewing bay, smiling to himself as he saw that Horus's fleet still had no idea that the entire 28th Expedition was within striking distance.

Fulgrim rested his hands on the command lectern as the enormity of his last thought settled on him. He could attack the Warmaster's expedition and destroy it utterly from here. His own warships were closing to the optimal firing distance, and he could unleash a devastating fusillade that would cripple the ability of the 63rd Expedition to respond in any meaningful way.

If Eldrad Ulthran had spoken the truth, then he could end the coming rebellion before it began.

'Plot firing solutions to the vessels before us,' he ordered.

Within moments, the guns of the 28th Expedition were trained on the Warmaster's ships, and Fulgrim licked his lips as he realised that he *wanted* to open fire.

'My lord,' said a voice beside him. He turned to see Lord Commander Eidolon holding out his sheathed sword, the silver hilt gleaming in the low light of the bridge. Fulgrim felt the dark, smothering weight of its presence settle upon him and said, 'Eidolon?'

'You asked for your sword,' said the lord commander.

Fulgrim could not remember issuing the order, but nodded and resignedly reached out to take the proffered weapon. He looped it around his waist as though it was the most natural thing in the world, and as he snapped the golden eagle buckle closed, the desire to order the attack faded like morning mist.

'Order all ships to unmask, but not to fire,' he ordered.

Captain Aizel leapt to obey, and Fulgrim watched as the fleet before the 28th Expedition suddenly became aware of his ships and began to scatter, desperately trying to manoeuvre into a position where it could avoid being blasted to pieces. Fulgrim knew that the frantic change of formation was a fruitless endeavour, for his vessels were in the perfect attack formation, and at the perfect firing range.

The vox-system burst into life as dozens of hails were received from the 63rd Expedition, and Fulgrim nodded as a channel was opened to the *Vengeful Spirit*, the Warmaster's flagship.

'Horus, my brother,' said Fulgrim, 'it seems I still have a thing or two to teach you.'

FULGRIM MARCHED ACROSS the docking umbilicus, towards the sealed hatch leading to the *Vengeful Spirit's* upper transit dock. Lord Commander Eidolon walked beside him, and Apothecary Fabius, Saul Tarvitz and the swordsman, Lucius, followed him. Fulgrim was disturbed to note that Lucius's face was heavily scarred with deep, parallel grooves. Many were fresh or recently healed, and he made a mental note to ask the warrior about them once their business with the 63rd Expedition was concluded.

He had chosen Tarvitz and Lucius because he had heard that they had forged friendships amongst the Luna Wolves, and such associations were never to be overlooked.

Eidolon accompanied him, for he feared for what Vespasian would make of what Horus might say in response to the allegations laid against him by the Council of Terra. As to why he had included Fabius, he wasn't sure, though he had a suspicion that the reason would be made clear to him soon enough.

As he drew near the hatch, the eagle-stamped pressure door began to rise, and warm air and light rushed to fill the umbilicus. Setting his face in an expression of calm reserve, Fulgrim stepped onto the metal decking of the *Vengeful Spirit*.

Horus was waiting for him, resplendent in gleaming armour of sea-green, with a brilliant amber eye at its centre. His brother's handsome, patrician features were alive with simple pleasure at the sight of him, and Fulgrim felt his worries fade at the sight of the magnificent warrior before him. To imagine that Horus might plan some treachery against their father was ludicrous, and his love for his brother swelled in his breast.

Four heroic specimens stood behind the Warmaster, who could only be the warriors that his brother called the Mournival, his trusted counsellors and advisors. Each was a warrior born, and carried himself proudly erect. Fulgrim easily recognised Ezekyle Abaddon from his bellicose stance, familiar topknot and martial bearing.

By the startling similarity between him and his primarch, the warrior next to Abaddon could only be Horus Aximand, Little Horus. The remaining two, he did not know, but each looked proud and noble, warriors to walk through the fire with.

Fulgrim opened his arms and the two primarchs embraced like long-lost brothers.

'It has been too long, Horus,' said Fulgrim.

'It has, my brother, it has,' agreed Horus. 'My heart sings to see you, but why are you here? You were prosecuting a campaign throughout the Perdus Anomaly. Is the region compliant already?'

'What worlds we found there are now compliant, yes,' nodded Fulgrim as his retinue stepped through the pressure door behind him. Fulgrim could see the pleasure the Mournival took in seeing their familiar faces, and knew he had chosen his companions wisely.

Fulgrim turned from Horus and said, 'I believe you are already familiar with some of my brothers, Tarvitz, Lucius and Lord Commander Eidolon, but I do not believe you have met Chief Apothecary Fabius.'

'It is an honour to meet you, Lord Horus,' said Fabius, bowing low.

Horus acknowledged the gesture of respect, and said, 'Come now, Fulgrim, you know better than to try and stall me. What's so important that you turn up unannounced and give half my crew heart attacks?'

The smile fell from Fulgrim's lips and he said, 'There have been reports, Horus.'

'Reports? What does that mean?'

'Reports that things are not as they should be,' he replied, hating that he had to bring the petty concerns of scribes and notaries to his brother's notice. 'Reports that suggest you and your warriors should be called to account for the brutality of this campaign. Is Angron up to his usual tricks?'

'Angron is as he has always been.'

'That bad?'

'No, I keep him on a short leash, and his equerry, Khârn, seems to curb the worst of our brother's excesses.'

'Then I have arrived just in time.'

'I see,' said Horus. 'Are you here to relieve me?'

Fulgrim forced himself to conceal the horror he felt that his brother could conceive of such a thing, and covered his consternation with a laugh.

'Relieve you?' he said. 'No, my brother, I am here so that I can return and tell those fops and scribes on Terra that Horus fights war the way it is meant to be fought, hard, fast and cruel.'

'War is cruelty. There is no use trying to reform it. The crueller it is, the sooner it is over.'

Fulgrim nodded and said, 'Indeed, my brother. Come, there is much for us to talk about, for we are living in strange times. It seems our brother Magnus has once again done something to upset the Emperor, and the Wolf of Fenris has been unleashed to escort him back to Terra.'

'Magnus?' asked Horus, suddenly serious. 'What has he done?'

'Let us talk of it in private,' said Fulgrim, desiring to end this public airing of such filthy accusations. 'Anyway, I have a feeling my subordinates would welcome the chance to reacquaint themselves with your… what do you call it? Mournival?'

'Yes,' smiled Horus. 'Memories of Murder no doubt.'

Horus indicated that Fulgrim should walk with him, and the two primarchs marched from the transit deck.

Eidolon followed in his footsteps, while Abaddon and Horus Aximand fell in behind the Warmaster, but Fulgrim could not fail to notice the accusing looks the Luna Wolves threw in the lord commander's direction. Fulgrim wondered what had passed between the warriors on Murder, as Horus led him through the halls of the mighty ship towards his personal staterooms.

Horus spoke volubly of shared memories of more innocent times, when all that had been before them was the simple joy of warfare, but Fulgrim heard none of it, too locked in his own private misery to listen.

At last, the journey ended at a pair of simple, dark wood doors, and Horus dismissed the two members of his Mournival. Fulgrim likewise dismissed Eidolon, ordering him to attend upon Apothecary Fabius.

'In many ways, it is fortuitous that you come to me now, my brother,' said Horus.

'How so?' asked Fulgrim, as the Warmaster opened the doors and stepped inside.

Horus did not answer, and Fulgrim followed him, seeing that an Astartes in armour the colour of weathered granite awaited them. The warrior was powerfully built and his battle plate was bedecked with parchments and tightly curled script work.

His head was shaven bare, the skin covered in angular tattoos.

'This is Erebus of the Word Bearers,' said Horus, 'and you are correct.'

'About what?' asked Fulgrim.

'That we have much to talk about,' said Horus, closing the doors.

HORUS'S STATEROOMS WERE spartan and austere compared to his own, without the lush decorations and fine artworks that hung on every wall and stood proud on golden plinths. This did not surprise Fulgrim, for his brother had always eschewed personal comforts in favour of appearing to share the discomforts of his warriors. Beyond an archway veiled in white silk, he could see his brother's personal chambers, and he smiled as he saw the mighty desk there, the piles of oath papers strewn across its surface, and the tome of astrology given to Horus by their father.

Thinking of their father, Fulgrim looked over to the wall upon which was painted a mural he had not seen in decades. It depicted the Emperor ascendant over all, with his hands outstretched, and above him spun constellations of stars.

'I remember that being painted,' said Fulgrim wistfully.

'Many years ago now,' agreed Horus, pouring wine from a silver ewer and handing the goblet to him. The wine was deep red, and Fulgrim felt as though he was staring into an ocean of blood as he raised it to his lips and took a long draught. Oily sweat bristled on his brow.

Fulgrim glanced over at the seated figure of Erebus, and felt an irrational dislike for the Word Bearer, despite never having met him or heard a single word pass his lips. He had never particularly relished the company of Lorgar or the warriors of the XVII Legion, finding their enthusiasms unwholesome, and their former zeal in proclaiming the Emperor as a figure of worship contrary to the central tenets of the Great Crusade.

'Tell me of Lorgar,' ordered Fulgrim. 'It has been some time since I have seen him. He prospers?'

'He does indeed,' smiled Erebus, 'like never before.'

Fulgrim frowned at the warrior's choice of words, and sat down on the couch facing the Warmaster's desk. The Warmaster sliced the flesh of an apple with a gleaming, serpent-hilted dagger, and Fulgrim's rarefied senses could feel an unspoken tension in the air, a miasma of things unsaid and great potential. Whatever Horus had in mind was clearly something of great import.

'You have recovered well from your wounds,' noted Fulgrim, catching the furtive glance shared between the Warmaster and Erebus. Precious little information had been released from the 63rd Expedition regarding the Davin campaign, certainly nothing to indicate that Horus had been wounded, but the Warmaster's reaction proved that at least part of the farseer's tale was true.

'You heard about that,' said Horus, taking a slice of apple into his mouth and wiping the juice from his chin with the back of his hand.

'I did,' nodded Fulgrim. Horus shrugged.

'I attempted to prevent word of it reaching the other expeditions for fear of the damage it might do to morale. It was nothing, a minor wound to the shoulder.'

Fulgrim smelled a lie and said, 'Really? I heard that you were dying.'

The Warmaster's eyes narrowed. 'Who told you that?'

'It doesn't matter,' said Fulgrim. 'What's important is that you survived.'

'Yes, I survived and now I am stronger than ever, revitalised even.'

Fulgrim raised his glass and said, 'Then let us give thanks for such a speedy recovery.'

Horus drank to mask his annoyance, and Fulgrim let a small smile creep across his face at the thrill of antagonising so powerful a being as the Warmaster.

'So,' began Horus, changing the subject, 'you have
been sent to check up on me, is that it? Is my compe-
tence as Warmaster in question?'

Fulgrim shook his head. 'No, my brother, though
there are those who question your means of advancing the Great Crusade. Civilians light years from the
battles we fight in their name dare question how you
make war, and seek to exploit our brotherhood by
tasking me to bring your war dogs to heel.'

'By war dogs, I assume you mean Angron?'

Fulgrim nodded and took a drink of the bitter wine.
'It cannot have escaped your notice that he is a far
from subtle weapon. Personally, I do not favour his
employment in theatres of war where anything less
that total destruction is called for, but I recognise that
there are times for subtlety and times for raw aggression. Is this war such a time?'

'It is,' promised Horus. 'Angron bloodies himself for
me, and at this moment I need him drenched in
blood.'

'Why?'

'I'm sure you remember what Angron was like after
Ullanor, Fulgrim?' asked Horus. 'He raged against my
appointment like a caged animal. His every utterance
was calculated to belittle me in the eyes of those who
thought my being named Warmaster an insult to
their pride.'

'Angron thinks with his sword arm, not his head,'
said Fulgrim. 'I remember that it took all my skill in
diplomacy to calm the thunder in his heart and
smooth his ruffled pride, but he accepted your role.
Grudgingly, it has to be said, but he accepted it.'

'Grudgingly is not good enough,' stated Horus
flatly. 'If I am to be Warmaster, I must have utter devotion and total obedience from all those I command

in the days of blood to come. I am giving Angron what he wants, allowing him to affirm his loyalty to me in the only way he knows how. Where others would pull tight the chain that binds him, I allow him his head.'

'And his loyalty to you is forged anew in blood,' said Fulgrim.

'Just so,' agreed Horus.

'I believe *that* is what the Council of Terra objects to.'

'I am the Warmaster and I make use of the tools available to me, moulding them to fit my purpose,' said Horus. 'Our brother Angron is raw and bloody, but he has his place in my designs. That place requires that his loyalty, first and foremost, is to me.'

Fulgrim watched the Warmaster's eyes as he spoke, seeing a passionate fervour he had not seen in many decades. His brother spoke of magniloquent designs and the fact that he required utter devotion from his followers. Was this the treachery the farseer had spoken of?

As Angron's loyalty was being won, was Horus swaying others to his cause? Fulgrim stole a glance at Erebus, seeing that he too was enraptured by the Warmaster's words, and wondered who laid first claim to the loyalties of the Word Bearers' primarch.

Patience… in time these truths will be known, said the voice in his head. *You have always looked up to Horus. Trust him now, for your destiny is linked inextricably with his.*

He caught a sudden, startled furrowing of Erebus's brow and experienced a moment's panic as he wondered if the Word Bearer had heard the voice too.

Fulgrim pushed aside such concerns and nodded at Horus's words. 'I understand perfectly,' he said.

'I see,' said Horus, 'and the Council's concern is simply with Angron's bloodlust?'

'Not entirely,' he replied. 'As I said, the Wolf of Fenris has been despatched to Prospero in order to bring Magnus back to Terra, though for what purpose I do not know.'

'He has been practising sorcery,' said Erebus. Fulgrim felt a spike of anger enter his heart at the warrior's temerity in addressing a primarch without a direct question being asked of him.

'Who are you to speak without leave in the presence of your betters?' he demanded, turning to Horus and waving a dismissive hand at the Word Bearer. 'Who is this warrior anyway, and tell me why he joins our private discussions?'

'Erebus is… an advisor to me,' said Horus. 'A valued counsellor and aide.'

'Your Mournival is not enough for you?' asked Fulgrim.

'Times have changed, my brother and I have set plans in motion for which the counsel of the Mournival is not appropriate, matters to which they cannot yet be made privy. Well, not all of them at any rate,' he added with a pained smile.

'What matters?' asked Fulgrim, but Horus shook his head.

'In time, my brother, in time,' promised Horus, rising from behind his desk and circling it to stand before the mural of the Emperor. 'Tell me more of Magnus and his transgressions.'

Fulgrim shrugged. 'You now know as much as I, Horus. All I was given to understand I have now told you.'

'Nothing of substance as to how Magnus is to travel to Terra? As a penitent or a supplicant?'

'I do not know,' admitted Fulgrim. 'Though to send one who dislikes Magnus as much as the Wolf to fetch him home suggests that he does not travel to Terra to be honoured.'

'It does not,' agreed Horus, and Fulgrim could see a glimmer of relief ghost across his brother's face. Had Magnus, like Eldrad Ulthran, seen a glimpse of the future and attempted to give warning of an imminent betrayal? If so, the Warmaster would need to deal with him before his return to Terra.

With the matter of the Lord of Prospero dispensed with to his apparent satisfaction, the Warmaster nodded in the direction of the mural and said, 'You said you remembered this being made.'

Fulgrim nodded, and the Warmaster continued. 'So do I, vividly. You and I, we had just felled the last of the Omakkad Princes aboard their observatory world, and the Emperor decided that such a victory should be remembered.'

'While the Emperor smote the last of their princes, you slew their king and took his head for the Museum of Conquest,' said Fulgrim.

'As you say,' nodded Horus, tapping a finger against the painting. 'I slew their king, and yet it is the Emperor who holds the constellations of the galaxy in his grip. Where are the murals that show the honours you and I won that day, my friend?'

'Jealousy?' chuckled Fulgrim. 'I knew you thought highly of yourself, but I never expected to see such vanity.'

Horus shook his head. 'No, my brother, it is not vanity to wish your deeds and achievements recognised. Who among us has a greater tally of victory than I? Who among us was chosen to act as Warmaster? Only

I was judged worthy, and yet the only honours I pos-
sess are those I fashion for myself.'

'In time, when the Crusade is over, you will be
lauded for your actions,' said Fulgrim.

'Time?' snapped Horus. 'Time is the one thing we
do not have. In essence, we may be aware that the
galaxy revolves in the heavens, but we do not perceive
it, and the ground upon which we walk seems not to
move. Mortal men can live out their lives undisturbed
by such lofty concepts, but they will never achieve
greatness by inaction and ignorance. So it is with
time, my brother. Unless we stop and take its measure, the opportunity for perfect glory will slip away
from us before we even realise that it was there.'

The words of the eldar seer echoed in his head as
though shouted in his ear.

He will lead his armies against your Emperor.

Horus locked his gaze with him, and Fulgrim felt
the fires of his brother's purpose surge like an electric
current in the room, feeding the flames of his own
obsessive need for perfection. As horrified as he was
by the things he was hearing, he could not deny a
powerful force of attraction swelling within him at
the thought of joining his brother.

He saw the rampant ambition and yearning for
power that drove Horus, and understood that his
brother desired to hold the stars in his grip, as the
Emperor did upon the mural.

Everything you have been told is true.

Fulgrim leaned back in his chair and drained the
last of his wine.

'Tell me of this perfect glory,' he said.

HORUS AND EREBUS spoke for three days, telling Fulgrim of what had befallen the 63rd Expedition on

Davin, of the treachery of Eugan Temba, the assault on the crashed *Glory of Terra*, and the necrotic possession that had taken his flesh. Horus spoke of a weapon known as the anathame, which was brought to his staterooms by Fulgrim's Apothecary after he had handed Fabius his seal to have it removed from the *Vengeful Spirit's* medicae deck.

Fulgrim saw that the sword was a crude thing, its blade like stone-worked obsidian, a dull grey filled with a glittering sheen like diamond flint. Its hilt was made of gold and was of superior workmanship to the blade, though still primitive in comparison to *Fireblade*, or even the silver sword of the Laer.

Horus then told him the truth of his injury, how he had, indeed, almost died but for the diligence and devotion of his Legion's quiet order. Of his time in the Delphos, the massive temple structure on Davin, he said little, save that his eyes had been opened to great truths and the monstrous deception that had been perpetrated upon them.

All through this retelling, Fulgrim had felt a creeping horror steal across him, a formless dread of the words that were undermining the very bedrock of his beliefs. He had heard the warning of the eldar seer, but until this moment, he had not believed that such a thing could be true. He wanted to deny the Warmaster's words, but each time he tried to speak a powerful force within him urged him to keep his counsel, to listen to his brother's words.

'The Emperor has lied to us, Fulgrim,' said Horus, and Fulgrim felt a knot of hurt anger uncoil in his gut at such an utterance. 'He means to abandon us to the wilderness of the galaxy while he ascends to godhood.'

Fulgrim felt as though his muscles were locked in a steel vice, for surely he should have flown at Horus to strike him down for such a treacherous utterance. Instead, he sat stunned as he felt his limbs tremble, and his entire world collapsed. How could Horus, most worthy of primarchs be saying such things?

No matter that he had heard them before from different mouths, the substance of their reality had been meaningless until now. To see Horus's lips form words of rebellion kept him rooted to his chair in horrified disbelief. Horus was his most trusted friend, and long ago they had sworn in blood never to speak an untruth to one another. With such an oath between them, Fulgrim had to believe that either his father or his brother had lied to him.

You have no choice! Join with Horus or all you have striven for will have been in vain.

'No,' he managed to whisper, tears welling in his eyes. The anticipation of this moment had fired his senses, but the reality of it was proving to be very different indeed.

'Yes,' said Horus, his expression pained, but determined. 'We believed the Emperor to be the ultimate embodiment of perfection, Fulgrim, but we were wrong. He is not perfect, he is just a man, and we strove to emulate his lie.'

'All my life I wanted to be like him,' said Fulgrim.

'As did we all, my brother,' said Horus. 'It pains me to say these things to you, but they must be said, for a time of war is coming, nothing can prevent that, and I need my closest brothers beside me when the time comes to purge our Legions of those who will not follow us.'

Fulgrim looked up through tear-rimmed eyes and said, 'You are wrong, Horus. You must be wrong. How could an imperfect being have wrought the likes of us?'

'Us?' said Horus. 'We are but the instruments of his will to achieve dominance of the galaxy before his ascension. When the wars are over, we will be cast aside, for we are flawed creations, fashioned from the wide womb of uncreated night. Even before our births, the Emperor cast us aside when he could have saved us. You remember the nightmare of Chemos, the wasteland it was when you fell to its blasted hinterlands? The pain you suffered there, the pain we all suffered on the planets where we grew to manhood? All of that could have been avoided. He could have stopped it all, but he cared so little for us that he simply let it happen. I saw it happen, my brother, I saw it all.'

'How?' gasped Fulgrim. 'How could you have seen such things?'

'In my near death state I was granted an epiphany of hindsight,' said Horus. 'Whether I saw the past or simply had my earliest memories unlocked I do not know, but what I experienced was as real to me as you are.'

The grey meat of Fulgrim's brain was filling fit to burst as he sought to process all that Horus was telling him.

'Even in my moments of blackest doubt, all that sustained me was the utter certainty of my ultimate achievement of perfection,' said Fulgrim. 'The Emperor was the shining paragon of that dream's attainment, and to have that taken away from me…'

'Doubt is not a pleasant condition,' nodded Horus, 'but certainty is absurd when it is built on a lie.'

Fulgrim felt his mind reel that he even entertained the possibility that Horus could be right, his words unravelling all that he had ever been and all he had ever hoped to achieve. His past was gone, destroyed to feed his father's lie, and all that was left to him was his future.

'The Emperor is a comedian playing to an audience too afraid to laugh,' said Horus. 'To him we are tools to be used until blunted and then cast aside. Why else would he leave us and the Crusade to retreat to his dungeons beneath Terra? His apotheosis is already underway and it is up to us to stop it.'

'I dreamed of one day being like him,' whispered Fulgrim, 'of standing at his shoulder and feeling his pride and love for me.'

Horus stepped forward, kneeling before him and taking his hands. 'All men dream, Fulgrim, but not all men dream equally. Those who dream by night in the dusty recesses of their minds wake in the day to find that it was vanity. For men like us, the dreamers of the day, our dreams are ones of hope, of improvement, of change. Perhaps we were once simply weapons, warriors who knew nothing beyond the art of death, but we have grown, my brother! We are so much more than that now, but the Emperor does not see it. He would abandon his greatest achievements to the darkness of a hostile universe. I know this for a fact, Fulgrim, for I did not simply receive this wisdom, I discovered it for myself after a journey that no one could take for me or spare me.'

'I cannot hear this, Horus,' cried Fulgrim, surging to his feet as his flesh threw off the paralysis that had thus far held him immobile. He marched towards the mural of the Emperor and shouted. 'You have no idea what you are asking me to do!'

'On the contrary,' replied Horus, rising to follow him. 'I know exactly what I am asking you to do. I am asking you to stand with me to defend our birthright. This galaxy is ours by right of conquest and blood, but it is to be given away to grubby politicians and clerks. I know you have seen this, and it must make your blood boil as it does mine. Where were those civilians when it was our warriors dying by the thousand? Where were they when we crossed the span of the galaxy to bring illumination to the lost fragments of humanity? I'll tell you where! They huddled in their dark and dusty halls, and penned diatribes like this!'

Horus reached down to his desk, snatched up a handful of papers and thrust them into Fulgrim's hands.

'What are these?' he asked.

'Lies,' said Horus. 'They call it the *Lectitio Divinitatus*, and it is spreading through the fleets like a virus. It is a cult that deifies the Emperor and openly worships him as a god! Can you believe it? After all we have done to bring the light of science and reason to these pathetic mortals, they invent a false god and turn to him for guidance.'

'A god?'

'Aye, Fulgrim, a god,' said Horus, his anger spilling out in a surge of violence. The Warmaster roared and hammered his fist into the mural, his gauntlet smashing the painted face of the Emperor to shards of cracked stone. Ruptured blocks fell from the wall to crash upon the metal deck, and Fulgrim released the papers he held, watching them flutter to the floor amid the ruin of the mural.

Fulgrim cried out as his world shattered into shards as fragmented as the rubble of the mural, his love for the Emperor torn from his breast and held up for the dirty, useless thing it was.

Horus came to him and cupped his face in his hands, staring into his eyes with an intensity that was almost fanatical.

'I need you, my brother,' pleaded Horus. 'I cannot do this without you, but you must do nothing against your conscience. My brother, my phoenix, my hope, wing your way through the darkness and defy fortune's spite. Revive from the ashes and rise!'

Fulgrim met his brother's stare. 'What would you have me do?'

EIGHTEEN

Deep Orbital/Excision/Separate Ways

THE FLIGHT DECK of Deep Orbital DS191 was a tangled mess of twisted metal and flames. The greenskins had occupied the orbiting defence platform for some time, and their unique brand of engineering had already begun to take root. Great idols of fanged iron behemoths squatted amid piles of wreckage, and machines that looked like crude fighter planes lay scattered and broken throughout the deck.

Solomon took cover from the chattering hail of gunfire spraying from the rude barricade that had been thrown together, 'constructed' was too elegant a word for what the greenskins had built, at the end of the flight deck.

Hundreds of roaring aliens had fired randomly, or waved enormous cleavers at the thirty warriors of the Second when they landed on the flight deck from their Thunderhawks. As part of the Emperor's

Children's assault, missiles had punched holes through the hull of the orbital with the intent of explosively decompressing the flight deck and allowing Solomon's Astartes to make an uncontested boarding at this supposedly unoccupied section.

The plan had proceeded without any problems until the tide of wreckage had plugged the holes and hundreds of bellowing, fang-toothed greenskin brutes had charged from the shattered wreckage of their fighters and bombers to attack with mindless ferocity. Wild gunfire ripped through the flight deck. Corkscrewing rockets burst amongst the Astartes, and crude powder charges exploded as hurled grenades burst among the charging Emperor's Children.

'Whoever said that the greenskins were primitive obviously never had to fight them,' shouted Gaius Caphen, as another greasy explosion of flame and black smoke erupted nearby, hurling spars of twisted metal into the air.

Solomon had to agree, having fought the greenskin savages on many occasions. It seemed as though there was no star system throughout the galaxy that had not been infested by the vermin of the greenskins.

'Any sign of our reinforcements?' he shouted.

'Not yet,' returned Caphen. 'We're supposed to be getting extra squads from the First and Third, but nothing so far.'

Solomon ducked as a rocket skidded from the knotted pile of metal he sheltered behind, with a deafening clang, and ricocheted straight up, before detonating in a shower of flame and smoke. Burning shrapnel fell in a patter of scorching scads of metal.

'Don't worry!' cried Solomon. 'Julius and Marius won't let us down.'

At least they better not, he thought grimly, as he bleakly considered the possibility of being overrun. With the unexpected counter-attack by the aliens, he and his warriors would be trapped on the flight deck unless they could fight their way through hundreds of shouting enemy warriors. Solomon wouldn't have given the matter a second thought against any other foe, but the greenskin warriors were monstrous brutes whose strength was very nearly the equal of an Astartes warrior. Their central nervous systems were so primitive that they took a great deal of punishment before they lay down and stopped fighting.

A greenskin warrior was not the equal of an Astartes by any means, but they had enough raw aggression to make up for it, and they had numbers on their side.

The Callinedes system was an Imperial collection of worlds under threat from the greenskins, and to begin the liberation of those worlds that had already fallen, the defence orbitals had to be won back.

This was the first stage in the Imperial relief of Callinedes, and would see the reuniting of the Emperor's Children and the Iron Hands as they assaulted the enemy strongholds on Callinedes IV.

Solomon risked a quick glance over the lip of the smoking metal, as he heard a strident bellow sounding from behind the spars of metal and wreckage that the greenskins were using for cover. Solomon had no knowledge of the greenskin language (or even if they had anything that could be described as language), but the warrior in him recognised the barbaric cadences of a war speech. Whatever passed for greenskin leadership was clearly readying their warriors for an attack. Tribal fetishes and glyph poles hung with

grisly trophies bobbed behind the rusted metal and
Solomon knew they were in the fight of their lives.

'Come on, damn you,' he whispered. Without support from Julius or Marius, he would need to order a
retreat to the assault craft and concede defeat, a
prospect that had little appeal to his warrior code.
'Any word yet?'

'Nothing yet,' hissed Caphen. 'They're not coming
are they?'

'They'll come,' promised Solomon as the chanting
bellows from ahead suddenly swelled in volume and
the crash of metal and iron-shod boots erupted from
beyond.

Gaius Caphen and Solomon shared a moment of
perfect understanding, and rose to their feet with
their bolters at the ready.

'Looks like they're going up the centre!' shouted
Caphen.

'Bastards!' yelled Solomon. 'That's my plan! Second, open fire!'

A torrent of bolter fire reached out to the greenskins, and the front line was scythed down by
rippling series of explosions. Sharp, hard detonations
echoed from the metal walls of the flight deck as the
Astartes fired volley after volley into the charging
enemy, but no matter how many fell, it only seemed
to spur the survivors to a greater frenzy.

The aliens came in a tide of green flesh, rusted
armour and battered leather. Red eyes like furnace
coals glittered with feral intelligence, and they bellowed their uncouth war cries like wild beasts. They
fired noisy, blazing weapons from the hip or bran-
dished mighty, toothed blades with smoke belching
motors. Some wore armour attached with thick
leather straps, or simply nailed to their thick hides,

while others wore great, horned helmets fringed with thick furs.

A huge brute in wheezing, mechanical exo-armour led the charge, bolter shells sparking and ricocheting from his protective suit. Solomon could see the rippling heat haze of a protective energy field sheathing the monstrous chieftain, though how such a primitive race could manufacture or maintain such technology baffled him.

The bolters of the Second wreaked fearful havoc amongst the aliens, blasting sprays of stinking red blood from great, bloodied craters in green flesh, or blowing limbs clean off in explosions of gore.

'Ready swords!' shouted Solomon as he saw that no matter how great the carnage worked upon the charge, it wouldn't be nearly enough.

He put aside his bolter and drew his sword and pistol as the first greenskin warrior smashed its way through the rusted girders, not even bothering to go around. Solomon swayed aside from a blow that would have hacked him in two, and swung his sword in a double-handed grip for his opponent's neck. His sword bit the full breadth of his hand into the greenskin's neck, but instead of dropping dead, the greenskin bellowed and savagely clubbed him to the ground.

Solomon rolled to avoid a stamping foot that would surely have crushed his skull, and lashed out once more. This time, his blade hacked through the beast's ankle, and it collapsed in a thrashing pile of limbs. Still it tried to kill him, but Solomon quickly picked himself up and stomped his boot down on the greenskin's throat, before putting a pair of bolt shells through its skull.

Gaius Caphen struggled with a greenskin a head taller than him, its great, motorised axe slashing for his head with every stroke. Solomon shot it in the face and ducked as yet another greenskin came at him. All shape to the battle was lost as each warrior fought his own private war, all skill reduced to survival and killing.

It couldn't end this way. A lifetime of glory and honour couldn't end at the hands of the greenskins. He had fought side by side with some of the Imperium's greatest heroes, and there was no way he was going to die fighting a foe as inglorious as these brutes.

Unfortunately, he thought wryly, *they* didn't seem to know that.

Where in the name of Terra were Julius and Marius?

He saw a pair of his warriors borne to the deck by a pack of howling greenskins, a roaring axe hacking their Mark IV plate to splintered ruins. Another was ripped almost in two by a close range burst from a monstrous rotary cannon that was carried by a greenskin as though it weighed no more than a pistol.

Even as he watched these tragedies play out, a rusted cleaver smote him in the chest and hurled him backwards. His armour split under the impact and he coughed blood, looking up into the snarling, fanged gorge of the greenskin leader. The hissing, wheezing armour enlarged its burly physique, its muscles powered by mighty pistons and roaring bellows.

Solomon rolled aside as the cleaver arced towards him, crying out as splintered ends of bone ground together in his chest. Momentary pain paralysed him, but even as he awaited another attack, he heard the sound of massed bolter fire and the high-pitched whine of a hundred chainswords.

The greenskin before him looked up in response to the sound, and Solomon did not waste his opportunity, unloading his weapon full in its face, pulping its thickly-boned skull in a torrent of explosive shells.

Its metal exo-skeleton kept it on its feet, but suddenly the greenskin force was in disarray as newly arrived Emperor's Children tore into the battle, delivering point blank shots from bolt pistols, or cutting limbs and heads from bodies with precisely aimed sword blows.

In moments, the fighting was done as the last pockets of greenskin warriors were isolated into smaller and smaller knots of resistance, and were mercilessly gunned down by the new arrivals. Solomon watched the extermination with cold admiration, for the killings were achieved with a perfection he had not seen in some time.

Gaius Caphen, bloodied and battered, but alive, helped him to his feet, and Solomon smiled despite the pain in his cracked ribs.

'I told you Julius and Marius wouldn't let us down,' he said.

Caphen shook his head as the captains who led the relief force marched over towards them. 'That's not who came.'

Solomon looked up in confusion as the nearest warrior removed his helm.

'I heard you could use some help, and thought we'd lend a hand,' said Saul Tarvitz. Behind Tarvitz, Solomon saw the unmistakable swagger of the swordsman, Lucius.

'What about the Third and the First?' he hissed, the fact that his battle-brothers had forsaken the Second more painful than any wound.

Tarvitz shrugged apologetically. 'I don't know. We were beginning our push to the main control centre and heard your request for support.'

'It's a good thing we did,' said Lucius, his scarred face twisted in amusement. 'Looks like you needed the help.'

Solomon felt like punching the arrogant bastard, but held his tongue, for the swordsman was right. Without their aid, he and his warriors would have been slaughtered.

'I'm grateful, Captain Tarvitz,' he said, ignoring Lucius.

Tarvitz bowed and said, 'The honour is mine, Captain Demeter, but I must regretfully take my leave of you. We must move on our primary objective.'

'Yes,' said Solomon, waving him away. 'Go. Do the Legion proud.'

Tarvitz threw him a quick martial salute and turned away, sliding his helmet back on and issuing orders to his warriors. Lucius gave him a mock bow and saluted him with the energised edge of his blade before joining his fellow captain.

Julius and Marius had not come.

'Where were you?' he whispered, but no one answered him.

'MY LORD!' CRIED Vespasian, marching into Fulgrim's staterooms without pause or ceremony. The lord commander was arrayed in his battle armour, the smooth plates oiled and polished to a reflective finish. His face was flushed and his stride urgent as he made his way through the mess of broken marble and half-finished canvases, towards where Fulgrim sat in contemplation before a pair of statues carved to represent the captains of two of his battle companies.

Fulgrim looked up as he approached, and Vespasian was struck again by the change that had come over his primarch since they had taken their leave of

GRAHAM MCNEILL

the 63rd Expedition. The four week journey to the
Callinedes system had been one of the strangest times
Vespasian could remember, his primarch sullen and
withdrawn and the soul of the Legion in turmoil. As
more and more of Apothecary Fabius's chemicals
were introduced to the Legion's blood, only a blind
man could fail to see the decline in the Legion's
moral fibre. With Fulgrim's and Eidolon's sanction,
few of the Legion's captains were willing to resist the
slide into decadent arrogance.

Only a very few of Vespasian's companies still held
to the ideals that had founded the Legion, and he was
at a loss as to know how to stop the rot. With the
orders coming directly from Fulgrim and Eidolon, the
rigid command structure of the Emperor's Children
allowed little, if any, room for leeway in the interpre-
tation of their orders.

Vespasian had requested an audience with Fulgrim
all through the journey to the Callinedes system, and
though his exalted rank would normally entitle him
to such a meeting without question, his requests had
been denied. As he had watched the battle hololiths
from the Heliopolis, and seen Solomon Demeter's
company abandoned, he had decided to take matters
into his own hands.

'Vespasian?' said Fulgrim, his pale features energised as he returned his gaze to the statues before
him. 'How goes the battle?'

Vespasian controlled his temper and forced himself
to be calm. 'The battle will be won soon, my lord,
but–'

'Good,' interrupted Fulgrim. Vespasian now saw
that his lord and master had three swords laid out
before him. *Fireblade* lay pointed at a statue of Marius
Vairosean, the damnable silver sword of the Laer

pointed at one of Julius Kaesoron. A weapon with a glittering grey blade and golden hilt lay in a shattered pile of marble sitting between the two statues, and Vespasian could see from the remains of a carved face that the statue had once been of Solomon Demeter.

'My lord,' pressed Vespasian, 'why were Captains Vairosean and Kaesoron held back from supporting Captain Demeter? But for the intervention of Tarvitz and Lucius, Solomon's men would be dead.'

'Tarvitz and Lucius saved Captain Demeter?' asked Fulgrim, and Vespasian was shocked to see a hint of annoyance surface on Fulgrim's face. 'How… courageous of them.'

'They shouldn't have needed to,' said Vespasian. 'Julius and Marius were supposed to support the Second, but they were held back. Why?'

'Are you questioning me, Vespasian?' asked Fulgrim. 'I am enacting the Warmaster's will. Do you dare to suggest that you know better than he how we should prosecute this foe?'

Vespasian was stunned at Fulgrim's pronouncement and said, 'With all due respect, my lord, the Warmaster is not here. How can he know how best to prosecute the greenskins?'

Fulgrim smiled, and lifting the grey sheened sword from the remains of Solomon's statue he said, 'Because he knows that this battle is not about the greenskins.'

'Then what is it about, my lord?' demanded Vespasian. 'I should dearly wish to know.'

'It is about righting a monstrous wrong that has been done to us, and purging our ranks of those without the strength to do what must be done. The Warmaster moves on the Isstvan system and on its bloody fields a reckoning will take place.'

'The Isstvan system?' asked Vespasian. 'I don't understand. Why is the Warmaster moving on the Isstvan system?'

'Because it is there that we will cross the Rubicon, my dear Vespasian,' said Fulgrim, his voice choked with emotion. 'There, we will take the first steps on the new path the Warmaster forges; a path that will lead to the establishment of a new and glorious order of perfection and wonder.'

Vespasian fought to keep up with Fulgrim's rapid delivery and confused ramblings. His eyes flickered to the sword in the primarch's hand, feeling a dreadful threat from the blade, as though the weapon itself were a sentient thing and desired his death. He shook off such superstitious nonsense and said, 'Permission to speak freely, my lord?'

'Always, Vespasian,' said Fulgrim. 'You must always speak freely, for where is the pleasure to be had in our facility for locution if we restrain ourselves from freedom? Tell me, have you heard of a philosopher of Old Earth called Cornelius Blayke?'

'No, my lord, but–'

'Oh, you must read him, Vespasian,' said Fulgrim, guiding him towards a great canvas at the end of the stateroom. 'Julius introduced me to his works, and I can barely conceive of how I endured this long without them. Evander Tobias thinks highly of him, though an old man such as he is beyond making use of such raptures as may be found locked within the pages of Blayke's work.'

'My lord, please!'

Fulgrim held up a hand to silence him as they arrived at the canvas, and the primarch turned him around to face it. 'Hush, Vespasian, there is something I wish you to see.'

Vespasian's questions fled from his mind at the horror of the picture before him, the image of his primarch distorted and leering, the flesh pulled tight over protruding bones and the mouth twisted with the anticipation of imminent violence and violation. The figure's armour was a loathsome parody of the proud, noble form of Mark IV plate, its every surface covered with bizarre symbols that appeared to writhe on the canvas, as though the thick layers of stinking paint had been applied over a host of living worms.

It was in the eyes, however, that Vespasian saw the greatest evil. They burned with the light of secret knowledge, and of things done in the name of experience that it would sear his soul to know but a fraction of. No vileness was beyond this apparition, no depths too low to embrace, and no practice too vile to be indulged in.

As he stared into the lidless eyes of the image, they fixed upon him, and he felt the painting's leprous visage peel back the layers of his soul as it hunted for the darkness within him that it would bring forth and nurture. The sense of violation was horrific. He dropped to his knees as he fought to avert his gaze from the burning cruelty of the painting, and the terrifying void that existed beyond its eyes. He saw the birth and death of universes in the wheeling stars of its eyes, and the futility of his feeble race in denying their every whim.

The painting's lips bulged, twisting in a rictus grin.

Give in to me… it seemed to say… *Expose your deepest desires to me.*

Vespasian felt every corner of his being dredged for darkness and spite, bitterness and bile, but his soul soared as he sensed the growing frustration of the violator as it found nothing to sink its claws into. Its anger grew, and as it did, so too did his strength. He tore his eyes from the painting, feeling its anger at the purity of his desires. He tried to reach for his sword to destroy this creation of evil, but the painting's monstrous will held his power of action locked in the prison of his flesh.

He harbours nothing, said the horrifying painting in disgust. *He is worthless. Kill him.*

'Vespasian,' said Fulgrim above him, and he had the vivid sensation that the primarch was not talking to him, but was addressing the sword itself.

He fought in vain to turn his head, feeling the sharp prick of the sword point laid against his neck. He tried to cry out, to warn Fulgrim of what he had seen, but his throat felt as though bands of iron had clamped around it, his muscles locked to immobility by the power of the image before him.

'Energy is an eternal delight,' whispered Fulgrim, 'and he who desires, but acts not, breeds pestilence. You could have stood at my right hand, Vespasian, but you have shown that you are a pestilence within the ranks of the Emperor's Children. You must be cut out.'

Vespasian felt the pressure on the back of his neck grow stronger, the tip of the sword breaking skin and warm blood trickling down his neck.

'Don't do this,' he managed to hiss.

Fulgrim paid his words no heed and, with one smooth motion, drove the blade of the anathame downwards through Vespasian's spine, and into his chest cavity until the golden quillons rested to either side of the nape of his neck.

THE CARGO DECKS of the deep orbital had been cleared of the greenskin dead by the Legion's menials, for a

portion of the Callinedes battle force to assemble and
hear the words of their beloved primarch. Fulgrim
marched behind a line of heralds, chosen from among
the young initiates who were soon to complete their
training as Emperor's Children. The trumpeters fanned
out before him, playing a blaring fanfare to announce
his arrival, and a thunderous roar of applause swelled
from the assembled warriors as they welcomed him.

Arrayed in his battle armour, the Primarch of the
Emperor's Children knew he was a truly magnificent
sight. His face was pale and sculpted, framed by the
flowing mane of his albino white hair. He wore the
golden-hilted sword that he had used to slay Vespasian, belted at his hip, eager to display the bond of
brotherhood that existed between him and the Warmaster.

Lord Commander Eidolon, Apothecary Fabius and
Chaplain Charmosian, the senior officers of his inner
circle, flanked him. They had been instrumental in
spreading the clarity of the Warmaster's vision to the
warriors of the Legion. The massive Dreadnought body
of Ancient Rylanor, the Emperor's Children's Ancient
of Rites, also accompanied him, through tradition
rather than loyalty to the Legion's new vision.

Fulgrim waited graciously for the applause to die
down before speaking, letting his dark eyes linger
upon those he knew would follow him and ignoring
those he knew would not.

'My brothers!' called Fulgrim, his voice lilting and
golden. 'This day you have shown the accursed greenskin what it means to stand against the Children of the
Emperor!'

More applause rolled around the cargo decks, but he
spoke over it, his voice easily cutting through the clamour of his warriors.

'Commander Eidolon has wrought you into a weapon against which the greenskins had no defence. Perfection, strength, resolve: these qualities are the cutting edge of the Legion and you have shown them all here today. This orbital is in Imperial hands once more, as are the others the greenskins had occupied in the futile hope of fending off our invasion.

'The time has come to press home this attack against the greenskins and liberate the Callinedes system! My brother primarch, Ferrus Manus of the Iron Hands, and I, shall see to it that not a single alien stands upon land claimed in the name of the Crusade.'

Fulgrim could taste the expectation in the air and savoured the anticipation of his next words, knowing that they carried death for some and glory for others. The Legion awaited his orders, most of them unaware of the magnitude of what he was to command, or that the fate of the galaxy hung in the balance.

'Most of you, my brothers, will not be there,' said Fulgrim. He could feel the crushing weight of disappointment settle upon his warriors, and had to fight to control the wild laughter that threatened to bubble up, as they cried out at what was to be a death sentence for many of them.

'The Legion will be divided,' continued Fulgrim, raising his hands to stem the cries of woe and lamentation his words provoked. 'I will lead a small force to join Ferrus Manus and his Iron Hands at Callinedes IV. The rest of the Legion will rendezvous with the Warmaster's 63rd Expedition at the Isstvan system. These are the orders of the Warmaster and your primarch. Lord Commander Eidolon will lead you to Isstvan, and he will act in my stead until I can join you once more.

'Commander, if you please,' said Fulgrim, gesturing Eidolon to step forwards.

Eidolon nodded and said, 'The Warmaster has called upon us to aid his Legion in battle once more. He recognises our skills and we welcome this chance to prove our superiority. We are to halt a rebellion in the Isstvan system, but we are not to fight alone. As well as his own Legion, the Warmaster has seen fit to deploy the Death Guard and the World Eaters.'

A muttered gasp spread around the cargo bay at the mention of such brutal Legions.

Eidolon chuckled. 'I see some of you remember fighting alongside our brother Astartes. We all know what a grim and artless business war becomes in the hands of such men, so I say this is the perfect opportunity to show the Warmaster how the Emperor's chosen fight!'

The Legion cheered once more, and Fulgrim's amusement turned instantly to sorrow as he understood that, but for Vespasian's stubbornness, a great many of these warriors would have made a fine addition to the army of the Warmaster's new crusade.

With such warriors fighting for the Warmaster, what heights of perfection would have been beyond them? Vespasian's refusal to allow his men to sample the heady delights of Fabius's chemical stimulants, or to undergo enhancing surgeries, had condemned the warriors once under his command to death in the Warmaster's trap of Isstvan III. He realised he should have disposed of Vespasian much sooner, and the mixture of guilt and excitement at the deaths he had set in motion was a potent cocktail of sensations.

'The Warmaster has requested our presence immediately,' shouted Eidolon through the cheering. 'Though Isstvan is not far distant, the conditions in the Warp have become more difficult, so we must make all haste. The strike cruiser *Andronius* will leave for Isstvan in four hours. When we arrive, it will be as ambassadors for our Legion, and when the battle is done the Warmaster will have witnessed war at its most magnificent.'

Eidolon saluted and Fulgrim led the applause before turning and taking his leave.

Now he had to deliver on the second part of his pledge to the Warmaster.

Now he had to convince Ferrus Manus to join their great endeavour.

NINETEEN

An Error of Judgement

THE BEAT OF hammers and the pounding of distant forges echoed through the Anvilarium of the *Fist of Iron*, but Gabriel Santar, First Captain of the Iron Hands, barely heard them. The Morlock Terminators stood sentinel around the edge of the chamber, the mightiest of them protecting the gates of the primarch's inner sanctum, the Iron Forge. Rendered ghostly by the hissing clouds of steam that billowed from the deck, the fearsome visage of the Morlocks put Santar in mind of the vengeful predators that howled across the frozen tundra of Medusa for which they were named.

His heart beat in time with the mighty hammers far below, the thought of once again standing in the presence of two of the mightiest beings in the galaxy filling him with pride, honour and, if he was honest, not a little trepidation.

Ferrus Manus stood beside him, resplendent in his gleaming, black battle armour and wearing a glistening cloak of mail that shone like spun silver. His high gorget of dark iron obscured the lower part of his face, but Santar knew his primarch well enough to know that he was smiling at the thought of a reunion with his brother.

'It will do my heart proud to see Fulgrim again, Santar,' said Ferrus, and Santar risked a sidelong glance at the primarch of the X Legion, hearing a note of wariness in his master's voice that echoed his own feelings on the matter.

'My lord?' he asked. 'Is something the matter?'

Ferrus Manus turned his flinty eyes on Santar and said, 'No, not exactly, my friend, but you were there when we parted from the Emperor's Children after the victory over the Diasporex. You know that our Legions did not part as brothers in arms should.'

Santar nodded, remembering well the ceremony of parting on the upper embarkation deck of the *Pride of the Emperor*. The ceremony was to be held aboard Fulgrim's flagship, for the *Fist of Iron* had suffered horrendous damage when it had intercepted the Diasporex cruisers closing on the *Firebird*, and the Primarch of the Emperor's Children had deemed it unfit for a ceremony of such magnitude.

Though such a proclamation had incensed its captain and crew, Ferrus Manus had laughed off his brother's hasty words and agreed to come aboard the *Pride of the Emperor*.

Surrounded by the Morlocks, Ferrus Manus and Santar had marched through the ranks of elaborately armoured Phoenix Guard towards the waiting forms of the Phoenician and his battle captains. The march had felt like they were running a gauntlet of enemy warriors instead of the praetorians of their closest brothers.

In Santar's eyes, the ceremony had been concluded with unseemly haste, Fulgrim taking his brother in an embrace that was as awkward as their first had been joyous. Ferrus Manus must surely have noticed the change in his brother's mien, but he had said nothing of it upon their return to the *Fist of Iron*. A tightening of the primarch's jaw as he watched the 28th Expedition translate into the churning maelstrom of the warp had been the only indication that he felt slighted by his brother's coldness.

'You think Fulgrim still feels affronted by what happened at the Carollis Star?'

Ferrus did not answer immediately, and Santar knew that was exactly what was bothering his primarch. 'We saved him and his precious *Firebird* from being blown to bits,' continued Santar. 'Fulgrim should be grateful.'

Ferrus chuckled and said, 'You don't know my brother then. That he needed saving at all is unthinkable to him, for it suggests that he acted in a manner less than perfect. Be sure not to mention it around him, Gabriel. I'm serious.'

Santar shook his head, his lip curled in a sneer. 'Too damn superior the lot of them, did you see the way their first captain sized me up when we first boarded the *Pride of the Emperor*? You didn't have to be old Cistor to feel the condescension coming from them. They think they're better than us. You can see it in every one of their faces.'

Ferrus Manus turned to face him, and the full power of his silver eyes bored in on Santar, their cold depths chilling in their controlled anger. Santar knew he'd gone too far, and he cursed the fire within him that surged in him at the thought of any insult done to his Legion.

'My apologies, lord,' he said. 'I spoke out of turn.'

As quickly as Ferrus's ire had risen at his fiery words, it subsided, and he leaned down close to Santar, his voice little more than a whisper. 'Yes you did, but you spoke from the heart, and that is why I value you. It's true that this rendezvous is unexpected, for I did not request the presence of the Emperor's Children to aid us. The 52nd Expedition needs no assistance in defeating the greenskins.'

'Then why are they here?' asked Santar.

'I do not know, though I welcome the chance to see my brother again and heal any rifts between us.'

'Perhaps he feels the same and comes to make amends.'

'I doubt it,' said Ferrus Manus. 'It is not in Fulgrim's nature to admit when he is wrong.'

THE GREAT BLACK iron gates of the Anvilarium swung open, and Fulgrim marched towards them with his flowing, fur-lined cape billowing in the heated gusts of air from the forges below. He stood for a moment at the chamber's threshold, knowing that to step across this line was to set foot on a road that might see him sundered forever from his closest brother. He saw Ferrus Manus with his first captain and chief astropath flanking him, the grim form of his Morlock bodyguards placed around the chamber's perimeter.

Julius Kaesoron, resplendent in his Terminator armour, and a full ten of the Phoenix Guard accompanied him to mark the gravity of the moment. When Fulgrim sensed the moment was right, he stepped into the dry heat of the Anvilarium and marched to stand before his brother primarch. Julius Kaesoron remained at his side, as the Phoenix Guard moved to join the Morlocks at the chamber's edge so that there was a purple and gold armoured twin for each of the steel-skinned Terminators.

The risk of approaching Ferrus Manus like this was great, but the rewards to be reaped upon the inevitable success of the Warmaster's ambition outweighed any doubts he might once have had.

The Warmaster had already begun the process of winning the other primarchs to his cause, and Fulgrim had promised that he could bring him Ferrus Manus without a shot being fired. Such was their shared history and bonds of brotherhood that Fulgrim knew Ferrus Manus could not fail to see the justice of their cause. The veil of lies had been lifted from Fulgrim's eyes, and it was his duty to reveal that lie to his closest brother.

'Ferrus,' he said, opening his arms to his brother, 'it gladdens my heart to see you again.'

Ferrus Manus embraced him, and Fulgrim felt his love for his brother swell in his breast as the primarch of the Iron Hands thumped his silver hands against his fur cape.

'It is an unexpected joy to see you, my brother,' said Ferrus, stepping back and looking him up and down. 'What brings you to the Callinedes system? Are we not prosecuting the foe quickly enough for the Warmaster?'

'On the contrary,' beamed Fulgrim, 'the Warmaster himself sends his compliments and bids me honour you for the speed of your conquests.'

He bit back a smile as he felt the pride of achievement fill every warrior of the Iron Hands in the Anvilarium. Of course the Warmaster had said no such thing, but a little flattery never failed to win over hearts and minds at such times.

'You hear that, my brothers!' shouted Ferrus Manus. 'The Warmaster honours us! Glory to the Tenth Legion!'

'Glory to the Tenth Legion!' bellowed the Iron Hands, and Fulgrim felt like laughing at such primitive displays of pleasure. He could show these dull warriors the true meaning of pleasure, but that would come later.

Ferrus clapped his silver hand on Fulgrim's shoulder and said, 'But come, brother. Aside from passing on the Warmaster's honour, what brings you here?'

Fulgrim smiled and placed his hand on *Fireblade's* golden pommel. He had deemed it impolitic to come before Ferrus without the sword his brother had forged beneath Mount Narodnya over two centuries ago, but he felt the absence of his silver blade keenly. Ferrus saw the gesture and reached behind him to lift *Forgebreaker*, the great hammer that Fulgrim had crafted.

The two primarchs smiled, and once again their brotherhood was obvious to all.

'You are right, Ferrus, there is more that I would speak of, but it is for your ears alone,' said Fulgrim. 'It concerns the very future of the Great Crusade.'

Suddenly serious, Ferrus nodded and said, 'Then we shall talk in the Iron Forge.'

MARIUS STOOD RIGIDLY to attention on the bridge of the *Pride of the Emperor*, his flesh alive with sensation as he watched the drifting slab of steel and bronze that was the *Fist of Iron* through the viewing bay. The ship was an ugly beast, decided Marius, its hull still scarred and unpainted after the damage done to it during the battle of the Carollis Star. What kind of Legion would travel in a vessel so unfitted to the glory of the warriors it carried? What manner of leader did not have the pride to embellish his fleet so that it displayed the perfection of the Legion it represented?

Marius felt his choler rise and struggled to control it as he found himself crushing the brass rails around the command pulpit. His anger stimulated the newly rewired pleasure centres of his brain, and it was only with a supreme effort of will that he forced himself to be calm.

He had explicit orders from his primarch, orders that might be the difference between life and death for all those aboard the *Fist of Iron*, and it would be the death of them all were he to fail when called upon. Fulgrim had specifically selected him for this role, for he knew there was no warrior more reliable than Marius in the Emperor's Children, who would not hesitate or suffer any conflict of conscience at doing what might have to be done.

Ever since going under the knives of Apothecary Fabius, Marius had felt as though his skin were a prison for the universe of sensation that seethed in the meat and bone of his body. Every emotion brought an ecstasy of joy, and every hurt a spasm of pleasure. Julius had instructed him on the teachings of Cornelius Blayke, and he had passed that knowledge throughout his company. Every one of his officers and many of the fighting Astartes had been sent to the *Andronius* for chemical and surgical enhancement. The demands on Apothecary Fabius had been so great that he had even established an entirely new corps of augmentative chirurgeons to meet the Legion's requirements for enhancements.

With the Legion's surprise attack on Deep Orbital DS191, the Iron Hands had welcomed them with open arms, renewing the oaths of brotherhood that had been sworn amid the corpses of the Diasporex fleet. The piquet vessels of the Iron Hands had stood down, and, discreetly and without provocation, the

Pride of the Emperor and her escorts drifted amongst the ships of the 52nd Expedition.

With one command, he could visit unimaginable destruction upon the Iron Hands. The thought made him sweat, and his every nerve ending leapt to the surface of his skin, singing with sensation.

If Fulgrim's mission was successful, such drastic action would not be necessary.

Despite himself, Marius realised that he hoped his primarch's mission would fail.

Ferrus Manus kept his most prized relics and personal creations within the Iron Forge. Its gleaming walls were fashioned from smooth, glassy basalt and hung with all manner of wondrous weapons, armour and machinery crafted by the primarch's silver hands. A vast anvil of iron and gold sat in the centre of the forge, and Ferrus Manus had long ago declared that none save his brother primarchs were permitted to enter this most private sanctum. Fulgrim himself had only set foot in it once before.

Vulkan of the XVIII Legion had once declared it a magical place, using the language of the ancients to describe the magnificence it contained. To honour Ferrus's skill, Vulkan had presented him with a Firedrake banner, which hung next to a wondrously crafted gun with a top loading magazine and perforated barrel formed in the shape of a snarling dragon. Its brass and silver body comprised the finest workmanship Fulgrim had ever seen, and he paused before it, its lines and curves so beautiful that to simply label it a weapon was to deny that it was in fact a work of art.

'I made that for Vulkan two hundred years ago,' said Ferrus, 'before he led his Legion into the Mordant Stars.'

'So why is it still here?'

'You know what Vulkan's like, he loves to work the metal and doesn't trust anything that hasn't had the beat of a hammer laid upon it or the fire of the forge in its heart.'

Ferrus held up his shimmering, mercurial hands and said, 'I don't think he liked the fact that I could shape metal without heat or hammer. He returned it to me a century ago, saying that it should remain here with its creator. I think Nocturne's superstitions aren't as forgotten as our brother would have us believe.'

Fulgrim reached up to touch the weapon, but curled his fingers into a fist before they touched the warm metal. To touch such a perfect weapon without firing it would be wrong.

'I understand that there is a certain attraction in a handsomely made weapon, but to apply such artistry to a thing designed to kill seems... extravagant,' said Fulgrim.

'Really?' chuckled Ferrus, hefting *Forgebreaker* and pointing it at *Fireblade* sheathed at Fulgrim's hip. 'Then what were we doing in the Urals?'

Fulgrim drew his sword and turned it in his hands so that it caught the light and threw dazzling red reflections around the forge.

'That was a contest,' smiled Fulgrim. 'I didn't know you then, and I wasn't going to have you outdo me, was I?'

Ferrus circled the Iron Forge, pointing his warhammer at the magnificent creations he had wrought, and which hung upon the wall. 'There is nothing in weapons, machinery, or engineering devices that obliges them to be ugly,' said Ferrus. 'Ugliness is a measure of imperfection. You of all people should appreciate that.'

'Then you must be perfectly imperfect,' said Fulgrim, his smile robbing the comment of malice.

'I'll leave being pretty to you and Sanguinius, my brother. I'll stick to fighting. Now come on, what's this all about? You speak of the future of the Great Crusade and then want to talk of weapons and old times? What's going on?'

Fulgrim tensed, suddenly anxious at what he was to ask of his brother. He had hoped to approach the matter circuitously, feeling out his brother's position and the likelihood of him joining them willingly, but with typical Medusan directness, Ferrus Manus had come right out and demanded to know his purpose.

How artless and blunt.

'When did you last see the Emperor?' asked Fulgrim.

'The Emperor? What has that to do with anything?'

'Indulge me. When was it?'

'A long time ago,' admitted Ferrus. 'Orina Septimus. On the crystal headlands above the acid oceans.'

'I last saw him on Ullanor at the Warmaster's coronation,' said Fulgrim, moving towards the great anvil and trailing his fingers along the cold metal. 'I wept when he told us that he believed the time had come for him to leave the crusading work to his sons, and that he was returning to Terra to undertake a still higher calling.'

'The Great Triumph,' nodded Ferrus sadly. 'I was on campaign in the Kaelor Nebula and too far distant to attend personally. It is the one regret I have, not being able to say my farewells to our father.'

'I was there,' said Fulgrim, his voice choked with emotion. 'I stood on the dais next to Horus and Dorn when the Emperor told us he was leaving, and it was the second most heartbreaking moment of my life. We begged him to stay, to see out what he had begun, but he turned his back on us. He would not even say what this great work was, only that were he not to return to Terra then all that we had won would crumble and fall into ruins.'

Ferrus Manus looked up at him, his eyes narrowed. 'You talk as if he abandoned us.'

'That was how it felt,' said Fulgrim, his tone bitter. 'How it still feels.'

'You said yourself that our father was returning to Terra to preserve all that we have fought and bled for. Do you really think he would not have wanted to see the final victory of the Crusade?'

'I don't know,' said Fulgrim angrily. 'He could have stayed, what difference would a few years make? What could be so important that he had to leave us there and then?'

Ferrus took a step towards him, and Fulgrim saw the reflection of his hurt anger in the mirrored eyes of his brother, the betrayal of everything he and the Emperor's Children had fought for over the last two hundred years.

'I do not understand what you imply Fulgrim,' said Ferrus, his words trailing off as the import of Fulgrim's earlier words came to him. 'What did you mean when you said it was the second most heartbreaking moment of your life? What could be greater than that?'

Fulgrim took a deep breath, knowing that he would have to come flat out and say what he had come to say.

'What could be greater than that? When Horus told me the truth of how the Emperor had betrayed us and planned to cast us aside in his quest for godhood,' said Fulgrim, relishing the horrified expression of surprise and fury on his brother's face.

'Fulgrim!' shouted Ferrus. 'What in Terra is wrong with you? Betrayed us? Godhood? What are you talking about?'

Fulgrim took quick steps to stand before Ferrus Manus, his voice passionate now that he had taken the final step and confessed his true reasons for coming here. 'Horus has seen the truth of things, my brother. The Emperor has already abandoned us and even now plots his apotheosis. He lied to us all, Ferrus. We were nothing more than tools to win back the galaxy in preparation for his ascension! The perfect being he pretended to be was a filthy lie!'

Ferrus pushed him off and backed away, his ruddy, craggy features pale and horrified. Knowing he had to press on, Fulgrim said, 'Others have already seen this truth and are moving to join Horus. We will strike before the Emperor is even aware that his designs have been unmasked. Horus will reclaim the galaxy in the name of those whose blood was spent to conquer it!'

Fulgrim wanted to laugh as the words spilled from him, the thrill of finally unburdening himself almost too great to stand. The breath heaved in his lungs, and he could not tell whether the thundering he could hear was the blood surging in his skull or the hammers of far away forges.

Ferrus Manus shook his head, and Fulgrim despaired as he saw his brother's horror turning to fury. 'This is the new direction of the Crusade you spoke of?'

'Yes!' cried Fulgrim. 'It will be a glorious age of perfection, my brother. What we have won is already being given away to imperfect mortals who will waste the glories we won for them. What we have earned in blood and tears will be ours again, can't you see that?'

'All I see is betrayal, Fulgrim!' roared Ferrus Manus. 'You are not talking about claiming back what we have won; you are talking about betraying everything we stand for!'

'My brother,' implored Fulgrim, 'please! You must listen to me. The Mechanicum has already pledged its support to the Warmaster, as have many of our brothers! War is coming, war that will engulf this galaxy in flames. When it is over, there will be no mercy for those on the wrong side.'

He saw the colour flood back into his brother's face, a raw and bellicose red that he knew all too well. 'Ferrus, I beg you for the sake of our brotherhood to join us!'

'Brotherhood?' bellowed Ferrus. 'Our brotherhood died when you decided to turn traitor!'

Fulgrim backed away from his brother as he saw the murderous intent in his blazing silver eyes. 'Lorgar and Angron are ready to strike, and Mortarion will soon be with us. You must join me or you will be destroyed!'

'No,' snarled Ferrus Manus, hefting *Forgebreaker* to his shoulder. 'It is you who will be destroyed.'

'Ferrus, no!' pleaded Fulgrim. 'Think about this. Would I come to you like this if I did not believe that it was the right thing to do?'

'I don't know what's happened to you, Fulgrim, but this is treachery and there is only one fate for traitors.'

'So… you are going to kill me?'

Ferrus hesitated, and Fulgrim saw his shoulders sag in despair.

'I am your sworn honour brother and I swear to you that I do not lie,' pressed Fulgrim, hoping that there was still a chance to convince his brother not to act in haste.

'I know you're not lying, Fulgrim,' said Ferrus sadly, 'and that's why you have to die.'

Fulgrim brought his sword up as Ferrus Manus swung his hammer for his head with blinding speed. The two weapons rang with a clash of steel that Fulgrim felt echo in the very depths of his soul. Flames blazed from his blade and lightning crackled from the head of Ferrus's hammer. The two primarchs stood locked together, Fulgrim pressing his fiery blade towards Ferrus, and the commander of the Iron Hands holding him at bay with the haft of his hammer.

Burning light and sound filled the Iron Forge, the weapons roaring as the unimaginable forces harnessed in their creation were unleashed. Ferrus dropped his guard and hammered his fist into Fulgrim's face, the force of the blow enough to crush the helmet of Tactical Dreadnought armour, but barely enough to bruise the flesh of a primarch. Fulgrim rode the blow and smashed his forehead into his brother's face, spinning on his heel and slashing his red hot blade towards Ferrus's throat.

The blade clanged on Ferrus's gorget, sliding clear without so much as scratching the black plate. Ferrus spun away from a return strike and swung his hammer one handed as he bought some space with his wide swings. The two warriors circled one another warily, both aware of how deadly the other could be, having fought side by side in decades of war. Fulgrim saw tears in his brother's eyes, and the mixture of sorrow and pleasure he took from the sight made him want to throw down his weapon and clasp his brother to his breast, that he might share such a stupendous experience.

'This is pointless, Ferrus,' said Fulgrim. 'Even now the Warmaster is preparing to expunge the weak from his forces at Isstvan III.'

'What are you talking about, traitor?' demanded
Ferrus.

Fulgrim laughed. 'The power of four Legions will
be unleashed against Isstvan III, but only those portions that are not loyal to the Warmaster and his
grand designs for the future of the galaxy. Soon, perhaps even already, those weak elements will be
dead, cleansed in the fire of a viral bombardment.'

'The Life Eater?' whispered Ferrus, and Fulgrim
relished the horror he saw in his brother's eyes.
'Throne alive, Fulgrim, how could you be party to
such murder?'

Wild laughter bubbled up inside Fulgrim, and he
leapt to the attack, his blazing sword cleaving the
air in a fiery arc. Once more, Ferrus's hammer came
up to block the blow, but it was not a weapon
designed for long duels, and Fulgrim rolled the
blade over the haft and stabbed for his brother's
face.

The burning blade scored along Ferrus's cheek,
the skin blackening to match his armour, and his
brother cried out as the sword he had forged dealt
him a grievous wound. Blinded for the briefest second, he staggered away from Fulgrim.

Fulgrim stepped in, not letting his brother widen
the gap, and smashed his fist repeatedly into Ferrus's face, hearing bone splinter beneath his assault.
Ferrus reeled from the punches, blood drenching
the lower half of his face. Fulgrim's senses shrieked
with pleasure at the sight of his brother's pain, and
his every sense was stimulated by what he was
doing.

As Ferrus stumbled, blinded and incoherent, Fulgrim closed and swung his sword for Ferrus's neck.
The sword arced towards Ferrus, but instead of raising

his weapon to block the blow, Ferrus dropped the hammer and turned into the blow, catching the descending blade in his molten silver hands.

Fulgrim cried out as the pain of the impact jarred his arms. He tried to pull his weapon free, but Ferrus had it locked tight in his hands. The blade was utterly immobile, the chrome-steel of his brother's hands swirling as though changing from solid matter to liquid metal. Fulgrim blinked as the metal of his sword seemed to liquefy and the fire of its blade rippled up Ferrus's hands.

Ferrus opened his eyes, and the fire of the sword was alive in the silver coins of his eyes.

'I forged this blade,' hissed Ferrus, 'and I can break it too.'

No sooner had the words left his mouth than *Fireblade* exploded in a bright flare of molten metal. Both primarchs were hurled from their feet by the force of the blast, their armour and flesh burned by white hot gobbets of molten metal.

Fulgrim rolled and blinked stars from his eyes, stunned by the force of the explosion. He still held the ruined *Fireblade*, though all that was left of the sword above the hilt was a smoking nub of hissing metal. The sight of the ruined blade penetrated the red mist of sensation that drove him and the symbolism of the weapon's destruction was not lost on him.

Ferrus was dead to him and would rather die than join the new galactic order of the Warmaster. He had hoped it would not come to this, but he knew that there was no other way this drama could end.

Ferrus lay insensible, his hands glowing with the wrath of the *Fireblade's* unmaking. His brother moaned in pain at the destruction he had wrought, and Fulgrim pushed himself to his feet as his brother groaned at the horror of what had transpired within his sanctum.

Fulgrim leaned down and took up his brother's warhammer, a weapon he had poured his heart and soul into, a weapon that had been forged for his own hand in a time that seemed as though it belonged to another age.

The weapon felt good, and he hefted it easily over one shoulder as he stood triumphantly over his brother's recumbent body. Ferrus propped himself up on his elbows and looked up through blood gummed eyes. 'You had best kill me, for I'll see you dead if you do not.'

Fulgrim nodded and raised *Forgebreaker* over his head, ready to deliver the deathblow.

The mighty warhammer trembled in his grip, though Fulgrim knew that it was not its weight that made it do so, but the realisation of what he was about to do. The darkness of his eyes met with the blazing silver of his brother's, and he felt his resolve waver in the face of the murder he was about to commit.

He lowered the hammer and said, 'You are my brother, Ferrus, I would have walked unto death with you. Why could you not have done the same for me?'

'You are not my brother,' spat Ferrus through the blood of his ruined face.

Fulgrim swallowed hard as he sought to summon the strength to do what he knew must be done. He heard a dim voice, a faraway whisper that screamed at him to crush the life from Ferrus Manus, but its entreaties were drowned by the memories of the great friendship he had once shared with his brother, for what could compete with such a bond?

'I will always be your brother,' said Fulgrim, and swung the hammer in an upward arc that connected thunderously with Ferrus's jaw. Ferrus's head snapped back and he collapsed to the floor of the Iron Forge, rendered unconscious by a blow that would have sent a mortal man's head spinning through the air for hundreds of metres.

The voice in his head screamed distantly for him to finish the killing, but Fulgrim ignored it and turned away from his brother. He kept hold of the hammer and made his way to the gates that led back into the Anvilarium.

Behind him, Ferrus Manus lay broken, but alive.

THE GREAT GATES to the Iron Forge swung open and Julius saw Fulgrim emerge bearing the mighty warhammer, *Forgebreaker*. Gabriel Santar also saw the weapon Fulgrim bore, but was not quick enough to realise its import until Julius turned and shouted, 'Phoenician!'

Instantaneously, the warriors of the Phoenix Guard swung the crackling blades of their golden halberds and beheaded the Morlocks they stood next to with chillingly perfect symmetry. Ten heads clattered to the floor, and Julius smiled as Gabriel Santar and the astropath spun in horrified confusion. The Phoenix Guard closed the noose on the centre of the Anvilarium with measured strides, their bloodied blades extended before them like those of executioners.

'In the name of the Avernii, what are you doing?' cried Santar as the gates of the Iron Forge closed behind Fulgrim with a hollow boom. Julius could see that the First Captain of the Iron Hands was itching to draw his weapon, but did not do so in the certain knowledge that his death would follow as soon as he reached for it.

'Where is Ferrus Manus?' demanded Santar, but Fulgrim silenced him with a shake of his head and a sly smile of pity.

'He is alive, Gabriel,' said Fulgrim, and Julius hid his surprise at this news. 'He would not listen to reason and now you will all suffer. Julius...'

Julius smiled and turned to Gabriel Santar, lightning sheathed claws sliding from the gauntlets of his Terminator armour. Even as Santar saw what must inevitably happen next, it was too late as Julius hammered the crackling blades into his chest and tore them downwards. The energised claws tore through Santar's armour, ripping through his chest cavity and exiting in a gory spray of blood at his pelvis.

The First Captain of the Iron Hands collapsed, his lifeblood flooding from his ruined body, and Julius savoured the delicious aroma of electrically burnt flesh.

Fulgrim nodded appreciatively and opened a channel to the *Pride of the Emperor*.

'Marius,' he said, 'we will be making our way to the *Firebird*, and could use something to keep the 52nd Expedition's ships busy. You may open fire.'

TWENTY

A Difficult Voyage/Isstvan III/Perfect Failure

DARK CURRENTS AND swirling colours, unknowable beyond the gates of the empyrean, flowed around the *Pride of the Emperor* and her small complement of escorts as they forged a passage through the warp. Fulgrim's flagship bore fresh scars of war, but for all that her hull was imperfect, her magnificence was undimmed. The guns of the Iron Hands warships had left their marks upon her once pristine hull, but the shots had been fired in spite and futile defiance, for the broadsides fired by Fulgrim's warships had caught the Iron Hands completely by surprise.

The battle had been short and one-sided, and though the vessels accompanying the *Pride of the Emperor* were few in number they had inflicted crippling punishment on those of their former allies, and disrupted their ability to respond in any meaningful way.

Much to Marius Vairosean's disappointment, Fulgrim had called a halt to the attack before the destruction of the *Fist of Iron* was complete. Leaving the crippled X Legion's fleet becalmed, the ships of the Emperor's Children had disengaged and made the translation into the immaterium to rendezvous with the forces of the Warmaster once more.

Initially, things had gone as smoothly as could be hoped for, but barely a week into the journey to Isstvan III, storms of fearsome power erupted in the warp, tsunamis of unreality that crashed around the vessels of the 28th Expedition and smashed one to destruction before the few surviving Navigators had managed to fight their way through the storms and guide the ships to relative safety.

Moments prior to the first maelstrom of force, terrifying shrieks of agony and terror had echoed the length and breadth of the *Pride of the Emperor's* astropathic choir chambers. Alarums had sounded, and one entire chancel was blown clear of the vessel by the force of the psychic forces unleashed, forks of purple lightning dancing across the hull before null-shields and integrity fields had contained the breach. Hundreds of telepaths were dead, and those wretched ruins of flesh that survived were reduced to babbling, moronic psychotics. Before their elimination, those that retained some form of communication spoke of terrifying, galaxy changing forces unleashed, a world devoured by a monstrous, creeping death, fires that reached to the heavens, and the ending of billions of lives at a single stroke.

Only Fulgrim and his coterie of most trusted warriors understood the truth behind these forces, and the feasting and carousing that greeted the news plumbed new depths of insanity. The Emperor's Children revelled in the Warmaster's strength of purpose with the abandon that was now commonplace in the Legion.

As the revelries of the Astartes continued, the preparations for Bequa Kynska's *Maraviglia* reached new heights of wonder and decadence, with each rehearsal discovering new and undreamt of raptures to include. Coraline Aseneca trod the boards nightly as she trained her voice to replicate the sounds recorded in the Laer temple, and Bequa's symphony soared passionately as she sought to encapsulate its power in musical form. As part of her quest, she developed new and outlandish musical devices, their melodies as yet unheard and unknown. Such was their scale and form that they more resembled weapons than instruments: monstrously oversized horns like missile tubes and stringed mechanisms with long necks like rifles.

La Fenice became a magical place of music and art, with the remembrancers working on the décor and embellishments of the theatre, excelling themselves as they strove to create a venue worthy of staging the *Maraviglia*.

Fulgrim spent a great deal of time in *La Fenice*, offering his insights to the artists and sculptors, and every suggestion was followed by frantic bouts of creativity as they were immediately implemented.

Fragmentary scraps of information trickled in from Isstvan III, and it was eventually discerned that the Warmaster's first strike against those whose loyalty remained with the Emperor had failed to wipe them out completely. Instead of viewing this as a setback, it appeared that the Warmaster had taken it as an opportunity to blood his loyal warriors and complete what had begun with the war against the Brotherhood of the Auretian Technocracy.

Warriors from the World Eaters, Death Guard and
Sons of Horus were at war in the fire wracked ruins of
a murdered world, hunting down and destroying the
deluded fools who believed they could oppose the
Warmaster's will.

Even now, declared Fulgrim, Chaplain Charmosian
and Lord Commander Eidolon would be earning the
Warmaster's plaudits as they displayed the battle perfection of their beloved Legion. When the killing on
Isstvan III was done, the chaff would have been cut
from Horus's force, and they would be a sharpened
blade aimed at the heart of the corrupt Imperium.

But the reunion of Fulgrim and Horus was to be
delayed it seemed.

With the death of the majority of the astropaths,
communication with the 63rd Expedition was problematic to say the least, with the shattered sanity of
those left alive making the precise exchange of information between the two fleets virtually impossible.
The Navigators could not discern a course through
the warp not wracked with heaving currents and battering storms, and declared that it would take at least
two months to reach Isstvan III.

Fulgrim chafed at such delays, but even a being as
mighty as a primarch was powerless to quiet the tem-
pests of the immaterium. In the enforced wait, he
studied more of the writings of Cornelius Blayke,
coming upon a passage that lodged like a splinter of
ice in his heart.

He tore the page from the book and burned it, but
its words returned to haunt him as the dark voyage
through the warp continued:

*"The phoenix is an angel; the clapping of whose wings
is the roar of thunder.*

*And this thunder is the fearful note that heralds the
cataclysm,
And the roar of the onrushing waves that will destroy
paradise."*

THE SCULPTURE WAS almost complete. What had begun
many months ago as a gleaming white rectangle
hewn from the quarries at Proconnesus on the Anatolian peninsula was now a towering, majestic
sculpture of the Emperor of the Imperium. Ostian's
workshop was almost tidy, only the tiniest chips and
flakes of marble drifting to the floor, for the last stage
of his statue's journey was being wrought with files
and rasps of greater and greater fineness.

It had been said that the point of a journey was not
to arrive, but to savour the experiences along the way.
Ostian had never understood that aphorism, believ-
ing that only the end result made the journey
worthwhile.

To anyone else, the statue would have been finished
some time ago, but Ostian had long ago realised that
only in these final stages could be found that which
would breathe the final life into the statue. At this cru-
cial stage, a true artist would find the last twist of
genius that lifted a statue from a thing of stone to a
work of art.

Whether that was in one last imperfection or a
human understanding of the frailty of life, he didn't
know and didn't want to know, for Ostian feared that
if he ever examined his talent too closely he would be
unable to piece it back together again.

In the months since their journey to the Callinedes
system (a pointless venture if ever there had been
one, for the 28th Expedition had tarried barely a week
and fought in only one battle as far as he could tell)

he had kept himself more or less confined to his studio and the sub-deck where meals were served. *La Fenice* had become a place of lewdness, where people who should know better drank too much, ate too much and indulged their every sordid appetite without regard for the mores of civilised behaviour.

The last few times he had visited *La Fenice*, he had been shocked and revolted by its appearance, the artwork and statuary taking on an altogether more sinister aspect as the primarch lent his vision to the final details of its renovation. Wild, orgiastic gatherings, like the debaucheries of the ancient Romanii Empire were now a frequent occurrence, and Ostian had chosen to stay away rather than be outraged on a daily basis.

The one time he had been forced to set foot in it since he had shared a drink with Leopold Cadmus, a man who, along with almost every remembrancer who had not journeyed to Laeran, appeared to have departed the 28th Expedition, he had seen Fulgrim directing Serena d'Angelus as she completed a great mural on the ceiling. Its proportions were monstrous and its subject matter a vile concoction of writhing serpents and humans engaged in unimaginable excesses.

Serena had spared him a brief glance, and he was ashamed as he remembered his harsh words to her when he had last visited her. Their eyes had met and, for a moment, he had seen a look of such anguished desperation that he had wanted to weep when he later recalled it.

Fulgrim had turned as though sensing his presence, and Ostian had been shocked rigid at the primarch's appearance. Brightly coloured oils rimmed his eyes and his silver hair was bound up in ludicrously tight plaits. The faint lines of what looked like tattoos curled on his cheeks, and his purple robe laid much of his pale flesh bare, revealing an inordinate number of fresh scars and silver rings or bars piercing the skin.

Ostian was transfixed by Fulgrim's dark eyes, the madness and driving obsession he had seen in his studio magnified to terrifying proportions.

The memory chilled him and he retuned his attention to the marble. Perhaps the remembrancers that had vanished from the 28th Expedition to greener pastures had the right idea, though a suspicious voice in the back of his head worried that some darker reason lay behind the sudden lack of dissenting voices.

Even the thought of such a suspicion was enough, and Ostian resolved that as soon as he found the spark of humanity that brought the statue to life, he would request a transfer to another expedition. The flavour of the 28th had become sour to him.

'The sooner I'm out of here the better,' he whispered to himself.

THOUGH HE COULD not know of it, Ostian Delafour's sentiment echoed Solomon Demeter's almost exactly, as he stared over the bombed out ruins of the Choral City and the Precentor's Palace. The desolate, fire-blackened landscape stretched out before him as far as the eye could see, as close to a vision of hell as he could ever imagine. This had once been a beautiful world, the obliterated perfection of its architecture in stark contrast to the rebellion that had fomented within its gilded palaces and the treachery that played out in its blackened remains.

A dark shroud had hung over Solomon ever since the battle on the deep orbital of the Callinedes system, though the reason for Julius and Marius's abandonment of the Second was now horribly apparent. He had seen neither of his brothers following the battle, and within hours he and the Second had been in transit to the Isstvan system to rendezvous with three other Legions to pacify the rebellious world of Isstvan III.

The heart of the rebellion was centred on a city of polished granite and tall spires of steel and glass known as the Choral City. Its corrupt governor, Vardus Praal had fallen under the influence of the Warsingers, rogue psykers that had supposedly been wiped out by the Raven Guard Legion over a decade ago.

Initial attacks on the Choral City had washed away many of Solomon's feelings of unease, the release of his anger and hurt in bloodshed reassuring him that things were as they should be, and that his earlier misgivings were no cause for concern.

Then Saul Tarvitz had arrived with an incredible tale of betrayal and imminent attack.

Many had scoffed at Tarvitz's warning, but Solomon had immediately known the truth of it, and had fought to make his brothers realise their danger. As the monstrous scale of the betrayal sank in, the Sons of Horus, World Eaters and Emperor's Children had raced to find shelter before the deadly viral payload struck the world intended to be their tomb.

Solomon had watched in horror as the first streaks of light lit up the sky and the detonations covered the skies in thick starbursts of deadly viral agents. The screaming of the city as it died haunted him still, and he couldn't even begin to imagine the horror that must have filled the minds of those who watched as the Life Eater devoured the flesh of their loved ones, before reducing them to disintegrated hunks of

rotted, dead matter. Solomon knew how deadly the
Life Eater was, and he knew that within hours the
entire planet would be a charnel house.

Then the firestorm had come and razed the surface
bare of any signs of its former inhabitants, burning
them to ashen flakes on the wind as it destroyed all in
its path and howled across the surface of Isstvan III in
a seething tide of flame. He shut his eyes as he
remembered the underground bunker that had sheltered both himself and Gaius Caphen from the viral
attack finally yielding to the molten heat of the
firestorm. The roar of the fire had been like that of
some ancient dragon of legend come to devour him,
and the agony as his armour melted in the heat and
seared his flesh was still fresh in his consciousness.

Trapped beneath the rubble, they had called for
help, but no one had come, and Solomon had wondered whether they were the only survivors of the
Warmaster's treachery. On the third day, Gaius
Caphen had died, his injuries finally claiming him as
sunlight filtered into their prison of rubble.

Eventually Solomon had been found by one of the
Sons of Horus, a warrior named Nero Vipus; barely
breathing, but clinging to life with the tenacity of one
who refuses to die until he has had his vengeance.

The first month of the battles that followed the
failed viral attack had passed in a blur of agony and
nightmares, his life hanging in the balance until Saul
Tarvitz had come to him and promised that he would
make the traitors pay for their betrayal.

Seeing the fires of ambition finally lit within the
young warrior had galvanised Solomon, and his
recovery had been nothing short of miraculous. An
Apothecary named Vaddon had found time, between
treating the wounded, to bring him back from the

brink, and as the war ground onwards, Solomon found his strength returning to the point where he was able to fight once more.

Taking the armour of the dead, Solomon had risen, phoenix-like, from what many had considered to be his deathbed, and had fought on with all the ferocity and courage for which he was renowned. Saul Tarvitz had immediately offered to transfer command to him, but he had refused, knowing that the surviving warriors of all the Legions looked to Tarvitz for leadership. To usurp that would be pointless, especially now that their heroic defiance of betrayal was almost at an end.

The massed forces of the Warmaster had driven them back into the heart of the palace, and the Sons of Horus had committed their best warriors to the assault. Solomon knew the end was not far off and had no wish to deprive Tarvitz of the glory of his last stand.

To Solomon's surprise, Tarvitz had not been the only warrior to excel in the crucible of this desperate combat, but the swordsman Lucius had also performed wonders, taking the head of Chaplain Charmosian in a duel atop the traitor's Land Raider for all to see.

As gratifying as it was to see these warriors come into their own, it was but a shadow compared to the anguish of Caphen's death and the revulsion he felt at what had become of their former battle-brothers. How could it have come to this, that warriors who had once stood shoulder to shoulder in forging the Emperor's realm could be locked in a bloody fight to the death?

What had happened to drive them to this?

It was beyond his understanding, and the aching hollowness inside him could not be filled with the deaths of his enemies. The dream of a galaxy for mankind to inherit was dying with this treachery, and the golden future that awaited them was slipping out

of reach forever. Solomon grieved for the future of
grim darkness that was being hammered out on the
anvil of Isstvan III, and hoped that those who would
come after them would forgive them for what they
had allowed to happen.

He hoped the future would remember the warriors
around him for the heroes they were, but most of all,
he hoped that Nathaniel Garro's *Eisenstein* could
escape this trap and take word of the Warmaster's
treachery to the Emperor. Tarvitz had told of his honour brother and how he had seized the frigate and
sworn to return with the loyalist Legions to crush
Horus utterly.

That hope, that tiny flickering ember of belief in sal-
vation, had kept the warriors defending the shattered
ruins of the Precentor's Palace fighting long after logic
and reason would have otherwise dictated. Solomon
loved each and every one of them for their heroism.

The distant thump of a bombardment drifted from
the western reaches of the city where the scattered
remnants of the Death Guard hunkered down in the
face of near constant shelling from the traitor forces.

Solomon limped through the eastern reaches of the
palace, the once mighty colonnades little more than a
series of empty, mosaic floored chambers whose fur-
nishings had long since been dragged out to form ad
hoc barricades. The domes of the chambers had
miraculously remained intact despite the months of
shelling, the blackened walls and scorched frescoes
an infinitely sad reminder that this had once been an
Imperial world.

When he heard the sounds, they were faint at first,
barely registering over the ever present crackle of
flames and relentless booms of explosions. The clash
of blades quickly penetrated the dull miasma of war,

and Solomon picked up his pace as he realised that the eastern approaches to the palace must be under attack.

Solomon ran as fast as his injuries would allow him, the pain of his burnt flesh acute, rendering his every footfall agonising. The sound of battle grew more strident and he could pick out the sharp clang of sword blades, though he dimly registered that there was no gunfire, no explosions.

The sounds came from ahead. Solomon skidded into a brightly lit dome, sunlight catching on the blades of the warriors who battled within. Captain Lucius commanded this sector of the defences with around thirty warriors, and Solomon saw the lithe figure of the swordsman at the centre of a tremendous battle.

Bodies littered the floor and a struggling mass of Emperor's Children filled the dome, surrounding Lucius as he fought for his life.

'Lucius!' cried Solomon raising his weapon and rushing to the swordsman's aid.

A flash of steel licked out and a warrior fell, cloven from neck to groin by the energised edge of Lucius's blade.

'They're breaking in, Solomon!' shouted Lucius gleefully, taking the head from another of his attackers with a deadly high cut.

'Not while I have my strength they won't!' bellowed Solomon, swinging his blade at the nearest of the attackers. His blow smashed the traitor to the ground in a welter of blood and shattered armour.

'Kill them all!' shouted Lucius.

'YOU DARE RETURN to me in failure?' bellowed Horus, the bridge of the *Vengeful Spirit* shaking with the fury of his voice. His face twisted in anger, and Fulgrim smiled as he watched the Warmaster struggle to hold his Cthonic fury in check. The *Vengeful Spirit* had changed a great deal since Fulgrim had last stood in the Warmaster's inner sanctum, its once open and brightly lit hubbub replaced with something far darker.

'Do you even understand what I am trying to do here?' continued Horus. 'What I have started at Isstvan will consume the whole galaxy, and if it is flawed from the outset then the Emperor will break us!'

Fulgrim allowed a smile of delicious insouciance to surface on his face, the excitement of finally arriving at Isstvan III, and the scale of the carnage wrought below, stimulating his taste for the excessive. Though the *Pride of the Emperor* had but recently arrived, Fulgrim had been careful to appear before the Warmaster as magnificent as ever, his exquisite armour worked with fresh layers of vivid purples and gold, with many new embellishments and finery added to complement the bright colours. His long white hair was pulled back, and his pale cheeks were marked with the beginnings of tattoos that Serena d'Angelus had designed for him.

'Ferrus Manus is a dull fool who would not listen to reason,' said Fulgrim. 'Even the mention of the Mechanicum's pledge did not–'

'You swore to me that you could sway him! The Iron Hands were essential to my plans. I planned Isstvan III with your assurance that Ferrus Manus would join us. Now I find that I have yet another enemy to contend with. A great many of our Astartes will die because of this, Fulgrim.'

'What would you have had me do, Warmaster?' smiled Fulgrim, being sure to twist his words with a sly mocking tone. 'His will was stronger than I anticipated.'

'Or you simply had an inflated opinion of your own abilities.'

'Would you have had me kill our brother, Warmaster?' asked Fulgrim, hoping that Horus would not ask such a thing of him, but knowing that it was what he wanted to hear. 'For I will if that is what you desire of me.'

'Perhaps I do,' replied Horus unmoved. 'It would be better than leaving him to roam free to destroy our plans. As it is, he could reach the Emperor or one of the other primarchs and bring them all down on our heads before we are ready.'

'Then if you are quite finished with me, I shall return to my Legion,' said Fulgrim, turning away with a flourish calculated to infuriate the Warmaster. He was not to be disappointed, and felt his heart pound as Horus said, 'No, you will not. I have another task for you. I am sending you to Isstvan V. With all that has happened, the Emperor's response is likely to arrive more quickly than anticipated and we must be prepared for it. Take a detail of Emperor's Children to the alien fortresses there and prepare it for the final phase of the Isstvan operation.'

Fulgrim recoiled and turned back to his brother, the disgust at such a menial role horrifying and repugnant. The exquisite sensations flooding his body at his baiting of the Warmaster faded and left him hollow inside. 'You would consign me to the role of castellan, as some housekeeper making your property ready for your grand entrance? Why not send for Perturabo? This kind of thing is more to his liking.'

'Perturabo has his own role to play,' said Horus. 'Even now, he prepares to lay waste to his home world in my name. We shall be hearing more of our bitter brother very soon, have no fear of that.'

'Then give this task to Mortarion!' spat Fulgrim. 'His grimy footsloggers will relish an opportunity to muddy their hands for you! My Legion was the chosen of the Emperor in the years when he still deserved our service. I am the most glorious of his heroes and the right hand of this new Crusade. This is... this is a betrayal of the very principles for which I chose to join you, Horus!'

'Betrayal?' said Horus, his voice low and dangerous. 'A strong word, Fulgrim. Betrayal is what the Emperor forced upon us when he abandoned the galaxy to pursue his quest for godhood and gave over the conquests of our Crusade to scriveners and bureaucrats. Is that the charge you would level at me, to my face, on the bridge of my own ship?'

Fulgrim stepped back, his anger fading as he felt Horus's rage wash over him, relishing the crawling sensations that filled him at the excitement of the confrontation. 'Perhaps I do, Horus. Perhaps someone needs to tell you a few home truths, now that your precious Mournival is no more.'

'That sword,' said Horus, indicating the venom sheened weapon that Fulgrim had been given at their last meeting. 'I gave you that blade as a symbol of my trust in you, Fulgrim. We alone know the true power that lies within it. That weapon almost killed me, and yet I gave it away. Do you think I would give such a weapon to one I do not trust?'

'No, Warmaster,' said Fulgrim.

'Exactly. The Isstvan V phase of my plan is the most critical,' said Horus, and Fulgrim could feel the Warmaster's superlative diplomatic skills coming to the fore as the dangerous embers of his ego were fanned.

'Even more so than what is happening below us. I can
entrust it to no other. You must go to Isstvan V, my
brother. All depends on your success.'

Fulgrim let the violent potential crackling between
them continue for a long, frightening moment,
before laughing. 'And now you flatter me, hoping my
ego will coerce me into obeying your orders.'

'Is it working?' asked Horus.

'Yes,' admitted Fulgrim. 'Very well, the Warmaster's
will be done. I will go to Isstvan V.'

'Eidolon will stay in command of the Emperor's
Children until we join you,' said Horus, and Fulgrim
nodded.

'He will relish the chance to prove himself further,'
said Fulgrim.

'Now leave me, Fulgrim,' said Horus. 'You have
work to do.'

Fulgrim turned smartly and marched from the Warmaster's presence, his breathing coming in shallow
bursts as he replayed the violent potential of the near
confrontation and allowed the memory of his
brother's anger once more to stimulate his senses.

The feeling was sublime, and he imagined greater
and headier delights ahead when the Isstvan V portion of the Warmaster's plan came to fruition: such
horrors, such death, such delights.

SOLOMON DROVE HIS roaring blade through the chest
plate of the warrior before him, twisting the weapon
savagely as it tore through the layers of ceramite, flesh
and bone. Blood sprayed from the ghastly wound and
the traitor crashed to the tiled floor. He spun
painfully to find another opponent, but the only figure left standing was Lucius, his scarred face flushed
with the energy of the battle. Solomon checked to

make sure there were no survivors before finally lowering his sword and acknowledging the pain of his many wounds.

Blood dripped from his sword as the whirring teeth slowly wound to a halt, and he took a deep breath as he saw how close they had come to being overwhelmed. The skill with which the swordsman had despatched his foes bordered on the miraculous, and Solomon knew that Lucius's reputation as the deadliest killer in the Legion was entirely justified.

'We did it,' he gasped, painfully aware of how dearly the victory had been bought. All the warriors under Lucius's command were dead, and as Solomon surveyed the carnage, he felt an immense sorrow as he saw that there was little to tell traitor from loyalist.

But for a twist of fate, might he too have turned on his brethren?

'We did indeed, Captain Demeter,' smirked Lucius. 'I couldn't have done it without you.'

Solomon looked up at the supercilious tone and bit back an angry retort. He shook his head at the swordsman's ingratitude and nodded wearily.

'Strange they came with so few warriors,' he said, kneeling beside the body of the last traitor he had killed. 'What did they think to gain?'

'Nothing,' said Lucius, cleaning the blood from his sword with a scrap of cloth, 'yet.'

'What do you mean?' demanded Solomon, fast growing weary of Lucius's obtuse answers. The swordsman's smiled, but didn't answer, and Solomon looked away, taking in the dead bodies and the stench of seared flesh and bone.

'Don't worry, Solomon,' said Lucius, 'it will all soon become clear to you.'

The smug gleam in the swordsman's eyes unnerved Solomon more than he cared to admit and a horrific, gut wrenching suspicion began to form in his mind.

He quickly looked around the dome, his eyes darting back and forth as he did a quick count of the bodies that lay silent and unmoving on the cratered floor. Lucius had been given the remains of four squads to defend this portion of the palace, some thirty warriors.

'Oh no,' whispered Solomon as he realised that there were around thirty corpses. He gazed at the battered armour plates, the blackened faces, and the damage that told him these warriors had not come fresh from their billets to attack the palace, but had been here all along. These dead warriors were not traitors at all.

'They were loyalists,' he whispered.

'I'm afraid so,' said Lucius. 'I am going to rejoin the Legion. The price for that is allowing Eidolon and his warriors a way into the palace. It was most fortunate you arrived when you did, Captain Demeter. I do not know if I would have been able to kill them all before the lord commander arrives.'

Solomon felt the walls of his existence come crashing down as the enormity of what he had done sank in. He dropped to his knees, and tears of horror and anguish spilled down his cheeks.

'No! What have you done, Lucius?' he cried. 'You have doomed us all.'

Lucius laughed and said, 'You were already doomed, Solomon. I just hastened the end.'

Solomon hurled aside his sword in disgust at what he had become, a killer no better than the traitors beyond the palace, and his anger at Lucius surged like a molten river.

'You took my honour from me,' he snarled, rising to his feet and turning to face the swordsman. 'It was all I had left.'

Lucius was right in front of him, that cocky, arrogant smile still plastered over his scarred features. The swordsman smiled and asked, 'How does it feel?'

Solomon roared and flew at Lucius, wrapping his hands around his foe's neck. Hate and remorse flooded his limbs with fresh energy to better strangle the life from this thief of honour.

A terrible pain erupted in his stomach, tearing upwards through his chest, and Solomon cried out as his ruined frame fell away from Lucius. He looked down to see the glowing blade of Lucius's sword protruding from his breastplate. The sizzle of burning meat and melting ceramite was strong in his nostrils as Lucius thrust his sword completely through his torso.

The strength fled from his body, and all the agony of the injuries he had fought to overcome since the firestorm returned a hundredfold. His entire body was a mass of pain, his every nerve-ending shrieking in agony.

Solomon dropped to his knees, his blood and life pouring from his body in a hot rush. He reached up to grip Lucius's arms, and fought to focus on the swordsman's face as death reached up to claim him.

'You... will... not... win...' he gasped, each word forced from his throat a small victory.

Lucius shrugged. 'Maybe, maybe not, but you won't be around to see it.'

Solomon fell backwards in slow motion, feeling the motion of air across his face and the crack of his skull against the hard floor. He rolled onto his back, looking out through the cracked dome to the clear blue sky beyond.

He smiled as the pain balms of his armour struggled uselessly to alleviate the mortal wound Lucius's blade had done to him, staring into the limitless expanse of the open sky and feeling as though his gaze might reach beyond the atmosphere to where Horus's fleet hung in space.

With a clarity denied him in life, Solomon saw where the Warmaster's terrible betrayal would inevitably lead, the horror and the long war that would surely follow. Tears spilled down his cheeks, but they were not shed for his own ending, but for the billions who would suffer an eternity of darkness for the sake of one man's dreadful ambition.

Lucius walked away from him, not even bothering to watch his final moments, and Solomon was glad of the peace. His breathing slowed and his eyelids flickered as the sky grew darker with each breath.

The light was dying with him, he thought, as though the world marked his passing by drawing a curtain across the day and ushering him into the final darkness with honour.

Solomon closed his eyes as a final tear fell to the ground.

PART FIVE

THE LAST PHOENIX

TWENTY-ONE

**Vengeance/The Price of Isolation/The
Prodigal/Death-Marked Love**

THE IRON FORGE had become Ferrus Manus's refuge
since the monstrous betrayal visited upon him by his
once-brother. Its gleaming walls were cracked, the primarch's hurt reaching out to destroy the things he
held dear in fury at the treachery given voice here.
Gabriel Santar stepped over weapons and armour
strewn across the floor, many pieces twisted as
though melted in the heart of a fire. He carried with
him a data-slate with fresh news from Terra. He
hoped that it would lift his primarch out of the anger
fuelled depression that had settled upon him like a
shroud in the wake of the traitor's scheme to sway the
Iron Hands to the cause of treachery.

Every artificer, forgemaster, Techmarine and
labourer had worked unceasingly to repair the damage done to their ships by the surprise attack of the
Emperor's Children fleet, and, in an unbelievable
time, the ships of the 52nd Expedition had been

413

ready to make for Terra and bring warning of the War-master's perfidy.

In this, however, they had been stymied as the ships' Navigators and astropaths had been unable to penetrate the warp, monstrous storms of terrifying force erupting through the depths of the immaterium, preventing any contact with or from Terra. To venture into the warp while it raged and seethed with unnatural vigour was tantamount to suicide, but it had taken all of Gabriel Santar's calming words to break through Ferrus Manus's towering fury and persuade him to await the end of the storms.

A hundred astropaths had died in attempts to penetrate the roiling miasma of churning warp storms, but though their heroic sacrifice was commemorated on the Iron Column, their efforts were in vain, and the Iron Hands remained incommunicado.

For weeks, the ships of the 52nd Expedition travelled by conventional plasma engines, hoping to locate a break in the warp storms, but it seemed as though the Realm Beyond was at odds with them, for the Navigators could see no way to break through and live.

Ferrus Manus had raged the length and breadth of the *Fist of Iron* at the injustice of surviving such treachery only to be prevented from bringing word of it to the Emperor by something as mundane as a warp storm.

When Astropath Cistor had brought word that his surviving choristers were at last receiving faint messages hurled out across the stars, the news had been greeted with great joy, until they had been deciphered and transferred to the command logic engines.

All across the Imperium, war was raging. On countless worlds, traitorous curs were revolting against their loyal leaders. Many Imperial commanders had declared for Horus and were denouncing the rule of the Emperor. Many of these traitors had launched attacks against neighbouring systems still loyal to the Imperium, and the rise of war was threatening to engulf the entire galaxy. Horus had spread his net of corruption wide, and it would take heroics the likes of which had forged the Imperium in the first place to save the Emperor's dream of a united galaxy.

Even the Mechanicum had been drawn into rebellion as warring factions fought for control of the great forges of Mars. The Astartes armour manufacturing facilities were coming under particularly heavy attack, and the Emperor's loyal servants cried out for reinforcements as their enemies deployed ancient weapons technologies that had long been forbidden.

Worse still, reports of alien attacks on human-held worlds were increasing with an alarming rapidity. The greenskins rampaged through the southern galactic rim, the savage hordes of Kalardun laid waste to newly compliant worlds in the Region of Storms, and the foul Carrion-eaters of Carnus V laid bloody claim to the Nine Vectors. As humanity was ripping itself apart with internecine warfare, countless xeno breeds were rising to feed on the carcass.

The Primarch of the Iron Hands hunched over the anvil in the centre of the forge, flickering blue fire blazing around his glowing silver hands as he worked a long length of gleaming metal upon it. The primarch's wounds had healed swiftly, but his jaw still jutted pugnaciously where his treacherous brother had smashed the stolen *Forgebreaker* against his skull. Even the mention of the traitor's name was forbidden, and Santar had never seen his primarch so wrathful.

Santar knew he himself was lucky to be alive, the
grievous wound inflicted by the First Captain of the
Emperor's Children having torn through his heart,
lungs and stomach. Only the timely ministrations of
the Legion's Apothecaries, and a determination to
wreak bloody vengeance upon Julius Kaesoron, had
kept him alive long enough for him to have his
ruined flesh replaced with bionic components.

The grim figure of Astropath Cistor followed
behind him, robed in cream and black, and clutching
his copper staff in a white knuckled grip. The
telepath's gaunt features were unreadable in the flickering firelight of the forge, but even one as dulled to
psychic vibrations as Santar was, could sense his concern.

Ferrus Manus looked up as they approached, his
grim, battered face a mask of cold iron anger. The
restriction on entry to the Iron Forge had been forgotten, such petty rules and regulations deemed
nonsensical in the face of the crisis facing the
Imperium.

'Well?' demanded Ferrus. 'Why do you disturb me?'

Santar allowed himself a tight smile and said, 'I
bring word from Rogal Dorn.'

'From Dorn?' cried Ferrus, the fire of his hands
diminishing and his face alight with sudden, savage
interest. He placed the glowing metal upon the anvil
and said, 'I thought the astropathic choirs could not
yet reach Terra?'

'Until a few hours ago, we could not,' agreed Cistor,
stepping forward to stand next to Santar. 'The warp
storms that frustrated our every effort at communication over the previous weeks have dissipated utterly,
and my choristers are receiving the most urgent com-
muniqués from Lord Dorn.'

'This is great news indeed, Cistor!' exclaimed Ferrus. 'My compliments to your staff! Now speak, Gabriel, speak! What does Dorn say?'

'My lord, if I may?' said Cistor before Santar could answer. 'This sudden calming of the warp disturbs me.'

'Disturbs you, Cistor?' asked Ferrus. 'Why? Surely it is a good thing?'

'That remains to be seen, my lord. It is my belief that some external force has acted upon the warp, aiding our efforts to navigate through it and to send messages across the void of space.'

'Why would you think this is a bad thing, Cistor?' asked Santar. 'Might not the Emperor have worked to achieve this?'

'That is certainly a possibility,' conceded Cistor, 'but it is only one of many. I would be remiss in my duties if I did not voice my concern that some other agent, perhaps one of our enemy's, is calming the Sea of Souls.'

'Your concerns are noted, astropath,' snapped Ferrus. 'Now, will one of you tell me what you have received from Dorn before I have to beat it out of you?'

Santar quickly held out the data-slate and said, 'The Emperor's Champion sends word of his plans to destroy Horus.'

Ferrus snatched the slate from him as Santar continued. 'It appears as though the Warmaster's treachery is confined to those Legions that fought with him at Isstvan III. As Cistor here says, the adepts of the Astropathic Corps have finally managed to establish contact with a great many of your brother primarchs, and even now they are mobilising against Horus.'

'At last,' snarled Ferrus, his silver eyes quickly scanning the data-slate. A grim smile of measured triumph spread slowly across his face. 'Salamanders, Alpha Legion, Iron Warriors, Word Bearers, Raven Guard and Night Lords... including the Iron Hands, that's seven entire Legions. Horus doesn't stand a chance.'

'No, he doesn't,' agreed Santar. 'Dorn is being thorough.'

'Indeed he is,' said Ferrus. 'Isstvan V...'

'My lord?'

'It seems Horus has established his headquarters on Isstvan V, and it is there we are to crush his rebellion once and for all.'

Ferrus handed back the data-slate and said, 'Send word to Captain Balhaan on the Ferrum that I shall be transferring my flag to his ship. Tell him to ready his vessel for immediate transit to the Isstvan system. Deploy as many of the Morlocks as are fit to fight into its barracks. The rest of the Legion will have to make best speed and join us as soon as they are able.'

Santar frowned, as Ferrus returned to the glowing metal on the anvil, and glanced down at the data-slate to ensure he had not misread the orders it contained, orders that came directly from the Emperor's Champion. He hesitated just long enough for Ferrus to catch his delay and said, 'My lord, our orders are to rendezvous with the full force of our Legion.'

Ferrus shook his head. 'No, Gabriel, I won't be denied my vengeance on... him by arriving late and allowing others to destroy him first. The Ferrum suffered the least amount of damage in the betrayal of the Emperor's Children and it's the fastest ship in the fleet. I... I need to face him and destroy him to restore my honour and prove my loyalty, Gabriel.'

'Honour? Loyalty?' said Santar. 'None could doubt your loyalty or honour, my lord. The traitor came to you with falsehoods and you hurled them back in his face. If anything, you stand as an example to us all, a faithful and dutiful son of the Emperor. How could you even think such a thing?'

'Because others will,' said Ferrus, picking up the long, flat metal on the anvil, an angry, fiery glow building in the silver depths of his hands. 'Fulgrim would not have risked attempting to turn me to the Warmaster's cause unless he truly believed I would join him. He must have seen weakness in me that made him think he would be successful. That is what I must purge in the heat of his blood. Though they might not voice such things openly, others will soon come to the same conclusion, you mark my words.'

'They would not dare!'

'They will, my friend,' nodded Ferrus. 'They will wonder what made Fulgrim risk such a dangerous gambit. Soon they will come to believe that perhaps he had reason to think I would follow him into treachery. No, we will make all speed for the Isstvan system to wash away the stain of this dishonour in the blood of traitors!'

IT TOOK AN effort of will not to approach the statue, and Ostian had to deliberately place the file on the battered metal stool next to him. Part of what made an artist great was knowing when something was finished, when it was time to put down the pen, the chisel or the brush and step away from it. The work belonged to the ages now, and as he looked up into the helmeted eyes of the Master of Mankind, he knew that it was finished.

Towering above him, the pale marble was flawless, every curve of the Emperor's armour rendered with loving care to exactly replicate his majesty. Great shoulder guards with eagles rampant framed a tall helmet of ancient design, topped with a long horse-hair crest of such fine carving that even Ostian expected it to ruffle in the cool air fluttering the papers and dust around him.

The great eagle on the Emperor's breastplate seemed as though it might burst from his chest, and the lightning bolts on his greaves and bracers exuded a raw power that energised the statue with a fierce anima. A long, curving cloak of white marble spilled down the back of the statue like a cascade of milk, and the Emperor's stature was such that he felt sure the Master of the Imperium might deign to look upon it with a moment of pleasure to see his image rendered so.

A wreath of gold set off the paleness of the marble, and Ostian felt his breath catch as something amazing took flight within him at the statue's perfection.

Ostian had been called many things in his career: a perfectionist, an obsessive, but to his way of thinking, it took obsession and a quest for the truth of the details for an artist to be worthy of the name.

Since receiving the block, the carving had taken him the best part of two years, his every waking moment spent working on the marble or thinking about the marble. Quick work by any method of measurement, but when placed against the final outcome, it was miraculous. Ordinarily, such a masterpiece would have taken much longer, but the changing character of the 28th Expedition had troubled Ostian greatly, and he had not ventured beyond his studio for many months.

He realised that he needed to reacquaint himself with events in the Great Crusade.

What new cultures had been met? What great deeds had recently been accomplished?

The thought of leaving his studio filled him with trepidation and excitement, for with the unveiling of his statue, he would be able to once again bask in the adulation of admirers; something he normally detested, but which, at moments like these, he craved.

No false modesty blinded Ostian to his talents, nay, his genius, in the moment following the completion of a piece of work. It would be in the days, weeks and months to come that flaws only he could see would become apparent, and he would curse his useless hands and begin thinking of how to improve on his next work.

If an artist should ever feel that he could no longer better himself then what was the point of being an artist? Each work should be like unto a stepping-stone that led to greater and greater heights of artistry, where a man could look back at his life's works and be satisfied that he had made the most of his allotted span.

Ostian removed his smock and neatly folded it before placing it upon the stool, taking exaggerated care to flatten the dulled fabric before stepping back. To admire his own work so avidly, now that it was finished, was unseemly, but when it was made public it would no longer be his and his alone. It would belong to everyone who saw it, and a million critical eyes would judge its worth or lack thereof. At moments like this he could begin to understand the self-destructive kernel of doubt that lurked in Serena d'Angelus's heart, or indeed any artist's, be they painter, sculptor, writer or composer. Within the artist's work was a portion of his soul, and the fear of rejection or ridicule was potent indeed.

A cold gust made him shiver and a lilting voice said, 'You have certainly captured him.'

Ostian jumped and spun around to see the terrifying, beautiful form of the Primarch of the Emperor's Children standing before him. Unusually, the Phoenix Guard was absent, and Ostian found himself beginning to sweat despite the coolness of his studio.

'My lord,' he said, dropping to one knee. 'Forgive me, I did not hear you enter.'

Fulgrim nodded and swept past him, swathed in a long purple toga embroidered with dazzling silver wrapped around his powerful physique. The golden hilt of a sword protruded from beneath the toga and a crown of barbed laurels sat upon his noble brow. The primarch's face was rendered doll-like by the application of thick, white greasepaint and brightly coloured, overpoweringly scented inks around his eyes and lips.

What the primarch hoped to achieve with his facial embellishments, Ostian did not know, but unless it was to appear vulgar and grotesque, it had failed completely. Like one of the theatrical performers of Old Earth, Fulgrim carried himself with regal authority. He waved Ostian to his feet as he stopped before the statue, his expression unreadable beneath the layers of paint.

'I remember him like this,' said Fulgrim. Ostian heard a note of sadness in the primarch's voice. 'That was many years ago, of course. He looked like this at Ullanor, but that's not how I remember him on that day. He was cold then, aloof even.'

Ostian rose to his feet, but kept his eyes averted from the primarch, lest he see his disquiet at his appearance. His earlier pride in the statue vanished the instant Fulgrim looked upon it and he held his breath as he awaited the primarch's critical opinion.

Fulgrim turned to face him, his grotesque mask of greasepaint and oil cracking in a smile. Ostian relaxed a fraction, and even though the flat, gem-like eyes of utter darkness remained unmoved, he saw a hostility there that terrified him.

The smile fell from the primarch's face and he said, 'That you carve a statue of the Emperor at a time like this shows either wilful stupidity on your part or reprehensible ignorance, Ostian.'

Ostian felt his composure crack at Fulgrim's pronouncement and he tried in vain to think of something to say in response.

Fulgrim walked towards him, and a suffocating fear rose in Ostian's fragile body, his terror at the primarch's displeasure rooting him to the spot. The commander of the Emperor's Children circled him, the towering presence of the primarch threatening to overwhelm what remained of Ostian's resolve.

'My lord...' he whispered.

'You spoke,' snapped Fulgrim, reaching down to turn him around so that his back was to the statue. 'A worm like you does not deserve to speak to me! You, who told me that my work was too perfect creates a work such as this, perfect in every detail. Perfect in every detail but one...'

Ostian looked up into the black pools of the primarch's eyes, but even through his terror, he saw a tortured anguish that transcended his own fear, a conflicted soul at war with itself. He saw the lust to do him harm and the desire to beg his forgiveness in the depths of the primarch's eyes.

'My lord, Fulgrim,' said Ostian through tears that spilled freely down his cheeks, 'I do not understand.'

'No,' said Fulgrim, advancing towards him and forcing him, step by step, towards the statue. 'You don't do you? Like the Emperor, you have been too enraptured by your own selfish desires to pay any mind to that which goes on around you; remembrancers vanished and friends betrayed. When all you once held dear is crumbling around you, what do you do? You abandon those closest to you and forsake them in the quest for something of supposedly higher purpose.'

Ostian's terror reached new heights as he bumped into the marble of the statue, and Fulgrim leaned down so that his painted face was level with his own. Yet even amid the flood of horror at what had become of the primarch, Ostian pitied him too, for there was great pain in his every tortured word.

'If you had bothered to take note of your surroundings and the great events in motion, you would have dashed this sculpture to ruins and begged me to become the subject of your latest work. A new order is rising in the galaxy and the Emperor is no longer its master.'

'What?' gasped Ostian in surprise. Fulgrim laughed, the sound bitter and desperate.

'Horus will be the new master of the Imperium,' cried Fulgrim, drawing the sword from beneath his toga with a flourish. The golden hilt shimmered in the brightness of the studio, and Ostian felt warm wetness run down his thighs at the loathsome sight of the soulless blade.

Fulgrim drew himself up to his full height, and Ostian sobbed in relief as the primarch's haunted eyes broke contact with his own.

'Yes, Ostian,' said Fulgrim, matter-of-factly. 'For the past week, the *Pride of the Emperor* has been in orbit over Isstvan V, a bleak and blackened world of no particular note, but one which will go down in history as a place of glorious legend.'

Ostian fought to control his breathing as Fulgrim circled behind the statue, and he sagged against the cool marble.

'For on this dusty, unremarkable world, the Warmaster will utterly destroy the might of the Emperor's most loyal Legions in preparation for our march to Terra,' continued Fulgrim. 'You see, Ostian, Horus is the rightful master of mankind. He is the one who has led us to triumphs undreamt of. He is the one who has conquered ten thousand worlds, and he is the one who will lead us in conquest of ten thousand more. Together we will cast down the false Emperor!'

Ostian's thoughts tumbled over one another as he struggled to come to grips with the enormity of what Fulgrim was suggesting. Betrayal dripped from every word, and Ostian was suddenly and horribly confronted with the fact that he was paying the price for his isolation. Shutting himself off from events simply because he did not care for them had led to this, and he wished he had taken the time to…

'Your work is not yet perfect, Ostian,' said Fulgrim from behind the statue.

Ostian tried to frame a reply when he heard a horrific scraping sound of metal on stone, and the tip of the primarch's alien sword burst through the marble plinth to spear between his shoulder blades.

The glittering grey blade emerged from his chest with a crack of bone. Ostian tried to scream in pain, but his mouth filled with blood as the blade pierced his heart. The primarch's strength drove the blade deeper into the statue, until the gold quillons clanged against the marble and the tip of the sword projected a full foot from Ostian's chest.

Blood flowed from his mouth in thick red runnels of saliva and his eyes dimmed. Ostian's life flowed from his body as though clawed out by some voracious predator.

Ostian looked up with the last of his strength as he dimly perceived Fulgrim standing before him once more.

The primarch looked at him with a mixture of contempt and regret, pointing at the blood-spattered statue he hung from.

'Now it's perfect,' said Fulgrim.

THE GALLERY OF Swords on the *Andronius* had changed a great deal since Lucius had last walked its length. Where once an avenue of monolithic statues of great heroes had stared down and judged the worth of a warrior as he walked between them, now those same statues had been crudely altered with hammers and chisels to resemble strange, bull-headed monsters with gem studded armour and curling horns of bone. Brightly coloured paints had been daubed over the statues, and the overall effect was like that of some garish carnival parade.

Eidolon marched ahead of him, and Lucius could feel the lord commander's dislike of him as an almost physical resentment. His killing of Chaplain Charmosian still sat ill with Eidolon, and he had called him a traitor twice over, but that seemed an age ago, when the loyalist fools on Isstvan III had still resisted the inevitable.

Lucius had given the lord commander the opportunity to win a great victory on a silver platter and, like

the fool he was, Eidolon had squandered his chance
for glory. When Lucius had slaughtered his warriors,
the eastern approaches to the palace were wide open
and Eidolon had led the Emperor's Children into the
palace to outflank the defenders and roll up their
pathetic defiance in a tide of fire and blood. But he
had overreached himself and left his forces exposed to
a counter-attack. It was an unforgivable oversight, and
one that Saul Tarvitz had punished him for, flanking
the flankers.

Lucius still smarted at his last confrontation with
Tarvitz, remembering the duel they had fought in the
ruined dome where he had killed Solomon Demeter.
Like Loken before him, Tarvitz had not fought hon-
ourably, and Lucius had been lucky to escape with his
life.

Still, it didn't matter anymore. After he had rejoined
his Legion, the Warmaster's forces had withdrawn
from Isstvan III, and commenced an orbital bombardment that had pulverised the surface of the planet
until not a single structure remained standing. The
Precentor's Palace was a ruin of vitrified stone, and the
force of the bombardment had levelled even the
might of the Sirenhold. Nothing lived on Isstvan III,
and Lucius felt a thrill of delicious excitement as he
considered the future the fates had opened up to him.

He paused to savour the heights of glory he would
rise to, and the new sensations awaiting him as he
marched at the side of his primarch once more. The
statue before him had once been Lord Commander
Teliosa, hero of the Madrivane campaign, and Lucius
remembered Tarvitz telling him that he had especially
honoured it.

He chuckled as he imagined what Saul Tarvitz
would make of the carved horns and exposed breast

that had been added to it by enthusiastic, if question-
ably skilled, sculptors.

'Apothecary Fabius is waiting,' snapped Eidolon
from up ahead, his impatience obvious.

Lucius grinned and spun on his heel to join
Eidolon at his leisure. 'I know, but he can wait a little
longer. I was admiring the changes you've made to
the ship.'

Eidolon scowled and said, 'If it were up to me, I'd
have left you to die down there.'

'Then I'm grateful it wasn't up to you,' smirked
Lucius. 'Still, after your defeat at Saul's hands, I'm surprised you retained your command.'

'Tarvitz…' growled Eidolon. 'A thorn in my side
from the day he made captain.'

'Well, he's a thorn no longer, lord commander,' said
Lucius, thinking back to his last sight of Isstvan III,
the swirling, cloud streaked glow of its atmosphere
flickering with the mushroom clouds of high yield
atomics and incendiaries.

'You saw him die?' asked Eidolon.

Lucius shook his head. 'No, but I saw what was left
of the palace. Nothing could have lived through that.
Tarvitz is dead and so are Loken and that smug bastard, Torgaddon.'

Eidolon at least had the good grace to smile at the
news of Torgaddon's death and he nodded reluc-
tantly. 'That at least is good news. What of the others?
Solomon Demeter, Ancient Rylanor?'

Lucius laughed as he remembered Solomon Demeter's death. 'Demeter is dead, of that I am certain.'

'How can you be so sure?'

'Because I killed him,' said Lucius. 'He happened
upon me when I was despatching the warriors
assigned to defend the eastern ruins of the palace and

happily joined in when I shouted to him that I was under attack.'

Eidolon smirked as he understood. 'You mean Demeter killed his own men?'

'Indeed he did,' said Lucius, 'with great gusto.'

Eidolon let out a burst of laughter, and Lucius could feel the lord commander's attitude thaw a fraction at the irony of Solomon Demeter's final moments.

'And Ancient Rylanor?' asked Eidolon, leading him further along the Gallery of Swords to the entrance to the apothecarion.

'I don't know for sure about that,' said Lucius. 'After the bombing, he took himself off into the depths of the Precentor's Palace. I never saw him again.'

'Not like Rylanor to run from a fight,' noted Eidolon, turning a corner and marching down a parchment lined corridor that led to the grand staircase of the ship's central apothecarion.

'No,' agreed Lucius, 'though Tarvitz did say something about him guarding something.'

'Guarding what?'

'He didn't say. Rumour was he'd found some kind of underground hangar, but if that were the case, then why didn't Praal use it to escape when the Legions arrived?'

'True,' agreed Eidolon. 'It is the nature of the coward to flee rather than fight. Well, no matter, whatever Rylanor's purpose, it is irrelevant, for he is buried beneath thousands of tonnes of radioactive slag.'

Lucius nodded and gestured down the stairs. 'Apothecary Fabius… what exactly is he going to do to me?'

'Is that fear I hear in your voice, Lucius?' asked Eidolon.

'No,' said Lucius, 'I just want to know what I am letting myself in for.'

'Perfection,' promised Eidolon.

THE CORRIDORS OF the *Pride of the Emperor* were never quiet now, hastily rigged mesh speakers blaring a constant cacophony of sound from *La Fenice*. After hearing a taster of the *Maraviglia's* overture, Fulgrim had commanded that his vessels be filled with music, and the weirdly distorted recordings of Bequa Kynska's symphonics echoed along every hallway, day and night.

Serena d'Angelus made her way along the dazzlingly bright corridors of Fulgrim's flagship, lurching from side to side like a drunk, her clothes stained with blood and ordure. The remains of her long hair were greasy, and matted clumps of it had been torn out in her ravings.

With the completion of the paintings of Lucius and Fulgrim, she had found herself without inspiration, as though the fire that had driven her to undreamt of highs and lows had burnt itself out. Days passed without her moving from her studio, and the months since the expedition had arrived in the Isstvan system had passed in a blur of catatonia and horrified introspection.

Dreams and nightmares had played out in her head like badly cut pict-reels, images of horrors and degradation she hadn't known she was capable of visualising, tormenting her with their intensity and hideousness. Scenes of murders, violations, desecrations and things so vile that surely a human being was incapable of indulging in them without losing their sanity, played out before her like some madman's fever dreams laid out for her unwilling scrutiny.

Occasionally she remembered to eat, not recognising the wild, feral woman she saw in the mirror or the scarred flesh that greeted her every morning when she awoke, naked in the ruin of her studio. Over the weeks the suspicion grew in her mind that the repeated visions that plagued her in the night were not simply delusions... They were memories.

She remembered weeping bitter tears as her suspicions were terrifyingly confirmed the day she had opened the stinking barrel in the corner of the studio.

A reek of decomposing human meat and acidic chemicals hit her like a blow, and the lid clattered to the floor as she saw the gooey, partially dissolved remains of at least six corpses. Smashed skulls, sawn bones and a thick soup of liquefying flesh sloshed around the barrel, and Serena vomited uncontrollably for several minutes at the horror of the sight.

She dragged herself away from the barrel and wept piteously as the full abhorrence of what she had done threatened to overwhelm her already fraying sanity.

Her mind had teetered on the brink of madness until a name had surfaced in the miasma of her consciousness, a name that gave her an anchor to cling to: Ostian... Ostian... Ostian...

Like a drowning woman clutching at a branch, she had pulled herself to her feet, cleaned herself up as best she could and stumbled, weeping and bloody, towards Ostian's studio. He had tried to help her and she had rejected him, seeing now the love that had motivated his altruism and cursing herself for not realising it sooner.

Ostian could save her. As she reached the shutter to his studio, she only hoped he had not forsaken her. The shutter was partially open and she slammed her palm against the corrugated metal.

'Ostian!' she cried. 'It's me, Serena... please... let me in!'

Ostian did not reply, and she beat her hands bloody on the shutter, screaming his name and sobbing as she cried and begged for his forgiveness. Still there was no reply, and in desperation she reached down and lifted the shutter.

Serena stumbled into the dimly lit studio, detecting a dreadful, familiar smell even before her exhausted eyes made out the loathsome sight before her.

'Oh, no,' she whispered as she saw the grisly sight of Ostian's body impaled upon a glittering sword blade protruding from a wondrous sculpture of the Emperor.

She dropped to her knees before him and screamed, 'Forgive me! I didn't know what I was doing! Oh, please forgive me, Ostian!'

What remained of Serena's mind finally buckled and collapsed inwards at this latest atrocity. She pushed herself to her feet and placed her hands on Ostian's shoulders.

'You loved me,' she whispered, 'and I never saw it.'

Serena closed her eyes and wrapped her arms around Ostian's corpse, feeling the sharp tip of the sword between her breasts.

'But I loved you too,' she said, and pulled herself hard onto the sword blade.

TWENTY-TWO

World of Death/The Trap is Set/Maraviglia

ISSTVAN V HAD been, so the exterminated Isstvanian myth-makers believed, a place of exile. Stories told that, in a time consigned to legend, Father Isstvan himself had sung the world into being with music for his Warsingers to hear and interpret. Father Isstvan was, it seemed, a fertile god and had spread his seed far and wide across the stars, nameless mothers bearing him countless children with which he had populated the first ages of the world.

Such allegorical concepts became night and day, the seas and the land, and countless other aspects of the world in which the Isstvanians lived. Within the Sirenhold, great towers and enormous murals had told these legends in great detail: intricate dramas of love, betrayal, death and blood, but these were gone forever, burned and pounded to oblivion by the War-master's bombardment.

Such wrath was no stranger to the myths of Isst-van, which told of the children of Father Isstvan who turned from his light and led their hosts against their benevolent sire. A terrible war followed. The Lost Children, as they came to be known, were finally defeated in a great battle and their armies destroyed. Instead of slaying his wayward children, Father Isstvan banished them to Isstvan V, a desolate place of black deserts and ashen wastelands.

Upon this nightmarish place of darkness, the Lost Children were said to brood upon their expulsion from paradise, bitterness twisting their beautiful countenances until no man could look upon them without revulsion. These monstrosities were said to dwell in cyclopean fortresses of black stone where they dreamed of returning to wreak vengeance on their enemies.

Such were the myths of Isstvan as preached by the Warsingers, cautionary tales that warned their people to follow the true path, lest the Lost Children return and finally take their long awaited vengeance.

Whether these myths were allegorical parables or were in fact history was irrelevant, for, in the shape of the Warmaster's Legions, the Lost Children had indeed returned.

THE SKIES OF Isstvan V were grey and ashen, dark clouds gathering in rumbling thunderheads to the south of where the first battle for the Imperium would be fought. As places of legend went, it was not particularly impressive, thought Julius Kae-soron. The air tasted of long vanished industry, and the ground underfoot was a dusty black powder, fine and granular like sand, but hard and crunching like glass.

When Julius had first set foot on the black deserts of Isstvan V, a howling wind had been whipping across the black dunes, echoing mournfully through the towers and weathered battlements of an ancient fortress, which stood atop a gently sloping ridge at the northern edge of a vast emptiness. Known as the Urgall Depression, it was the planet's largest desert, a featureless plain of bare rock and scattered scrub that rose gently to low hills upon which was built the fortress. Who had raised it was unknown, though the Mechanicum adepts postulated that it belonged to a civilisation that predated humanity by millions of years.

Its walls were formed of enormous blocks of a hard vitreous stone, each one the size of a Land Raider, and carved with such precision that there was no evidence of any bonding agent between them. Its builders were long dead, but their architectural legacy had endured the passage of aeons, though long stretches of the wall had collapsed over the millions of years. Such ruin rendered it untenable as a fortress, but ideal as a bulwark against which to mount a defence. The wall stretched for nearly twenty kilometres and rose to heights of thirty metres in places, with slopes of gritty sand banked against it and filling the hallways of its mighty, turreted keep.

Fulgrim had set up his command within the remains of the keep and begun the work of ensuring that it would be a bastion worthy of the Warmaster.

Together with Marius, Julius followed the Primarch of the Emperor's Children as he toured the mighty works of fortification being undertaken here. Vast teams of Mechanicum earthmovers were shifting the sand from before the walls of the fortress and using it to form a vast network of earthworks, trenches, bunkers and redoubts that stretched along the ridge before the fortress. Laagers of anti-aircraft batteries were set up in the shadow of the walls, and mighty orbital torpedoes on mobile launch vehicles hid in the warrens of the fortress. If the Emperor's Legions wanted to destroy them, they were going to have to come down to the surface to do so.

The Primarch of the Emperor's Children was arrayed in his plate armour, the gleaming ceramite burnished to a brilliant purple, though Julius's newly enhanced vision detected hundreds of subtle variations of hue within each plate. Legion artificers had added many layers to the armour, its sweeping curves accentuated in new and wondrous ways, the Imperial Eagle removed from his breastplate and replaced with gracefully carved bands of lacquered ceramite.

Silver and gold edged every plate and scenes representing the Legion's new loyalties were carved onto every surface, lending the armour the appearance of something purely ceremonial, though such an impression could not be further from the truth.

'A fine sight is it not, my friends?' asked Fulgrim as he watched a gigantic bulldozer the size of a Titan lander scooping hundreds of tonnes of sand and rubble into a similarly gigantic hopper.

'Majestic,' said Julius without enthusiasm. 'The Warmaster will be pleased, I'm sure.'

'He will indeed,' replied Fulgrim, oblivious to the irony in his tone.

'Do we know yet when Horus will grace us with his presence?' he asked.

Fulgrim turned, finally hearing Julius's ennui. He smiled, sweeping a hand through his unbound white hair, and Julius felt his spirits aroused by the sight of the beautiful primarch. In deference to the

Warmaster, Fulgrim had dispensed with the powder and paints on his face and more resembled his old self, a glorious warrior of utmost perfection.

'The Warmaster will join us soon, Julius,' said Fulgrim, 'and so too will the Legions of the Emperor! I know this work seems tedious to you, but it is necessary if we are to achieve the great victory Horus requires.'

Julius shrugged, his senses crying out for stimulation. 'It is humiliating. The Warmaster could have thought of no greater punishment than denying us a place in the battle for Isstvan III and consigning us to become ditch diggers and grubby labourers on this desolate rock.'

'We all have our part to play,' said Marius, ever the sycophant, but Julius could see that he too did not relish this work and smarted at missing the glory of expunging the imperfect from their Legion. The battles on Isstvan III had been glorious, and Eidolon had sent word of the perfection of the Legion's conduct as well as the fact of Solomon Demeter's death.

Unlike when Lycaon had died fighting the Diasporex, Julius hadn't known what to feel upon hearing of his former battle-brother's end. His senses were heightened to the point that only the most shocking things could evoke more than a glimmer of passing interest. He felt no sadness, only a mild regret that a warrior as fine as Solomon had proved to be imperfect, and thus deserving of his fate.

'That we do, Marius,' agreed Fulgrim. 'The work we do is vital, Julius, that is why Horus has entrusted it to us. Only the Emperor's Children bring the perfection required to ensure that this phase of the Warmaster's plan plays out as ordained.'

'This work is fit only for the workers of the Mechanicum and perhaps the dour Iron Warriors of Perturabo's Legion. For it to be foisted upon the Emperor's Children is demeaning,' said Julius, unrepentant in his defiance. 'We are being punished for our failure.'

Though Fulgrim had been devastated at his exclusion from the battles raging on Isstvan III following the disastrous mission to bring over Ferrus Manus, he had nevertheless thrown himself into the preparations for Horus's triumphant arrival like a man possessed.

The Legions of the Emperor were massing to destroy them and soon the battle that might very well determine the fate of the Imperium would be fought on this desolate plain.

'Maybe so,' growled Fulgrim, 'but it will be done.'

WITH THE DESTRUCTION of the last surviving warriors on Isstvan III, the Legions of Horus made their way to Isstvan V, a flotilla of powerful warships and carriers bearing the martial pride of four Legions, their ranks fully comprised of those whose loyalty was to Horus and Horus alone.

Mass conveyers of Lord Commander Fayle's Army units brought millions of armed men and their tanks and artillery pieces. Bloated Mechanicum transports bore the Legio Mortis to Isstvan V, dark priests of the Machine ministering to the *Dies Irae* and its sister Titans as they prepared to unleash the unimaginable power of these land battleships once more.

Final victory on Isstvan III had been bought with many lives, but in its wake the Legions were tempered in the crucible of combat to do what must be done to save the Imperium. The process had been long and bloody, but the Warmaster's army was ready and eager to fight its brothers, where the lackeys of the Emperor would find their readiness to strike down their kith and kin untested.

Such mercy would be their undoing, promised Horus.

THE ATMOSPHERE IN *La Fenice* was tense and ripe with potential. Thousands packed its stalls and boxes, the vividness of the art, sculpture and colours overwhelming the senses with their extravagance. Nearly three thousand Astartes warriors had returned to the *Pride of the Emperor* from the surface of Isstvan V, and some six thousand remembrancers and ship's crew jammed themselves between the warriors wherever a space could be found. The excited hubbub of conversation filled the theatre.

For tonight would see the unveiling of Bequa Kynska's long-awaited *Maraviglia*.

The auditorium was painted in a riot of colours with gold trim throughout, and ornamental plasterwork and mouldings divided the wall areas into large, well-proportioned panels decorated with all manner of splendidly overwrought artworks. In magnitude, *La Fenice* had few superiors, even in the largest and most urbane of the Terran hives, and was finished in a style that had clearly involved the most lavish expenditure of resources.

Parquet spread from the front of the stage in wide, concentric arcs, the mosaic floor invisible beneath the sandals of the thousands who had come to see this most magnificent spectacle. Semi-circular niches to the side of the parquet accommodated busts of renowned impresarios of Terra and other, more exotic, statues of hedonistic libertines. Amongst these

sculptures were other, less recognisable statues of
mightily muscled androgynous figures with bulls'
heads and bejewelled horns.

To the rear of this area, six mighty columns of solid
marble supported the dress circle, and the front of the
balcony was decorated with exquisite plaster
appliqué.

Brass cages containing brightly coloured songbirds
were suspended from the base of the balcony and
their frantic music added to the din of the orchestra
and audience. A sweet scented musk drifted from
hanging incense burners and the air was almost
unbearably humid. The sense of fevered anticipation
was palpable as scores of musicians tuned their instruments in the bow shaped orchestra pit before the
stage. Each instrument was a monstrous contraption
of pipes, bellows and crackling electrical generators,
which in turn were hooked to towering stacks of
mighty amplifiers, created specifically for this performance, and designed to replicate the magical music of
the Laer temple.

Coloured lights and strategically placed prisms
filled *La Fenice* with blinding rainbows and cast beams
of a million different hues to every corner of the theatre. An army of seamstresses had worked tirelessly to
create the stage curtain, and the glaring footlights illuminated the vividness of the red velvet and the
wondrously embroidered images of decadent legends,
cavorting nudes, animals and scenes of battle.

On the vast pediment above the stage, illuminated
by a single spotlight, was the late Serena d'Angelus's
painting of the Emperor's Children's primarch. Its terrible aspect, unendurable finish, and the passion of its
outlandish colours rendered those who saw it dumb,
and robbed them of coherent thought.

More of Serena's work could be seen on the vaulted ceiling of the theatre, a colossal, multi-coloured mural of serpents and ancient beasts of legend, which sported with naked humans and beasts of all description.

The sheer bulk of the Astartes filled much of the enormous theatre, even though they were stripped of their armour and wore only simple training robes. Those remembrancers that found themselves behind one of the giant warriors danced from foot to foot as they sought to obtain a better view of the stage.

The captains of the Legion sat in the comfort of the boxes, arranged in two tiers on either side of the stage. The boxes overlooked the proscenium with an unobstructed view, and their façades were of a classical design with fluted pilasters to either side.

The box with the most perfect viewpoint was known as the Phoenician's Nest, its interior painted with frescoes of gold and silver, and decorated with yellow satin draperies that overhung lace curtains. Over it all, a valance of gold silk shimmered in the light of hundreds of candles fixed upon a great chandelier above the centre of the stage.

A movement in the Phoenician's Nest drew the gaze of the gathered audience and soon every eye was fixed upon the magnificent warrior standing there. Dressed in his finest toga of regal purple, Fulgrim raised his hand to the crowd and basked in the adoration displayed by his Legion as thunderous applause built and shook the rafters with its volume.

His senior commanders accompanied the primarch, and as he took his seat the lights began to dim. A brilliant spotlight shone on the stage as the great velvet curtain parted and Bequa Kynska made her entrance.

✠ ✠ ✠

JULIUS WATCHED WITH barely contained excitement as
the blue haired composer crossed the stage and
descended into the orchestra pit to take her place on
her conductor's podium. Dressed in a scandalously
translucent dress of gold and crimson, the gossamer
thin material hung with precious stones that glittered
like stars. The cut of her dress plunged from her
shoulders to her pelvis, the swell of her breasts and
the hairlessness of her flesh clearly visible beneath.

'Magnificent!' cried Fulgrim, clapping furiously
with the audience at Bequa's appearance, and Julius
was amazed to see tears in his eyes.

Julius nodded, and though he had no real memory
of feminine splendour or any frame of reference
against which to compare her, the composer's curves
and obvious womanhood stole away his breath.
Julius had felt such stirrings of emotion when he
gazed upon his primarch, heard a particularly inspiring piece of music or went into battle, but to feel his
senses aroused by a mortal woman was a new experience for him.

Thick silence enveloped the audience as they waited
for the magic to happen, the collective breath of
nearly ten thousand throats held fast as the moment
of anticipation stretched to breaking point. Bequa
selected a mnemo-baton and tapped it on the libretto
stand before launching into the opening bars of the
Maraviglia's overture.

Tremendous noise erupted from the orchestra pit as
the first notes blared from the newly conceived
musical devices, the sound reaching to every corner of
La Fenice with its wonderful instrumentation,
romantic beauty and hints of themes yet to come.
Julius felt himself carried on a journey of the senses
as the music rose and fell, emotions he had never

experienced plucked from the depths of his soul and brought joyously to the fore as the crashing beats and wild, skirling tunes wound their way through the audience.

He wanted to laugh and then cry, and then he felt a terrible anger build, before it bled away and a great melancholy settled upon him. Within moments the music had torn that loose, and a soaring elation asserted itself with the utmost lucidity and force, as though all that had gone before was merely the prelude to some grand design yet to be unveiled.

Bequa Kynska thrashed like a lunatic atop her conductor's podium, jabbing and slashing the air with her baton, her hair a wild comet of blue as it whipped around her head. Julius tore his eyes from the magnificent sight of her and looked out over the audience to witness its reaction to this sublime, raucous music.

He saw faces rapt in stunned disbelief, eyes wide as the power and majesty of the dissonant sounds penetrated every skull and spoke to every soul of the sensations evoked. But not every member of the audience appeared to appreciate the wonder of what they were privileged to witness, and Julius saw many with their hands clamped over their ears in the throes of agony as the music swelled once more. Julius caught sight of the slender figure of Evander Tobias in the audience, and his anger grew as he watched the ungrateful wretch lead a group of his fellow scriveners through the crowd towards the exit.

Scuffles broke out and the recalcitrant archivist and his fellows were attacked, fists pummelling them to the ground where they were kicked and beaten. Without pause, the audience returned its attention to the stage, and Julius felt a fierce pride swell in his breast as he watched a heavy boot crunch down on Tobias's

GRAHAM MCNEILL

skull. None remarked upon the sudden, bloody violence, as if it had been the most natural reaction, but Julius could see the bloodlust spread throughout the audience like a virus or the shockwave of a detonation.

The music swept onwards, rising and sweeping around *La Fenice* like a whirlwind, until at last it reached the thunderous crescendo of its climax, whereupon the curtain rose in a flurry of dramatic and spectacular sensations.

Julius rose to his feet as the peals of music drove ever onward, the overture continuing in an unbroken melody of sounds, and the sheer visceral emotions that filled him on seeing what lay beyond was like a punch to the guts.

The interior of the Laer temple had been recreated in painstaking detail, its eye-watering colours and dimensions faithfully recreated by the artists and sculptors who had walked within its magnificence.

Vivid lights flashed around the theatre, and Julius felt a momentary disorientation as more music blasted from the orchestra, a new piece with darker overtones and an aching sense of imminent tragedy. The waves of sound and harmony flowed outwards from the stage and over the audience, immersing them in the power and sensations he had first felt when he had followed Fulgrim into the temple.

The effect was immediately obvious, and a shudder of pleasure rippled through the audience as the powerful notes flowed into and through them. Dizzying colours flashed through the air, and as the music built to yet another high, a second spotlight stabbed onto the stage. The slender form of Coraline Aseneca, the prima donna of the *Maraviglia*, appeared.

Julius had never heard Coraline's voice before and was unprepared for the sheer virtuosity and power of her singing. Her tone was in perfect, discordant harmony with Bequa's music, reaching heights no human voice could possibly attain. Yet attain them she did, the energy of her soprano's voice reaching beyond the realms of the five senses, all of which were being stimulated it seemed to Julius.

He leaned forwards, laughing uncontrollably as an intoxicating rush of emotions seized him, and he clasped his hands to his head at such over-stimulation. A chorus joined Coraline Aseneca on stage, though Julius hardly noticed them, their intermingled voices allowing the soprano's voice to swoop through even more unfeasible notes, which reached into the very hindbrain to pluck at sensory apparatus Julius was not even aware he possessed.

Julius forced himself to look away from the stage, enthralled and terrified by what he was seeing and hearing. What manner of being could hear music of such terrible power and retain his sanity? Man was not meant to listen to this, the birthing cry of a beautiful and terrible god as it forced its way into existence.

Eidolon and Marius were as ensnared by the spectacle of the *Maraviglia* as he was, pinned to their seats in rapture. The jaws of both warriors were locked open as though they entertained the idea of joining with Coraline Aseneca in song, but there was panic in their eyes as their mouths stretched wide in silent screams, bones cracking as they distended like a snake about to devour its prey. Hideous, soundless shrieks issued from their throats, and Julius forced himself to look at Fulgrim for fear that he might strike down his friends in his fugue state.

Fulgrim gripped the edge of the Phoenician's Nest, leaning forward as though forcing passage through a powerful wind. His hair writhed around his head and his dark eyes burned with a violet fire as he revelled in the cacophony.

'What is happening?' cried Julius, his voice swept up and becoming part of the music. Fulgrim turned his dark eyes upon him, and Julius cried out as he saw an age of darkness within them, galaxies and stars wheeling in their depths as unknown power flowed through him.

'It's beautiful,' said Fulgrim, his voice barely above a whisper, but sounding deafening to Julius as he propelled himself from his seat and fell to his knees at the edge of the box. 'Horus spoke of power, but I never imagined...'

Julius watched in wonder, realising the he could actually see the soprano's music as it reached out into the audience and slithered amongst them like a living thing. Their shrieks and cries penetrated the fog of music that writhed in his brain, and he saw all manner of horrors enacted throughout the audience, as friends turned and fought each other with fists and teeth. Some audience members fell upon one another with carnal lust, and the heaving crowd soon resembled a great wounded beast, convulsing in agonised throes of death and desire.

Nor was it simply mortals who were affected. The Astartes too were swept up in the surging power generated by the *Maraviglia*. Blood was spilled as the emotions of the Astartes were overloaded with sensational excess, and were vented in the only way men bred as warriors knew how. An orgy of killing spread from the stage, blood running in rivers as the power of the music thundered through *La Fenice*.

Julius heard a great buzzing, creaking sound, like a great sheet of sailcloth being ripped to shreds, and he turned to see the mighty portrait of Fulgrim writhing and stretching at the canvas as though its painted subject fought to be free of the constraints of the frame. Fires blazed in its eyes and a howling shriek that sounded as though it echoed down an impossibly long tunnel filled his skull with a monstrous thirst and the promise of horrific splendours.

Lights blazed around the theatre, flowing from the orchestra pit like liquid, the greasy, electrical fire lifting from the bizarre instruments and achieving physicality as they became liquid serpents of myriad colours. Madness and excess followed the light, and all those it touched gave themselves over to the wildest, darkest delights of their inner psyches.

The orchestra played as though their limbs were not their own, their faces twisted in horrified rictus masks and their hands frenziedly dancing across their instruments with violent life. The music held them in its grip and was not about to let any weakness on the part of its creators deny its existence.

Julius heard notes of agony enter Coraline Aseneca's voice, and managed to lift his eyes to the stage, where the prima donna danced in a wild, exuberant ballet as the choristers screamed in unnatural counterpoint. Her limbs snapped and twisted in a manner no human limb was designed to, and he could hear the cracking of her bones as it became part of the million melodies filling the theatre. He could see that she was dead, her eyes lifeless. Every bone in her body turned to powder, and yet the song poured from her still.

The madness and frenzy engulfing *La Fenice* soared to new heights of excess as all flesh was infected with the maelstrom of sights and sounds coming from the stage. Julius watched as Astartes clubbed mortals to death with their fists and drank their blood or ate their flesh, scarring their skin with the broken bones and draping the torn skin of their victims about them like grisly shawls.

Vast orgies of mortals shuddered on the blood slick parquet as the living and the dead became vessels for the dark energies pouring into the world, every violation imaginable willingly inflicted.

At the centre of the madness, Bequa Kynska conducted the chaos with a delirious smile of triumph plastered across her face. Julius saw the knowledge that this was her greatest work in the light of her eyes as she stared in rapt adoration at Fulgrim.

Then, without warning, a terrifying scream cut through the crescendo of noise, and Julius saw the abused form of Coraline Aseneca twist into the air, her limbs spread-eagled as some unknown power seized the broken meat and gristle of her body and warped it into some new, hideous form. Her shattered limbs straightened, becoming lithe and graceful once again, the flesh taking on a pale lilac hue. Where before Coraline had been clad in a shimmering dress of blue silk, the fabric transformed into a harness of gleaming black leather that revealed the supple beauty of the soft flesh formed from the ruin of her corpse.

A horrific wet sucking noise engulfed the prima donna and whatever force had previously held her aloft released her. The thing Coraline Aseneca had become landed with supple grace in the centre of the stage.

Julius had never seen anything so simultaneously beautiful and repellent, a naked female creature that evoked both a potent loathing, and a perverse sensuality that gnawed at the pit of his stomach. Hair like needle horns swept back from her oval face, with its green, saucer-like eyes, fanged mouth and luscious lips. Her body was sculpted perfection, lithe and sensuous, but with only a single breast, and her skin was loathsomely tattooed and pierced. Each of her arms terminated in a long crab-like claw of glistening red chitin and moist flesh. Despite the lethal claws, the creature was disturbingly seductive, and Julius felt moved in a way he had not been since he had been elevated to the ranks of the Astartes.

She moved with languid, cat-like grace, her every movement redolent with sexuality and the promise of dark pleasures and excesses unknown to the minds of mortal men. Julius ached to taste them. The she-creature turned her ancient eyes upon the choristers behind her and threw her head back to emit a siren song of such longing and heartbreaking beauty that Julius wanted to climb from the box to join her.

Even before the note of summoning had dissipated, it was taken up by the frenzied orchestra, and grew louder and louder. Julius saw the members of the chorus spasm and twist as Coraline Aseneca had, the same bone-cracking harmonies transforming five of them into more of the hauntingly alluring creatures. The remaining choristers fell to the stage as dried husks of flesh, drained of their life, as though merely fuel to power the transformation of the cavorting creatures that leapt from the stage in a flurry of slicing claws and bestial shrieks.

The six creatures moved with sinewy, supple grace, the caress of their razor sharp claws opening arteries and severing limbs with every lissom movement.

Bequa Kynska was the first to die, a monstrous claw impaling her from behind and ripping from her chest in a fountain of blood. Even as she died, she smiled in delight at the wondrous things she had done. The rest of the orchestra was torn to pieces as the beautiful monsters ripped through them with a speed and sensual malice that Julius could barely imagine.

At last, the music of the *Maraviglia* fell silent as the musicians were slaughtered in the caress of razor claws, their lives torn from their quivering flesh. Julius cried out in the sudden void, the absence of the music like a physical pain in his bones. Though the music had fallen silent, *La Fenice* was still a deafening arena. The killing and copulation continued unabated, though the shrieks of agony and ecstasy turned to wails of anguish as the music's demise was mourned in renewed bouts of bloody madness.

Julius heard Marius give a howling cry of loss and turned to see his battle-brother leap from the Phoenician's Nest to the stage. Fulgrim watched him go, his body quivering with emotion and pleasure, and Julius pushed himself unsteadily to his feet. He watched as Marius dropped into the bloody ruin of the orchestra pit and lifted one of Bequa Kynska's bizarre instruments.

Marius hefted the long, tubular device and hooked it into the crook of his arm like a boltgun, running his hands along the length of the shaft until it produced a monstrous vibration like the roar of a chainsword. Even as Julius watched Marius's futile attempts to recreate the music, more of the Emperor's Children rushed to join him, each picking up one of the orchestral instruments and attempting to conjure the magic of the music once again.

Julius felt the breath heave in his lungs and gripped the edge of the balcony for fear that his legs would not support him.

'I… what…?' was all he could manage as Fulgrim moved to stand next to him.

'Wondrous was it not?' asked Fulgrim, his skin glowing with renewed vigour and his eyes alight with fresh purpose. 'Mistress Kynska was a fiery comet. Everyone stopped to look at her and now she is gone. We will never see anything like her again, and none of us will be able to forget her.'

Julius tried to reply, but a vast explosion of noise erupted from behind him and he turned to see a portion of the stage wreathed in smoke and collapsing rubble. Marius stood in the centre of the orchestra pit, electrical fire dancing across his flesh as he strummed his hands across the screaming instrument. A howling, pyrotechnic blast of sonic energy shot from it and ripped one of the balconies from the wall in a devastating explosion. Chunks of marble and plaster flew through the air and the sound of the instrument drew howls of pleasure from Marius's fellow Astartes.

Within moments, each had mastered his device and a renewed crescendo of howling, shrieking blasts of energy began ripping the theatre apart. The monstrously beguiling she-monsters gathered around Marius, adding their own unnatural shrieks of pleasure to the delirious music he was making.

Marius turned his instrument into the crowd and unleashed a thrumming bass note that built to an explosive climax. Clashing chords like howls of ecstasy tore through a dozen mortals with an earsplitting concussion, and each of Marius's victims thrashed helplessly as their bones snapped and heads exploded beneath the barrage of noise.

'My Emperor's Children,' said Fulgrim, 'what sweet music they make.'

Explosions of flesh and stone bloomed throughout *La Fenice* as Marius and the rest of the Astartes filled it with the music of the apocalypse.

TWENTY-THREE

The Battle of Isstvan V

CAPTAIN BALHAAN STOOD immobile at his command lectern, and tried to control his breathing as he watched the three majestic figures gathered on the bridge of the *Ferrum*. Iron Father Diederik stood by helm control, similarly awed by the towering figures of the three primarchs as they discussed how best to destroy the enemy forces on Isstvan V. His readings of history had spoken of the charisma of ancient heroes of legend, the mighty Hektor, brave Alexandyr and the sublime Torquil.

Tales spoke of how men had been struck dumb by their sheer majesty, and thus these heroes had been described in terms of wondrous hyperbole that were clearly exaggerated and designed to inflate their reputations. Balhaan had discounted most such stories as overblown fabrications, until he had first laid eyes upon a primarch and knew them to be true, but to see three of them gathered together was like nothing he could describe. No mere words could hope to convey the fearful awe he felt at beholding such perfect visions of warriors as stood on the bridge of his ship.

Ferrus Manus, clad in his shimmering fuliginous armour, stood a head taller than his brothers, pacing like a caged Medusan snow lion as he awaited news of the rest of his Legion. He punched one silver fist into his palm as he paced, and Balhaan could see the urgent need to take the fight to the traitors in his every movement.

Next to the broad, mightily muscled Primarch of the Iron Hands, Corax of the Raven Guard was tall and slender. His armour was also black, but it seemed to be utterly non-reflective, as though it swallowed any light that dared to fall upon it. The white trim of his shoulder guards was fashioned from pale ivory, and great wings of dark feathers swept upwards to either side of his pallid, aquiline features. His eyes were murderously dark coals, and long, gleaming talons of silver were unsheathed over his gauntlets. So far, the Primarch of the Raven Guard had said nothing, but Balhaan had heard this of Corax, that he was a taciturn warrior who kept his counsel until he had something of worth to impart.

The third of the primarchs was Vulkan of the Salamanders, a brother with whom Ferrus Manus had a great friendship, for both were craftsmen as well as warriors. Vulkan's skin was dark and swarthy, and his eyes carried a depth of wisdom that had humbled the greatest scholars of the Imperium. His armour was a shimmering sea green, though each gleaming ceramite plate was embellished with images of flame picked out in a profusion of coloured chips of quartz. One shoulder guard was fashioned from the skull of a great firedrake, said to have been the beast Vulkan had hunted in his contest with the Emperor hundreds of years ago, while over the other was draped a long mantle of iron-hard scales taken from the hide of another mighty drake of Nocturne.

Vulkan bore a wondrously crafted weapon with a top-loading magazine and perforated barrel formed in the shape of a snarling dragon. Balhaan had heard of the gun, its brass and silver body having been crafted by Ferrus Manus many years ago for his brother primarch. Balhaan had watched as his primarch had presented it once again to Vulkan, and felt great pride swell within him as the dark-skinned warrior had graciously accepted the legendary weapon and sworn to bear it in the coming battle.

To stand in close proximity to such mighty warriors was an honour Balhaan knew would never be equalled. He resolved to remember every detail of this moment and record it as best he could, so that future captains of the *Ferrum* would know the honour accorded their vessel in times past.

Balhaan had pushed the crew of his ship to its very limit to reach the Isstvan system with such speed, and now that they had arrived, it was to find that they had come alongside the fleets of the Raven Guard and Salamanders. Discreet reconnaissance had identified enemy positions, and the primarchs had mapped out landing zones as well as optimal attack patterns, but without the other Legions tasked with destroying Horus's rebellion, nothing could be done.

To have reached their destination and be unable to enact the Emperor's will was a supreme frustration, but even Ferrus Manus's rage had recognised that they could not overwhelm the Warmaster's forces without support.

Ten companies of the Morlocks were berthed throughout the *Ferrum*, the deadliest and most experienced warriors of the Legion, and Balhaan knew that whatever force was arrayed against the Terminators, it could not survive their wrath. The Iron Hands would undertake the initial assaults with the veterans of their Legion, and Balhaan felt that it was appropriate that the Legion's best warriors should be first into battle. Led by Gabriel Santar, the Morlocks hungered to confront the Emperor's Children and make them pay for the dishonourable murders done to their number in the Anvilarium of the *Fist of Iron*.

The rest of the 52nd Expedition was following behind the *Ferrum*, but when they might arrive in-system was unknown, and every second their assault was delayed gave the traitors more time to fortify their positions.

The Legions of Corax and Vulkan were in position to commence their attack runs on Isstvan V, but Astropath Cistor had received no word from Ferrus Manus's brother primarchs of the Word Bearers, Night Lords, Iron Warriors or Alpha Legion.

'Are all units ready and in position?' asked Ferrus Manus without turning from the viewing screen.

Balhaan nodded and said, 'They are, my lord.'

'Still no word from the rest of the Legions?'

'None, my lord,' said Balhaan, checking the link to the choral chambers of the Legion's few surviving astropaths. The same ritual had been repeated every few minutes as Ferrus Manus chafed at the delay in ordering the attack, the waiting interminable for warriors who lusted to strike back at those who tarnished the honour of their brothers with their treachery.

The hatch to the bridge slid open and a pair of the Terminator armoured Morlocks entered, followed by the gaunt figure of Astropath Cistor.

Barely had he stepped within the bridge than Ferrus Manus was at his side, his gleaming hands taking the astropath by the shoulders in a crushing grip.

'What news of the other Legions?' demanded Ferrus, his craggy features and blazing silver eyes centimetres from Cistor's.

'My lord, I have personally received word from your brother primarchs,' said Cistor, squirming in the primarch's grip.

'And? Tell me, are they en route? Can we commence the attack?'

'Ferrus,' said Corax, his voice soft, yet laden with quiet authority, 'you will crush him to death before he tells you. Release him.'

Ferrus let out a shuddering breath and stepped back from the quivering astropath as Vulkan stepped forward and said, 'Tell us what you have heard.'

'The Legions of the Word Bearers, Alpha Legion, Iron Warriors and Night Lords are mere hours behind us, my lord Vulkan,' said Cistor calmly. 'They will break warp close to the fifth planet.'

'Yes!' shouted Ferrus, punching the air and turning to his brother primarchs. 'The honour of drawing first blood in this battle falls to us, my brothers. We go for full planetary assault.'

Ferrus's enthusiasm was infections, and Balhaan felt his blood fire with the knowledge that they were soon to take the wrath of the Emperor's judgement to the traitors. His primarch resumed his pacing of the bridge as he threw out orders to his brothers.

'The Morlocks and I will take the vanguard,' said Ferrus. 'Corax, your Legion is to secure the right flank of the Urgall Depression and then push into the centre. Vulkan, you have the left wing.'

The primarchs nodded at Ferrus's words, and Balhaan could see that even the normally stoic Corax relished the prospect of destroying the enemy below.

'The other Legions will make planetfall as soon as they break warp. They will secure the dropsite and reinforce our assault,' cried Ferrus, his eyes ablaze with magnesium fire.

He shook his brothers' hands and turned to address the crew of the *Ferrum*. 'The traitors are not expecting us to assault so soon, and we have the advantage of surprise. The Emperor damn us if we waste it!'

THE DELAYS ENFORCED upon Ferrus Manus had not been wasted by the Warmaster's forces. Since their arrival at Isstvan V, eight days ago, the warriors of the World Eaters, Death Guard, Sons of Horus and Emperor's Children had deployed throughout the defences constructed along the ridge of the Urgall Depression, making ready for the howling storm of battle that was soon to descend upon them. Behind them, long range, support squads manned the walls of the fortress, and Army artillery pieces waited to shower any attacker with high explosive death.

The *Dies Irae* stood before the wall, its colossal guns primed and ready to visit destruction on the enemies of the Warmaster, Princeps Turnet personally swearing to atone for the treachery that had engulfed his command during the Battle of Isstvan III.

Nearly thirty thousand Astartes hunkered down on the northern edge of the Urgall, their guns ready and their hearts steeled to the necessity of what must be done.

The skies remained an unbroken canopy of slate grey clouds, and the only sound to break the ghostly howl of the wind was the scrape of metal on metal. A sense of historic solemnity hung over the black desert, as though all gathered knew that these were the last moments of quiet in what was soon to be a bloody battlefield.

The first warning came when a dull, red orange glow built behind the clouds, bathing the Urgall in a fiery light. Then came the sound: a low roar that built from a deep, thrumming bass to a shrieking whine.

Alarms sounded and the clouds split apart as individual streaks of light burned through and fell in a cascading torrent of fire. Thunderous explosions ripped along the edge of the Urgall, and the entire length of the Warmaster's forces was engulfed in a searing, roaring bombardment.

For long minutes, the forces of the Emperor pounded the Urgall from orbit, a firestorm of unimaginable ferocity hammering the surface of Isstvan V with the power of the world's end. Eventually, the horrific bombardment ceased and the drifting echoes of its power faded, along with the acrid smoke of explosions, but the Emperor's Children had performed perfectly in creating a network of defences from which to face their former brothers, and the forces of the Warmaster had been well protected.

From his vantage point in the alien keep, the Warmaster smiled, and he watched the sky darken once again as thousands upon thousands of drop-pods streaked through the atmosphere towards the planet's surface.

He turned to the bellicose, armoured figure of Angron and the gloriously presented Fulgrim and said, 'Mark this day well, my friends. The Emperor's loyalists are heading to their doom!'

THE NOISE WAS horrendous, a never-ending howl of fire that turned the interior of the drop-pod into a blisteringly hot oven. Only the ceramite plates of their armour allowed the Astartes to launch an attack in this manner, and Santar knew that their lightning assault would catch the traitors at their most vulnerable while they reeled from the power of the orbital barrage.

Ferrus Manus sat opposite Santar, an unfamiliar sword across his lap, and the fire of their descent reflected in the silver of his eyes. Another three of the Morlocks filled the drop-pod, the greatest warriors of the Legion, and the bloody tip of the spear that would drive hard in the foe's vitals.

The skies above the Urgall Depression would be thick with drop-pods, the combined might of three Legions slashing through the air to exact a blood vengeance upon their erstwhile brothers, and Santar could feel the powerful desire to destroy the Warmaster's traitors in every breath he took through the new metallic chassis of his body.

'Ten seconds to impact!' screamed the automated vox-unit.

Santar tensed and pressed himself hard against the central core of the drop-pod, the servos of his Terminator armour locking in place in preparation for the colossal force of impact. He could hear thunderous, booming explosions from beyond the armoured petals of the drop-pod, recognising them as enemy battery fire. It seemed inconceivable that any enemy had survived the bombardment.

The jerk of retro-burners, followed by the crushing hammer blow of the landing, tore at his grav-harness, but Santar was a veteran of such assaults, and was well used to the violence of such screaming deceleration. No sooner had the drop-pod hit than explosive bolts blew out the hatches and the scorched panels fell outwards. The grav-harness released and Santar charged out onto the surface of Isstvan V.

His first sight was of mountainous flames as the fire of thousands of drop-pods turned the grey skies into a weave of light and smoke. Explosions marched across the ground as artillery shells smashed into the earth, and armoured bodies were pulped by the monstrous shockwaves. The ridge before him was awash with gunfire, streams of it flickering back and forth as thousands of Astartes engaged in a furious firefight.

'Onwards!' shouted Ferrus Manus, setting off towards the ridge. Santar and the Morlocks followed him into the crazed maelstrom of the battle, seeing that the bulk of the Iron Hands had impacted in the very heart of the enemy's defences. The black desert burned in the aftermath of the bombardment, and the twisted remains of shattered bunkers, redoubts and collapsed trenches were a grisly testament to its power.

Nearly forty thousand loyal Astartes fought along the length of a ridge before the towering walls of an ancient fortress, the speed and ferocity of their assault catching the traitors completely off guard. Even with the filtering of his armour's senses, the noise of battle was appalling: gunfire, explosions and screaming cries of hatred.

The flames of war lit up the clouds above, and streaks of fire whipped across the battlefield in deadly arcs of bullets and high-energy lasers. The ground rumbled with the footfalls of an angry leviathan as the *Dies Irae* strode through the flurries of missiles

and gunfire, its mighty weaponry blazing and goug-
ing huge tears through the loyalist ranks. Miniature
suns exploded in the desert as the Titan's plasma
weaponry blasted craters hundreds of metres in diameter, obliterating hundreds of Astartes at a stroke and
turning the sand to shimmering dark glass.

Ferrus Manus was a god of war, smashing traitors to
the ground with blows from his shimmering fists or
blasting them apart with an ornately crafted pistol of
enormous calibre. The sword he had brought was
belted at his side, and Santar wondered what it was
and why he had bothered to bring it.

A hundred traitors emerged from a ruined trench
complex before them, a mix of Death Guard and
Sons of Horus, and Santar slid the lightning-sheathed
blades from his gauntlets. Amid the riotous confusion of the battle, Santar relished this chance for
simple bloodletting. The traitors stood their ground,
firing their guns from their hips as the Iron Hands
smashed into them. Santar disembowelled his first
opponent, and waded into the rest with a speed that
would have done any warrior in Mark IV plate proud.
Bolts and the roaring blades of chainswords struck
him, but his armour was proof against such things.

Ferrus Manus slaughtered enemy warriors by the
dozen, their traitorous nerve failing in the face of
such a majestic avatar of battle.

The trenches and bunkers were a mass of thousands
of struggling warriors, against a backdrop of explosions and the tremendous noise of slaughter. Orders,
and cries of victory or despair flashed through his helmet vox, but Santar ignored them, too caught up in
the cathartic release of killing to pay them any mind.

Even amid the chaos of fighting, Santar could see
that the battle for the Urgall Depression was going

well. Hundreds, perhaps even thousands of traitors had been slaughtered in the opening moments of the assault. Entire Chapters of the Salamanders pressed home the shock of their attack with flame units cleansing the trenches and dugouts of enemies in stinking promethium tongues of fire. Streaks of sun-fire stabbed through the smoke-wreathed darkness, and Santar recognised the light as fire from the weapon his primarch had gifted to Vulkan.

Sure enough, the mighty figure of Vulkan strode through the torrents of bolts, killing with every sweep of his sword and shot of the weapon his brother had forged in his name. A colossal explosion erupted at the primarch's feet, wreathing him in killing fire, and dozens of his Firedrakes were hurled through the air, their armour molten and the flesh seared from their bones. Vulkan marched through the fire unscathed, continuing to kill traitors without missing a beat.

Ferrus Manus pushed deeper into the ranks of the traitors. Their training had never prepared them to face the wrath of a primarch. The Morlocks followed behind their lord and master, a fighting wedge forging a bloody path through the filthy traitors with every shot and blow.

BEHIND THE TREMENDOUS thunder strike of the assault, the heavy landers of the loyalist fleets braved the storm of anti-aircraft fire ripping upwards from inside the ancient fortress. Burning craft spiralled to the ground, ripped apart in streams of tracer fire, or blown apart by mass-reactive torpedoes. Hundreds of aircraft jostled for position as they descended to the dropsite, bringing heavy equipment, artillery, tanks and war machines to the surface of Isstvan V.

Billowing clouds of granular dust obscured much of the landing zones as cavernous holds disgorged scores of Land Raiders and Predator battle tanks. Entire companies of armoured vehicles roared onto the surface of the planet, churning the sand beneath their tracks as they raced to join the battle on the ridge.

Whirlwinds and Army artillery units deployed on the desert flats, spreading out and zeroing in on enemy emplacements, added their own thunder to the constant crack and rumble of battle. Even heavier craft descended on burning columns of fire, and the super heavy tanks of the Army rumbled out, the barrels of their massive guns hurling huge shells against the glassy walls of the fortress.

What had begun as a massed strike against the traitors' position was rapidly turning into one of the largest engagements of the entire Great Crusade. All told, over sixty thousand Astartes warriors clashed on the dusky plains of Isstvan V, and for all the wrong reasons, this battle was soon to go down in the annals of Imperial history as one of the most epic confrontations ever fought.

The loyalist attack was bending the line of the traitors back, a curving arc of battle with Ferrus Manus at its centre. The screaming raptors of Corax's Raven Guard cut a swathe through the enemy's right flank, his fearsome assault wings dropping from above on the fire of jump packs, and slaughtering their foes with shrieking sweeps of curved blades. Corax darted like a dark bird of prey, leaping through the air with his winged jump pack and killing with every stroke of his mighty talons. Vulkan's Salamanders burned the traitors' left flank, plumes of fire marking the extent of their advance.

But for every success, the traitors thus far had an answer. The terrifying form of the World Eaters primarch cut through hundreds of loyal Astartes as they tried to force a crossing through a killing zone of World Eater support squads. Angron bellowed like a primordial god of battle, his twin swords carving bloody ruin through any who dared stand before them. As easily as the traitors died at the blades of Corax, Ferrus Manus and Vulkan, so too did the loyalists die at those of the Red Angel.

In contrast to the brute savagery of Angron, Mortarion, the Death Lord, killed with a grim efficiency, harvesting scores of loyalist lives with every sweep of his terrifying war-scythe. His Death Guard fought with grim tenacity. Where the traitor primarchs stood, none could live, the loyalist assault breaking against them like the tide on immovable cliffs.

Throughout the traitor lines, the Sons of Horus fought with bitter hatred in their hearts, First Captain Abaddon leading the Warmaster's finest in battle, his wrath terrible to behold. He killed with unremitting savagery, while Horus Aximand fought beside him, his blows mechanical and forlorn as his haunted eyes took in the scale of the slaughter.

In the centre of the traitor line, the Emperor's Children fought with unremitting cruelty, its warriors howling with savage glee as they killed their former brothers. Unnatural horrors of mutilation and degradation were visited upon the living and the dead as Fulgrim's Legion repulsed every attack, though their primarch was yet to be seen.

Bizarrely clad warriors in Mark IV plate draped in stretched skin cavorted in the midst of the deadliest combats, fighting without helmets, their jaws wired open as they unleashed a hideous screaming. They

bore unknown weaponry and fired echoing blasts of
atonal harmonics that ripped bloody canyons in the
massed ranks of the Iron Hands. Great pipes and
loudspeakers fixed to their armour amplified the
screaming vibrations of their killing music, and deafening sound waves tore apart warriors and armoured
vehicles.

As the bulk of the heavier equipment was landed
behind the ferocious battle, more and more explosions erupted in the traitors' lines, and even Angron
and Mortarion were forced to pull back out of range
of the loyalist artillery. In the centre of the battle, Ferrus Manus pushed ever onwards, his Iron Hands
pushing deeper and deeper into the heart of the
enemy defences as they sought to punish the traitors
and unleash their wrath on the Emperor's Children.

Thousands were dying every minute, the slaughter
terrible to behold. Blood ran in rivers down the
slopes of the Urgall Depression, carving thick, sticky
runnels in the dark sand. Such destruction had never
yet been concentrated in such a horrifically confined
space, enough martial power to conquer an entire
planetary system having been unleashed in a line less
than twenty kilometres wide.

Entire squadrons of armoured vehicles fought to
reach the front lines, but the press of armoured bodies was so thick that their commanders were
frustrated in their desire to crush the traitors beneath
their armoured bulk. Firing lines of Land Raiders
formed and collimated lines of ruby laser fire stabbed
towards the fortress and the leviathan-like form of the
Dies Irae.

Void shields flickered and, realising the danger, the
monstrous Titan switched its fire from the infantry to
the armour. Rippling blasts of plasma energy sawed

along the line of tanks, and a dozen exploded as the white heat of fire torched their energy magazines.

The slaughter continued unabated, on a scale never before seen, with neither side able to press home their advantages. The traitors were well dug in and had defensible positions, but the loyalists had landed virtually directly on top of them with vast numerical superiority.

The bloodletting was a truly horrific sight as warriors who had once sworn great oaths of loyalty to one another fought their brothers with nothing but hatred in their hearts. No Legion fared well in the slaughter, the scale of the fighting rendering tactics meaningless as the two armies battered each other bloody in a remorseless conflict that threatened to destroy them all.

JULIUS DANCED THROUGH the combat, the sights and sounds of the killing causing rushes of physical pleasure to spasm through his body as he fought with savage joy. His armour was dented and gashed in a dozen places, but the wounds he had suffered only spurred his frenetic killing dance to greater heights. In preparation for the fighting, he had repainted its every surface in a riot of colours that stimulated his freshly reborn vision.

He had similarly enhanced his weapons, and the looks of horror and disgust that accompanied his every killing blow fired his senses.

'Look upon me and realise the greyness of your lives!' he screamed as he fought, delirious with slaughter. He had long since discarded his helmet to better experience the chaos of the battle, the roar of guns, the buzz of swords through flesh, the explosions and the vividness of shell traceries across the heavens.

He ached to have Fulgrim next to him in this most exquisite of battles, but the Warmaster had plans enough for the Primarch of the Emperor's Children. A petulant frown creased Julius's ecstatic features, and he spun to deliver a perfectly aimed decapitating strike at a dark armoured Iron Hands warrior. Horus and his plans! Where amongst these plans was the time to enjoy the spoils of victory? The powers and desires awakened within him by the *Maraviglia* were for the using. To deny them was to deny one's own nature.

Julius swept up the helmet he had just cut from his enemy and plucked the head from within, taking a moment to savour the stink of the blood and scorched flesh where his blade had cauterised it.

'We were brothers once!' he cried with mock gravitas. 'But now you are dead!'

He leaned in and kissed the cold lips of the Iron Hand, laughing as he hurled it high into the air, where it was ripped apart in the near constant hail of bolts. Whooping howls of manic laughter and thrumming bass explosions swept towards him, and he threw himself flat as a killing wave of sound roared overhead. The musical wave was excruciatingly loud, but Julius screamed in pleasure as the noise sluiced through his flesh.

Julius rolled to his feet in time to see a burnished group of Terminators lumbering towards him, and he grinned in feral glee as he saw they were led by Gabriel Santar, the first captain's markings on his armour standing out like a beacon in the darkness.

A whooshing roar of clashing noise tore a great furrow in the ground beside him and blasted upwards from the black sand like a volcanic eruption. Behind him, Julius saw the flesh-wrapped form of Marius, and roared with the pleasure of seeing his fellow captain alive and fighting.

Marius Vairosean had embellished his armour with jagged iron spikes, and had torn the skin from the dead of *La Fenice* to decorate its blood-slathered plates. Like Julius, he had not walked away from the *Maraviglia* without alteration, the monstrous distension of his jaws locking his mouth open in a constant, howling scream. Where his ears had once been were two great gashes carved in his flesh, and his eyes were stitched open, forever prevented from closing.

He still carried the great musical instrument he had taken from Bequa Kynska's orchestra, modified to bear spiked handles and grips to render it into a terrifying sonic weapon. Together, he and his fellows unleashed a barrage of discordant scales that sent a dozen of the Morlocks into convulsions, and Julius screamed his appreciation as he leapt to meet Gabriel Santar with his sword aimed at his throat.

THE HORROR OF what he was seeing almost cost Gabriel Santar his life. The Emperor's Children before him were like nothing he could ever have imagined in his worst nightmares. Though the enemies he had fought before had been honourless traitors, at least they had still been recognisable as Astartes. These were degenerate perversions of that perfect ideal: warped and twisted freaks who openly displayed their perversions.

A mutilated monster in power armour draped with bloody flaps of skin shrieked as he swept some bizarre weapon back and forth, its deadly sonic energies tearing warriors apart in explosions of ruptured armour and liquefied flesh.

Even as Santar raised his energised fist to block a sword cut aimed at his head, he recognised the twisted features of Julius Kaesoron. The warrior was a thrashing dervish, laughing and howling as he spun like a lunatic around Santar, slashing wildly as he attacked. Kaesoron's weapon was a fearsome, energised glaive that was easily capable of carving through his armour, and Santar turned as fast as he was able to block each ferocious stroke of the blade, but even one as fast as he could not hope to match his opponent's serpent-like speed.

He caught the descending blade of his opponent's weapon between the digits of his energy wreathed fist and a fiery explosion burst between them. He twisted his wrist, and Julius's blade snapped, leaving only the length of a forearm above the quillons.

Santar grunted in pain as he felt the skin of his fist fuse with the melted plates around his hand. He saw Julius sprawled on his back, the ceramite armour of his breastplate bubbling with the residue of the explosion, his face a screaming, burnt horror of seared flesh and exposed bone.

Despite the pain of his burned claw of a hand, Santar grinned beneath his helmet and stomped forwards to deliver the avenging deathblow to his hated enemy. He raised his foot to stamp down on Julius's chest, the power of his Terminator armour easily able to crush Astartes plate.

Then he saw that Julius wasn't screaming in pain, but in orgasmic pleasure.

He paused in revulsion for the briefest second, but that second was all that Julius needed. Sweeping up the broken edge of his glaive, the blade alive with flaring energies, he rammed it into Santar's groin.

The pain was unimaginable, surging agonisingly around his body. Julius Kaesoron tore the remains of the weapon upward, molten gobbets of armour dropping to the dark sand in the midst of a spraying rain of Santar's blood. The blade tore through his pubis and ripped into his breastplate as Julius rose to his feet with the motion of his sawing weapon.

Santar's entire body convulsed in agony, not even the frantically pumping pain balms able to mask the horrifying agony of having his torso carved open. He tried to move, but his armour was locked in place as Julius looked directly at him. His face was horrifically illuminated in the firelight of the battle, the skin peeled away from the musculature beneath, and the white gleam of bone jutting through his cheeks.

Even amid the thunder of battle and with his lips burned away, Julius's next words were horribly clear to Santar as his life slipped away.

'Thank you,' gurgled Julius. 'That was exquisite.'

THE BATTLEFIELD OF Isstvan V was a slaughterhouse of epic proportions. Treacherous warriors twisted by hatred fought their once-brothers in a conflict unparalleled in its bitterness. Mighty gods walked the planet's surface and death followed in their wake. The blood of heroes and traitors flowed in rivers, and hooded adepts of the Dark Mechanicum unleashed perversions of ancient technology stolen from the Auretian Technocracy to wreak bloody havoc amongst the loyalists.

All across the Urgall Depression, hundreds were dying with every passing second, the promise of inevitable death a pall of darkness that hung over every warrior. The traitor forces were holding, but their line was bending beneath the fury of the loyalist assault. It would take only the smallest twists of fate for it to break.

And then they came.

Like fiery comets from the heavens, the thrusters of countless drop-ships, landers and assault craft broke through the fire-shot clouds of smoke and descended to the loyalist landing zone on the northern edge of the Urgall Depression. Hundreds of Stormbirds and Thunderhawks roared towards the surface, their armoured hulls gleaming as the power of another four Legions came to Isstvan, their heroic names legendary, their mighty deeds known the length and breadth of the galaxy: Alpha Legion, Word Bearers, Night Lords, Iron Warriors.

TWENTY-FOUR

Brothers with Bloody Hands

FERRUS MANUS SMOTE all around with his fists, twin
balls of silver steel that crushed bone and clove
armour wherever they struck. His gun was discarded,
his load of ammunition long since expended, but he
needed no mere weapon to be a lethal killing
machine. No blade could wound him and no shot
could penetrate his armour, his every movement a
fluid economy of motion as he killed with every
stride, pushing the fighting wedge of the Morlocks
deeper into the traitor lines.

The sword at his waist hung like a lead weight of
cosmic justice at his side, but he would not draw it,
not until he faced his traitorous brother and revealed
its terrible purpose before taking his revenge.

He longed to push ahead of his warriors, to carve a
bloody path through the traitors in search of Fulgrim,
but while the battle still hung in the balance he could
not set aside his duty of command, and seek a duel

with the viperous primarch to settle once and for all the enmity between them.

The fire and clamour of war surrounded him. Smoke boiled from wrecked tanks and shattered defences, and explosions of gunfire filled the air with bullets, bolts and lasers. Screams and blood filled his senses, the chaotic nature of the battlefield a morass of thousands upon thousands of warring Astartes. Even through his fury, Ferrus saw the horrific tragedy being played out upon the stage of Isstvan V. Nothing would ever be the same again after this battle, even in their final victory.

This betrayal would stain forever the honour of the Astartes, no matter the outcome.

Men will fear us from this day onwards, and they will be right to, thought Ferrus.

He heard the cries of jubilation behind him, but it was some moments before their substance penetrated his killing rage. He crushed the skull of a warrior of the Sons of Horus in his mighty fist and turned to see the welcome sight of an aerial armada of gunships dropping from orbit.

'My brothers!' he yelled triumphantly as he recognised the familiar iconography of his fellow loyalists. Alpha Legion Thunderhawks screamed over the battlefield, and the midnight-skinned vessels of the Night Lords swooped in to take position on the flanks to envelop the Warmaster's forces. Word Bearer Stormbirds howled in on screaming jets, the gold wings on the glacis of their craft shimmering as though afire in the glow of battle. Heavy transports of the Iron Warriors slammed into the Urgall Depression and disgorged thousands of warriors, who immediately began fortifying the landing zones with armoured barricades and looping coils of razor wire.

Tens of thousands of his fellow Astartes poured onto the surface of Isstvan V, and in a single stroke, the loyalist force was more than doubled in size. Ferrus punched the air in righteous vindication as he watched the power and might of his brothers' Legions fill the black desert behind him, their warriors, fresh meat for the battle.

His vox-unit chimed urgently as a ripple of fear visibly passed along the traitor lines at the sight of such a terrifying display of martial power. His practiced eye could see that the traitor forces had lost their stomach for the slaughter, entire cohorts pulling back from their prepared positions in dismay. Even the *Dies Irae* was retreating, the mighty Titan cowed in the face of such overwhelming force.

Ferrus saw the distant form of Mortarion ushering his warriors back towards the ruined fortress, and even Angron was retreating, his bloodstained World Eaters like some monstrous, bloody tribe of head-hunters. But the Emperor's Children...

The smoke parted before him, and Ferrus saw what he had been looking for ever since he had set foot on this damned planet.

Clad in shimmering armour of purple and gold, he saw Fulgrim.

His former brother drew his most debased followers to him, waving them back to the black walls with long sweeps of a glittering silver blade. A long haft of ebony, worked with silver and gold extended behind his shoulder, and Ferrus smiled grimly as he realised that his brother had also understood that the fates had ordained this duel must take place upon the blasted plain of Isstvan V.

Twisted freaks in flesh-covered armour surrounded the Primarch of the Emperor's Children, and a monster with red, seared flesh attended at his right hand. Only now, at the end, did Fulgrim dare to reveal himself.

Even as Ferrus finally saw Fulgrim, he knew that his brother too was aware of him. He felt hate and betrayal rise in him like a suffocating wave.

The traitors were falling back from the loyalists with increasing speed, leaving thousands of corpses behind them, both friend and foe. The scale of the slaughter was not lost on Ferrus, and though his blood sang with this victory and his imminent confrontation with Fulgrim, he was not blind to the fact that the loyalist Legions had suffered appalling casualties to win it.

He watched the enemy line melt before him, the loyalist warriors exhausted by the furious battle, stumbling as their enemy fled before them. He called his Morlocks to him before opening a channel to Corax and Vulkan.

'The enemy is beaten!' he shouted. 'See how they run from us! Now we push on, let none escape our vengeance!'

Grainy static washed through the reply, Corax's words almost lost amid the rumbling thunder of explosions and the descent of yet more allied dropships.

'Hold, Ferrus! The victory may yet be ours, but let our allies earn their share of honour in this battle. We have achieved a great victory, but not without cost. My Legion is bloodied and torn, as is Vulkan's. I cannot imagine yours has not shed a great deal of blood to carry us this far.'

'We are bloodied, but unbowed,' snarled Ferrus, watching as the distant figure of the fabulously bedecked Fulgrim climbed to the top of a jagged spur of black rock and spread his arms in blatant challenge. Even from hundreds of metres away, the mocking smile twisting his features was clearly visible.

'As are we all,' put in Vulkan. 'We should take a moment to catch our breath and bind our wounds before again diving headlong into such a terrible battle. We must consolidate what we have won and let our newly arrived brothers continue the fight while we regroup.'

'No!' shouted Ferrus. 'The traitors are beaten and all it will take is one final push to destroy them utterly!'

'Ferrus,' warned Corax, 'do not do anything foolish! We have already won!'

Ferrus snapped off the vox-channel and turned to face the surviving Morlocks of his bodyguard. A half century of Terminators surrounded him, their clawed gauntlets crackling with blue arcs of energy and their proud stances telling him they would follow whatever order he gave, whether it be to retreat or to march into the hell of battle once more.

'Let our brothers rest and lick their wounds!' he yelled. 'The Iron Hands will let no others have the satisfaction of settling our affairs with the Emperor's Children!'

FULGRIM SMILED AS Ferrus Manus renewed his attack into the heart of the defensive lines atop the Urgall Depression. Backlit by the flaring strobe of battle, his brother was a magnificent figure of vengeance, his silver hands and eyes reflecting the fires of slaughter with a brilliant gleam. For the briefest second, Fulgrim had been sure that Ferrus would pause to muster with the Raven Guard and Salamanders, but after his daring challenge atop the rock, there would be no restraining his brother.

Around him, the last of the Phoenix Guard awaited the blunt wedge of the Iron Hands, their golden halberds held low and aimed towards their foes. Marius and his wailing sonic weapon howled in anticipation of the combat, and Julius, almost unrecognisable with his skin burnt from his bones, ran a blistered tongue around the lipless ruin of his mouth.

Ferrus Manus and his Morlocks charged through the shattered ruin of the defences, his black armour and their burnished plates scarred and stained with the blood of enemies. Fulgrim's fixed smile faltered as he truly appreciated the depths of hatred his brother held for him and wondered again how they had come to this point, knowing that any chance for brotherhood was lost.

Only in death could this end.

The retreat of the Warmaster's forces appeared ragged and faltering, exactly as Horus had planned it. Warriors streamed back from the front lines of battle in determined groups, their spirits apparently broken, but gathering in knots of resistance behind shelled ruins and fire-blackened craters.

The Iron Hands pushed through the defences, the bulky Terminators unstoppable in their relentless advance. Lightning crackled from the claws of their gauntlets and their red eyes shone with anger. The Phoenix Guard braced themselves to meet the charge, fully aware of the power of such mighty suits of armour.

Marius released a howl of ecstatic joy, and his bizarre weapon amplified it into a screeching wail of deadly harmonics that ripped through the ground in a roaring sonic wave to explode amongst the front ranks of the Morlocks.

The giant warriors were torn apart in a clashing shriek of aural power as the apocalyptic noise made play of their armour and butter of their flesh. The Emperor's Children screamed in pleasure at the sound, their enhanced senses and augmented brain paths rendering the discordant sounds into the most vivid sensations imaginable.

'When they come,' shouted Fulgrim, 'leave Ferrus Manus to me!'

The Phoenix Guard answered with a terrible war cry and leapt to meet the Morlocks in a searing clash of blades. Electric fire leapt from the golden edges of the halberds and claws of the warriors, and a storm of light and sound flared from each life and death struggle. The battle engulfed the Primarch of the Emperor's Children, but he stood above it, awaiting the dark armoured giant who strode inviolate through the lightning shot carnage as brothers hacked at one another in hatred.

Fulgrim nodded in greeting as Ferrus reached towards a sword belted at his waist, and he smiled as he recognised *Fireblade's* hilt.

'You remade my sword,' said Fulgrim, his voice cutting through the atrocious din of fighting. Though the ferocious battle between the Morlocks and the Phoenix Guard surrounded them, neither primarch's praetorians dared approach them, as though aware that to transgress this fateful confrontation would be a heinous crime.

'Only to see you dead by a weapon forged by my own hand,' spat Ferrus.

In response, Fulgrim sheathed his silver sword and reached behind him to unlimber the great warhammer held at his back. 'Then I shall do likewise.'

The great weight of *Forgebreaker*, the weapon his own skill and energies had crafted beneath the peaks of Mount Narodnya, felt good in his hands as he descended the rock to face his erstwhile brother.

'It is fitting we face one another with the weapons we forged long ago,' said Fulgrim.

'I have long waited for this moment, Fulgrim,' replied Ferrus, 'ever since you came to me with betrayal in your heart. For months I have dreamt of this reckoning. Only one of us will walk away from this, you know that.'

'I know that,' agreed Fulgrim.

'You betrayed the Emperor and you betrayed me,' said Ferrus, and Fulgrim was surprised to hear genuine emotion in his brother's voice.

'I came to you because of our friendship, not despite it,' answered Fulgrim. 'The universe is changing, the old order upset and a new dawn approaching. I offered you the chance to be part of the new order, but you threw it back at me.'

'You sought to make me a traitor!' snarled Ferrus. 'Horus is mad. Look at all this death! How can this be right? You will hang from Traitor's Gibbet for this sedition, for I am the Emperor's loyal servant and through me his will and vengeance will be done.'

'The Emperor is a spent force,' snapped Fulgrim. 'Even now he whittles away on some trivia in the dungeons of Terra while his realm is in flames. Are those the actions of a being fit to rule the galaxy?'

'Do not think you can win me to your cause, Fulgrim. You failed once and you will not get a second chance.'

Fulgrim shook his head. 'I am not offering you a second chance, Ferrus. It is already too late for you and your warriors.'

Ferrus laughed at him, but he could sense the despair in it. 'Are you mad, Fulgrim? It's over. You and the Warmaster are defeated. Your forces are routed and the power of another four Legions will soon crush your attempt at rebellion utterly.'

Fulgrim was unable to keep the sensations seething in his head contained any longer and he shook his head as he savoured his next words. 'My brother, how naïve you are. Do you really think Horus would be foolish enough to trap himself like this? Look to the north and you will see that it is *you* who are undone.'

THE FORCES OF the Raven Guard and Salamanders fell back in good order to the drop zone, where their reinforcements were deploying to join the fight. The drop-ships of the Iron Warriors, armoured bastions connected by high walls of spiked barricades, formed an unbroken line of grim fortifications on the northern slopes of the Urgall Depression.

A force larger than that which had first begun the assault on Isstvan mustered in the landing zone, armed and ready for battle, unbloodied and fresh.

Corax and Vulkan led their forces back to regroup and to allow the warriors of their brother primarchs a measure of the glory in defeating Horus, dragging their wounded and dead with them. The victory had been won, but the cost had been steep indeed, with thousands of all three Legions lost to the betrayal of the Warmaster. Horus's forces were in retreat, but there would be no celebration of the slaughter, no joyous victory feasts or glorious days of remembrance, only another sad scroll added to a banner that would never again see the light of day.

Scorched tanks rumbled alongside the Astartes, their ammunition expended and their hulls battered by the impact of shot and shell.

Unanswered vox hails requested medical aid and supply, but the line of Astartes at the top of the north ridge was grimly silent as the exhausted warriors of the Raven Guard and Salamanders came to within a hundred metres of their allies.

A lone flare shot skyward from inside the black fortress where Horus had made his lair, exploding in a hellish red glow that lit the battlefield below like a madman's vision of the end of the world.

And the fire of betrayal roared from the barrels of a thousand guns.

FULGRIM LAUGHED AT the stunned look on Ferrus's face as the forces of his 'allies' opened fire upon the Salamanders and Raven Guard. Hundreds died in the fury of the first moments, hundreds more in the seconds following, as volley after volley of bolter fire and missiles scythed through their unsuspecting ranks. Explosions flashed to life in their midst, vaporising warriors and tearing through tanks as the force of four Legions ripped the beating heart from the first wave of loyalists.

Ferrus Manus watched in mute horror as he saw a storm of fire engulf Corax, and a titanic explosion mushroom skyward from where Vulkan stood in astonished outrage at what was happening.

Even as terrifying carnage was being wreaked upon the loyalists below, the retreating forces of the Warmaster turned and brought their weapons to bear on the enemy warriors within their midst. Hundreds of World Eaters, Sons of Horus and the Death Guard fell upon the veteran companies of the Iron Hands, and though the warriors of the X Legion continued to fight gallantly, they were hopelessly outnumbered and would soon be hacked to pieces.

Ferrus Manus turned to face Fulgrim, and the Primarch of the Emperor's Children could see the despair etched into his brother's features, his silver eyes dull and lifeless. To have so great a victory snatched away in an instant must be the most sublime sensation. Fulgrim almost wished to switch places with his brother just to taste that feeling for himself.

'Only dismal defeat and death await you, Ferrus,' said Fulgrim. 'Horus has commanded your death, but for the sake of our past friendship I shall plead your case to him if you throw down your arms. You have to surrender, Ferrus. There is no escape.'

Ferrus Manus tore his eyes from the slaughter of the loyalist forces, his teeth bared with the volcanic fury of his home world.

'Maybe not, traitor, but only dishonour holds any terror for me,' spat Ferrus. 'The Emperor's loyal warriors will not surrender to you, not now, not ever. You will have to kill every last one of us!'

'So be it,' said Fulgrim, launching himself towards Ferrus Manus, swinging his mighty warhammer. The primarchs' weapons, forged in brotherhood, but wielded in vengeance, met in a blazing plume of energy, and the battlefield was illuminated for hundreds of metres by their ferocious energies.

The two primarchs traded blows with their monstrously powerful weapons, the strength to defeat armies and topple mountains unleashed as they fought like gods forced to end their dispute in the realm of mortals. Ferrus Manus wielded his flaming blade in fiery slashes, his every blow defeated by the ebony hafted hammer he had borne in countless campaigns.

Fulgrim swung his hammer in great, looping arcs, its heavy head powerful enough to crush the armour of a Titan to paste. Both warriors fought with the hatred only brothers divided can muster, their armour dented, torn and blackened by the fury of their conflict.

To fight an opponent of such magnificence was a privilege, and Fulgrim savoured every clash of hammer and sword, every fiery line cut across his flesh and every grunt of pain torn from his brother's mouth as *Forgebreaker* glanced his armour. They circled in the midst of cries of pain and roaring savage glee, the Morlocks of Ferrus Manus slain, but for a last few desperate heroes.

Ferrus cut the shoulder guard from Fulgrim's armour and spun inside his guard to deliver a lethal thrust towards his groin. Fulgrim stepped to meet the blow, batting aside the tip of the fiery sword with the haft of *Forgebreaker*, and hammering the warhammer's head towards Ferrus's skull.

The Primarch of the Iron Hands took the blow, dropping to one knee and lashing out with his blade as blood streamed from the terrible wound in his temple. The sword's fiery tip cut across Fulgrim's stomach, opening his armour and tearing through his flesh. The pain was indescribable, and Fulgrim fell back, dropping his hammer as his hands sought to stem the blood pouring from his body.

Both primarchs faced each other on their knees through a haze of pain and blood, and Fulgrim once again felt an ache of sadness well within him. The pain of his wounds, and the sight of his brother's broken skull coated in blood, tore a window into his mind. The sensation was like a powerful gust of fresh mountain air, clearing away the fog that had wrapped him in a suffocating embrace for so long that he no longer noticed it until it was gone.

'My brother,' he whispered, 'my friend.'

'You have long since lost the right to call me friend,' snarled Ferrus, pushing himself to his feet and staggering towards Fulgrim with *Fireblade* raised to smite him.

Fulgrim cried out, and his hand leapt unbidden to his waist as the flaming blade carved a burning path towards his neck. Silver steel flashed as he drew the sword he had taken from the Laer temple and blocked the descending weapon. Ferrus's sword hissed and spat as it bit into the silver blade, the Primarch of the Iron Hands' strength forcing the blazing metal, centimetre by centimetre, towards Fulgrim's face.

'No!' cried Fulgrim. 'This is not right!'

The amethyst stone at the hilt of Fulgrim's sword pulsed with an evil light, bathing Ferrus Manus's face in a leering purple glare. Energy streamed from the blade, and musky smoke billowed around them, deadening sounds and obscuring sight. Fulgrim felt a monstrous presence swell around him, its power and nameless essence more intoxicating and dreadful than anything he could ever have imagined.

Diabolical strength flooded his limbs and he pushed against the power of Ferrus Manus, feeling his brother's surprise at his resistance. With a cry of animal rage, he surged to his feet and hurled Ferrus Manus back, spinning and lashing out with his sword.

The silver edge bit deep into the breastplate of his brother's armour, and the Primarch of the Iron Hands cried out, falling to his knees once again as the blade's flaring energies parted his dark armour like a fingernail through cold grease. Hot blood sprayed from the wound and *Fireblade* slid from Ferrus's hand as he gasped in fierce agony.

Finish him! Kill him! the voice screamed, and to Fulgrim it seemed as though it echoed across time and space as well as within his skull. He staggered with the blunt force of its imperative, lurching as though his limbs were not his to control.

His normal grace and élan were forsaken as he falteringly raised the silver sword in preparation of delivering the deathblow to Ferrus Manus. Unknown energies coruscated along the notched blade and down the length of his arms into the meat and bone of his wounded body.

Fulgrim was wreathed in purple fire. Crackling arcs of lightning caressed him with a lover's tenderness, seeking out his open wounds and licking them with balefire as they sought entry to his flesh.

Fulgrim stood above Ferrus Manus, his chest heaving convulsively as his entire body shook with the violence of the power that sought to claim him.

He must die! Otherwise he will kill you!

Fulgrim looked down at his defeated opponent and saw his own reflection in the mirrors of Ferrus's eyes.

In an instant that stretched for an eternity, he saw what he had become and what monstrous betrayal he had allowed himself to be party to. He knew in that eternal moment that he had made a terrible mistake in drawing the sword from the Laer temple, and he fought to release the damnable blade that had brought him so low.

His grip was locked onto the weapon and even as he recognised how far he had fallen, he knew that he had come too far to stop, the realisation coupled with the knowledge that everything he had striven for had been a lie.

As though moving in slow motion, Fulgrim saw Ferrus Manus reaching for his fallen sword, his fingers closing around the wire-wound grip, the flames leaping once more to the blade at its creator's touch.

Kill him before he kills you! NOW!

Fulgrim's blade seemed to move with a life of its own, but it had no need of such impellents, for he swung the blade of his own volition.

The silver blade clove the air as it swept towards Ferrus Manus, and Fulgrim felt the ancient triumph of the presence that he now knew had dwelt within it all this time. He tried desperately to pull the blow, but his muscles were no longer his own to control.

Unnatural warp-forged steel met the iron flesh of a primarch, its aberrant edge cutting through Ferrus's skin, muscle and bone with a shrieking howl that echoed in realms beyond those knowable to mortals.

Blood and the monumental energies bound within the meat and gristle of one of the Emperor's sons erupted from the wound, and Fulgrim fell back as the searing powers blinded him, dropping the silver sword at his side. He heard a shrieking wail, as of a choir of banshees, whip around him as phantom, skeletal hands clawed at him, and a thousand voices tore at his mind.

Ghostly whirlwinds seized him and spun him around, twisting him like a limp rag in their grip, and threatening to tear him limb from limb in retribution. Even as he welcomed such oblivion, he felt another presence move to protect him, the same presence that had guided his sword arm, the same presence that had been his constant companion since Laeran, though he had not known it.

Fulgrim fell to the ground as the winds released him, and faded with a shrieking howl of anguished frustration. He landed heavily and rolled onto his side, heaving great gulps of cold air into his lungs as the sound of battle returned to him. He heard cries of pain, gunfire, explosions and the rhythmic crack of bolters as they fired relentless volley after volley. It was the sound of death.

It was the sound of a massacre.

His entire body aching with pain and loss, Fulgrim pushed himself upright. Blood and the detritus of battle surrounded him, the stoic figures of armoured warriors staring in wonder at the headless body that lay on the black ground before him.

Fulgrim took a shuddering breath and raised his hands to the heavens, screaming his loss at the sight of his brother so cruelly murdered.

'What have I done?' he howled. 'Throne save me, what have I done?'

What needed to be done.

Fulgrim heard the voice as a sibilant whisper in his ear, the breath of the speaker hot on his neck. He twisted his neck, but there was nothing to be seen, no unseen speaker or mysterious presence.

'He's dead,' whispered Fulgrim, the aching loss and guilt of his crime too monstrous to believe. 'I killed him.'

Yes, you did. With your own hands, you struck down your brother, he who had only thought well of you and fought faithfully with you through all the long years.

'He… he was my brother.'

He was, and all he ever did was honour you.

The looming presence that surrounded him and spoke to him seemed to claw at his eyes with insubstantial fingers, and Fulgrim felt his mind wrenched into the realm of memory, seeing once again the battle against the Diasporex and the *Fist of Iron* coming to the rescue of the *Firebird*. He saw the resentment he had picked at for months, only now understanding the altruism of Ferrus Manus's deed and the loss of life his selfless act had incurred. Where before he had seen only self-aggrandisement in his brother's action, he now saw it for the heroic deed it had truly been.

His brother's critical comments, the wounding darts meant to undermine him, he now saw had been jests designed to puncture his self-importance and restore his humility. What he had perceived as Ferrus's prideful boasts and rash actions had been deeds of courage that he had spitefully dismissed.

Ferrus's rejection of his attempt to betray him was the act of a true friend, but only now did he see how his brother had, even then, tried to save him.

'No, no, no,' wept Fulgrim as the true horror of what he had done struck him with the force of a thunderbolt. He looked around through tear-filled eyes and saw the horrific changes wrought upon his beloved Legion, the perversions that masqueraded as epicurean pleasure.

'Everything I have done is ashes,' he whispered and swept up the golden *Fireblade*, so recently wielded by his brother in an attempt to undo the evil Fulgrim had embraced.

Fulgrim reversed the blade and held its fiery tip against his body, the edge blackening his hands and burning the skin through the rents torn in his armour.

To end things now would be the easiest thing in the world; to take away the guilt and wash the pain away in a sharp thrust of steel into his vitals. Fulgrim gripped the sword tightly, drawing blood from his palms where the blade's edge sliced his skin.

No, noble suicide is not for the likes of you, Fulgrim.

'Then what?' howled Fulgrim, hurling away the sword his brother had forged.

Oblivion: the sweet emptiness of eternal peace. I can grant you what you crave... an end to guilt and pain.

Fulgrim rose to his feet and stood tall beneath the storm wracked clouds of Isstvan V, his once beautiful face streaked with tears, and his pristine armour stained with the blood of his beloved brother.

Fulgrim lifted his hands and looked at the blood there.

'Oblivion,' he said, his voice hoarse. 'Yes, I crave the boon of nothingness.'

Then leave yourself open to me and I will put an end to it all.

Fulgrim took a last look around. The grim-faced warriors who had foolishly thrown in their lot with the Warmaster: Marius, Julius and thousands more were damned, and they could not see it.

All around him, he could hear the sounds of the future, of warfare and death. The thought that he shared the guilt of the destruction of the Emperor's dream was the greatest shame and sorrow he had ever known.

An end to it all would be a blessed relief.

'Oblivion,' he whispered as he closed his eyes. 'Do it. End me.'

The barriers in Fulgrim's mind dropped and he felt the elation of a creature older than time as it poured into the void in his soul. No sooner had its touch claimed his flesh for its own than he knew he had made the worst mistake of his life.

Fulgrim screamed as he fought to keep it out, but it was already too late.

His consciousness was crushed into the dark, unused corners of his mind, forever to be a mute witness to the havoc wrought by his body's new master.

One moment Fulgrim was a primarch, one of the Emperor's Children, the next he was a thing of Chaos.

TWENTY-FIVE

Massacre/Daemon/The Last Phoenix

LESSER TROOPS WOULD have given up and accepted their fate in the face of such overwhelming opposition, but the warriors of the Salamanders and Raven Guard were Astartes. So they fought like never before, knowing their doom was at hand, and desiring to make the traitors pay in blood for every one of their number that fell.

Caught between two armies, the first wave of the loyalist forces was being systematically massacred. Unrelenting gunfire from the Iron Warriors at the drop-site, and the resurgent forces along the Urgall Depression crushed the Salamanders and Raven Guard in a terrifying vice, and cut them to pieces in a murderous storm of fire and blood.

Warriors of the Alpha Legion and Word Bearers followed their leaders onto the black plains of Isstvan V, their guns blazing and their chainswords bright as they cast off the last remnants of their loyalty to the Emperor and turned their weapons on their brothers.

The *Dies Irae* killed scores with every shot of its mighty weaponry, striding like a giant daemon of legend through the benighted slaughter. White-hot fire blossomed amongst the loyalists and killing flames sawed across the black desert, vaporising men and turning sand to glass. Traitor tanks roared from the Urgall Hills, weapons blazing and crushing the wounded beneath their tracks. The Iron Hands were lost, the fate of their primarch a mystery as his last known position was overrun by hordes of screaming enemy warriors.

Let slip from his false retreat, Angron carved a bloody path through the loyalists, his swords reaping a bloody tally through the ranks of his enemies. The Red Angel fought in a barbaric frenzy, his mind lost to all but the killing rage that drove his blades. His warriors hacked and chopped their foes like butchers, in a killing frenzy of berserk rages, slathering their armour in the blood of the fallen.

If the noise of battle had been incredible before, it was deafening now, no voices heard that were not screams of pain or hate. Individual sounds were lost amid the constant roar of gunfire and rumbling explosions, melding into one long immense howl of murder. What had begun as a battle had become a massacre, each pocket of loyalist resistance gunned down with overwhelming superiority of fire, before the shredded survivors were hacked apart with bloody chainswords.

Mortarion harvested loyalists with great sweeps of his scythe, his ragged cloak billowing in the hot winds of the battlefield's fires, as the Death Guard crushed their foes beneath the relentless pounding of marching feet and the disciplined volleys of gunfire.

At the forefront of the Emperor's Children, Lord Commander Eidolon and the swordsman Lucius led a contingent of their warriors into the heart of the enemy, killing with wondrous displays of bladework and howling shrieks of raw sonic power. The swordsman danced through the battle, his Terran blade carving a screaming, bloody path as he laughed in time with music only he could hear.

Marius Vairosean and his orchestra of damnation ploughed the bloody sand with their terrifying harmonics, ripping open flesh and metal with shrieking chords and howling scales. In contrast, Julius Kaesoron took little part in the fighting, expending his energies in the mutilation and defilement of the corpses left in his brother's wake. Trophies of flesh hung from his armour, each violation he wreaked on the flesh of the enemy more extreme than the last.

Apothecary Fabius picked his way through the carnage like a vulture, pausing here and there at fallen Astartes to perform some gruesome extraction. A coterie of warriors protected him and hideous homunculi assisted him in his loathsome labours, the fruits of which were borne behind them in a vile procession of bloodstained organ bearers.

Fulgrim was nowhere to be seen, the magnificent primarch lost amid the destruction of the Iron Hands' Morlocks, but even without him, his warriors fought with savage and exquisite glee.

With victory in his grasp, the Warmaster took to the field of battle, surrounded by Falkus Kibre and his Justaerin Terminators. The remnants of Horus's Mournival fought alongside him, the Warmaster's magnificent black armour and amber chest adornment gleaming bloody in the firelight.

The killing fields of Isstvan V ran red with the blood of the loyalists, their brave attempt to halt the rebellion of Horus little more than ragged flesh and blood that fought for the last shreds of honour left to them.

Here and there, fierce resistance overcame the traitorous forces and desperate bands of heroes fought their way clear of the trap, dragging their wounded with them towards the few surviving drop-ships.

A band of Raven Guard smashed through a cordon of Emperor's Children who shrieked in orgasmic pleasure as they were cut down, too immersed in the sensations of their own pain and death to fight back. A black-armoured captain led the breakout, fighting his way towards a miraculously undamaged Thunderhawk as his warriors bore the grievously wounded body of their primarch towards escape.

Of Vulkan there was no sign, his warriors cut off and surrounded by the Night Lords and Alpha Legion. Gales of bolter fire hammered the brave warriors of Nocturne and obliterated them. Not all the Salamanders were so cruelly slaughtered, others following the Raven Guard's example and battling their way to their aircraft and the hope of escape.

The few remaining Iron Hands, bereft of their primarch's leadership, banded together with the Salamanders and a brave few managed to break out of the hideous massacre, but such successes were the merest fraction of the battle.

Within hours the slaughter was complete and almost the entire strength of three complete Legions lay silent and dead on the tortured sands of Isstvan V.

THE ONCE-GREY skies of the planet burned orange with the reflected glow of a thousand pyres. The firelight bathed the rippling, glassy sands in a warm radiance, and towering pillars of black smoke from the burning corpses filled the air. Lucius watched the blizzard of ash fall like snow from the skies and stuck out his tongue to taste the greasy, ashen tang of the dead.

Beside him, Lord Commander Eidolon, the skin of his face stretched and waxen over his bones, watched the cremation of the dead with dull, glassy eyes.

'We need to be moving again soon,' said Eidolon. 'We have no time to waste with pointless ritual.'

Privately, Lucius agreed, but he kept his counsel as the thousands of Astartes loyal to Horus filled the broken desert of the Urgall Depression. They gathered before a great reviewing stand, constructed by the dark priests of the Mechanicum with astonishing speed. As the sun began to sink beyond the horizon, the smooth black planes of the stand shone with a blood red glow.

The stand was erected as a series of cylinders of ever decreasing diameter, one standing atop another. The base was perhaps a thousand metres in width, constructed as a great grandstand upon which the Sons of Horus stood, their pre-eminent position as the elite of the Warmaster in no doubt after this great victory. Each warrior bore a flaming brand, and the firelight cast brilliant reflections from their armour.

Atop this pedestal of flame was another platform, occupied by the senior officers of the Legion. Lucius could see the familiar, hulking form of Abaddon together with Horus Aximand. The others he didn't recognise, but his attention was drawn higher before he could linger on their identities.

Above the senior officers of the Sons of Horus stood the primarchs.

Even rendered miniscule by distance, the sheer magnificence of such a gathering of might was breathtaking. Seven beings of monumental power stood on the penultimate tier of the reviewing stand, their armour still stained with the blood of their foes, their cloaks billowing in the winds that swept the Urgall Depression.

He had known Angron and Mortarion since the bloody days of Isstvan III. Their might had been demonstrated to him time and time again during that campaign. His own primarch had been a source of inspiration to Lucius for decades, though Fulgrim stood curiously apart from his brothers on the podium, as though disdainful of them.

But the others... the others had been unknown to him until now, their power and presence filling the plain before the stand with a hushed awe.

Lorgar of the Word Bearers, who had only recently arrived, stood proud and tall with his red cloak wrapped around his granite grey armour like a shroud. Alpharius, resplendent in purple and green held himself erect, as though attempting to match the beings around him in stature. Grim-faced Perturabo stood apart from his brothers, the firelight reflecting red from the burnished plates of his armour and mighty hammer. The lightning-streaked armour of Night Haunter seemed darker even than the black podium, his skull-faced helmet a spot of white amid the shadows that wreathed him.

Finally, the uppermost tier of the reviewing stand was a tall cylinder of crimson that stood a hundred metres above the primarchs. The Warmaster stood on top of it, his clawed gauntlets raised in salute. A furred cloak of some great beast hung from his shoulders, and the light of the pyres reflected from the amber eye upon his breastplate.

The Warmaster was illuminated from below by a
hidden light source, bathing him in a red glow that
gave him the appearance of the statue of a legendary hero, as he stood looking down on the
endless sea of his followers from the towering platform.

As the sun finally dipped below the horizon, a
flight of assault craft roared over the Urgall Hills,
their wings dipping in salute to the mighty warrior
below. Solid waves of cheering crashed against the
reviewing stand, howls of adulation torn from tens
of thousands of throats.

Lucius found himself swept up in the glory and
added his voice to the din, his enhanced senses
screaming in pleasure at the sheer, deafening volume of the cries. High, screaming voices from the
Emperor's Children echoed weirdly over the plain,
ecstatic shrieks of pleasure and debasement like
nothing that should ever have been given voice by a
mortal throat.

No sooner had the aircraft passed overhead than
the massed Astartes began to march around the
reviewing stand, their arms snapping out and hammering their breastplates in salute of the Warmaster.
At some unseen signal a flame ignited on the northern slopes of the Urgall Depression and a blazing
line of phosphor leapt across the ground in a
snaking arc that described the outline of an enormous blazing eye upon the hillside.

The adulation soared to new heights as the Eye of
Horus seared itself into the sands of Isstvan V, the
Warmaster's forces roaring themselves hoarse in his
praise. Super-heavy tanks fired in salute of Horus,
and the towering immensity of the *Dies Irae*
inclined its massive head in a gesture of respect.

The ashes of the dead fell like confetti over the War-master's mighty army. Lucius felt a huge surge of purpose fill his heart and made a vow to never once rest in the service of the power Horus represented. Not even death would contain his might. He gripped the hilt of his sword tightly as loudspeakers placed around the desert erupted with sound, the booming, stentorian voice of the Warmaster sweeping over the Astartes.

'My brave warriors!' began Horus. 'We have achieved much, but there is still more for us to do. With courage, vision and power we have defeated those who sought to prevent us from realising my great dream, but our victory here will count for little if we do not press onwards.'

Horus punched his clawed gauntlet into the air and shouted, 'The road to Terra is open. The time has come for us to take the war to the Emperor in his most impregnable fastness! We will make immediate preparation for the invasion of Terra and an assault on the Imperial Palace. Make no mistake, and it will be ours, my brothers! This will be no easy task, for the Emperor and his deluded followers will fight hard to prevent us from interfering with his plans for god-hood. Doubtless much blood has yet to be spilled, theirs and our own, but the prize is the galaxy itself.'

Horus paused as he let the weight of the stakes sink in before bellowing across the fields of Isstvan V, 'Are you with me?'

Lucius joined the cheering as it reached into the fire-lit skies, and cries of 'Hail Horus! Hail Horus!' resounded long into the darkness.

WITHIN THE RUINED keep of Isstvan V, shadows cast by the funeral pyres were thrown out on the smooth, basalt flagstones. Dust motes shaken from the ceiling and walls by the rumble of thrusters hung heavily in the air as the Warmaster's army took its leave of the fifth planet. Horus watched as yet another squadron of Stormbirds lifted off in clouds of dust lit by blue fire, satisfied that all was proceeding as he desired.

His brother primarchs were mustering their forces for the invasion of Imperial space, and he was certain that each and every one understood the need for unquestioning obedience to his orders. As Warmaster, the armies of the Imperium had been his to control, from the mightiest fleet of battleships to the lowliest Army soldier, but to see such martial power gathered in one place was truly inspiring.

Not since Ullanor had he witnessed such a gathering of heroes, and his mood soured as he thought once again of the devastated greenskin world and the last time he had seen his father. Time had moved on and revealed much that had been hidden, but still the unease that events were moving too fast for him to control gnawed at the furthest corners of his mind.

He turned from the window and poured himself a cup of wine from a brass pitcher he lifted from a nearby table. He drained the wine in a single swallow and poured another as a rapid knocking sounded at the chamber's entrance.

Horus looked up, his mood souring further as he saw Fulgrim standing in the doorway, a gilt inlaid box held before him.

Once they had shared a brotherhood as close as any, but in the years since they had fought together, something had changed within Fulgrim. His brother had been a warrior of perfection, but now he simply revelled in the sensations of battle and the adrenaline high of ferocious combat instead of the precise application of force.

His brother wore his battle armour, the plates gleaming and new once again, as though he had never set foot upon a battlefield. He wore a long cape of fiery golden scales at his shoulders, and a mail shirt of glittering silver hung beneath his breastplate. What had once been a magnificent, all-enclosing suit of armour now resembled a theatrical costume.

'Warmaster,' said Fulgrim.

Horus detected a subtle difference in his brother's tone, something so slight that it would have escaped anyone else's notice but his. He lifted his cup and drank a mouthful of wine, beckoning Fulgrim into his chambers.

'You requested a private audience with me, Fulgrim,' he said. 'What is so important that you could not tell me in front of our brothers?'

His brother smiled and bowed before opening the box he carried. 'My esteemed lord and master of Isstvan, I have brought you a trophy.'

Fulgrim reached into the box and withdrew a grisly prize lifted from the field of battle. Horus felt a momentary shiver of horror as he saw the severed head of Ferrus Manus.

The flesh was grey and dead, his erstwhile brother's silver eyes plucked from his head, and the sockets raw and bloody. His jaw hung open and a splintered nub of bone projected from where his skull had been caved in on one side.

Ferrus had become an enemy, but to see his flesh violated so brutally was repugnant to Horus, though he was careful to keep his feelings veiled.

With a casual flick of the wrist, Fulgrim tossed the bloodied object at Horus's feet. Ferrus Manus's head rolled across the black floor and came to rest with the ravaged eye sockets staring up at Horus in blind accusation.

Horus looked up from the head and turned his gaze on Fulgrim, seeing again the insouciance that had infuriated him so when his brother had returned in failure from his attempt to win over the Primarch of the Iron Hands.

As distasteful as it was, he knew he would have to offer congratulations. 'Well done, Fulgrim. You have slain one of our greatest foes as you said you would, but I fail to see why you make this presentation in so private an audience. Surely you would wish our brothers to revel in your triumph?'

Fulgrim laughed, but there was a timbre to his brother's amusement that sent a chill down Horus's spine as he recalled where he had heard such ancient malice before... in the voice of Sarr'Kell, the entity Erebus had summoned in the heart of the *Vengeful Spirit*.

'Fulgrim?' asked the Warmaster. 'Explain yourself.'

The Primarch of the Emperor's Children shook his head and wagged his finger at Horus. 'With the greatest respect, mighty Horus, you do not address Fulgrim any more.'

Horus looked into his brother's dark eyes, seeing beyond the arrogance and superiority to what lay within. Darkness filled his brother's core, an ancient darkness that had torn itself from the womb of a dying race with a bloody birth scream.

Its existence was as old as the heavens and as fresh as the dawn. Its life was immortal and its capacity for malice infinite.

'You are not Fulgrim,' he breathed, suddenly wary of this intruder in his midst.

'No,' agreed the thing with his brother's face.

'Then who are you?' demanded Horus. 'A spy? An assassin? If you are here to kill me then I warn you I am no weakling like Fulgrim. I will break you before you can lay a hand upon me!'

Fulgrim shrugged and tossed the box he carried onto the floor with a clatter. It landed next to Ferrus's severed head. Horus let the energised claws of his gauntlets slide out in warning.

'Perhaps you can defeat me,' said Fulgrim, crossing the room to pour himself a cup of wine, 'but I have no wish to test either of us in such a fruitless and wasteful trial of combat. On the contrary, I am here to pledge myself to your cause.'

Horus glanced towards Fulgrim's waist, and relaxed as he saw that this thing masquerading as his brother had come before him unarmed. Whatever its purpose in unveiling itself, it had not come with violence on its mind.

'You still have not answered my question,' said Horus. 'Who or what are you?'

Fulgrim smiled and licked his lips with a long sweep of his tongue. 'Who am I? I should have thought that would be obvious to one who has had dealings with other creatures of my ilk.'

Once again, Horus felt the chill that he had experienced when the Lord of the Shadows had manifested in the stone-walled lodge, raised in the heart of his flagship.

'You are a creature of the warp?' he asked.

'I am indeed. What your insufficient language might call a "daemon". A poor word, but it will have to suffice. I am a humble servant of the Dark

Prince, an emissary come to aid you in your little war.'

Horus felt his anger towards this impudent creature grow with every patronising syllable that dripped from its lips. It had usurped the body of one of his underlings, the fate of the galaxy was at stake, and it dared to call such a conflict 'little'!

The Fulgrim thing turned away from him and paced the length of his chambers, as though it had never seen a room quite like it. 'I have claimed this mortal shell as my own, and I must admit that it is most pleasing to me. The sensations one experiences when clothed in flesh are quite unique, though I daresay I shall have to make some alterations to its form in time.'

Horus felt his skin crawl at the idea of such a hideous violation. 'What of Fulgrim? Where is he?'

'Fear not,' laughed the warp creature. 'We have a long and… involved history, Fulgrim and I, and I certainly do not wish him any lasting ill. For some time I have been his conscience, quietly advising him in the lonely watches of the night, advising him, cajoling him, comforting him and steering his course of action.'

Horus watched as the daemon ran its hands along the sand-blown walls of the chamber, its eyes closing as it enjoyed the rough texture of the stone surface.

'Steering his course of action?' prompted Horus.

'Oh, yes!' exclaimed the warp creature. 'I made him believe that he should not doubt your course of action. Of course, he resisted, but I can be very persuasive.'

'You made Fulgrim join with me?'

'Of course! Did you really think you were *that* good an orator?' chuckled the daemon. 'You have me to thank for clouding his perceptions and adding his strength to yours. But for me, he would have run to his Emperor screaming of your imminent betrayal.'

'And you think I owe you something, is that it?' asked Horus.

'Not at all, for in the end, Fulgrim was weak, too weak to finish what his own desire had begun,' explained the creature. 'His obsession led him to launch the deathblow at his brother, but his weakness would not allow him to land it without my help. I merely gave him the strength to do what he wanted to do.'

'But where is he now?'

'I have already told you, Horus,' cautioned the daemon. 'Fulgrim's anguish at what he had done proved too great for him to bear. He begged me to help him extinguish his life, but I could not destroy him, that would have been far too prosaic. Instead, I gave him eternal peace, though not, I think, in the way he actually desired it.'

'Is Fulgrim dead?' asked Horus. 'Answer me, damn you!'

'Oh no,' smiled the daemon, tapping an elongated finger with a sharpened nail against his temple. 'He is here inside me, utterly aware of all that transpires, though I do not suppose that he is happy pressed into the furthest reaches of his soul.'

'You have already claimed his flesh,' snarled Horus, taking a thunderous step towards the daemon-Fulgrim. 'If he is of no more use to you then let him die.'

The daemon shook his head with an amused sneer. 'No, Horus, I shan't be doing that, for his cries of horror are a great comfort to me. I am unwilling to let him fade away, since our discussions offer me much amusement and I do not suppose I shall ever tire of them.'

Horus felt nothing but revulsion at the fate his brother suffered, but forced his disgust to one side. After all, had not the daemon already pledged its allegiance to him? It was patently a creature of great power, and to allow the knowledge that their primarch was as good as dead, would certainly cost him the loyalty of Emperor's Children Legion.

'You may have Fulgrim for now,' said Horus, 'but keep your identity a secret from all others, or I swear I will see you destroyed.'

'As you wish, mighty Warmaster,' said the daemon-Fulgrim, nodding and giving an unnecessarily ostentatious bow. 'I have no particular desire to reveal myself to others anyway. It will be our secret.'

Horus nodded, though he made a silent vow to free his brother as soon as he was able, for no one deserved to endure such a terrible fate

But what power could unmake a daemon?

ORBITAL SPACE AROUND Isstvan V was as busy as any fleet docking facility around the lunar bases, with the vessels of eight Legions assuming formation prior to transit to the system jump point. Over three thousand vessels jostled for position above the darkened fifth planet, their holds bursting with warriors sworn to the Warmaster.

Tanks and monstrous war machines had been lifted from the planet with incredible efficiency and an armada greater than any in the history of the Great Crusade assembled to take the fire of war into the very heart of the Imperium.

The fleets of Angron, Fulgrim, Mortarion, Lorgar and the Warmaster's own Legion would rendezvous at Mars, now that word had come from Regulus of the planet's fall to Horus's supporters within the Mechanicum. With the manufacturing facilities of Mondus Gamma and Mondus Occullum wrested from the control of the Emperor's forces, the forges of Mars were free to supply the Warmaster's army.

The eager warriors of the Alpha Legion were singled out by Horus for a vital mission, one upon which the success of the entire venture could depend. Following the Warmaster's misdirection of Leman Russ, the Space Wolves were known to be operating in the region of Prospero after their attack on Magnus's Thousand Sons. In the nearby system of Chondax, the White Scars of Jaghatai Khan were sure to have received word of Horus's rebellion and would no doubt attempt to link with the Space Wolves. Horus could not allow such a grave threat to appear, and so the warriors of Alpharius were to seek out and attack these Legions before they could join forces.

Night Haunter's fleet had already departed, bound for the planet of Tsagualsa, a remote world in the Eastern Fringes that lay shrouded in the shadow of a great asteroid belt. From here, the Night Lords' terror troops would begin a campaign of genocide against the Imperial strongholds of Heroldar and Thramas, systems that, if not taken, would leave the flanks of the Warmaster's strike on Terra vulnerable to attack. The Thramas system was of particular importance, as it comprised a number of Mechanicum forge worlds whose loyalty was still to the Emperor.

The ships of the Iron Warriors prepared to make the journey to the Phall system where a large fleet of Imperial Fists vessels were known to be regrouping after a failed attempt to reach Isstvan V. Though Rogal Dorn's warriors had played no part in the massacre, the Warmaster could not allow such a powerful force to remain unmolested. The enmity between bitter Perturabo and proud Dorn was well known, and it was with great relish that the Iron Warriors set off to do battle.

With his flanks covered and the forces that could potentially reinforce the heart of the Imperium soon to be embroiled in war, the gates of Terra were wide open.

One by one, the fleets of the Warmaster's rebellion began the long journey to the planet from which they had begun the Great Crusade, each Legion's ships diminishing to silver specks in the darkness before vanishing utterly.

Soon, only the Sons of Horus remained in orbit over Isstvan V.

From the strategium of the *Vengeful Spirit*, the War-master looked down upon the dark orb through the circular viewing bay above his throne, his expression unreadable as he watched the elliptical curve of the fifth planet recede.

He turned as he heard the sound of footfalls behind him and saw Maloghurst limping towards him with a data-slate in his hand.

'What do you bring me, Mal?' asked Horus.

'A communication, my lord,' replied his equerry.

'From whom?'

Maloghurst smiled. 'It's from Magnus the Red.'

LA FENICE WAS a ruin. The daemon that had claimed Fulgrim's body strode through the wreckage of Bequa Kynska's last and greatest performance, smiling as it remembered the scenes of destruction and wanton lust enacted here. The glow of a handful of dim footlights flickered in the gloom. The air stank of blood and lust, and the parquet was sticky with fluid and strewn with bone.

The power of its dark prince had poured through the mighty theatre and entered every living thing within it, breaking down the barriers of inhibition between desire and action.

Truly it had been a great performance, and the lesser avatars of its master had feasted well on the excess of sensation unleashed, before discarding their borrowed flesh and returning to the warp.

All around it were the signs that its master's power had been unleashed: the remains of a defiled carcass, a gaudy masterpiece of blood and ordure daubed on the wall or a sculpture of flesh formed from a multitude of body parts.

Outwardly, the daemon still resembled the body it had stolen, but already there were hints that the flesh was soon to be reshaped in an image more pleasing to it. An aura of power vibrated the air around it and its skin held a soft shimmer of inner luminosity.

The daemon hummed the opening bars of the *Maraviglia's* overture and drew the sword sheathed at its waist, the golden hilt shimmering in the fading glow of the wavering footlights. It had retrieved the anathame from Ostian Delafour's studio, surprised and amused to find another body impaled on its lethal point. The shrivelled husk of flesh was barely recognisable as Serena d'Angelus, but the daemon had honoured her corpse with the most sublime ruin before making its way to *La Fenice*.

It held the sword up to its face and laughed as it saw the tortured soul of Fulgrim behind its eyes reflected in the shimmering depths of the blade. The daemon could hear his pitiful cries echoing within his skull, the torment in every desperate shriek the sweetest music.

Such things pleased the daemon, and it stood for a moment to savour the fruits of its influence on Fulgrim. The fools who served in the III Legion had no idea that their beloved leader was clawing ineffectually at the bondage in which he was held.

Only the swordsman, Lucius, had appeared to realise that something was amiss, but even he had said nothing. The daemon had sensed the burgeoning warp touch upon the warrior and had presented him with the silver blade within which the Laer had bound a fragment of its essence. Though the weapon was now bereft of its spirit, there was still power within the blade, power that would empower Lucius in the years of death to come.

The thought of the coming slaughters made the daemon smile as it imagined what it might accomplish with this stolen flesh. Sensations that could only be imagined in the warp would be made real in this mortal realm, and a galaxy's worth of blood, lust, anger, fear, rapture and despair awaited it on the march to Terra. A billion souls were at the mercy of the Warmaster, and with the power of a Legion at its command, what heights of sensation might it experience?

The daemon made its way to the front of the stage and looked up towards the great portrait that hung above the smashed wreckage of the proscenium. Even in the dying light, the portrait's magnificence was palpable.

A glorious golden frame held the canvas trapped within its embrace, and the daemon smiled as it took in the wondrous perfection of the painting. Where before the image had been a garish riot of colours with a terrible aspect that horrified those mortals who dared to look upon it, it was now a thing of beauty.

Clad in his wondrous armour of purple and gold, Fulgrim was portrayed before the great gates of the Heliopolis, the flaming wings of a great phoenix sweeping up behind him. The firelight of the legendary bird shone upon his armour, each polished plate seeming to shimmer with the heat of the fire, his hair a cascade of gold.

The Primarch of the Emperor's Children was lovingly portrayed in perfect detail, every nuance of his grandeur and the life that made Fulgrim such a vision of beauty captured in the exquisite brushwork. The daemon knew that no finer figure of a warrior had ever existed or ever would again, and to even glimpse such a flawless example of the painter's art was to know that wonder still existed in the galaxy.

The painted Fulgrim stared down upon the ruin of the theatre and the monster that had claimed his mortal shell. The daemon smiled as it saw the horror within his eyes, a horror that had not been rendered by any skill of the painter. Perfect, exquisite agony burned in the portrait's gaze, and as the daemon sheathed the anathame and bowed to the silent stage, the dark pools of its painted eyes seemed to follow its every movement.

The daemon turned from the portrait and made its way from the theatre as the last of the footlights guttered and died, leaving the last phoenix forever shrouded in darkness.